Ple

`

fatal impact

KATHRYN FOX

fatal impact

HODDER &
STOUGHTON

First published in Great Britain in 2014 by Hodder & Stoughton
An Hachette UK company

1

A CIP catalogue record for this title is available from the British Library.

Hardback ISBN 978 1 444 75469 8

Printed and bound by Clays Ltd, St Ives plc

Hodder & Stoughton policy is to use papers that are natural, renewable
and recyclable products and made from wood grown in sustainable forests.
The logging and manufacturing processes are expected to conform
to the environmental regulations of the country of origin.

Hodder & Stoughton Ltd
338 Euston Road
London NW1 3BH

www.hodder.co.uk

To Duncan, for giving me the courage to fly.

1

The technician anchored the small pack to her waist band and clipped the microphone to her jacket lapel.

'Please welcome to the stage the internationally renowned forensic pathologist and one of the world's foremost experts in forensic medicine, Tasmania's own Dr Anya Crichton.'

Lecture notes in one hand, Anya wiped her spare hand on her trouser leg as she climbed the steps to the stage amidst loud applause. A quick glance confirmed the auditorium was filled to capacity.

'Thank you,' she began. 'I'm sorry to be here. In fact, I'm sorry that any of us has to be here to discuss violence against women and children.'

The audience was silent. Anya had their attention.

She brought up the first slide with a handheld remote: a clean skull projected onto the giant screen.

'Some of you will find this talk disturbing, but I don't do victims any favours if I censor the effects of the violence. If there are any family members present or victims of violent crime, I'd ask you to consider leaving this session. I have chosen to show specific images to discuss. Despite being unidentifiable, they may cause distress.'

She paused. An elderly couple rose, shuffled to the aisle

and exited the auditorium.

Anya wondered if her own father, an advocate for victims of homicide, had been delayed or chosen to sit this session out. He normally texted or emailed as soon as he arrived. She cleared her throat and presented the next slide: a side view of the same skull. 'The skull is a series of bones joined together by what we call sutures. Here, a section made of up of right temporal and frontal bones is depressed.' She used the laser pointer to demonstrate. 'This was a fatal injury caused by a blow with a blunt object.'

The next slide showed a bruised and swollen face, a digital black band obscured the eyes. The only hint at the victim's sex was the long blood-matted hair to the side of the head.

Anya suspected that few in the room knew about this case. 'This was a twenty-five-year-old woman with two children. She was pregnant with her third child, but the uterus was ruptured during this latest beating. This woman endured at least twice-weekly beatings.' Anya moved to a drawing of the human body and with each click, revealed a new red mark, indicating a fracture or significant injury. Broken wrists, elbow, tibia, jaw, ruptured spleen, torn liver, fractured eye socket.

There were audible gasps throughout the theatre.

'This woman was found at the base of the Gap in Sydney. Her husband told friends and family she had left him and her children for another man. Her body wasn't found for three days.' She paused. 'Cause of death was multiple trauma, but there were multiple bone fractures at various stages of healing. The woman suffered regular beatings and disclosed to her mother, who lived overseas, that she wanted to leave her violent husband. When friends and the local doctor asked about the injuries, she repeatedly denied her husband's involvement. It's typical in these cases that victims remain silent, for fear of escalation of the violence, or even being killed.'

She let the words hang. The room remained silent. 'Police found traces of her blood in the family home and the husband was charged. He used the previous beatings as a defence because if he had wanted her dead, he could have killed her any time. He maintained that she had left him.'

She drew in a breath. 'Tragically, he later boasted about killing her to a friend, but had already been tried and acquitted by then. By remaining silent about the pattern of behaviour, which would have alarmed anyone and highlighted how much risk she was in, this woman helped her husband get away. With her own murder.'

She paused and then showed another slide: of a small skeleton found burnt in bushland behind a town. 'I did the post-mortems on all of these cases. We sometimes get a history, and this is what I received for this boy. In this child's seven years, he was like a ghost. Neighbours barely saw him, and he didn't attend school or socialise with others. He lived with various relatives and at one stage was forcibly removed from his mother, but she regained custody. Community service workers' calls often go unanswered or the families refuse to open the door to them. Even if friends reported seeing bruises on the face and neck, he most likely would have been failed by the system.' She hit the next slide. 'There was a litany of old healed and healing fractures. I found teeth in what was left of the stomach, dislodged from the mouth by a blow. Exact cause of death was impossible to establish due to the fact the body had been severely burnt, and that also made homicide difficult to prove.'

Studying the slide, Anya couldn't help make comparisons to her eight-year-old son, Ben, who was full of life, hope and love. Things this poor child had been deprived of.

She turned to face the audience. 'One of these cases attracted nationwide media attention and affected changes to law. But which one?' She paused. The audience muttered quietly amongst themselves.

Anya took a sip of water from a glass on the lectern.

'The first case,' she clicked forward to another slide of the skull, 'was that of an eighteen-year-old law student.

Four friends went out for a night in the city. Only three came home. This was considered a random act of violence. He had his life ahead of him. According to witnesses, there was no provocation. The young man was out with his girlfriend, celebrating turning eighteen and being legally able to drink. All it took was one blow with an iron bar to kill him.' She showed a photo of a handsome young face that had filled the newspapers. 'The offender was drunk and admitted to looking for a fight. He was evicted from a couple of venues earlier in the night for being intoxicated. He claimed he didn't remember hitting the student, or why he chose to target him.

'This case outraged the country and every talkback radio show. It should be a basic right to go into the city and come back alive. Laws about late-night opening and responsible alcohol service were changed within weeks, with bipartisan support.'

She could see some of the audience lean forward. 'There is no doubt we should all be safe to walk around our cities at night. But what about the right to sleep safely in our own beds? To be safe at home without being murdered by a person who is supposed to love us? To grow up without being tortured?

'For those who were wondering, The woman at the Gap had migrated from India to marry her husband, in the hope of a better life. The little boy was born in a remote community to an Indigenous mother and died in a small town in the house of a stepfather and uncle. His death barely rated a mention in the press.'

Anya noticed a middle-aged woman on crutches heading down the central aisle towards a standing microphone set up for questions. Two security guards quickly descended and blocked her path. Words were exchanged and the woman began shouting as the guards moved back. The house lights came up.

The emcee quickly moved to Anya's side and explained, 'There's a protest group outside. Looks like one of them somehow managed to slip through security.'

The disabled woman didn't appear to be much of a threat, but Anya appreciated the security concerns. The front-row seats were occupied by prominent state and federal politicians, community leaders and the odd sports star. She wondered who the protesters were targeting. The woman in the aisle continued to call out until she was escorted out the doors.

The emcee switched on his hand mike as the woman's muffled voice receded. 'Ladies and gentlemen, apologies for that interruption. May I take this opportunity to remind you to wear your conference lanyard for all sessions. For security reasons, no one will be allowed in without their access pass. Once again, I apologise for the interruption.' He turned to Anya. 'Back to you, doctor.'

The crowd applauded, and Anya continued. 'In no way is this conference intended to diminish the impact of the violence many men experience. Clearly, we are not silent about some forms of violence – on our streets, for example. As a pathologist, I've seen far too many murder victims, both men and women. But it wasn't until I became a forensic physician – and documented injuries on surviving victims as well – that the true scope of violence against women and children became apparent to me. I liken it to unfinished murder.'

A man in jeans and a loose shirt approached the central microphone, holding up a lanyard in one hand to declare his right to be present. Anya opted to accept the question at this stage in the talk.

'I respect your opinion, doctor, but there are also women who abuse their partners and their children. Men are more likely to die from violence than women, if the facts are told. Why aren't you and everyone else here standing up for those men as well? The media coverage of street violence has been too long coming, and now you criticise it!'

Anya suspected he had experienced violence or abuse himself.

'I'm not criticising, just contrasting cases that invoke public outrage. You're right. What's reported is merely the tip of the iceberg. Every boy who witnesses or experiences violence is five times more likely to abuse his partner and children,' she held up one hand, fingers spread. 'Every girl who witnesses or experiences violence as a child is five times more likely to be abused by her partner. Is it any wonder we're seeing increased episodes of violence generation by generation, among both men and women? Stopping violence in the home is a major societal issue. I honestly believe that by preventing violence against women and children, all men benefit.' She clicked forward to a new slide, but the man wasn't finished.

'After we separated, my ex-wife falsely accused me of stalking her and abusing our children,' his voice was now raised. 'I was home alone and couldn't prove it. The kids were too young to be credible witnesses. Then she got an appre-hended violence order taken out so I couldn't see my kids.' He jabbed a finger in her direction. 'How can we protect ourselves when society's first reaction is to punish men? You didn't even bother to mention the high rate of male suicide.'

A few people in the audience clapped loudly. Anya felt for the man but did not want to allow the discussion to veer away from the main focus of the conference.

'I'm sorry about your personal situation, but there are moves to help men – to vindicate those who are falsely accused, and to prevent violent offenders from doing more harm.

'I'm currently involved in a trial program that puts GPS monitors on men who have apprehended violence orders taken out against them. Up until now, it is the women and children who have had to move, hide, change their behaviour, completely abandon their routines and support networks. We all know that AVOs don't stop bullets, knives or fists. Based on their history of abuse, personality, and a number of other factors, men are rated in terms of the risk of violence they pose. Those deemed at highest risk of committing further violence are fitted with a GPS monitor in addition to receiving counselling. If they go anywhere stipulated under the AVO, police can immediately intervene before anyone is hurt. In your case, this would have confirmed you were not a threat to your former wife and had been nowhere near the children when she claimed. The point, however, is that men are now being compelled to modify their behaviour and learn what is acceptable and what isn't.'

'Guilty until proven innocent,' the questioner responded.

'It may appear that way, but it is saving lives. And the futures of men who may have been imprisoned otherwise. It may not be perfect, but it's better than the situation we have now. Ninety women murdered by spouses in the past two years and how many more living with the constant fear of being murdered? Even one is far too many.'

The audience erupted in applause.

'Now, let's go over some of the physical things to look for in abuse victims,' Anya continued. 'Injuries on the dead look vastly different from on the living. Scars and wounds are enhanced when blood is no longer pumping. It's the wounds and injuries on children at most risk we need to become more adept at recognising.'

Myriad cases flashed through Anya's mind as she presented some slides, the identities of the children masked with black blocks across their eyes. Some members of the audience audibly repositioned in their seats, while others gasped. The men in the front row sat with arms folded, legs extended.

The slides were shocking. Cigarette burns, belt-buckle bruises, fractured jaws, faces so swollen their features were unrecognisable.

Then Anya showed some slides of minor bruising and asked the audience if the examples were normal or abnormal. At the end of the session, Anya collected her USB and descended the stairs.

'Excuse me, doctor.'

A young man dressed in a grey suit and black tie greeted her. 'Fantastic talk. Absolutely riveting,' he said and shook

Anya's hand. 'Ryan Chapman, I work for Minister Moss. He's asked for a quiet word outside. And perhaps a photo op.'

The emcee came over and collected Anya's microphone, then addressed the audience. 'Our next session will begin in five minutes, so if you can please resume your seats.' Anya excused herself from the group and moved outside to the foyer, where she greeted the minister. She noticed the protesters outside the glass auditorium foyer, chanting and carrying placards about 'Frankenfoods'.

'Christian Moss. Welcome back to Hobart, Doctor,' the minister effused. 'Apologies for the rabble-rousing. They're demanding we end progress and make the state a national park.'

Anya had assumed the protesters were objecting to some aspect of the conference. She often received a barrage of insulting emails after presenting. The most frequent of late was that she was a man-hater and was jealous because she was too disgusting to rape. Trolls often flooded her inbox, and she had learnt over time to ignore the anonymous bile, but report particularly threatening messages to police. Luckily, the threats were rare.

'Have to say that was really compelling. As Minister for Community Services and Policing, I hear a lot of speeches, and that was extraordinary. I think your GPS program may go down very well here,' said the minister, with an oily smile.

Anya was more than a little surprised. It wasn't often politicians approached her about starting preventive projects. Cost and lack of immediate benefits didn't often translate to votes, particularly when it came to subjects that polarised voters. 'What about funding and police support?' she asked.

'We can always find the funds, and leave the support to me.' Moss winked. 'I'm here to make a real difference. Sometimes there's a greater good at stake.'

'Excuse me, sir, press are waiting, cameras are set up.' Ryan Chapman appeared at the minister's elbow, checking his smart phone. 'And we have to avoid the street closures.' He raised the phone. 'A quick photo?'

Anya stood beside Moss for the picture, unsure whether to be excited about the possibility of trialling GPS devices to curb domestic violence in the state, or suspicious that she was being used to boost Moss's standing with female voters.

'We'll be in touch,' Ryan Chapman assured her, and passed over a business card. She reached into her bag and returned the gesture with one of hers. Moss pocketed it before following his assistant out to address the sea of protesters. Anya decided to go back to her room to freshen up before a pre-arranged coffee with the police commissioner.

Checking her phone, she headed across to the adjoining hotel lobby, glad to avoid the press conference out on Davey Street. A text message confirmed her father had arrived in time to hear her speak and was proud of how well she'd done. He was racing off to run a legal workshop for social workers and GPs, and would see her for dinner. She messaged back: *7 pm Constitution Dock.*

In the lobby, the woman who had attempted to interrupt her talk sat on a lounge, crutches leaning against the side of her chair. A hotel security officer stood by her, speaking into a walkie-talkie.

'I'm not leaving until I've seen her,' said the woman tartly.

'Madam, you are trespassing. We are going to ask you one more time to leave, or you'll be forcibly removed. No one wants that.'

'I have every right to be here.' The woman remained defiant. 'I'll tell you exactly what I told your minion. I'm waiting for one of your paying guests.'

'Madam, does she even know you're coming?'

There was the slightest hesitation. 'Of course.'

The security man rubbed his forehead and looked around. 'You can't camp here hoping to see a conference participant. We take our guests' privacy very seriously.'

'I'll sit here all day and night if that's what it takes.'

Metres away from the exchange, Anya's phone rang. It was the front desk from the Grand Chancellor, asking if she was expecting a guest in the lobby.

Anya glanced across at the woman. 'Does she walk with crutches?'

'Yes.' The receptionist sounded surprised. 'You do know her?'

Anya breathed out. 'I'll go and talk to her now.'

She hung up and approached the lounge.

'Dr Crichton,' the woman exclaimed, and attempted to get up but struggled against the deep cushion. 'My name is Beatrice Quaid. I have been waiting to see you.'

Anya extended her hand and said hello. The woman was hardly a threat and this was a very public place. She didn't seem to have anything to do with the protest outside.

'Apologies, madam, doctor, for any misunderstanding.' The security man stepped back. 'If we can be of further assistance . . .'

'You'll be the first to know,' the woman said, sarcastically. She must have been in her late sixties, dressed in elasticised pants and a floral appliquéd T-shirt. Anya sat on the adjacent chair.

'The papers said you helped people and that you would be here for a conference. I'd almost given up hope.' Her breathing was laboured and she wheezed intermittently. Arthritic fingers dug inside her open handbag to a set of rosary beads. 'I've been praying for help and here you are.' The woman's eyes were dark and soulful. 'You're my last chance.' The woman was determined, if nothing else.

'For what?' Anya asked.

Mrs Quaid swallowed. 'To prove a woman murdered her child.'

Anya was surprised. 'My job is to determine cause of death and the nature of injuries, and I specialise in sexual assaults. If you think a death may have been suspicious, you need to tell the police.'

'If money's an issue, I can pay.' The fingers grabbled with an envelope from the bag, stuffed with dollar notes. 'I'll do whatever it takes for justice.' Her eyes welled. 'Please help me, I'm begging you.'

Anya lightly touched the woman's elbow. 'Have you spoken to the police?'

Mrs Quaid wheezed. 'They treat me like I'm crazy. One said I could be charged with making a vexatious claim. The security guard over there wanted to have me charged with trespass and creating a public disturbance.'

Anya glanced around the foyer, which was congested with a group checking in or out. It was easy to see why the hotel security discouraged loiterers, and the woman's manner had not endeared her to them. That didn't mean she was crazy.

'Who do you think was murdered?'

'I don't think. I *know*. My grandson was murdered. By my own daughter.'

2

'How did your grandson die?' Anya asked carefully.

Beatrice dabbed at a tear with bulbous arthritic fingers.

'Little Tom's death was horrific. The coroner said it was whooping cough.'

Anya felt for the grieving grandmother. Even so, infections happened. Whooping cough was one of the most fatal. 'Unless your daughter or someone she knows deliberately injected Tom with a lethal infection, it can't be considered murder.'

Beatrice looked across, dark eyes pleading. 'She might as well have. She refused to vaccinate him, and my two granddaughters.'

Anya took a deep breath. As devastating as this was, murder charges could never be brought against the mother. 'I'm afraid—'

'I know what you're going to say. I've heard it all before. It may be the parents' right to refuse to vaccinate, but what about the rights of the children? Isn't that what your conference is about?'

The woman had a point, but Anya knew too well that it wasn't that simple.

'Our Jenny's not that bright. Never has been. My husband made a lot of money on the share market, and left me comfortable. I want to provide for the girls, but I can't give Jenny anything. It'll just go to that hippie cult she's caught up in.'

Anya knew of a number of religious groups in the state that could be deemed cults. 'Who is she involved with?'

'Jenny and the others live on a few acres in the Huon Valley, in Bellamy. They're all about natural healing, organic foods and going back to basics. Mind you, our taxes support them and the poor children are neglected and subjected to cruel treatment. These people manipulated her and refused to get Tom medical help until it was too late. Now they've got my granddaughters as well.'

She pulled out a photo from her bag. In the image, two little girls looked to be around 12 months and eight or nine. The smaller one sat on her sister's lap. Both had scraggly hair and grinned at the camera.

'Mia's three now, and Emily, well, she's ten. I've postponed my knee replacement surgery to fight for custody of them.'

If this was the most recent photo the grandmother owned, she hadn't had contact with her daughter in a while.

'Jenny and her friends don't believe in doctors. They believe some charlatan who thinks he can heal everything. And there's always a hefty price attached.'

Anya had been involved in cases in which children had been neglected and refused medical aid that could have saved their lives. If it could be shown that Jenny or her fellow commune members had known how ill the child was and refused medical intervention, there might be a case for manslaughter. In those cases, irrespective of a verdict, no one really won.

'Please understand, I don't want to hurt Jenny. It isn't her fault. She never fitted in at school and got pregnant to the first boy who looked at her. Then she had two more to a couple of other no-hopers.'

The woman put her weight forward, wincing as she

supported one knee. 'Please help those girls. They don't stand a chance with Jenny and the people she's in with.'

Anya pulled out her iPad. Bellamy wasn't familiar. 'Are they affiliated with any other group?'

Beatrice reached down into her bag. 'They put out a news-letter called *Back to Basics, Nature's Only Way*. I printed out everything I could find on them.' She handed a plastic sleeve containing newspaper cuttings and articles across to Anya.

'They live on communal land. Jenny lives on the outer part of the acreage. Jenny moved into that house just over a year ago. The rent was cheap, then I found out it was because those people owned the land. That was just before Tommy got sick. I've tried to call, but the phone just rings out. The phone company says there isn't a fault. I went there a couple of months ago but no one would let me see Jenny or the kids. They threatened to call the police and have me charged with trespassing.' The old woman's shoulders drooped and she looked away. 'I just wanted to see that my grandchildren were well and safe.'

'Have you applied for visitation rights?' Grandparents were often the casualties when relationships broke down, and were regularly forgotten or ignored by the courts and parents.

'Jenny ignores my lawyer's letters. I even rang the local police to go around there.' Beatrice reached over and clutched Anya's hand. 'Please help me, the police won't do anything. Community services went out there and said there was no case to answer.'

A question needed to be asked. 'Do you think they're at risk of physical harm – abuse, or even sexual interference?'

'I don't know. You read about these sorts of groups, how they treat women and children—' She stopped herself. Anya could feel the woman's pain and fear.

'How long was Tom sick with the infection?'

Beatrice shook her head. 'We only know what Jenny said, and she's protecting the charlatan I told you about. The local doctor eventually saw him and sent Tom straight to hospital.

He was put on a breathing machine, but . . .' She took a shallow breath. 'By then, it was all too much for his tiny body.'

Anya could imagine the tragic scene. The little boy had died in hospital. There were no guarantees earlier intervention could have saved him.

'When was the last time you spoke to, or had contact with Jenny?'

'After Tom's funeral. I asked about whether the other children had been vaccinated, she said they were getting natural medicine instead. Please, doctor, you're my last chance. Jenny isn't fit to raise those children on her own. I feel it in my bones. Something terrible is going to happen to them if we don't do something.'

Anya thought for a minute. The Huon Valley wasn't far from Hobart. 'I could pay your daughter a visit and see the girls if she'll let me in. I can also go over the death certificate and medical history of your grandson if you give me the details. Names, dates of birth and death, and the names of any doctors who might have seen Jenny and the kids.'

'I have a list.' Beatrice's pained frown softened. 'Here's Jenny's address, my details, and oh, yes, the names of the doctors who've treated the kids in the past, and a signed consent for me to access their records. Jenny signed it before Tom . . .' Beatrice trailed off and paused.

'One more thing,' Beatrice Quaid said. 'If you see the girls, could you please let them know Nanna loves them.'

Anya passed over her business card. She hoped Beatrice was being completely honest and didn't have another agenda. 'My assistant will be in touch regarding my fees for private consulting.'

'I don't know how to thank you, doctor.'

Anya helped the arthritis sufferer to her feet and handed across both forearm crutches. She wondered how the grandmother would ever be able to manage two young girls even if she were given custody.

3

The meeting with the police commissioner was productive. He was open to the concept of GPS monitoring of violent male offenders. Anya took the opportunity to ask about the community in Bellamy that Jenny Quaid was part of. As far as he was concerned, they lived an alternative lifestyle, kept to themselves and didn't cause trouble.

Free for the afternoon, Anya decided to hire a car a day earlier. She had planned to drive north to see her mother in the morning. She could be at Jenny Quaid's house in around half an hour. The ten-year-old should be on school holidays. If she couldn't see the mother and daughters, the local doctor might at least discuss Tom's death.

Anya collected the car and called her assistant about fee structures for Mrs Quaid. Thankfully, nothing urgent had arisen, so she was still free to stop in on her mother for a couple of nights as planned.

Out of Hobart, it felt good to be amongst scenery she had always loved. Heading southwest on the Huon Highway, she was reminded of the breathtaking greenery of her birth state, and the abundance of produce for which it was world renowned. This really was the 'apple isle', highlighted by the signs for apple cider, juice and fresh fruit at almost every turn-off.

The town of Huonville sat on the banks of the Huon River. Just past the town, Anya turned down a remote road. At an intersection, a tie-dyed flag flapped beside a row of letterboxes. Anya stepped out of the car, engine still running, and lifted the flap behind 4033. Inside, snails had eroded the corners of a white envelope. Behind the plastic window, the addressee showed Ms J. Quaid. Anya dialled the number Beatrice Quaid had provided. The engaged signal continued to beep. Anya felt the sting in her face from the unfiltered sun and wiped perspiration from the back of her neck.

As she drove down the winding drive, past a burnt-out house on one side, she could see a raised garden bed several metres long. The block number 4033 was graffitied in white paint on its corrugated-iron support. Anya parked on a verge and stepped out. In the front yard, away from the house, a rusted car shell lay amidst metre-high grass.

The place looked derelict, apart from the garden beds. Fruit was withering in the heat and the soil cracked beneath her fingers. There were few weeds, so the garden had been tended at least until recently.

Anya wondered if the mother and daughters had gone away for a few days. A chainsaw whirred somewhere in the distance.

Anya wiped her forehead as she climbed the verandah and knocked on the front door. A set of chimes on the verandah clinked in the hint of a breeze.

No answer. Glancing down, she noticed something protruding from under a tattered doormat. Lifting the corner, Anya saw that the local police had left a calling card, as had a telephone company worker. She replaced the mat and stepped down off the verandah. To the right of the house, the garage door was half-open. Blowflies flew out and buzzed around Anya's head as she approached. She swiped at them and tentatively stepped inside.

'Hello. Is anyone home?'

A noxious smell flooded her nostrils. Concerned and uneasy, she continued through to the back of the garage, which led through to a small courtyard. A clothesline was mounted against the back wall. Tattered towels hung limply amongst rows of children's underwear, shorts and T-shirts. More raised garden beds contained silver beet, wilted lettuce and a number of yellow and red cherry tomato plants which had shrivelled in the dry soil. Flies swarmed around a plastic bowl by the fence. As Anya neared it, she saw maggots wriggling their way through the rotting contents. Pet food. Anya headed back to the front of the house.

'You right?' An older man called from the street, dirt staining a once-white singlet.

Anya raised her hand to block the sun. 'I'm looking for Jenny Quaid. Do you know if she's home?'

The man held a chainsaw in large, suntanned hands. 'Don't have much to do with the tree huggers. If you ask me, they're all feral. Filthy buggers, ought to piss off, the lot of 'em.'

The neighbour swatted flies from his face.

'Have you seen their pet?' Anya asked.

'That bloody feral cat? It's feral too. Should be shot if you ask me. Found another dead rosella on my doorstep this morning.'

'Could the Quaids have gone away and left the cat?'

'That'd be right. If I see that bloody animal, it's a goner.' He marched off, chainsaw at the ready. He had obviously seen her arrive; probably took note of who came and went. Anya suspected curiosity had prompted his visit rather than any desire to be helpful.

She sensed something wasn't right. If Jenny had gone away, it seemed odd that she would leave the garage door open and all that washing on the line. Anya moved back to the courtyard, used her shoe to flip the bowl over and cover the rotting mess of animal food.

It didn't put her at ease. Off the courtyard, a glass sliding door provided access to the house. Peering through, she could make out the kitchen and living area. As her eyes adjusted to the dimness inside, she saw tins and utensils strewn across the bench. She knocked and the door moved a little. With her left hand, she manoeuvred the glass, careful to avoid the handle. It clunked then gave way enough for her to put her foot inside and lever it open further.

'Hello? Jenny?' Anya stepped inside and startled as a mottled cat sprinted out the partially opened door. A chill went through her. Plastic dolls, balls and blocks littered the floor. The handset of an old-fashioned corded phone dangled over the kitchen bench.

In the eerie quiet, she could hear a slow drip coming from another room. She pulled out her mobile phone and a fly hit her in the face. Then another. She clasped the handset tightly and tracked along the skirting boards of the corridor – force of habit, to preserve evidence in case of a crime scene. Leaning into the bathroom, she caught her breath. Dark smears spread across the white tiled floor. A stained towel, with the distinct smell and colour of stale blood, lay near the door. A bird squawked outside the part-open window. Without stepping inside, she stood on her toes to see more. Another soiled towel had been thrown inside the otherwise empty bath.

Her heart galloped as she dialled the police. While waiting for an answer, she quickly surveyed both bedrooms, calling out one more time then straining to hear a response that didn't come.

There was no sign of life.

Or death.

4

Anya waited in her car, running through the scene again in her mind. It was impossible to judge the volume of blood on the bathroom floor because it had been wiped. It could look like a massacre had taken place even if only one tablespoon of blood had been spilled. Gut feeling told her the amount on the tiles was significant blood loss for an adult. It was even more alarming if it had come from a child.

Maybe there had been an injury, or a blood nose, and the mother had rushed the children to hospital. Calls to the two closest hospitals excluded any admissions with the name Quaid. Anya drummed her fingers on the steering wheel. And waited.

The patrol car was first to arrive, quickly followed by Hobart detectives. After speaking to Anya, they immediately called the homicide squad, who took another forty minutes to reach the house. Inside her hired Commodore, the air-conditioning blasted. When she'd failed to find any sign of life, she had retraced her steps in order not to further contaminate the scene. Three people were missing, and the scene was suspicious. The local detectives had gone to the neighbours to ask if anyone had seen or heard anything unusual, and establish when Jenny and the girls had last been seen. Despite chainsaw man's nosy interference, she doubted he would have been much help.

A car parked behind the crime scene van, and two men stepped out. The swagger of one suggested a homicide detective. Anya abandoned the cool air. The taller man peeled off sunglasses.

'Not often a pathologist drums up business. Conference not interesting enough?' He stood with hands on hips.

Anya extended her hand. He reluctantly shook it.

'Detective Sergeant Jim Bowden.'

'Dr Anya Crichton.' His grip was strong. 'Crime scene are still inside.'

'Steve Schiller, detective constable,' the shorter and younger man offered. 'Interesting talk this morning, by the way.'

Bowden shot him a silencing look. 'What do we know about the family so far?'

'Twenty-five-year-old woman and two daughters, ten and three, live here. They're part of a community that aims to get back to nature, eat organic foods.'

Bowden rolled his eyes. 'Dog shit's natural but you don't put that in your pie hole.' He tugged at his belt. 'What exactly are you doing out here?'

'Phone's been off the hook and the grandmother was concerned something was wrong. She asked me to pay a visit.'

'Police should have handled it.' The senior detective flipped open a notebook. 'Grandmother's name?'

Anya could feel his resentment. 'Beatrice Quaid. She did contact the local uniforms. They left a calling card when no one answered the door.'

Bowden just perceptibly shook his head and replaced the sunglasses.

'They took a lot of care with the garden,' Schiller volunteered.

'Yeah, looks like they're real house-proud.' Bowden nodded towards the overgrown grass and car chassis in the front.

'I'm serious. Look at this permaculture bed.' Schiller wandered over to the raised garden. 'Silverbeet is, or was, shading the lettuce. Roma tomatoes, basil.' He found a stick and dug down. 'They've used seaweed and leaves on a bed of branches. Composts well and limits fungal growth. This is cheap, efficient and productive.' He lurched away as a rat scampered across the bed and into the grass.

At the sight, Anya took a few steps back and quickly surveyed the ground around them.

'Must be good,' Schiller added, 'if the rats love it.'

'Some recommendation.' Bowden pointed to a dark green plant with cauliflower-type foliage. 'Whatever that is it looks like a giant weed.'

'It's kale,' Schiller responded. 'Considered a superfood. Full of nutrients and antioxidants.'

'And with the added benefits of rat shit,' Bowden sniped.

The detective was right about the care in the planting. Anya wondered if Jenny had done the gardening on her own or with help. Beatrice had spoken about Jenny as if she were intellectually challenged. Either she had a talent for growing produce, or she had help with the property.

'Wonderboy here has an environmental science degree. Likes to remind us every chance he gets.' Bowden checked his watch. 'How long did you say crime scene have been inside?'

Bowden was typically old-school, not tertiary educated, Anya assumed. Schiller was part of the new breed, brought into police forces with degrees, but not necessarily appreciated by Bowden and his ilk who valued experience and street smarts above formal education.

The three walked around to where the cat food had been rotting. 'My first impression,' Anya said, 'was that the family could have just popped out. If it hadn't been for the flies in the cat food, I may have left as well.'

Bowden's phone rang and he listened to the caller. 'Pathologist's here now.' His eyes remained on Anya as he hung up. 'Turns out you were right. They just found a body inside.'

Anya's body tensed.

Schiller broached, 'The mother?'

Bowden shoved both hands into his trouser pockets and

shook his head. 'There's some international pathologists' meeting and Hobart's short-staffed. They've asked if you'd mind examining the scene while you're here.'

Anya could hardly refuse. Since the amalgamation of state medical boards, she could easily step into the role in Tasmania. And she was present. She agreed to do whatever she could to help and moved to the crime scene van and steeled herself. After pulling on white overalls over her trousers and shirt, she grabbed an evidence collection box. The homicide detectives followed her.

Once inside the front door, all three donned gloves and shoe covers.

'Through here.' A scene of crime officer with 'SOCO' printed across his back ushered them in and indicated the children's bedroom. His face was solemn. 'We've taken photos but didn't want to disturb anything before you . . .' His voice trailed off.

'Appreciate it,' Anya said as they headed past the bathroom and into the bedroom.

'In there.' A SOCO with a camera jerked his head towards the wardrobe. Inside, Anya saw a pink plastic container. It resembled the box that her son Ben kept his toys in. Sturdy, but not heavy enough to cause damage if the lid shut on a child.

Schiller fell in behind.

Bowden hovered a little longer by the door. 'We'll give you some space.'

The lid was up, and inside was a khaki army disposal blanket. Anya turned to the SOCO with the camera. 'Have you taken all the photos you need yet?'

'I haven't disturbed anything apart from the corner of the blanket we moved. As soon as it was clear it was a body, we called for you.'

He stood to the right of Anya, camera poised. She gently peeled back a section of blanket to the chest. A small pale hand was visible against a bony forearm. Anya held her breath and lowered it further. The photographer snapped with the flash on.

The child's body was curled into an almost foetal position, clutching a stuffed duck. A girl. Blood was smeared around her mouth and had dripped onto her threadbare butterfly night-dress. Fine, shoulder-length brown hair framed the pale face. On the exposed skin, collar bones appeared prominent.

'She's too big for a three-year-old but small for a ten-year-old,' Anya commented.

'Any obvious trauma?' Bowden remained a few steps behind.

'Not that I can see.' She gently lifted the nightie. 'Blood stains on the underpants, though. We have to consider sexual assault, so the implication is, a man is likely to be involved in the death.'

'Which means,' Schiller said what they were all thinking. 'The mother probably knows him. She's either involved in the death or taken off with the other child.'

'Or, it's possible whoever did this has the mother and the three-year-old,' Anya said. 'Either way, it's urgent you find Jenny and her younger daughter.'

'If a whack-job raped and killed the girl then took the mother and kid, they could be dead already,' Bowden said solemnly.

Another officer entered and immediately had everyone's attention. 'Rest of the property is clear. No more remains.'

Anya was concerned about the amount of blood in the bathroom. There didn't appear to be trauma to the girl's face, or that much blood on her clothes. It was possible the blood in the bathroom came from someone else. 'Did you find anything that could have been used to inflict trauma?'

He shook his head.

Bowden took command. 'Listen up, everyone. We have a missing mother and her three-year-old child. We need a description of them and recent photos. Someone in this freakin' community knows something.'

'Judging by the blood in the bathroom,' Anya reminded them, 'if Jenny and Mia are alive, one or both could be critically injured.'

'For now we treat this as a homicide and a missing persons investigation,' Bowden ordered, before punching numbers into his phone and heading out of the room.

The message was clear. If Jenny or Mia had bled in the bathroom, they had to be found quickly to have any chance of surviving.

5

Anya suggested she visit the GP on Beatrice's list whose surgery was nearby. Bowden immediately volunteered Schiller to tag along with Anya in her car.

Beatrice Quaid would have to formally identify the young body back in Hobart, to establish whether it was, in fact, Emily. Anya could only imagine her grief at losing a second grandchild, and being told that Jenny and Mia were missing, possibly murdered. There was nothing she could do directly for Beatrice now. Besides, as a family member who had raised the alarm, Mrs Quaid might find herself a person of suspicion in the initial stages of the investigation. Except the older woman didn't appear capable of lifting a child into a toy box by herself, or dexterous enough to wipe the bathroom floor. And there was the issue of a possible sexual assault.

Anya and the detective stood in the waiting room amongst sniffles, babies, bandaged limbs and the elderly. A woman in her forties appeared from an end room, seemingly unperturbed by the noise or number of filled seats in the waiting area. Blue earrings matched the frames on her glasses.

A receptionist handed her a file with sticky notes attached. 'There's a policeman and doctor here to see you. They said it's urgent.'

'Thanks.' Dr Debra Wilson scanned the messages. A toddler in the waiting area let out a scream and her focus temporarily diverted. 'Sorry, but we're short-staffed today. How can I help you?'

In a low voice, Schiller said, 'A patient of yours was found today. Dead.'

She let out a sigh. 'You need a death certificate?'

It was a natural assumption to make. Elderly and chronically ill people died at home. Without certification by a doctor who could establish cause of death, it became a coroner's case and required a post-mortem.

'I'm afraid it's more than that. I'm Detective Constable Schiller. Dr Crichton is assisting with a homicide investigation. Is there somewhere we can speak in private?'

Suddenly, the area went silent. Patients could have been forgiven for assuming the doctor was under suspicion.

Anya hastened to add, 'We just need to find out if you know anything that could help us.'

'Of course.' The GP ushered them into a consulting room and closed the door. 'Who was the patient?'

'We suspect it was Emily Quaid.'

The doctor's eyes widened. 'Not little Emmy?' She turned to Anya. 'What do you mean *suspect*?'

'The body was found at the Quaid home. We're still awaiting formal identification, but it appears to be a small child around eight to ten.'

The GP sank into her consulting chair, hand over her mouth for a few moments. 'The poor family. After everything they've been through.'

With the desk butted against the wall opposite the door, Schiller pulled the corner chair closer. 'The mother and sister are missing.'

'Missing? I don't understand.'

Anya sat in the extra chair. 'Emily's body was found in a toy box in the wardrobe. There were blood stains on the bathroom floor. At this stage, it isn't clear whose blood it is.'

Dr Wilson seemed stricken. 'You think . . . Emmy was murdered?' Her eyes darted from the detective to Anya for answers. 'Jenny and Mia?'

'That's what we're trying to find out. And why time is so pressing,' Anya explained.

'I understand.' She straightened. 'How can I help?'

Schiller cleared his throat. 'Do you know the mother well?'

'I saw her fairly frequently until about a year ago. I heard she was seeing some alternative practitioner instead. From what I know of her, she seems like a loving, caring parent. After the death of her little boy, she threw everything she had into protecting those two little girls.'

Anya let the detective take the initial lead. After that, she would ask about any family or medical history that would be valuable at Emily's post-mortem.

Schiller took rapid notes. 'When did the boy die? What happened?'

'It was a while ago. I can check the exact dates.' Dr Wilson wheeled her chair back to the keyboard.

Anya glanced around the office. As well as a Fellowship with the College of GPs, a Medical Degree with Honours and a Paediatric diploma hung above her desk. A jungle mural on the opposite wall with a vertical ruler measured children's height. In the corner were two plastic crates, one containing wooden toys and the other well-worn picture books. Two bright yellow toddler-sized chairs sat in front of the toys. The practice clearly comprised a significant proportion of children.

A few seconds later, a file appeared on the computer screen. 'Tom's file has been archived, but I've got the family history on Emily's notes . . . He contracted whooping cough last January . . . He was eight months old.' She looked up. 'I saw him one night when he was in acute respiratory distress and immediately called an ambulance. He was intubated and spent the next day in intensive care, where he died.'

'How long had the child been ill before the mother sought medical attention?' asked Schiller.

'A couple of days,' she said. 'Respiratory infections are common in infants.'

'Was he vaccinated?'

'No. To my knowledge, none of the children were.' She locked eyes with the detective. 'Emmy's dead and Jenny and Mia are missing. Shouldn't you be out there looking for them?'

Schiller leant forward. 'I realise this is difficult for you, but two kids have died on this woman's watch and it's our job to protect the other one, who may or may not still be alive.'

Dr Wilson seemed to freeze. 'I can't believe it. It doesn't make sense.'

Doctors became attached to patients when they lived and worked in a small community. Anya knew that from her own mother. She had grown up thinking her mother's patients often meant more to her than family.

'The police need to know as much as possible about Jenny and Mia. Anything you can tell us will help,' Anya reassured her.

'Did she have any religious beliefs that prevented her seeking medical help?' asked Schiller.

Anya suspected he was alluding to the Bellamy commune and their lifestyle.

'Being anti-vaccination is a choice, not a religion, and it's not a crime, as much as you or I may disagree with it. A large number of people around here believe in natural healing. It's a battle we constantly fight. We have to be accredited, satisfy stringent professional reviews, but anyone can call themselves a healer.'

Anya tried a different approach. 'How did Jenny react when Tom died?'

'She was devastated. As any mother would be. She wasn't the same after.'

'In what way?' Anya had seen the changes in her own parents after losing a child.

'More withdrawn, but she refused counselling and didn't come in for a follow-up. I saw her at the markets recently, selling bread she'd made, and she seemed a lot brighter.'

Schiller resumed. 'Were there ever unexplained bruises, head injuries, broken bones on the children?'

'I would have noticed if there had been anything. And there was nothing about the children's behaviour to suggest abuse or neglect. They were a bit scruffy, usually covered in dirt, the usual bruises on the shins.'

'Dirty and scruffy?' Schiller noted the description.

Dr Wilson stressed, 'As in normal, healthy, active kids.'

'Except that two of these healthy kids are dead.'

'With all due respect, detective, I'd be more concerned if I didn't see routine bruises on shins. To me that would suggest something was stopping the child from playing and doing normal activities. Illness, delayed milestones, or a child who was cocooned in virtual bubble wrap.'

Anya had seen too many cases in which failure of a child to grow was the result of physical or emotional neglect. 'What were the children's growth patterns?'

The GP referred back to the computer. For her age, Emily was on the twenty-fifth percentile for height and the twentieth for weight. 'Emily was smaller than average for a ten-year-old, but her growth was consistent. Mia was bigger, on the eightieth percentile for height and the seventieth for weight. At least, that was the case five months ago.'

Schiller scribbled. 'Was Emily being smaller than her sister a concern?'

'What matters is consistent growth rate, not size. Different fathers means different genes. Emmy was born petite and stayed that way.' She typed away at her keyboard. 'The last time I saw Emily was to suture a finger.' She scrolled down the records. 'She got it caught in the spoke of her sister's tricycle. That was in . . . August. I always thought Jenny was an amazing mother under the circumstances.'

'Circumstances?' the detective asked.

'Being a single mother. From what she told me, she left school pretty early and fell in with the wrong crowd, experimented with drugs.'

Schiller looked up. 'Did she still use?'

'No. She was poorly educated, not stupid, detective. Those children mean the world to her. Tom's death made her more protective.'

Anya knew the blood on Emily's underwear suggested sexual assault. A de facto or boyfriend would be high on the suspect list. 'Did Jenny have–'

'Discussing her relationships would breach patient confidentiality.' Dr Wilson sounded conflicted.

'I get that, I really do.' Schiller leant in closer. 'But a ten-year-old girl's body was shoved into a toy box. We've got blood all over the bathroom floor and we don't know whose it is. Jenny or Mia could be seriously injured and in desperate need of help. If you know anything that can help us, you owe it to them to tell us.'

A long silence followed.

Anya tried another tack. 'The grandmother told me that there were three different fathers. The question is, were any of them involved in the kids' upbringing, or was there another man in the girls' lives? If you can't tell us, is there anyone who might know?'

The GP rubbed her forehead before looking back to the screen.

'According to my notes, Emily's father died from some neurological condition and never even knew her. Jenny was afraid Emily might have inherited it. As part of the family history, I can tell you there was also a maternal history of clotting disorders.'

Anya read between the lines. A clotting disorder meant the pill and certain hormone contraceptives were too dangerous to prescribe.

'Theoretically, would contraception be a concern for someone with that history?'

The GP nodded. 'Only if a patient was sexually active. Like I said, Jenny was dedicated to those kids. She is anti-vaccination, but has no problem with certain modern medicines. Mind you, she wouldn't necessarily have confided in me. Like I said, it's been some time since I saw her in the rooms.'

Anya knew GPs were part of the local communities, and this one was small. 'Outside the surgery, have you ever seen Jenny with a man?'

'Socially, I've seen her at the fresh food market I mentioned. She seemed to be friendly with the people there. They barter fruit and vegetables for haircuts, gardening and the like. Jenny makes gluten-free bread, which is much better than store-bought versions. We share a hairdresser at Hairtastic.'

'What about the other fathers? Are they involved?' Schiller enquired.

'Last Jenny heard, Mia's dad was working on a fishing trawler off the Western Australian coast, and Tom's was in the army, from memory. I remember he came back for the funeral and that was it. I just can't believe anyone who knew them would hurt Emily or Mia.'

Schiller stood. 'We appreciate your time. Just one more question. You mentioned an alternative therapist who's involved with the Bellamy group. Do you happen to know his name?'

'Dylan something . . . Hey, no. Heyes. That's it. Dylan Heyes.'

Schiller wrote down the name, thanked the doctor and left the room.

'You've been incredibly helpful.' Anya stood.

'Whatever the police think, I can't believe Jenny would have ever intentionally harmed her children.'

The word 'intentionally' caught Anya by surprise. 'Meaning?'

'From what I can tell, she's fairly simple and trusting. She'd ask me questions about cooking, how to use cleaning products, that sort of thing. Things you'd assume were basic common sense. Then again, common sense is a misnomer. It's a lot rarer than it should be.'

Anya wondered if Jenny had inadvertently put the children and herself at risk.

6

Outside the police station, Anya called her former husband in the hope of speaking to their son, Ben. Martin's home number went straight to voicemail. School was still out for another week and the pair could have been at the beach, or on their way to or from Sydney. She tried his mobile.

'Leave a message and I'll get back to you ASAP.'

She wanted them to know she'd called, that she was thinking of them – both.

'Hi guys, Mum here, just wanted to say how much I'm missing you. I'm seeing Poppy tonight for dinner, then should be at Nanna's tomorrow. All going well, I'll see you in a few days. Talk soon, love you.'

The beep sounded again and she instantly regretted leaving the message. Martin had always been frustrated by the unpredictable nature of Anya's work. He saw it as being unreliable where family was concerned. She could hardly reveal that instead of just attending a conference, she'd attended the scene of a dead child in a toy box. Things with Martin were complicated enough right now.

He had to assume the 'love you' was for Ben.

A tap on the hood of the car interrupted her thoughts. She wound down the window.

Steve Schiller stepped off the kerb. 'I know we were going to take your formal statement, but Jenny Quaid's natural healer has turned up with his lawyer. He wants to talk.'

Anya grabbed her bag and left the car with a sense of foreboding. They may have the break they were hoping for. If he'd killed Emily, he most likely knew where Mia and Jenny were. That was, if they were still alive.

Schiller showed her to an adjacent interview room with a small monitor, then excused himself. The junior detective then joined Bowden next door. Opposite them at the table sat a man in his mid-thirties with wavy dark hair and a few days' growth of stubble. To his side was an older man dressed in an open-necked shirt and grey suit jacket. The lawyer.

'We appreciate you coming in, Mr Heyes.' Schiller flipped to a blank page on his notepad.

Bowden cleared his throat. 'Do you want to make a formal statement?'

'Hold on,' the grey jacket interrupted. 'There's been a misunderstanding. I'm here as an observer. The Quaids belong to a small, close community. Every one of our members is suffering the loss. Dylan is here of his own volition, to minimise trauma to everyone concerned.'

Bowden was unmoved. 'Most people would think about the suffering a ten-year-old child went through, and care more about the welfare of a missing mother and child.'

'It's why we're here.' Heyes interlocked his fingers in front of his mouth. 'Jenny is one of the kindest and most giving souls I've ever met, and those girls are a gift.'

'I didn't know you people had a religious bent,' Bowden said without looking up from his notes.

'You don't have to be religious to be spiritual, detective. That's all I meant. Jenny is a wonderful human being. I wanted to help you in any way possible catch whoever, or whatever, did this to Emmy.'

Anya wasn't sure if Bowden's silence meant he was taken aback by the comment.

The lawyer broke the tension. 'Dylan here is the community's mayoral equivalent. He speaks for everyone who lives within the boundaries of Bellamy.'

Schiller and Bowden exchanged glances.

The younger detective asked, 'How long have the Quaids been your patients?'

'Actually,' Heyes rubbed his hands along the thighs of his jeans, 'I don't have patients.'

Bowden interrupted, 'I have it here that you're a natural healer, practitioner of holistic kines . . .' He faltered.

'That's correct.' Dylan straightened.

'So what should we call people who come to you for treatment?'

The lawyer was quick to make the distinction. 'For the record, Dylan sees "clients".'

The word jarred for Anya. Traditionally, the medical profession used the word 'patient', which implied a duty of care to relieve suffering. The word 'client' was used more by lawyers, as someone for whom they provided a service. Customers.

Bowden frowned. 'Prostitutes have clients too.'

Dylan unlinked his fingers and swept a piece of hair from his forehead. 'Medicine is about control, and money. Doctors assume they have all the knowledge and make unilateral decisions about what is best for patients. My clients enter into an equal relationship with me and together we choose the best holistic program for their wellbeing. People who come to me are equal in the relationship.'

Schiller referred to Heyes's business card. 'I see you have an Advanced Diploma in something called HSc, ATMS, AKA, ICMA. Sounds like you're pretty knowledgeable.'

'And I share that knowledge, to empower my clients.'

'That must be pretty time consuming,' Bowden quipped.

Anya suppressed a smile as the lawyer interjected.

'Is there a point to this? What's this got to do with Emily Quaid's death?'

Schiller resumed the lead. 'It would be helpful to establish the relationship between Mr Heyes and the Quaid family.'

'It's okay, I'm happy to clarify,' Heyes said. 'I met Jenny when she moved here. After Tom died, I helped her address some problems she was having with anxiety and some, well, you could say, alarming behaviour, particularly regarding the children.'

Bowden didn't miss a beat. 'Are you saying the kids were neglected, or mistreated?'

Heyes put both hands up. 'I'm just saying she had a litany of problems like insomnia, depression, general amotivation.'

'You mean grief?' Schiller retorted. 'She had just lost a child.'

Heyes's eyes flared. 'That's right. But this was a downward spiral. She had wild swings in blood sugars, which made her crave toxic foods like chips, fried foods.'

'Sounds like most of us on a good day.' Bowden patted his belly.

The lawyer glared at him but the officer appeared unfazed.

'And how did you treat that?' Schiller enquired.

'For the record, I don't diagnose and treat as such, but address the relative underlying stress patterns associated with bodily imbalances. Traditional medicine would have pumped her with antidepressants and sleeping tablets. Her hormones were out of balance and her cranial structures were out of alignment, including her sphenoid.' He paused, as if waiting for a response.

Anya moved closer to the monitor. The sphenoid bone was inside the skull, with a small section connected to the temporal and frontal bones on each side. She hoped he wasn't talking about manipulating it in some way.

'It could have happened when she was assaulted a few years ago. She mentioned a violent boyfriend.' He reached for the cup of water and took a gulp. 'The sphenoid bone,' he tapped just above each of his temples, 'is crucial to spinal, cerebral and spiritual function. Emily was also affected. It's possible she was assaulted in the past.'

'Hang on.' Bowden raised a hand. 'Are you telling us Emily Quaid's skull was damaged?'

'No, I'm saying it was out of alignment and required restoration of balance. After Tom's death, they were consuming food containing all sorts of toxins. Colourings, artificial flavourings, preservatives.'

Schiller sat back. 'Feeding children junk food isn't a crime. If it was, we'd be arresting almost every parent in the country.'

Anya respected his approach.

'That food is criminal. It was damaging Emily, causing all sorts of illness in the child.'

Anya remembered the growth chart shown to them by the GP at the surgery. Emily had normal growth patterns and was thin, but hadn't appeared malnourished.

'What illnesses in particular?'

'Candida infection.'

'Like in thrush?' Schiller asked. Bowden shot him a quizzical look.

'That's a small part of it. I'm talking about candida of the bowel. It can cause all number of symptoms and usually goes undiagnosed by doctors. They choose not to believe it exists.'

Anya had seen the infection in patients who were severely immunocompromised such as cancer patients undergoing chemotherapy, or in cases of overwhelming infection. Natural therapists seemed quick to diagnose it on history alone in patients who had any number of non-specific symptoms.

Heyes was in his element. 'In the early stages it caused Emily constipation and diarrhoea, bloating, food allergies, intolerances, flatulence and poor concentration, then as it spread it led to coughs and colds, ear infections and asthma. It was responsible for her nightmares and detachment anxiety. She never wanted to be away from her mother's side.'

Anya rubbed the back of her neck. The child had lost a baby brother and her mother was grieving. Heyes could have just described her own son, Ben, who had a run of viral infections when he started school, which was a normal part of childhood. Candida had nothing to do with it.

Bowden asked, 'The treatment is?'

'Initially I conducted food allergy and intolerance tests. She was having problems with gluten, dairy and eggs, so she commenced a diet of organic, raw foods to detox completely. A cleansing broth helped rebuild her immune system.'

Anya listened intently. Detoxing a child was dangerous. It could cause fatal dehydration and electrolyte deficiencies.

Schiller looked up. 'When was that?'

'Three weeks ago.'

'When was the last time you saw Emily and her mother?'

'A week ago today, when I performed the Neurocranial Realignment therapy.'

Anya sighed. This had to involve the sphenoid bone he had mentioned earlier. She didn't like where this was heading.

'You're going to have to explain that one.' Bowden remained curt.

'I don't expect you've heard of it; it's a ground-breaking physical treatment. Doctors look at the superficial, but the sphenoid bone is the key to so much illness. Its job is to milk the pituitary gland as it moves. And that is the true centre of our cosmic force.'

Schiller glanced at the camera. Anya listened closely for any clues as to specifics she should be looking for at the post-mortem.

'I performed Bilateral Endonasal Balloon therapy. Using a blood pressure bulb covered in a lubricated finger-sized covering, I insert the finger cot into the nasal passages and when the client breathes out, the bulb delivers a controlled burst of pressure into each side. Sometimes the lower nasal passageways need a double dose, but the effect is immediate. It causes a shift in the sphenoid that realigns the cranial bones and opens up cerebrospinal fluid and blood flow, and helps the sinuses to drain better and stimulates the pituitary gland. The effects are immediate. Emily left the room a different child.'

Anya tried to imagine how difficult it would be to get a ten-year-old to be compliant with such an invasive and uncomfortable procedure. At the post-mortem, she would need to ask the pathologist to look closely for signs of trauma to the nasal bones and areas surrounding the sphenoid.

The lawyer reached into his bag and extracted a series of papers. 'Dylan has kindly outlined the treatments. Here are the instructions for the cleansing broth and the detox diet, and NCPT, which Jenny Quaid has copies of as well. You'll notice there is information about what to do if the child became unwell. You'll also find a waiver signed by Jennifer Quaid.'

Schiller glanced at his partner. 'Waiver? Don't you mean consent?'

'No, detective, you'll find it's a waiver. Dylan doesn't claim to treat clients. As he explained, he addresses bodily imbalances.'

There was a prolonged silence in the room as the detectives surveyed the papers.

Bowden spoke first. 'Do you charge for these services?'

'Yes, but in Jenny's case, she provided fresh bread in exchange for my services.'

Bowden nodded. 'Did you hear from Jenny Quaid again, about how her daughter was doing?'

'The lines of communication were open. In my field, no news is good news. You have to remember, I offer clients hope; the rest is up to them.'

'In our experience no news is never good news.' Schiller rose. 'And hope is never a solution.' Collecting his notes, he added, 'We'll be in touch. Thanks for your time.'

Bowden remained seated. 'Couple more things: could Jenny Quaid have been seeing other therapists?'

Heyes straightened and puffed out his chest. 'No. No way.'

'Needed to check. Are you sure because you were in an intimate relationship with her?'

'This interview is over,' the lawyer snapped, and stood. 'That would be completely unprofessional. Dylan is a health therapist.'

'Who has just gone to great pains to explain that he has "clients", not patients. As far as I know, lawyers don't have ethical problems consummating relationships with female clients, so why would Mr Heyes?'

The therapist's face reddened. He and the lawyer pushed past Schiller on their way out.

In their wake, Bowden stood, hands on hips. 'My gut screams this guy did something to Emily. How can shoving tubes into a kid's nose and blowing pressure up the brain be safe?'

Anya waited until Heyes was out of sight before joining the detectives. She had wondered the same thing, particularly if the child had moved suddenly as pressure was applied. It would be like trying to hold down a greasy cat. 'It depends on the amount of pressure, and how compliant Emily was. Either way, he says he performed the procedure a week ago. If it caused damage, then you'd think it would have manifested pretty quickly.'

Schiller leant on the table. 'Are you sure the mother would have known if something had gone wrong? She was pretty vulnerable and this guy is good at care without responsibility.'

They headed for the main office. 'Beats me,' Schiller threw his notepad down on a desk, 'How people get suckered by these whack jobs.'

It was easy to see how a mother who had lost a child would fear hospitals. Heyes was right about some things. Issues with gluten and lactose were common, but could be accurately diagnosed with medical tests. The results of detox therapy for a child, however, could be catastrophic. The liver and kidneys could be important in Emily's case.

A phone rang and they glanced around, hoping someone else would answer it. Someone else did.

Schiller sat back against a desk. 'The way he lawyered up, he's protecting his own backside.'

It was possible Emily had died from complications of Heyes's recommended treatments. It left a lot unexplained, though, such as why the body was found in the toy box, and why Jenny and Mia were now missing.

The waiver had caught Anya's attention. 'You might want to look into his other "clients". He may have been through this before. This time he came prepared with his lawyer and defence. And he doesn't seem to have a problem with breaching client confidentiality.'

'I'm on it.' Schiller moved to the photocopier. 'You should take a copy of his miracle cure notes. You may be able to tell the mumbo jumbo from what is safe.' Bowden shook his head. 'We've got to stick with the big picture. That guy's pretty convincing, and it sounds like Jenny trusted him. We can't forget the fact that there was blood on the girl's underpants . . .'

The comment hung heavily.

Schiller's phone rang. 'Doctor, you've been invited to the autopsy at four o'clock. Would you care to come along as an observer?'

Anya checked her watch. 'I'll see you there.' She grabbed her bag and car keys. It was important to have as much information for Beatrice Quaid when they eventually spoke.

A uniformed officer entered the room and handed Schiller an envelope before retreating. Crime scene had already printed off some of the photos from the house. 'Hey wait,' the young detective said. 'Anya, what do you make of this?'

The image was of a photo of Jenny Quaid and two little girls. One was a baby in pink, the other looked around five or six. 'It had to have been taken before Tom was born. That means it was Mia as a baby, and that must be Emily. She looks young because of her size.'

'Yeah, but what about what she's holding.'

Anya looked closer. Under her arm was a soft toy. A yellow duck. Identical to the one wrapped in the blanket with Emily's body. Anya felt her pulse quicken. Whoever put Emily in the box knew she loved that toy.

'You're looking for someone who knew her well. If a man murdered Emily, Jenny may well be involved.'

Dylan Heyes was their prime suspect.

7

The image of Mia, Emily and Jenny replayed in Anya's mind. Someone who knew the family well had been involved in leaving the duck with Emily's body. If it was an abduction, there was no obvious motive. If Dylan Heyes was involved, he'd seemed calmer and more controlled than she would have imagined – until the question of sexual relations with Jenny arose.

Anya drove along the main street in Huonville and found a car park a few doors down from the hair salon. It was a hunch that may just pay off. It if didn't, she wouldn't have wasted valuable police time. In her experience, there was always someone women confided in. If it wasn't some kind of therapist, this was the next person on the list. The GP had mentioned Hairtastic as the place Jenny went for haircuts.

A man with a buzz cut greeted her from behind a tall reception desk. A blow dryer blasted in the background.

'Can I help you, madam?'

Anya always felt old when anyone called her that. 'Dr Wilson mentioned that someone here cut her hair.' A rail-thin woman with copper-red, shoulder-length hair interrupted her cutting to look up. The man glanced at a computer screen on the desk. 'Do you want to make an appointment with Wendy?'

'I just wondered if it was possible to have a quiet word.' Anya tugged at a loose piece of hair that had escaped her hair knot.

The man looked sympathetically at Anya's hair and quickly moved from his stool. He whispered into the ear of the woman who had looked up. She studied Anya before saying something to the person in the chair and putting down the hair dryer.

'How can I help you?' Anya was greeted with a look of concern. Did her hair really look that bad?

'Dr Wilson mentioned your name.'

The woman's shoulders relaxed. 'We all love Debbie. Come and have a seat.' The pair sat at a lounge near the front window. 'Are you thinking of a bob, longer in the front, shorter in back?'

'This isn't about me. I'm here about Jenny Quaid.'

The woman scanned Anya's face with wide brown eyes. 'Are you from some government department? Please don't tell me she owes money again.'

Anya realised the news hadn't reached the salon yet.

'No. Have you seen or heard from her in the last three days?'

Curiosity quickly turned to concern.

She checked her watch. 'Not since last week. There's a farmers' market on Sunday. She'll be working at the co-op today. Why?' She dipped into her pocket and lifted out a phone, pressed a number and listened before clicking the end button.

'It's going to message bank. Look, if she owes money, I might be able to help out. Some months the bills just mount up, but she'll pay every cent back when she can.'

Anya touched the woman's hand. 'I'm sorry. This isn't about money.'

There was no way to break the news gently.

'A child was found in Jenny's house today. Dead. The police think it might be her daughter, Emily. Jenny and little Mia are missing.'

The man behind the desk covered his mouth. 'Oh my–'

'I need air.' Wendy grabbed something from behind the desk. It was a pack of cigarettes and a lighter.

The man moved from the desk to the seated customer.

Outside, Wendy stopped a few shops away and lit a cigarette. Her hands were shaking. 'What happened. To Emmy?'

'She was found at the house. It's too early to know how she died.' Anya decided honesty was the only way to gain the woman's trust. 'There was no sign of Jenny or Mia. It looked like they hadn't been there for a couple of days.'

One arm folded against her waist, Wendy took a long drag and exhaled. 'No way she'd leave Emmy. Jen would never ever do that.' Her eyes suddenly widened. 'How can they be missing?' She flicked a strand of copper hair from her eye. 'Someone has to be keeping her from Em . . . This is bullshit. This can't be happening.'

Anya spoke softly, even though the street was quiet. 'I was at the house. There was blood in the bathroom that someone had tried to clean.'

The hairdresser puffed on the cigarette and shook her head, as if it would make reality go away.

'Do you know if Jenny is seeing anyone? Is there anyone who might want to hurt her or the kids?'

The hairdresser locked eyes with her. 'You think someone killed Emmy. And Jenny and Mia too?' She clutched her stomach. 'I'm going to be sick.' She gagged and dry-retched a number of times, then wiped her mouth.

Anya stood close, offering physical support if needed. A couple across the road had stopped and were watching.

'I only babysat Em and Mia two weekends ago. I took over my Wii and we played every single game. They had a ball.'

The man from inside the salon had obviously been watching and tentatively appeared with a glass of water containing a lemon slice.

'You can talk in the back room, stop the whole town gawking at you. I'll make sure you have privacy.'

Wendy stubbed out her cigarette on the footpath.

Before heading inside, Anya phoned Steve Schiller and explained where she was. She asked him to email images of the interior of the Quaid house. Kitchen, living areas and bedrooms, apart from the wardrobe. A babysitter would be familiar with them.

Anya walked back through the salon. The smell of ammonia perm solution initially made her eyes water. In a back room shelves contained rows of shampoo, conditioners and hair dyes. The reception man carried in a second chair. He patted Wendy on the back before lighting another cigarette for her. 'I'll get you a strong coffee.' He closed a sliding door behind him.

Anya was aware of how pressing time was now. 'I need to ask some personal questions about Jenny, because it's critical the police find her and Mia quickly.'

Wendy tucked her feet up onto the chair and hugged her knees. 'I understand.'

'Would you know if Jenny has a boyfriend?' she asked again.

'There isn't anyone.' Wendy leant closer. 'Those kids are her world. Some people think she's over-the-top protective, but who can blame her?'

'Did any men show a particular interest in her or the girls?'

'Only that snake-oil merchant, Dylan Heyes. He made Emily his pet project, even gave Jenny "discount rates".'

Anya recalled that Heyes had mentioned bread in exchange for his services. 'Did anything sexual ever happen between him and Jenny?'

Wendy took another drag. 'He specialises in bored house-wives. I could tell you some stories.'

That's exactly what Anya was hoping. Hairdressers seemed to know all about who was sleeping with whom in the community.

'Does Jenny have many friends out at Bellamy?'

The hairdresser let the cigarette burn down. 'She works with them. She loves being part of their "family" as she calls them but they're pretty full on and half of them are squatting out there, without electricity or hot water. Jenny wants more than that for her kids. When she needs money for bills, or just some space, she knows she can call me. I take DVDs out there for the kids, and games.' She stubbed the butt into a glass bowl. 'I don't understand. If she was in trouble, why didn't she call?'

'Did Emily have school friends or spend time with other kids?'

'Emmy's gorgeous, bright and sensitive. A real old soul.' Tears welled. 'She was always helping her mum and preferred to spend time with her. They were more like sisters. They have the same birthday, fifteen years apart.'

'Can you think of anywhere else Jenny might go, if she needed to get away in a hurry?'

Wendy thought for a while. 'She would have come to my place. I'd have to pick her up. She can't drive.

Anya heard a ping from her bag. She pulled out her iPad and checked the emails. Schiller had sent through the pictures she'd asked for. 'If I show you some pictures of how the house was found, do you think you'd know if anything was out of place?'

'I guess.' Wendy put her legs down and moved her chair closer to see the screen. Looking at the first photo she said, 'Wednesdays and Saturdays are her bread-baking days. Like clockwork. Although she never leaves the flour or yeast out like that. And she always wipes the bench clean between each batch.'

Today was Friday. If the kitchen had been abandoned on Wednesday, Emily can't have been dead for more than forty-eight hours. Anya scrolled to the next image.

'That's wrong. The milk on the bench. She would never leave it out.'

Anya became more concerned that the mother and daughter had been abducted.

Inside the fridge, items were stacked neatly in containers. Either Jenny Quaid was incredibly organised, or she had an obsessive-compulsive disorder. The rest of the house didn't seem to have the same level of order.

'We talked about kitchen hygiene a lot after Tom died. I saw Jenny putting meat on the shelf above vegetables in the fridge. She didn't realise how quickly foods go off if you leave them out. She'd leave cooked sausages on the bench overnight, then have them for tea the next night. Money was tight; she had to make the most of leftovers.'

'So she learnt. The fridge was evidence of that.'

'Oh yeah, she always wants to learn more about things. Leaving school so early really bothers her. Those girls of hers had better finish high school or . . .' Her voice trailed off.

The next images appeared on the iPad, these of the living areas and bedrooms.

'Can you see anything out of place? Or maybe something that isn't there that should be, like a computer?'

'She didn't own one, or any real jewellery, for that matter.' A dye-stained finger pointed to the television, which sat on a piece of wood held up by milk crates. 'She found that left out for council pickup. Worked fine. She loves watching the ads, thinks those are better than the shows. Never met anyone like her.' The hairdresser fought back tears. 'Everything looks normal.'

They moved to the girls' bedroom. Both beds were unmade.

'Did Jenny ever discipline the girls?'

'All the time. She didn't want them growing up disrespectful.'

'In what way?' Anya probed.

Wendy looked directly at her. 'Never hit them, if that's what you mean. Sure, she could yell. What mother doesn't? But the way she handled those kids was amazing. Most of the time, all she needed to do was say their name, or give them a look.' The sliding door opened and a woman in a black vinyl cloak appeared, hair wrapped in a towel. They could hear a blow dryer back inside.

'Sorry. Bathroom.'

Wendy opened the back door for her, which led outside and the woman shuffled off, presumably to a toilet shared by the businesses.

'Can you go back to the photos in the kitchen?' Wendy leant in again. 'That's weird. Jenny's recipe book isn't there.'

'Where did she keep it?'

'On two hooks on the pantry door.'

An enlarged image showed the empty hooks.

'Emily had the brilliant idea of doing up cards for Jen's birthday. To show her the quantities in the recipes and how long to bake each dish. I got them laminated and punched holes in one side. Em strung them together into a book so they could hang where Jen could easily see them.' Wendy became more animated. 'The number of chef's hats showed how much Em liked the foods. That way, Jen could always make perfect bread and cakes, even roasts.'

'You said the cards *showed* the quantities.' Anya didn't follow. Recipes always listed quantities and cooking times. Why would they need to be shown on handmade cards?

'With cups, different-sized spoons and drawings. Only Jenny wanted me to think they were for Emily and Mia, not her.'

Anya suddenly understood. Rather than being overprotective, Jenny Quaid was hiding a secret that kept her vulnerable and isolated. She was too ashamed to share it with her closest friend.

The twenty-five year-old couldn't read. With the death of Emily, she had lost her protector.

'Don't you see?' Wendy pleaded. 'Jenny could never hurt Emily. That child was her eyes to a world she couldn't otherwise be a part of.'

Anya became even more afraid for what had happened to Mia and her mother.

8

As she left Hairtastic, Anya noticed a heightened police presence in the main street. Uniformed officers had begun door-knocking the shops with photos of Jenny and Mia. Anya headed back to Hobart for Emily's post-mortem, hoping someone would know enough to help the investigation. On the way, she called Schiller and filled him in on what she had learnt.

Along the A6 past colourful orchards, she left the pristine Huon River behind. It always amazed her that she could be in planted orchards and a relatively short drive away lay the rugged World Heritage Southwest Forests. Tasmania was full of contrasts and contradictions, she remembered all too well.

After parking near the hospital and locating the morgue, she braced herself before entering through the plastic screen doors. Inside lay the small, pale body. Emily Quaid had acted beyond her years, translating the world for her mother.

Dr Clive Arneil and a technician were already inside the suite, along with Schiller. 'Anya, it's good to have you here. Last time we worked together, it must have been Bali, wasn't it?'

'After the hotel bombing.'

'You two identified those bodies?' Schiller seemed impressed.

Anya nodded. 'We all do disaster work, there aren't enough pathologists to go around so we all do what we can when there's an emergency.'

Clive went back to the task. If the case of a child bothered him, he hid it well. He had once quietly admitted to her that he preferred dead people. He found them less complicated than live ones. He avoided conferences, and preferred to correspond with colleagues via letter or email, such was his shyness with strangers.

Schiller retreated closer to the doors. 'Detective Bowden decided he was better off going over the Quaid house again for evidence.'

'Anything so far?' She averted her eyes from the table.

Clive had already opened the chest plate. 'External examination is a female child, 134 centimetres, weight 22 kilograms.'

Anya knew that was small for a ten-year-old girl. Ben, now eight, was 130 centimetres and weighed more than that.

'Skin turgor was increased, suggesting dehydration. Otherwise, unremarkable.'

'A natural therapist had her on a diet of raw foods and "detox" recipes,' Anya said. She also explained the procedure Dylan Heyes had performed through the nose and asked Clive to check for damage to the nasal cavity and sphenoid bone.

Clive didn't look up. 'That doesn't explain a distended abdomen. There were no other distinctive markings, wounds or injuries. I noted blood and faecal matter around the anus.'

Anya stepped forward and had a look for herself. Emily's skin was like alabaster. There were no visible contusions, bruises or dot-like haemorrhages. Nothing to suggest trauma, no ligature marks. 'External genitalia?' she asked.

'Hymen was intact with no signs of perineal trauma. Nevertheless, I took swabs.'

That suggested Emily hadn't had vaginal interference. But the blood around her rectum remained a concern.

Anya moved to the lit up viewing boxes. X-rays of the skull, limbs and chest failed to reveal any fractures, new or healed. There was no evidence of foreign bodies either. The chest appeared congested and loops of bowel were enlarged.

A rancid smell Anya recognised suddenly filled the room. Schiller covered his nose. Anya moved closer to the abdomen. In his gloved hands, Clive held a stretch of large, perforated intestine. 'Appendix isn't inflamed,' he announced. Anya's attention was drawn to the wall of the bowel. It was oedematous, swollen.

The pathologist dissected a section, opening it up, continuing to dictate into the hanging microphone above his head. 'The wall is friable and tore on minimal disruption. There are longitudinal ulcers near the caecum.' He extended the cut. 'And in sections of the large bowel.'

Schiller reached over to see. 'Could she have had Crohn's?' He added, 'When we were fourteen, my twin brother got sick and lost all this weight. They diagnosed it on colonoscopy. He used to pass blood.'

'Crohn's is a possibility, but it's too early to reach a conclusion.'

An inflammatory bowel disease might explain what they were seeing, but Anya was drawn to the appearance of the kidneys.

Clive pulled a stretch of bowel to the side and exposed them. Like the bowel, both were congested and inflamed. He asked for a needle and syringe, which the technician prepared. Inserting it into the tiny bladder, he pulled back on the plastic syringe. He repeated the process. The syringe remained empty. 'Looks like she was anuric.'

'Anuric?' The detective took notes on a small pad.

'She wasn't producing any urine,' Anya answered. 'You'd expect the bladder to have something in it, even if she had recently voided.'

The phone in the centre rang. The technician answered and handed it to Anya.

'Ken Kuah, Professor of Haematology. I'm told this is an urgent police investigation so I had a look at the blood films myself.'

Dr Arneil asked Anya to place the handset on speakerphone and open the email on the desk laptop. Anya clicked on the message sent by Kuah. Multiple images downloaded. Anya enlarged the first one. 'We're looking at the first slide now. Full blood count showed leucocytosis, white cell count was forty-one. Haemoglobin's down but haematocrit's up. There's a marked thrombocytopenia. As you can see, there are significant numbers of schistocytes.'

'What are they from?' Schiller was understandably impatient to know what it all meant.

'The Greeks, of course,' Clive answered. '*Schistos* – divided, and *kytos* – cell.'

To save time, Anya pointed to the screen. 'Can you see how these cells are irregular and look like broken pieces?'

'Yeah, compared to the red, round ones.' Schiller was concerned with their relevance to the investigation. 'Do they happen with physical trauma? Maybe as a result of what that Heyes did to the nasal area?'

'They are damaged, but at a microscopic level, when they pass thrombi, or clots,' Dr Kuah commented. 'We didn't receive a clinical history, just a date of birth. Did the child have an artificial heart valve?'

'No,' Clive said. 'I'm looking at a friable, ulcerated large intestine.'

'Sorry,' the detective interrupted, 'you're talking about clots? If the blood was full of clots, doesn't that mean she won't bleed much? I mean, someone's blood was all over that bathroom floor and if it isn't hers . . .'

Anya clarified, 'Microscopic clots occur in vessels and organs, using up things called thrombocytes or platelets. They're what stop you bleeding to death if you have a simple nose bleed or a cut.'

'Okay,' Schiller reasoned, 'so once they are all used up . . .'

'Inflammation leads to leaking blood vessels. Without platelets, bleeding gets out of control. It means,' Anya deduced, 'the blood on the floor in the bathroom could have come from Emily's bowel.'

Schiller asked quietly, 'Just so we're all clear. Did outside interference, like a sexual assault, cause the bowel inside to bleed?'

'Detective,' Clive interrupted, 'in this case the rectum was doing what it was designed for. It is an exit, not an entrance. There is nothing to suggest sexual assault in this instance.'

Anya felt relieved for Emily. She clicked the next image on the computer. 'I'm looking at the electrolytes. Raised serum creatinine, lactic dehydrogenase, low sodium, elevated potassium. Kidney failure and severe dehydration, to the point that she could no longer produce urine.'

'There's blood in the lungs as well,' Clive added.

'Could those results be caused by something like leukaemia?' Schiller asked. The question was reasonable.

Dr Kuah spoke again. 'I believe we're looking at a haemolytic anaemia. The faecal smear is overrun with gram-negative bacteria that also appear on portions of the blood film. The child had an overwhelming form of sepsis, or infection, if you like. I'll organise serology for antibodies to E. coli strains.'

Schiller suddenly looked pale. 'Infection? So Emily wasn't murdered but she still ended up stuffed in a box?'

'Stomach's full of blood,' Clive announced. 'That would cause vomiting, another potential source of the bathroom blood stains.'

Anya thought about what Beatrice Quaid had said. She believed Jenny was guilty of negligent homicide by refusing to get Tom vaccinated. If Emily had developed a serious infection and hadn't been taken for medical treatment, Jenny could be considered responsible as well.

She turned to Schiller. 'We won't know for sure until we have the blood cultures back, and they may not grow anything anyway. But it looks like Emily died from Haemolytic Uraemic Syndrome, or HUS for short. It's caused by a bacteria that produces its own toxin, which is why it causes so much damage.'

'Then why the hell put her body in a box?' Schiller's brow furrowed. 'Unless you're guilty, or trying to cover up something else.'

It was possible Jenny had panicked. With two children dead, she could have been frightened of losing Mia, her only surviving child.

Schiller said, 'Any chance the brain-bone shifting nose treatment caused or introduced the infection? If it did, I'm going straight for that snake, Heyes.'

'The bacteria is transferred via the faecal-oral route,' Clive muttered.

'The family friend I spoke to was adamant, Jenny was meticulous about kitchen hygiene and safe food storage,' Anya said.

'Then how did she get it?' Schiller pulled out his phone. 'Is it contagious?'

'No,' Dr Kuah said down the phone line, 'but cases like this are rarely isolated. They usually occur as part of an outbreak. The sufferer ingests the bacterium in either uncooked, under-cooked or contaminated foodstuffs.'

'In lay terms,' Clive said, 'it's a deadly form of food poisoning.' He moved to examine the skull.

'So if Jenny Quaid did all the cooking and even made their bread,' Schiller reasoned, 'chances are . . .'

The answer hung in the air. Mia and her mother could be in desperate need of medical assistance. Not to mention that any number of other people might have come into contact with the source of the infection.

'This is a notifiable infection. The public health unit has to be told,' Clive said flatly. 'This could be the first case of an epidemic.'

'Or, it may have been confined to Jenny's home.' Schiller suggested. 'Remember the rat on the garden bed?'

Irrespective, given the attention a child death and missing family garnered, Anya knew it would be made public before long. 'If you and Bowden don't mind, I'd like to let the grandmother know how Emily died. Once public health know, it will be open to the media. Mrs Quaid deserves to hear it from someone other than a reporter.'

Schiller checked his watch.

'Uniforms brought her in to ID the body about an hour ago. She went home to wait by the phone for word.'

'Good news,' Clive interrupted. 'About that intranasal business. You'll be pleased to know, the sphenoid bone is intact.'

9

After the post-mortem, Bowden called Schiller back to the Quaid home to check the scene one more time and interview anyone who might know where Jenny and Mia may have gone. They hoped to find out how close the community members were and if any of them had been ill.

On the way to the car park, Anya dialled Beatrice Quaid's number. It answered on the first ring.

'We have nothing to say. Please respect that,' a male voice pleaded.

'My name is Dr Anya Crichton. I met with Mrs Quaid this morning. May I speak with her?'

There was a muffled conversation in the background. At least someone was screening the calls to the home. The media would be on Beatrice's doorstep and were probably calling for comments.

'Have they found Jenny and Mia yet?' Beatrice sounded raspier than earlier.

Anya closed her eyes. The waiting had to be intolerable. 'They're still searching everywhere possible. I'm calling about Emily.'

Beatrice took an audible gasp.

'It looks like she died from a severe gastrointestinal

infection.' She deliberately avoided using the term *food poisoning* over the phone, in case the grieving and worried grandmother misheard and believed Emily had been poisoned. 'The source was most likely something Emily ate. It isn't contagious and there's no vaccine that could have prevented it.'

There was a prolonged silence on the line.

'I don't understand. The police said she was . . . they said foul play. It's why they were so worried about Jenny and Mia.'

'Initially, that's what they thought. Blood tests confirm the presence of the bacteria, but they can take a couple of days.'

'Then where are my daughter and grandchild?' Beatrice's voice was strained. 'Did Jenny . . . did she just let Emily die?' She swallowed. 'Then shove the dead child in a box and run away, as if no one would ever know? Not even Jenny could be that cold.'

Anya didn't have the definitive answer. 'Maybe Jenny panicked.' It was difficult to imagine how any mother could let a child suffer without getting help. Especially when Emily was so close to Jenny. She had previously lost her son to an infection, and could have feared Mia would be taken away from her. By her own mother.

Without a car, it would have been almost impossible to take a three-year-old far, and even harder if the child were sick as well. Unless she had hitchhiked or someone had offered her a ride. But the house looked as if she'd left in a rush. The phone was off the hook. Records would show who she'd last spoken to, if she had, in fact, called for help.

'The police are chasing up medical centres and hospitals, in case Jenny presented at one of them.'

'Do you think Mia could have the same infection as Emily?'

Anya couldn't lie. As difficult as it was for the grandmother, she deserved to know the truth.

'It's possible, if they ate the same contaminated food. Jenny as well. Public health and food inspectors will swab the contents of the home fridge. If this bacteria is there, they'll find it.'

'Thank you, doctor, for keeping me informed. I'm sorry, I have to go now.'

Anya wondered about Jenny Quaid's mind-set. The woman had shunned conventional medicine and lost her baby in a hospital. Dylan Heyes came across convincingly with his pseudoscience and medical jargon. To perform his intra-nasal therapy, he had to have had Jenny's complete trust. Anya wondered if he had dissuaded her from seeking medical help in the past. Or if he had advised that diarrhoea and vomiting were a normal part of his detoxification program. Without answers, and nothing more to offer the investigation tonight, she drove back to the hotel, showered and washed the day out before changing for dinner.

The loose cotton dress she'd chosen billowed as she approached the harbour. The sea air, and all her memories of watching the ocean, were invigorating. She pulled out her ponytail and let the breeze dry her wavy mane.

Her phone rang and she answered as soon as she saw the number.

'Hi, Mum,' Ben enthused.

She almost missed being called Mummy, but those days were past.

'Hey, gorgeous boy, I've been looking forward to hearing all about your day. How was it?'

'Good. We went to this really great zoo. I patted wallabies. The emus tried to eat my lunch but Dad chased them away. They're cranky and I didn't really like them much. They really need to learn manners.'

Anya smiled. At times the eight-year-old sounded more like an old man. 'Lots of animals get rude when food's around. Some people, too. Did you see the giant crocodiles?'

'They didn't move. All you could see was their noses sticking out of the water. Are you with Poppy yet?'

'No, but I'll give him a big hug for you. We're having dinner at Constitution Dock. It's a big harbour and there are lots of fishing boats, yachts, cruisers.'

'Can you take some pictures? We had schnitzel and chips tonight at a cafe.'

Anya could hear Martin in the background say, 'Don't tell Mum all our secrets. Sorry, mate, we gotta go. Tell Mum I'll call her later, visiting hours finish soon. You can talk to her tomorrow.'

'Did you hear Dad?'

'Yes, it's okay. You need to go.'

'Mum,' his voice lowered. 'We're going back to see Nita. She's got "*ammonia*",' he emphasised the pronunciation, 'and is sick in hospital.'

'I know, sweetie. Pneumonia is pretty serious.'

'I have to put my shoes on. Say hi to Poppy for me. I love you.'

'Love you all the way to the sky and back again.'

'Love you all the way to the sky and never back again.' He went one better every time.

10

Anya glanced around at the boats and snapped some pictures to show Ben. He loved all things water and everything nautical.

She turned and saw her father. Instantly recognisable in sunglasses, striped polo shirt and knee-length shorts, he was more tanned and leaner than when she'd last seen him, a couple of months ago. It made his silver hair more distinguished.

He stood, removed his glasses and smiled, creating the long dimple creases she had adored as a child. As they hugged, he held her tightly and kissed her head. Bob Reynolds had always been the most affectionate in the family, and through his work he had been known to embrace victims and sometimes even violent offenders.

'Hey, kiddo, you looked as if you had the weight of the world on those shoulders, just then.' He stepped back. 'Everything okay back home?'

'Just tired. Long day. Ben sends his love and a big hug.'

Bob grinned. 'I'm sending a giant one back at him.'

Anya was thinking about Ben's life compared to Emily and Mia's. How lucky he was to have two loving parents, even if they didn't live together.

Bob looked out towards the eclectic collection of boats in dock. Sloops, schooners and maxi yachts bobbed amongst fishing trawlers and traditional wooden boats.

'Remember all the times we sat here watching the finish of the Sydney to Hobart?'

The sounds of seagulls and metal clunking on masts always took her back to those times. The yacht race that began on Boxing Day was one of the world's top ocean races and a highlight of childhood summers. It had been a welcome break from her grandmother's farm.

'Seeing them sail through the harbour was always special.'

'And there I thought I had to bribe you to come, with the world's best fish and chips.'

Anya smiled. 'There was that too.' Her stomach gurgled at the mention of food.

'I know just the place where we can sit, enjoy some unusual decor and indulge again.'

It sounded perfect, although the decor had her intrigued. 'Is Evelyn coming?'

Her father usually stayed with his favourite cousin when he visited.

'She's sorry but she's come down with some sort of virus. Hopefully it's just a twenty-four-hour thing.'

They walked in the breeze around to Hunter Street, to the old wharf. Anya savoured the salty air and turned to admire the view across to Mount Wellington.

'Here we are,' Bob announced, directing her attention to a wooden sign hanging above them, adorned with a skull and crossbones and reading *The Drunken Admiral*. 'Sorry, they don't have outside tables, but Evie says this place is her top pick.'

As they entered, the smell of cooking oil and deep-fried fish filled Anya's nostrils. The place was full with families and conversation. She glanced around at the wooden tables and nautical decor. A skeleton was propped up against a ship's wheel. Barrels hung from the ceiling and a fake hand protruded from the mouth of a shark's head. Doubloon-style coins were scattered between iron candlesticks and burning white candles on a display table.

Her father nodded. 'It's exactly how she described. Even though you half expect Captain Jack Sparrow to pop out, they tell me the food is incredible.'

'Ben would have a conniption if he saw this place.'

A friendly waitress greeted them.

Bob said, 'I have a booking under Reynolds. Do you have anywhere a little quieter?'

'I've put you at a table in the quietest room.'

They followed her to a room with a small window, filled mostly with tables for two. Anya's father held the chair out for his daughter. 'Neither of us has to drive, so what would you like to drink?'

'Pina colada, thanks,' Anya said to the waitress.

'I'll have a scotch on the rocks. And I hear your tempura olives are a specialty.'

'They are good, I'll bring you some with your drinks.' The waitress handed them menus.

Anya's work at the conference had finished, and she was keen to know how Bob's workshop had gone. 'Did you have a good turnout today?'

'Full room, definitely got some people thinking outside the square.' He unfolded the napkin. 'Yours was a cracker talk this morning, apart from the protester coming in. You handled it with great aplomb, I must say.'

'She wasn't a protester, Dad. She was desperate for help to prevent what she thought was child abuse. It's complicated.'

'Anything I can help with, legal or otherwise?'

Anya shook her head. 'At the moment it's a missing persons case.'

The waitress returned with their drinks and placed a tray of tempura olives on top of a treasure map paper placemat.

'Not that case that's been on the radio – a child's body and two others missing?'

Anya took a sip and scanned the menu. 'Unfortunately,

she has been affected by that. And it's part of my job to be involved.'

Reading the menu, she considered the source of Emily's fatal infection. E. coli, a bacteria rampant in humans and animals, mostly came from contaminated food. Cooking should kill the bacteria if it were on meat, but raw and undercooked foods and salads were another possible source. And Heyes had had Emily on a raw foods diet.

'Few people appreciate what goes on behind the scenes when death occurs. I just know how busy you've been since you came back from overseas.' He raised his glass. 'I have Diana, but who's looking after you?'

Her father still worked for legal aid part-time, but spent the majority of his days working in prisons and with victims of violent crime. Anya clinked her glass with his and took a long, cool sip. 'I'm glad you remarried, honestly. Trust me, I'm fine. I love what I do. And Ben is the most wonderful thing to have ever happened to me.'

Bob wiped his lips. 'Any chance I'll see my wonderful grandson for his birthday?'

'We're not sure where he'll be on the day.' He was with his father and – Anya still found it difficult to know what to call Nita. Martin had been about to break up with the woman, or so he said, when she'd called with the news that she had malignant melanoma.

'Martin and Ben are at Westmead Hospital. They'll be in Sydney until the end of next week.' She took another drink and felt her face flush with the alcohol. 'Nita's still on the melanoma vaccine trial. It looks like some of the brain tumours are shrinking, but she's developed pneumonia.'

Her father popped an olive into his mouth. 'That's great news about the tumours . . . for her.'

Anya knew where this was heading. 'Please don't.'

'Something happened on that cruise between you and Martin. Ben thought you were a family again. How confusing do you think this is for him?'

It was confusing enough for the adults involved. Nita had been about to leave for England, and Martin wanted to separate. Then she'd received the news about having metastatic melanoma, with a very poor prognosis. Everything had changed.

The waitress reappeared. Anya decided on hot rock salmon with wasabi for a main.

'I'll have the Yachties Seafood mixed grill,' Bob said, 'with a giant bowl of chips. We can share starters, bloody mary oysters and the chorizo entrees would be great. And some bread, too, thanks.' The waitress cheerily retrieved the menus.

'It's a long way from the newspaper-wrapped fish and chips we used to have.' Keen to change the subject, Anya glanced around and noticed a replica musket on the wall, complete with barnacles along the barrel and handle.

Bob lowered his gaze to meet Anya's. 'What are you doing about Martin?'

Reluctantly, she admitted, 'Nita needs him now. More than—'

'I get it. More than you do, because you're healthy. But when are your needs going to be considered? It's sad about Nita. Tragic, in fact, but do you think she wants to be in a pity relationship right now?'

A waiter delivered a piping hot loaf of bread, on a tray with balsamic vinegar, sea salt and olive oil.

Anya grasped the hot loaf. As she sliced through the crust, steam escaped from the soft centre. 'It isn't like that.'

She cut a second piece for herself.

'Let's consider the options.' Bob was used to negotiating and confronting violent offenders with the consequences of their crimes, with the hope of them taking responsibility for their actions. He dipped his bread in the oil, then vinegar, and sprinkled sea salt on top.

'Even if he's trying to be honourable, if Martin is waiting until she gets better before he leaves, then he's living a lie. If he's waiting until she dies, then he's depriving her of the chance to find real love. If he doesn't have the courage to leave her and never really wanted to, then he's lying to you.' He took a large bite.

Anya felt a slight draught on her legs. 'You never liked Martin. No matter how much he grows up, changes or how responsible he's become, he'll never be good enough in your and Mum's eyes.'

Bob finished chewing and swallowed. 'I'll concede that in the beginning, and through the divorce, I had my concerns about Martin. He was emotionally immature and when he threatened to take Ben away and deny you any access . . . Let's just say that was unforgivable, even if it was cooked up by his lawyer.'

Anya had to admit that was the lowest point in the relationship and the most hurtful thing Martin had done or said. But things had changed. Neither of them was the same person.

'People do thoughtless things when they're hurt. Remember you and Mum?'

'I do, and it's something I'll always regret. Sometimes people are broken and you just can't fix them. I tried with your mother. God knows I did.' He paused and looked at a couple being seated across the room. 'This isn't about us, it's about you. Anyone can see Martin is a great father to Ben. Realistically, when has he ever put your needs first?'

The divorce occurred when Martin decided to leave his job nursing. They were living in England at the time, and Anya had to work full-time to pay the bills. When they separated, Martin was the stay-at-home parent, and the judge awarded him custody on that basis, to minimise disruption to Ben.

'He wanted full custody to hurt you, and he got it.'

'Dad, I'm always on call, my job doesn't exactly lend itself to a stable home life.' Between her locum pathology work with the department of forensic services, and part-time work at the sexual assault unit, her work hours were unpredictable enough. Rapes and murders didn't conveniently occur during weekdays from 9 am to 5 pm. Something that had always frustrated Martin about their family life was the fact that she could be called out at any time, day or night. Outings and functions were often interrupted by her work. She had attempted to decrease her on-call hours by giving freelance expert opinions in trials, but it had only increased her need to travel and be away from home. Now she needed to work the hours to pay maintenance and child support, while paying off her own mortgage and business costs.

'Plenty of parents go through that. They hire nannies, or arrange after-school care, without being denied access to the children.'

'Dad, Ben is happy, and that's what's most important.'

He reached across and touched her hand. 'You deserve to be happy. Never forget that.'

She was beginning to wonder if the reconnection she and Martin had experienced on the cruise was merely a holiday fling. Except that instead of disembarking and never seeing each other again, they shared a child together.

The entrees arrived and Anya was glad of the distraction. She started with an oyster. The Russian vodka had a surprising kick.

Bob stabbed another olive with his fork. 'Got a call from Damien last week.'

Her father had an unnerving knack of provoking thought, then moving on. She was grateful the conversation now turned to her brother. At thirty, he worked as a forensic lab technician in London, but was adolescent in his refusal to settle down in the one place for very long.

'How is he?'

'Skiing with the new girlfriend in Europe. He says hello, and asked about Ben, of course.' He picked up some capsicum and chorizo with his fork. 'You know he never forgets birthdays . . . anniversaries.'

Anya's brother was eight years younger and had been born after three-year-old Miriam had been abducted. Mimi's birthday had been on the seventeenth of January, a week ago. There was only one date worse than the seventeenth, and that was the date of her disappearance. In July it would be thirty-three years since she'd vanished. With the disappearance of a mother and child, Anya braced herself for the comparisons to other missing persons cases, like that of Mimi Reynolds, which would be peppered through the media.

'He's worried about your mother.'

Anya collected another oyster. 'Why?'

Bob put down his cutlery. 'He rang yesterday, in the middle of the night, his time.'

As the baby of the family, Damien had always been closest to their mother. He constantly complained that she worked too hard, didn't take holidays, didn't see her kids or her grandson often enough. He couldn't seem to fathom that this was their mother's choice, or that she had changed irrevocably the day Miriam disappeared. Anya dipped some bread in the vinegar.

'Dad, he'll never understand completely and can't be expected to. This time every year Mum becomes withdrawn. I called her that day too, and she didn't ring back until yesterday. I emailed her saying I'd be down here. She gets busy with work.'

The waitress delivered the mains. Anya's salmon with Japanese spices sizzled on its hot rock base. The other dish contained scallops, garlic prawns and fish cooking on its own barbecue plate, alongside chips, salads and sauces. The food was mouth-watering.

'This looks and smells sensational. Dig in,' Bob encouraged, and tasted a prawn.

The first bite of salmon melted in Anya's mouth.

'Damien's concerned about her state of mind and may have good reason.'

'She's always on call,' Anya defended. 'Did she forget to call him back?'

'Kiddo, she'd forgotten what day it was.' He cut into a scallop. 'Thirty-two years of buying Mimi a present for that day. This year she suddenly forgets?'

Jocelyn was sixty-four years old now, and had a strong

family history of dementia. Her mother, grandmother, aunts and uncles all had it.

'There's bound to be a simple explanation. Maybe she'd been up all night on call and got the date wrong in her mind. I'll see her tomorrow anyway, and call Damien to let him know she's fine.'

Bob's phone chimed a song from Herman's Hermits. 'It's Evelyn,' he whispered to Anya. He listened for a moment. 'You did the right thing calling the ambulance and me . . .' His eyes widened. 'I'll go straight to the hospital.'

Anya grabbed her bag and caught the eye of the waitress for the bill.

'I don't understand it,' Bob said. 'She had a bit of an upset stomach when I left. Lucky her neighbour checked. She was on the floor, bleeding.'

11

They arrived in emergency as the ambulance transporting Evelyn pulled into the bay. She was pale, lying flat with fluid infusions in both arms. Blood stained a section of her hair and shoulder. Visibly shaken by his cousin's appearance, Bob bent over and held her hand. One look at the patient and the triage sister rushed them inside, ambulance officers describing the vital signs as they went.

Bob was asked to speak to another nurse. They needed Evelyn's medical history and details. Anya stayed with him.

'When can I see her?' he repeatedly asked.

'The doctors are assessing her, then you'll be allowed in.'

As they spoke a large man pushed past them.

'Excuse me,' the nurse said, and quietly asked a ward clerk to call security. 'Sir, before you leave, I need to take that cannula out of your arm.'

The man responded with a choice set of expletives directed at the staff and ripped out the tube, spilling blood on the floor. Another nurse ran to his aid wearing gloves and holding a dressing pad. He pushed her aside and staggered off. Bob watched in disbelief.

'A Friday night special?' Anya asked.

'And it isn't even a full moon. They're starting early tonight.

Drunks, drugs, who knows what else?' the nurse attending them said. 'Sorry you had to see that.'

Bob was distracted. 'Will Evie be okay?'

'She's in the best place,' Anya comforted. After giving the admission details, they retreated to the waiting room and found the only two vacant seats. Bob sat, face in his hands.

He and Evelyn had grown up a street apart and were closer than most brothers and sisters. Anya finished quizzing him on any medical details he knew about his favourite cousin. He stressed how many close relatives had died of heart attacks at an early age and how Evie had tried hard to prevent developing it with a healthy lifestyle.

Anya had enough to at least give the doctors a list of Evelyn's medications and major conditions. She excused herself to speak with the registrar or specialist on duty. The triage nurse looked her up and down. 'They're very busy.'

'I'm a doctor. I have some background on the woman who was just brought in.'

The ward clerk dialled the phone on her desk and said something Anya couldn't hear over the waiting-room noise.

'I'll take you through,' she said through the glass window. 'Meet you round the side. Dr Saba's the specialist on duty.'

When they entered through the plastic doors, they were greeted by a petite woman with short black hair, stethoscope and pen dangling from her neck.

'Dr Anya Crichton.' The pair shook hands.

'I know. I saw you speak this morning,' the woman said.

It made sense an emergency specialist would attend the conference.

'Ranu Saba. What brings you here?'

'Miss Reynolds. Found collapsed on her floor. My father is her cousin and next of kin. He's been staying with her for a couple of days. Only meds we know of are antihypertensives and cholesterol tablets.' Anya handed over a piece of paper with the names of the treatments. 'I can check the doses later.'

'What is her normal health status?'

Phones rang at the desk behind them. Every bed appeared full. Someone moaned in pain behind a curtain.

'She's fully independent, works full-time as a special needs teacher, doesn't drink alcohol, is a non-smoker and is allergic to penicillin. Strong family history of ischaemic heart disease. Both parents and a brother died of myocardial infarcts in their forties. Dad says she complained of stomachache earlier and thought she had a virus. He wasn't there when she collapsed.'

'She hit her head when she fell and needs sutures, so we're trying to assess her neurological function. However, she is hypotensive and tachycardic. Any history of inflammatory bowel disease, ulcers?'

'No, as far as I know, she's otherwise healthy and doesn't take NSAIDs or aspirin.'

A younger doctor brought a green bowl with fresh blood in it.

'Bed nine just had a haematemesis and dropped her BP.'

'Get two units of O-negative ready for transfusion and cross-match her for four. I'll call the gastro registrar. She'll need an urgent scope.'

'Dr Saba, we're ready for the lumbar puncture.' A fresh-faced male stood proud in a white coat, but his forehead was damp with perspiration. He was either a student or an intern.

'I'll be there shortly. You scrub.'

The month was January, when new doctors began working, and residents rotated to new departments. A month ago, many of the doctors on duty would have been at least a year more experienced.

'We're doing fourteen-hour shifts for the first month to cover the new interns. I'm sorry, doctor, but I need to go. Thank you for your assistance.'

A nurse handed Dr Saba a message. 'Two more D&Vs, an MVA and a GI bleed coming in.' Anya stepped back.

'You might need to put the D&Vs in the holding room, for now,' Dr Saba said.

D&V stood for diarrhoea and vomiting. Anya said quickly, 'Can I ask, how many cases of gastro have you seen today?'

'I think this will be four tonight. Why?'

A monitor alarmed for a few seconds then continued its regular beeping.

'I was at the PM today of a child who died of what looks like Haemolytic Uraemic Syndrome.'

'Were they in our intensive care?'

'She never made it to hospital. Blood film had gram-negative organisms. The lab is trying to determine what strain of E. coli, but we have to wait for cultures.'

Dr Saba sighed. 'Meanwhile other patients could be incubating. Any idea of the source?'

Another nurse interrupted. 'Can you please write up another pethidine? The ankle fracture's in distress and our favourite orthopaedic registrar forgot before disappearing back to theatre.'

Emergency medicine was multitasking at its best. The doctor obliged.

'No. But she'd been on a raw foods diet.'

A heart monitor alarmed and Dr Saba moved to the bedside of a man on life support. A nurse handed her a printout of an ECG and a drug chart. 'We'll give him another 0.5 mg of atropine and repeat in two to three minutes if the rate doesn't pick up.'

They moved out of the way of a radiographer with a portable X-ray machine who scanned the patient list near the desk.

'Bed nine,' Dr Saba instructed. 'Tell me her BP.'

A buzzer rang three times. 'I'm sorry, I have to go,' Dr Saba said again. 'We'll do our best for your cousin.' She disappeared behind a cubicle curtain followed by two nurses and two more doctors. It was a cardio-respiratory arrest.

A male nurse rushed past with a defibrillator on a trolley. A ward clerk showed Anya to a relatives' kitchen where she could make a cup of tea. Staff would find her if there were any changes. A row of grey plastic chairs were outside and more private than the waiting room. It could be hours before they knew more.

On the way out of the department, Anya noticed the whiteboard with patient and bed names. Evelyn Reynolds was listed as bed nine.

Her father looked numb when she returned with two black coffees. 'She was fine when I left, just an upset stomach. I mean, she's never even taken a sick day. Is it her heart?'

'No. She just vomited blood so they're going to have to do an endoscopy, to look inside her food pipe and stomach, to make sure she's not bleeding from an ulcer. They're organising it now.'

They sat for a moment in silence. Four cases of gastroenteritis brought in tonight so far. Anya was beginning to be more fearful that the organism that had killed Emily hadn't come from the Quaid garden. 'Dad, it's possible she has a kind of food poisoning. Can you remember what you've each eaten over the last few days?'

If they had eaten the same thing, he, too, could be incubating the bacteria. 'Meat, vegetables, salads, anything that may not have been properly cooked.'

She pulled out a notebook and a pen from her bag. 'Jot down what comes to mind, and where Evie gets her groceries from, if you know.' Bob silently took notes. They'd bought food at the local supermarket.

Anya remembered the hairdresser talking about Jenny volunteering at the food exchange for the farmers' market.

'Does she eat much organic or fresh food?'

'She gets those from the fresh food market on the weekend. Lamb and vegies.'

Anya pulled her iPad out of her bag and accessed the photos of Jenny Quaid's kitchen. Tomatoes, carrots and spinach were in the vegetable drawers. No processed meats, just a small pack of sausages. Anya hoped the swabs came back quickly, so they could at least identify the source and recall whatever carried the bacteria. Or at least warn people and whoever produced it.

The emergency ward clerk left her office again, this time asking Anya if Dr Saba could see her – alone.

She left Bob and re-entered the ward.

Dr Saba peeled off surgical gloves and stood at the sink. 'Thought you should know. There's another confirmed case, a seventy-five-year-old man who came in a couple of hours ago. Blood film shows E. coli. His daughter called an ambulance when he didn't answer the phone.'

'Is he from anywhere near Huonville?' Anya hoped he may have been part of Jenny Quaid's food exchange. That would at least limit the number of people potentially exposed to the contaminated food.

'No, Battery Point, here in Hobart. Why?'

Anya sighed. The source was unlikely to have come from the vegetables Jenny Quaid had grown.

'Can you find out what he's eaten and where? We need to identify the source.'

Dr Saba shook her head. 'I'm sorry. He was in renal failure when he arrived. He died five minutes ago.'

12

Anya returned to the hotel and slept for a couple of hours. Bob remained by Evelyn's side in the high dependency unit. The gastroscopy showed tearing in the oesophagus from the strain of vomiting. Bloody diarrhoea had begun a couple of hours ago. By then Evelyn had developed kidney failure and fluid on the lungs. Her condition was critical, but stable. For the moment.

Further, a blood smear had confirmed an E. coli infection. Through Dr Saba, Anya now knew of five confirmed cases, including two new cases that had come in overnight in Hobart alone. So far, the death count was two. She hoped Evelyn and the others could survive.

Her father had given her a key to Evelyn's home, so in the early morning light she drove over to collect a change of clothes for him. A knock on the door at 8 am was a food inspector from the department of health. She appeared at the door with a large box briefcase containing forms, swabs and collection packs.

She handed across a piece of paper. 'The information on here informs you what I have to do. Can you tell me where the kitchen is?'

Anya showed her through. The woman was no-nonsense,

and didn't bother with small talk. Anya appreciated that. 'I guess you won't be wanting a glass of water, tea or a coffee.'

'Never eat or drink on the job.'

It was easy to see why. The purpose of visits was to swab for potentially lethal infections.

The stainless-steel fridge was immaculately clean, with not even a finger mark on the door. Different from Anya's white fridge, adorned with artwork by Ben and pictures of them together.

On the top shelf was a plastic bowl covered in cling wrap, half-filled with lamb stir-fry, one of Bob's favourites. The inspector used plastic tweezers to take a sample from the centre and placed it into a small sealed container. She labelled the location, date and time. Sauces were lined up in a slide-out container. None of them were of interest to the inspector. Grapes half-filled a dessert bowl. A number of grapes were collected, this time with fresh tweezers.

'Do you know if the resident has visited a petting zoo or dairy farm recently?' The woman scratched her neatly trimmed grey hair with a plastic pen.

'Not as far as I know.'

'Any unpasteurised products? Milk, cider?' Anya checked the inside of the door: supermarket-lite milk, and orange juice in a one-litre container, unopened. 'No.'

'What's in the freezer?'

Homemade frozen lasagne, dairy-free mango gelato, and half a spinach quiche accompanied a pack of frozen plain pizza bases. A mango-marinated flat chicken lay in its original packaging. The health inspector selected samples from the quiche and lasagne. Two fillets of supermarket fish caught her attention.

'Confidentially,' she said, 'I've swabbed cholera on fish like this.' She opened the pack with gloved hands. 'Imported from Thailand. The water was infected and froze along with the fish. That's why it's worth identifying as soon as possible, even on a Saturday.'

Cholera infection had never occurred to Anya. As far as she knew, it hadn't ever caused infection within Australia, instead being found in people who had returned from endemic areas.

Inside the vegetable drawer were tomatoes, capsicum, corn on the cob, eggplant and broccoli, which were all sampled. 'We all get worried about meat not cooked properly. Most people forget that vermin and insects defecate on the foliage. Can't tell you how many times broccoli, sprouts and spinach cause trouble. Being an island, at least we don't have to deal with cockroaches here. Did you know they vomit on food?'

Anya had to learn to live with cockroaches in Newcastle, then Sydney. Despite being one of evolution's most successful creations, they had not managed to infest Tasmania – yet.

Two green plastic bags were labelled *Livelonger Organics* and sealed with plastic bread ties. Inside one were spinach leaves. The other contained potatoes.

'Aha. I've seen one of these before.'

'In Bellamy?' asked Anya.

'No. At a place outside Signet.' The inspector stopped. 'How did you know I've been to Bellamy? That was late yesterday.'

'I was at a house there when a body was found.'

'You with the police?'

'No, I'm a pathologist.'

The woman looked Anya up and down. 'Don't look like one, not that I've ever met any, come to think of it.' She turned back to her work.

'You don't normally see potatoes in the fridge,' she continued. 'Unless there are vermin in the pantry. With all the recent rain, mice and rats are moving into roofs and cupboards.'

Decomposing and dismembered bodies didn't bother Anya. The mere mention of rats and mice was another story.

After taking samples of all the vegetables, the inspector looked at the fruit in a wooden bowl on the table. Oranges, bananas, red and green apples provided a colourful display. Swabs of the apples were taken and meticulously labelled.

Anya opened the pantry. Generic plastic bags hung in a dispenser inside the door, and green bags were stacked inside one another on the floor. There was no sign of mice droppings. She opened the kitchen drawers. Inside the second one was a book titled *Budget*. Attached to the pages were grocery, clothes and bill receipts. Either money was tight, or her aunt had become more organised.

The inspector flicked through the food receipts. She photographed the ones for the past month with a digital camera. 'Sometimes we can identify the batches from the factories via the codes on the receipts. Not often we get a month's worth of receipts. With incubation being anything from one to ten days, sometimes we can't confirm the source. Unless we can trace it back to one factory of smallgoods, or cheese, like they did with the recent listeria outbreak.'

The inspector moved to the bathroom, Anya suspected, to swab the toilet seat for E. coli. Not yet satisfied with her collection, she examined the kitchen bins and scraps container, before asking about the recycling and rubbish bins. To her frustration, they'd been collected the previous night.

Anya's phone rang. Steve Schiller's focus remained on Jenny and Mia. 'As a priority, the stations have agreed to run TV ads asking for Jenny Quaid to come forward. Good thing you picked up her reading problem, 'cause the brass were planning to leak the story to newspapers in the hope she'd see it.'

'There've been more cases.'

'I heard. I also know you were at the hospital last night. Are you okay?'

'My father's cousin is in a critical condition. She's one of the cases.'

'Sorry. I had no idea there was a connection. If there's anything I can do . . .'

Anya watched the food inspector check under the sink. Her neck ached from being in a hospital waiting room for so many hours. 'Did you need me for anything?'

'Oh, right. Wanted you to know I've been looking into that therapist's background. He's definitely a scammer. Weight-loss tea, miracle powders, new healing techniques. Stays a couple of years in one place, just long enough to gain trust and exploit people and then runs out. He deals in cash and kind, and has so far managed to stay under the tax man's radar. So far, no one's nailed him, but Jim's doing some more digging. All those qualifications came from an alternative medicine school. Run and owned solely by him.'

It was no surprise to Anya. The information he had given Jenny about the raw food diets included the comment that diarrhoea was natural once the diet began, and was proof the body was detoxifying.

'If he misrepresented himself as a qualified practitioner and gave out medical advice, we can charge him with fraud,' Schiller concluded. 'And he lied to us. The last number dialled from Jenny Quaid's phone was to our Mr Heyes on Wednesday.'

Anya suspected that if the call was the reason Jenny hadn't sought medical help for Emily, Heyes could be charged with manslaughter, or even negligent homicide. Then again, even with medical intervention, there was no guarantee every sufferer would survive. She thought about Evie Reynolds, whose organs were already shutting down.

'He lied with his lawyer present as well.'

'Jim and I will go back and interview him. Convenient that Jenny's not around to tell her side of the story, don't you think?'

13

After delivering toiletries and a change of clothes to her father, Anya left to visit her mother. She would return to Hobart if there was any change in Evelyn's condition, but Bob would keep vigil by the bedside in the meantime, and there was nothing more she could do, apart from offer moral support.

The drive up to the midlands took just on two hours, and passing familiar towns reminded her of how much time she'd spent in this part of Tasmania as a child. The last time she had seen her late grandmother's homestead, now her mother's home, it had been in sad need of maintenance. Weeds ravished the once prided rose garden, and the rusted verandah roof had lifted and exposed the already weathered wooden supports.

Pulling up in the gravelled drive, Anya could barely believe the impact of the changes. New cream pillars and painted wood windowpanes complemented the stone. With slate tiles all in place and the corrugated-iron verandah roof repaired, the house looked modern but with all of its colonial character. The property had taken her mother two years to restore before she could move in six months ago. It was a shame Grandma hadn't lived long enough to see it.

Like guard dogs, chickens clucked frantically somewhere behind the house. Anya climbed the stairs to the verandah and knocked on the security grille. No one answered. The gravel drive crunched underfoot as she walked over to the small cottage to the side of the main house. The two-bedroom shack had been converted to a small waiting area, treatment room and consulting office, for weekends and emergencies.

Jocelyn Reynolds opened the door. The physical changes were immediately marked. Gone was the apple shape her mother had developed since menopause. Weight loss had aged her once rounder face. Anya reached out to greet her for the requisite hug, during which she was kept at elbow's distance by her mother. From the residual smell of latex gloves, she had seen patients in her Saturday morning surgery.

'I didn't expect you yet.' Her lips forced a smile, but her eyes remained static above hollowed cheeks.

'If it's easier, I'm happy to stay at a motel. We can have dinner–'

'Nonsense. What would people think?'

Anya had never really cared what people thought. In her experience, they were far more interested in themselves.

'You can stay in my old bedroom.' Jocelyn closed the door behind her and locked it.

Less than a minute, and Anya already felt awkward. Discussing the renovation would be a good subject to start with. 'The place looks amazing. Grandma Burgess would be so proud.'

'Nothing a lot of hard work couldn't achieve.'

They walked on towards the main house, chickens squawking in the distance.

Jocelyn stopped and unlocked her car door. 'Now you're here, you'd better come with me to Audrey's for lunch. I'll never hear the end of it if she knew you were here and didn't see you.'

Audrey was her mother's closest friend and Anya's godmother. Jocelyn and Audrey had grown up together. Anya couldn't understand why her mother had made plans when she was only here for such a short time.

'Mum, I came to see *you*, and hoped we could just spend some time together. Catching up. It's been a while.'

Anya tried to remember how long it had been since Jocelyn had seen her only grandson. At eight, Ben barely knew his grandmother. She was always too busy working to visit, and refused to have anything to do with Ben's father. That was unlikely to change as long as Martin had custody. It had been many years since Anya had seen this house.

'You can talk on the way.' Jocelyn got into the driver's seat.

A few minutes later they were headed into the centre of Longford. Anya's mind drifted back to a time when she and Damien had swum with Grandma Burgess in the river at the mill dam. It had been her favourite part of the school holidays. Grandma used to jump in wearing rolled-up trousers and an old shirt. She'd joke she could avoid washing day if she threw herself around enough in the water. The memory still made Anya smile.

'How have you been?' Anya didn't want to make a feature of the weight loss but wanted to know if everything was all right.

'Why does everyone keep asking? I'm fine.' Jocelyn tugged at a scarf tied roughly around her neck. Her chambray shirt had sweat patches under the arms.

'Damien was worried.'

'Whatever for? He always catches me at a bad time. Last time we spoke was just after Christmas. I suppose I was short with him. I was in the shower when the phone went.' She glanced sideways. 'No son wants to hear he's talking to his mother while she's in the shower, stark naked.'

Anya didn't mention the call on Miriam's birthday.

Jocelyn's phone bleeped. 'Can you check that?'

It was inside the middle console. A text read, *Swelling down. Now wanting hot bath.* Anya read it out for her mother.

Jocelyn smiled. 'Wayne Bitford got stung by wasps again. He's had an antihistamine and ice bath to take the heat out of the stings. His daughter-in-law's visiting from Melbourne and panicked. I'd be more concerned if that man didn't complain. Can you text back, *Good news. Call if you need me?*'

Anya had forgotten how stoic many of the people who lived rurally could be. When a doctor was an hour's drive away, they did what they could in terms of first aid and survival.

'That means we've got time to stop at the bakery and beat the coach.' She turned into Wellington Street and parked in a small car park in front of an antiques shop and gallery, adjacent to a bakery.

Outside the car, her mother waved to a woman walking a pram further down the street. 'The flour mill's been here for over a hundred and fifty years. It's been a skin and wool store, even a soap factory in its day.'

Inside, the array of breads on display would have put a Leichhardt bakery to shame. Gone were the days when the only choice was a white loaf or soft white roll.

'Audrey aims for lunch at one, but we won't eat until at least three, so we might as well order something.'

After deciding on a cappuccino and a short black, Jocelyn included a request for a dozen cupcakes in a box, and two sausage rolls with sauce. She passed one in a paper bag to Anya.

Coffees in hand, they headed towards the car. The sun was struggling to peek through a cloud mass. Her mother detoured to the park and sat at a wooden table and bench. She tore open her bag and emptied two sachets of tomato sauce on her sausage roll.

It instantly reminded Anya of Saturdays in winter when Damien played soccer. Afterwards, her mother would tend to house calls and her father would cook hot dogs, party pies or sausage rolls. The smell of pastry cooking in the oven as they tried to warm up by the fire was one of her favourite childhood memories.

Jocelyn emptied two sachets of sugar into her cup. 'How long are you staying in Tassie?'

'I thought I'd go back on Monday. Evelyn's in hospital with Haemolytic Uraemic Syndrome, in a critical but stable condition. I'll stay as long as necessary for Dad's sake.'

'I had no idea she was ill.' She took off her sunglasses. 'I know how close your father and Evelyn have always been.'

'He was staying with her yesterday when she was admitted to hospital. He sat with her all night.'

'Do they know what caused it?'

Anya took a sip and wiped the froth from her top lip. 'It's E. coli and there have been two deaths in the Hobart region already.' She ripped opened her paper bag and pulled off a piece of flaky pastry. 'If you see any cases of severe vomiting and diarrhoea . . .'

Two little girls danced around the rotunda in the park. Jocelyn watched them for a while.

Anya said, 'A little girl died from E. coli and her mother and sister are missing.'

'I saw that on the news but they didn't mention the infection. The poor family must be going through hell.' Jocelyn's pale blue eyes seemed grey in the sunlight. 'First that little girl is found, then the others go missing. I pray they're both safe . . .'

'I was thinking about Miriam, how long it's been.' There was a moment's silence.

'They say time heals everything. It doesn't.'

'Damien said he rang you the other day, on the seventeenth.' She waited for some recognition.

'Our Mimi would be thirty-six.' Jocelyn sipped her coffee. 'I didn't speak to your brother that day, or anyone except Audrey. I got your message. I was too tired to talk anyway.'

Anya noticed a clavicle pressing against her mother's skin when the wind blew her shirt open a little. 'Has your workload decreased since leaving Launceston and joining the practice here?'

'Let's not play mind games. I think I'd know if I spoke to my own son, Anya. Did you speak to him directly, catch him in between ski fields?'

Anya shook her head. 'He rang Dad.'

'You came all this way to check up on me because of something secondhand your father, or that interfering wife of his, passed on?' She gathered her rubbish. 'That's just great.' She stood and slammed the papers into a dark green park bin. 'We need to go. Audrey will be waiting.'

Anya caught up. 'You knew I was coming to see you. We talked about it weeks ago. Dad only said something because he wanted to know you were okay.'

'He gave up the right to know anything about me when he left.'

Forgiveness and understanding weren't in her mother's vocabulary where Bob was concerned. The way Anya saw it, Jocelyn had shut down emotionally the day of Miriam's abduction. Bob had tried to keep the family together, but in the end, nothing could ease Jocelyn's grief. He hadn't met his second wife until long after the divorce. Time and distance hadn't mellowed Jocelyn's perception of any part she may have played in the marriage breakdown.

They headed back to the car and drove along the Midlands Highway towards Gibbett Hill. The sun disappeared behind dark grey clouds. In winter, with fog, the area looked like an English moor. As a child, Anya had been frightened by the story of a ghost who haunted travellers. Locals claimed their cars had filled with a black smoke as they drove past the site where a violent murder had taken place in the 1830s. Anya looked to the side where the body of an executed bushranger had been hung in chains from a tree for three years, as a deterrent to other criminals. There was no sign of the particular tree, but she still twisted in her seat to look. Like so much of the mainland, Tasmania had a barbaric history, not easily forgotten.

Jocelyn glanced sideways. 'Remember this place? I always thought it's where you developed your obsession with death and gore.'

The comment sounded disapproving. Anya preferred to think that the public display of a body decomposing and being picked at by birds would have disturbed any child. Being told the man's family saw the body every day bothered her the most.

As they wound around the back of the historic town of Perth, a sea of white poppies swayed in the breeze. The sight was nothing short of spectacular. Jocelyn spoke like a tour guide. 'We're still the world's largest producer of opium alkaloids. Humbling to think something grown here can be used to treat patients on the other side of the world.'

Anya felt a burst from the air-conditioning and closed the vents on the passenger side.

Some things hadn't changed. Born and bred Taswegians, like her mother, were exceptionally proud of their state – more so than anyone anywhere else Anya had lived. The geographically isolated state had a number of claims to fame, and this was just one of them. It produced fifty per cent of the world's concentrated poppy straw, which was used by pharmaceutical companies to make morphine and codeine. Less pristine were the electric fences plastered with warning signs about trespassing.

'Has security become an issue?'

'More about insurance. It's only the odd fool who tries to steal anything. The industry brings a lot of jobs to this area and it's worth protecting. You have no idea how many people are doing it tough. Really struggling.'

Anya could imagine. With a high Australian dollar, imports were at record levels. A large exporting agricultural industry like this would be suffering. Her mother opened her window despite the air-conditioning. It had to be in the mid-twenties outside, but beads of perspiration appeared over Jocelyn's forehead and top lip. She reached down to the cup holder for a water bottle filled with a tea-coloured liquid and took a few swigs.

'So how is Evie doing?'

Anya thought she had explained. 'Still in a critical condition.'

Jocelyn tightened her tanned hands on the steering wheel. Anya took in the smaller silhouette. The weight loss was dramatic, but she had devoured the sausage roll. Her mother seemed preoccupied and defensive, particularly about Damien's supposed call. Something seemed wrong. Damien was a stickler for dates and had never missed calling Jocelyn on Miriam's birthday, no matter where he was in the world. He'd been concerned enough about Jocelyn to call their father, knowing the pair rarely spoke.

Anya checked her email on her smart phone. Damien had sent a message.

> *Dad emailed and told me about Evie. He's really worried. What are her chances of getting through this?*
>
> *He also said you're with Mum. Can you please check her out? Something's wrong. She didn't remember it was Miriam's birthday. You know she ALWAYS remembers. When I rang her that night, she was slurring her words over the phone and didn't make any sense. She sounded drunk. Then she said she had to go and see a patient. Annie, she was in no state to drive or see a patient. Like I said, can you check her out? I wouldn't normally ask, but you're the only person she might listen to.*

What Damien said was more than disturbing. If she'd been drinking that night and had no memory of his call, that was one thing. If she'd gone out to see patients in that state, she'd risked lives and her medical registration.

Anya watched Jocelyn take another slurp from the drink bottle.

14

Jocelyn turned into the drive. They were heading towards Audrey Lingard's home.

The property bore little resemblance to the place Anya remembered. The paddocks were still green, but the fibro house was dilapidated. Pale blue paint peeled off the exterior and some of the roof capping was noticeably loose. A downpipe had been punctured to release water on one side of the front.

Before the car had stopped, Audrey was outside the screen door. Jocelyn's best friend since childhood was still glamorous, wearing a flowing top that tastefully covered her very large bust, and white jeans. The shirt was a striking combination of aqua and blue chiffon, set off by cobalt crystal earrings.

Audrey's face beamed when she saw Anya and she hurried to the passenger side, arms outstretched.

Jocelyn turned off the engine and left the keys in the ignition.

Anya peeled herself out of the seat and was greeted with a bear hug. Audrey hung on and rocked from side to side with enthusiasm.

'Can't believe you are here. Look at you, the spitting image of your auntie Maisy.' She pulled back, gripping Anya's hands with her rough calloused fingers.

'What's it been? Ten years?'

'Twelve,' Jocelyn clarified, before stepping forward for her own half-hug.

'It was after Anya's graduation, before she married that no-hoper.' Jocelyn looked upwards. 'What was his name?'

'Martin.' Anya swallowed.

Jocelyn reached into the back seat for the box of cupcakes and some freshly cut gerberas.

'Well, we all thought it. Your mother has always been a good judge of character and knew it wouldn't last. He was rude. Never met anyone so full of himself, have we, Josie?' Audrey gestured towards the house. 'Good riddance, I say. Now you've got the bad one out of your system, you're free to find Mr Right.'

'Actually, Martin and I are considering a reconciliation.' Anya instantly regretted saying it out loud. She would have loved to be able to talk to her mother about the relationship and receive some of the insights Jocelyn's patients received. It was no secret her mother had never liked the man she'd married. Jocelyn had conveniently forgotten that her parents had disapproved of Bob as well. No one was ever good enough for the daughters in the family. Jocelyn could be a loyal friend, but once a negative judgement had been made about someone, there were no second chances given.

'You just can't teach common sense,' Jocelyn muttered. 'As Einstein said, the definition of insanity is doing the same thing over and over and expecting a different result.'

Ever a peacemaker, Audrey took the flowers. 'He'll always be Ben's father. We should be grateful for that.'

Anya allowed them to go up the stairs first and took a full, deep breath. Martin had changed. Grown up. She thought of their time together on the cruise ship, and how he would have risked his life for her. Talking to her mother about him was pointless.

'Some things don't change,' a man's voice said behind her.

She hadn't seen Glenn Lingard in many years, not since he

was pimply faced and off to university in Melbourne. He was more muscular, but still lean, with brown-rimmed glasses and a gleam in his round brown eyes.

He took a couple of strides up the stairs and kissed Jocelyn's cheek. Her mother's face relaxed into a broad smile. She had always been fond of Glenn, who was two years older than Anya. Despite being forced to spend holidays together, the children had never been close. Anya extended her hand to the man who was now a stranger.

'Anya, you look exactly how I remember.' Glenn stepped back, with a cheeky glint. 'Same unruly hair, spidery limbs. Bet you can still outrun me too.'

'I doubt it.' She felt awkward again. His round face was thinner but the dimple in his chin could still hold a pencil. His forearms were tanned and muscular. 'No one could call you Tubby anymore.'

He laughed. 'Some people still do. Suspect half the kids at school never knew my real name.'

Once inside, the two older women chatted comfortably while Audrey fussed with a crystal vase on the island bench. Her mother was never more relaxed than with her oldest friend. Anya almost envied their easy and comfortable relationship. If anyone had noticed a change in her mother's behaviour, it should have been Audrey. First chance she got, she'd try and catch her alone to ask.

'I've read about your work,' Glenn said. 'And I hear about you whenever you call home.' Hands in pockets, he scuffed the carpet. 'Mum does like to pass on news.'

'Don't worry, I've heard all about the countries you worked in, and how well you're doing.'

He half smiled again. 'Funny, it never occurred to me she'd brag the same way.'

The two women had little in common apart from a family history and children. Jocelyn had left for university in Hobart, and Audrey had married at eighteen. Her husband was arrested for indecent exposure in a park and left when Glenn was small.

Jocelyn had heard he'd died of AIDS in a South Australian nursing home but it had never been spoken about. Audrey had never remarried and had cared for her elderly parents until both their deaths.

'Actually, I'm on my way to collect the eggs,' Glenn offered, 'if you'd like an excuse to escape.'

Anya didn't need to be asked twice. They quickly headed out the back door, as they had done when they were kids. Outside, they swapped their shoes for gumboots and ventured into the chicken pen. At least a dozen Isa browns rushed at them. Some rammed the boots with their beaks. Anya's mind flashed back to being a child again at her grandparents' farm. The chickens used to scare her, so she had loathed collecting the eggs.

First, Glenn explained, they had to eat high-protein feed so they could lay good eggs. After that came the kitchen scraps. Glenn carried in his hand a bucket with remnants of lettuce, bread crusts, vegetable skins and crushed eggshells, from which he threw handfuls away from the roost.

'Don't suppose you have a pair of gloves?' She checked the undersoles of her boots. Chook poo was everywhere.

'Never did like getting your hands dirty,' he joked.

The smell of the birds and the fertiliser they produced filled the area. The clucking was strangely comforting. Glenn wandered to the coop in the corner and lifted the feed bucket over the fence, out of reach. He replaced it with an empty one. The chickens raced from one handful to the next, pushing and shoving each other according to the pecking order.

'Are you really seeing your ex or did you say it to give them something to gossip about?'

Anya stumbled over what should have been a simple answer. 'It's complicated.' The smell of chicken excrement intensified.

'Still, did you see the look on your mum's face?' He laughed. It was hearty, and infectious.

Anya lowered her head on the way into the coop. Dozens of eggs were scattered on top of shredded newspaper. She tentatively picked up one at a time, gently putting each in the empty container Glenn had placed on the ground.

'I'd forgotten how good these are at laying.'

A number of chickens squawked loudly outside. 'We usually get one a day from every chicken, except in winter when the laying slows. They're bred especially for laying.'

Anya deposited the last egg into the container as Glenn grabbed a shovel and rake from the back of the pen. She took the rake from him and dragged the sullied paper into a pile. 'Where are you working now?'

'The Tasmanian Institute of Agricultural Advancement, or TIAA as it's known. It brings scientists, industry and government together. It's Mecca for researchers like me. Our work is attracting a lot of overseas interest.' He scooped up the mess, left the coop and deposited it in a large plastic tub on the other side of the fence.

The sun was beating down on the corrugated-tin roof and sweat was forming around Anya's hairline and neck.

Glenn pointed to a wheelbarrow with a hessian cover weighed down with a brick. 'There's more paper in there. For the first time, I feel like my work is respected and really understood. The state government is putting a lot into the institute and are big supporters of innovations in science, which is a lot more than can be said for the other states. They're lagging way behind.'

She wheeled the barrow to the coop entrance and lifted the hessian. She dug both hands into the densely packed paper and spread what she could manage over the empty laying area. No bit of newspaper or advertising material would have been wasted on this property.

'What area are you working on?'

'There are a few great projects I'm involved in. At the moment we're fine-tuning a tea bag that can filter out cholera in water. Imagine the lives that will save, and for a negligible cost.'

Anya was impressed. Applied science and medical advancements were sorely underfunded by governments, who tended to budget for the short-term. Scientific breakthroughs like the cholera bag took years, and possibly decades to develop.

'That's something I'd invest in,' she said.

'See, you get it. Not everyone around here feels the same way. There's a lot of ignorance and fear about doing anything different. The old ways aren't necessarily the best, as you know.'

He had a good point.

They exited through the gate while the chickens continued to race around in tangential sprints without any obvious reason. Glenn led her to the rear of the main house and they dipped their boots into a tray of chlorine disinfectant before replacing them on the shoe rack by the back door. 'Hope you're hungry, Mum always over-caters.'

They scrubbed their hands in the metal laundry tub with yellow Sunlight soap, and dried them with the towel hanging from a hook. Her mind returned to a time when she had to stand on a crate to reach these very taps.

'There's plenty of food,' Audrey announced. The table was covered in platters of cold cuts, cheeses, pâté and fresh bread. 'Entree's served.'

'Glenn, can you get Anya a drink? There's wine, water and lemon, iced tea, or coffee.'

'Anything cold would be great, thanks.'

Jocelyn headed over to Glenn and they were quickly engaged in an animated conversation. Anya took the opportunity to talk with his mother. 'Need any help?'

Audrey put her arm around Anya. 'It's so good to see you again. It's been far too long. Look at those two. Can't be in the room without disagreeing on everything.'

She watched the interaction. 'Mum's lost a lot of weight. How's she been?'

'Fine. Patients have given her a difficult time about leaving the Launceston practice. She was supposed to cut back by moving here, but she's busier than ever. We're so short of doctors around here. It's a strain, always being on call, and with looking after that house. She never stops, as you know.'

'Have you noticed any changes, like her getting a bit forgetful?'

'Your mother is as strong as a mallee bull. She just has too much on her mind right now with work, and . . . certain people demand far too much of her.'

Glenn's voice stressed whatever point he was making and Jocelyn fired back something Anya couldn't make out.

She quietly asked Audrey, 'Who? Maybe I can do something to help, but she doesn't tell me much.'

'I can't say, but some things are too big to fight. You know how she gets. Like a dog with a bone when she thinks there's an injustice in the world.'

'What's she crusading about now?'

Jocelyn turned their way and gave Audrey a steely look.

'I've said too much.' Audrey became flustered and turned her attention to the others. 'Would you two please agree to disagree, and we can eat in peace.'

Anya wondered what new cause her mother had taken on, who was demanding too much of her, and what was going on with her health.

As Glenn handed her a glass of iced tea, her phone rang. She recognised Steve Schiller's number from earlier and was quick to ask, 'Any word on Jenny or Mia?'

'No, but the lab confirmed the blood in the bathroom was Emily's. We're still waiting to question Dylan Heyes, more formally this time. His lawyer is at a luncheon, apparently. I get the feeling he'll only talk if there's something in it for him.'

Anya wiped her forehead. 'Are you any closer to knowing where the infection came from?'

'The lab said it's a Shigella-producing bacteria.'

'That's the name of the specific toxin made by the E. coli,' Anya explained.

'There are three more cases here, and we just got word there have been another three, in Launceston. Once we know

what caused it, the brass wants us to charge whoever's responsible with homicide. The faster the better, whether it's Heyes,
Jenny Quaid, or some food manufacturer.'

Either way, it was unlikely Jenny Quaid was responsible
for the outbreak. Chances were there would be more cases
with potentially fatal consequences before they could stop the
spread.

15

After lunch, Jocelyn handed Anya a spare set of keys and dropped her off at the door. She had one more house call to attend. Anya collected her laptop and carry-on from the rental car and carried them up the verandah steps. The screen door didn't have a lock, but the front door had two. Juggling her handbag and laptop, she pushed her case over the threshold. The metal screen door slammed against the back of her foot and pain shot through her heel. It had taken a chunk of skin just above the shoe line.

She steered the bag further along the corridor, dropped her handbag on the floor and entered the first room on the left, Jocelyn's childhood bedroom. Slipping out of her shoes, she dropped the laptop on the double bed. The bedspread was a quilt her grandmother had made out of clothing her children and grandchildren had worn. Anya bent down and touched it, and noticed blood on her heel.

Holding a tissue from the bedside table against the wound, she hobbled towards the kitchen, careful not to bleed on the wooden floorboards. She stopped short at the family room to her left, shocked by the scene. Manila folders were piled high on the lounge, rug and on the television cabinet, obscuring half the screen. Some were opened and spread out across the floor. A bookshelf was half-empty, rows of books collapsed into the spaces. She counted three separate A4 notepads with scribbles on them. There was barely room for anyone to step without treading on something. Yellow sticky labels were plastered across a whiteboard with arrows and circles drawn to connect them.

Her mother had always been house-proud and obsessively tidy. A plate that had hung in the kitchen in their old home read, *Cleanliness is next to Godliness*. Jocelyn had moved in months ago, but this was not the result of interrupted unpacking. It had the hallmarks of frenetic activity and disorganised thinking. Anya's heart lurched. Damien had good reason to be worried about their mother; only alcohol may not be the issue.

In the dining area, papers obliterated the surface of the mahogany table and there were more stacks of what looked to be patient files. The kitchen bench had medical books and reference papers spread out in piles. Dirty mugs and plates were stacked in the sink and spilled over to the stove top. Anya opened the oven. The clean glass door suggested it hadn't had much use. The microwave had food spatters visible from where she stood.

It didn't appear cooking, cleaning or eating were any longer a priority for Jocelyn.

Anya took a step and felt her heel throb again. She needed a Band-Aid to stop the bleeding. The kitchen drawers only contained eating utensils and bills. She checked the cupboards. Many were empty, or contained the odd tin of tomatoes or bean salad mix. No sign of a first aid kit.

She opened the fridge door, to see if her mother had it better stocked than the cupboards. Milk, cheese, carrots and a bag of drooping spinach inside a bag marked *Livelonger Organics* caught her attention. She lifted the bag out. The bin contained a couple of papers and the plastic lid from a jar; no empty alcohol bottles. Anya recalled that Livelonger was the brand she had seen at Evelyn's home, and that the health inspector had mentioned. It wasn't worth taking a chance in case it contained the lethal bacteria. The spinach went in with the rubbish.

She moved to the main bathroom to wash her hands. There were no towels, so she decided to try the ensuite off the main bedroom. There had to be a Band-Aid or plaster strip somewhere in the house. In the bedroom, the sheets and doona had been pulled up, and pillows unevenly placed at the head. An empty glass and a half-full bottle of iced tea sat on the bedside table. In the ensuite, a wet towel hung over the shower recess, and a linen basket was overflowing.

Anya felt uncomfortable violating her mother's privacy when she opened the bathroom cabinet doors. Inside she found a packet of thin strip-plasters, which she grabbed. After removing a couple and applying them to her heel, she put the packet back, next to a half-used pack of Panadol, an aspirin and a small prescription bottle. She hesitated with her hand on the door. Her mother was a practising doctor, and if she was ill or impaired, patients could be compromised.

Slowly, Anya reached for the prescription bottle and read the label. *Thyroxin 50 micrograms once daily.* Treatment for an underactive thyroid gland. The seal was still intact. Instead of weight loss, hypothyroidism usually caused slow metabolism and weight gain. The prescribing doctor was listed as Jocelyn Reynolds. She closed the cupboard door.

Stepping back, she caught a glimpse of something reflected in the mirror. From under the bed, a scrapbook pad, like the ones she and Damien had drawn on as children, caught her attention. Beside it was a pack of coloured markers. She sat on the bed and lifted page after page of flow charts and arrows, pointing from one name to another. Another page, in red pen, repeated the letters, MIV, circled over and over. It looked like something someone with mania and delusions would have written.

The third bedroom door had been closed when she arrived. Reluctantly, Anya headed back to the corridor, searching for more evidence to explain what might be going on in her mother's mind. Turning the enamel knob, the door clicked open. She stepped back, nausea rising in her gullet.

Inside was Miriam's old bed, with the few photos they had of her framed on the tallboy. A second white metal bed that had once been Anya's was on the other side, piled high with wrapped presents. There was no need to count them; Anya knew there was one for every birthday and Christmas since her sister's disappearance. Thirty-three years later, the bedroom was set up exactly as it had been: a shrine to Jocelyn's lost child.

Anya felt winded. She thought the move would be positive for her mother, and give her the chance to finally move on. A soft pink blanket lay scrunched at the foot of the bed and there were indentations on the mattress. Miriam's second-favourite cuddly toy lay against the pillow. Her favourite had been with her when she was taken.

Anya stepped inside and reached for the pale pink bear with piercing blue eyes. She thought of Emily Quaid being put in the box with her favourite yellow duck. She hoped and wanted to believe that whoever took Miriam had let her keep her Blinky bear with her for as long as she had lived. Blinky had gone everywhere with her and she'd needed it to sleep. The police knew that it was unlikely her sister had lived very long, and was probably buried or dumped in some remote part of the bush – something her father accepted but her mother would not. Wherever Miriam lay, Anya hoped Blinky was with her. She sat on the bed and held the pink bear. Damien had been right to be worried. Their mother was behaving strangely and the house was disorganised and nothing like how she had lived in Launceston. Anya put the conversation with Damien aside for the moment and thought about her mother's weight loss. Anya had seen the pattern before, many times in her mother's family. Jocelyn's mother, aunts, uncles and older brother had developed dementia in their sixties. For them, it began with weight loss from disinterest in cooking, and forgetting to eat. If diagnosed with the brain disorder, Jocelyn could no longer practise medicine. It was her reason for living.

Anya sat for a while in the room, desperately trying to work out what to do. Her mother wouldn't take kindly to being forced into a medical assessment of any variety, no matter the ruse. And she was self-prescribing medication. Anya decided to stay a few days longer. She needed to call Martin.

Reaching for her bag, she felt a presence and half turned. The barrels of a shotgun were less than a metre from her face.

16

Anya froze where she stood. The man pulled the magazine handle back, then forwards. The pump action meant the barrel was loaded.

'Don't move or so help me, I'll blow your head off.'

Trapped between the shooter and the door, heart hammering in her chest, she had little choice but to act calm.

'I don't have much cash.' She caught sight of the man's bearded face as he stared at her, gun mounted on his shoulder. A red cap made his eyes difficult to see. He was wearing a fluorescent safety vest. She quickly established that he was much heavier and taller than she was, even hunched over the barrel.

'I don't want your money,' he almost shouted. 'I knew something was up when the door was open. Jocelyn never leaves it like that.'

He had to be a friend or caretaker of some sort. Anya relaxed and breathed out. 'Mum's gone to a house call and gave me the keys.'

The man was unmoved, finger still on the trigger. 'Her kid lives on the mainland. Let's start again. Who sent you?' It suddenly occurred to Anya that the paranoid writings may have come from this man. Maybe he was one of Jocelyn's patients?

The screen door banged. Anya flinched, but the man remained fixed.

'Len, what the hell are you doing?'

'I caught her going through your things. Call the police.'

Jocelyn pushed the gun barrel down towards the floor. 'Don't be ridiculous. She's my daughter. I dropped her off before checking on the Lovetts.'

Gun now by his side, the man pulled off the cap and revealed a mess of wiry hair. 'Sorry. Thought you were someone else.'

Anya wondered who he'd imagined was in the house, uninvited.

'Who's been in Miriam's bedroom?' Jocelyn's voice was calm but forceful.

'Joss, you know I'd never stick my nose in your business.'

'You came into the house uninvited and pointed a gun at me, why?' Anya wanted to know. And what was he doing with a gun in the first place?

'Regardless, that room is off-limits. To everyone. Do you understand?'

The man unloaded the chamber of its shell and propped the gun in the corner near the now closed front door.

Anya couldn't fathom why it didn't seem to bother her mother that this man had held a gun to her head.

'Well, I should probably introduce you properly,' Jocelyn said, kicking her shoes off near the door. 'Len, meet my older daughter, Anya.'

'Do you pull a gun on every new person you see?' Anya asked, not even half-joking.

'Not normally,' he mumbled. 'I did apologise.' Under the safety vest, he was wearing dirty jeans and a dark blue shirt. Black socks covered enormous feet. He'd removed his boots before entering the house. That's how he had approached her so quietly, she realised.

Jocelyn remained nonplussed by the event and was in the kitchen busying herself with washing out three pottery mugs from the sink.

'I'll make a pot.' She turned on the kettle with wet hands. Len pulled a tea towel from the bottom drawer and dried the mugs.

Anya's phone bleeped from the corridor. Concerned about leaving her mother alone for too long with Mr Gun Happy, she checked the text message. Two more E. coli cases, according to Schiller. The swabs taken from the food speci- mens could confirm the source within the next few hours if they were lucky. Not so lucky for the sufferers still incubating the infection.

She made her way back to the kitchen area. Jocelyn had cleared off three chairs at the table, and deposited the paperwork on top of already towering piles. The pair were in animated conversation and went silent when she re-entered the room.

'Made you a cuppa,' Jocelyn said. 'Milk's in the fridge door. If you want sugar, you'll have to wait until I go back to town.'

Anya helped herself, and subtly sniffed the milk before pouring any into her tea. It was within its use-by period.

She still couldn't believe the man at the table had held her at gunpoint and her mother was chatting away with him as if nothing odd had occurred. He had to be a patient. Didn't it unnerve Jocelyn that he had entered her house, uninvited and with a gun? He could have killed her daughter. Anya couldn't get the image out of her mind. Her mother didn't appear to have taken the threat seriously. She wondered whose beha- viour was the least rational. She sat on the chair her mother had cleared.

'Sorry about all the mess, but I'm working on something,' Jocelyn said defensively.

'Anything I can help with?' Anya asked, keen to know if there was a reasonable explanation for what she was seeing and the changes in her mother.

'Just an audit of my patients. Part of my CME.'

'What's that?' Len took a gulp of tea.

'Continuing medical education. It's compulsory in order for doctors to keep their registration and stay up to date.'

It seemed logical, but it was strange that it seemed to have taken over her home, that she hadn't kept it in the surgery, or done the work via computer. That was one of the advantages of computerised medical records. It was easy to establish patterns of disease and illness, in order to effect preventive strategies in communities.

Anya sipped. 'How do you two know each other?'

'We're neighbours. We keep an eye out for each other.' Jocelyn smiled at Len, who kept his head down.

It still didn't explain the gun. Len must have sensed this, because he added, 'I was in the ute and saw Jocelyn's car drive out. I came over to drop off some mail for her, and saw that the door was open. The gun was on the front seat, so I went back and got it.'

Anya had always thought the area was safe. At least it used to be. 'Have there been break-ins around here?'

'The service station got held up, but people are just being more careful these days.' Jocelyn glanced at Len. 'Isn't that right?'

'Yep, can't be too careful.' He slurped his tea.

'Mum, I was wondering if we could have a quiet word. In private.'

'Better go outside, Joss, the walls have ears, you know.'

Anya headed out the back door. Her mother brought her mug of tea and lowered herself into the old bamboo sofa chair.

'Mum, is he one of your patients?'

She sighed. 'When you live in a small community, everyone becomes your patient when there's no one else to see them. He's harmless.'

'Harmless?' Anya paced up and down the verandah. 'He could have killed me. That gun was loaded and he was ready to shoot. He sounds completely paranoid. Who did he think I was? And all this, "the walls have ears" talk. What part of that is normal?'

Jocelyn surveyed the backyard. 'He's a farmer. They carry guns. You've been away far too long. Things have changed. Life is different now.'

'How? Explain it to me.' Anya sat beside her mother and pleaded, 'Whatever is going on, I want to help. You just have to help me understand.'

'The Dengate farm used to be one of the biggest properties in the area. When the old man died, he left it to his two sons, but Len had been a bit of a black sheep and was more interested in producing quality organic food than maximising profits. His father left him forty-five acres. Len's entrepreneurial brother got the rest. No surprise, the brother quickly sold his share to an international consortium over at Emerald Vale and made a fortune.' She blew air across her mug before taking a large sip.

'Now Len's is the only property under fifty acres for tens of miles, apart from mine, that is. There are a few interests hoping his business will fail.'

'Okay, but you have to admit, Len's an unusual character. Has he just wandered into your house uninvited before?'

'For Pete's sake. Of course he's welcome. He's my neighbour. You have no idea what he's been through. He's no bother. In fact, I enjoy his company and he is a good, honest man.'

Anya was still concerned about his mental state. Coming around with a gun, ready to shoot, wasn't exactly acceptable behaviour. 'Are you too close to see that he has some paranoid tendencies? I mean, are those his conspiracy theories in the scrapbook in your room?'

Jocelyn's face tightened. 'You went through my room as well?' She stood up. 'You had absolutely no right.'

Anya pointed at her heel and tried to explain. 'I was looking for a Band-Aid to stop bleeding on your floor.'

Len popped his head out the back. 'Thanks for the tea. Left Ros outside. Didn't want hair all over your floor.' He seemed to sense something was wrong. 'I'll just show myself out and grab my gun on the way.'

Jocelyn pushed past him and Anya heard the door to her bedroom slam shut.

The two were left standing there. 'No hard feelings, eh?' he tried.

Anya didn't respond. Len's vest had slipped and she saw a logo on his shirt.

Livelonger Organics.

17

Anya locked the front door and stopped outside her mother's bedroom. She was trying to look out for Jocelyn and wanted to explain that. Jocelyn saw the fact that Anya had gone through her things as the ultimate betrayal. But it seemed like an overreaction, as if her mother had something to hide. Anya wished that for once they could talk about problems without defensiveness, accusations or tempers flaring.

She decided to give her mother some time to calm down. Back in the spare bedroom, she logged on to her computer and checked emails. Martin had sent a photo of Ben at the petting zoo, bending down looking into the eyes of a wallaby. She replied by saying how much she wished she could have been there as well. She would have given anything to have been with them today if it had been possible.

Her default page was a news site. Images of Jenny and Mia Quaid appeared, appealing for them to come forward, or for anyone who had seen them to notify police. *Grave fears are held for their safety*, a caption read. There was mention of two deaths from a gastroenteritis infection with a warning about foods and use-by dates, the importance of hand washing before handling food, and avoiding raw fish and meat until the source of the infection could be identified.

The only link she knew of between cases so far was Livelonger Organics. It may not be a coincidence that Len Dengate was involved in the company. Jocelyn had said the land had been sold and one son was left with a small parcel for his organic farm. She Googled Len's name.

He was a vocal member of the Organics Association of Australia, and outspoken about natural foods and using modernised techniques for cultivation. An opinion piece he'd written that had appeared in the *Hobart Sentinel*, outlining the dangers of giant corporations controlling the food chain, was eloquent and informative. He was a proud proponent of using science to increase yields, but only if the methods were tested and proven safe. He seemed to have an issue with genetically modified foods, which he referred to in one interview as 'a bigger threat to world health than polio, measles and malaria combined'.

She watched an interview he had given just over a week ago with the local *Lie of the Land* show, highlighting the latest agricultural developments. He was dressed in the same uniform, but presented his information clearly, and logically handled the questions about his farming techniques and the profitability of organics. Footage of Livelonger's farm showed a production line with sprays hosing every piece of produce before they were packaged for distribution. The reporter described the company created by Len Dengate as one of Tasmania's most innovative agricultural enterprises.

'It's a certified organic farm that produces top-quality vegetables and has been supplying the state's best restaurants for years. With such fertile land, this time of year the strawberries, raspberries, cherries and stone fruits like peaches are exceptional.' The interview finished with Len espousing the virtues of 'nature's finest': more vitamins, better flavour and stays fresher for longer. The reporter bit into a piece of fruit and urged viewers to support Tasmanian natural food companies.

Anya paused the video clip. Emily's mother may not have vaccinated her children, but her ten-year-old had most likely

died from eating 'healthy, natural food'. Few people remembered that death was natural too.

Emily had been on a raw food diet thanks to the naturopath, and one of those foods had very probably killed her.

Anya had to admit that Len Dengate presented well and
had answered the interviewer's questions with spontaneity
and wit. There was no sign of paranoia or any hint of odd
behaviour. And no shotgun in sight.

If there was a connection between the E. coli and Len's
farm, he would be shut down and the company's name most
likely ruined. Her mother had said things were tough, and he
was already under pressure from larger corporations to sell out.
Nevertheless, if Livelonger Organics was responsible for the
outbreak, it had to be identified as quickly as possible, or more
people like Emily and Evelyn would be infected.

She phoned her father and the call diverted to voicemail.
She decided not to leave a message. He'd know she had called
by the missed number.

Anya decided to make herself useful, so she sorted dirty
laundry piled on the washing machine into coloureds and whites.
She put the dark load on then checked in the pantry for something to eat. Tinned tomatoes, a packet of dried pasta and a pack
of vegetables in the freezer, non-organic, were all that was edible.
She found a frying pan and saucepan and prepared a tomato sauce
first. She would cook the pasta when her mother came out.

While the sauce was simmering, she took her laptop
outside and sat on the old cane chair. If she closed her eyes
she could smell the cigarillos Grandma Burgess would sneak
when she thought no one would notice. The chair still gave
off the vaguest scent of them. She vividly remembered her
grandmother beating the old rug on the clothesline while she
and Damien chased down chickens that had escaped from a
much more primitive pen than the one that stood in its place.
The chickens squawked inside. Behind the apple and lemon
trees, about fifty yards from the house, this one was modern
and freshly painted. Someone had to have built it for Jocelyn.

Anya thought of Grandma spending hours tending the vegetable patch and exchanging her produce with her neighbours for rabbits, sheep or even beef. Jenny Quaid cooking bread in exchange for food and services was not that different. It was the old way.

The sun faded and Anya moved back inside. This time, her mother's door was open. On the kitchen bench was a note.

Going out, don't wait up.

Anya walked back to her bedroom and peered through the curtains. Her mother's Mazda had gone. She sat on the bed, wondering how it had happened that she knew so little about Jocelyn's life. The sobering fact was, she barely knew her mother at all. So much time had passed, and there had been so much bitterness since Miriam's disappearance. She hoped more than ever that Mia and Jenny would be found alive.

18

The next morning, the roosters woke Anya around six. Even the pillow couldn't smother the noise. She had eaten alone, and stayed awake until she heard the Mazda pull up at midnight. Jocelyn had gone straight to her bedroom without speaking.

Anya showered and dressed and made a pot of tea. Her mother's bedroom door remained closed.

By nine, there was still no sign of Jocelyn, so Anya grabbed her keys and bag and decided to pay the Livelonger farm a visit. She wanted to know if Livelonger had anything to do with the co-op that the hairdresser said Jenny Quaid worked for, or sold food at the farmers' market Jenny attended. If the answer was no, it was unlikely Livelonger had been the source of the infection. Hopefully, the owner wouldn't greet her with a shotgun if she entered legitimately through the front of his property. He had already seen her car and should recognise it. And would have been up as long as she had by now.

On the way to the entrance Anya passed fields of potatoes and spinach. Pivot irrigators anchored at one end watered the crops, by computer-control, she assumed. At one stage, Tasmania had produced most of the potatoes for the largest fast food outlet along with the largest supplier of frozen chips nationwide. From what Jocelyn had said, times had changed. In a global world, even local land was being outsourced.

She drove through the entrance marked with a weathered billboard – *Livelonger Organics – Nature's Finest. Showroom open Monday to Friday 10 am–3 pm, Saturdays 9 am–12 am. Sundays 11 am–3 pm.* It wasn't open yet, but someone should be around. For farmers, there were no days off and this was already mid-morning in their working day.

She drove slowly towards a large industrial shed with a Land Rover parked outside. Security cameras were placed at intervals along the tin roof. After locking the car, she looked for an open entrance. Outside on a table in the shade was a box marked, *Sorry, we are closed. Please try some of our sumptuous treats.* It was very homely and inviting, in contrast to the impression the cameras and Len Dengate presented.

A woman came out of the shed door. 'Can I help you?' Her hair was bound in tiny braids all tied back into one ponytail. Her skin was the colour of dark chocolate, highlighted against the vibrancy of her orange and yellow kaftan.

'I'm just visiting. My mother, Jocelyn Reynolds, is a friend of Mr Dengate.'

'You must be the world-famous doctor.' The woman smiled broadly. 'You look very much like your mother.' Her accent was slightly clipped.

Anya felt at a disadvantage. 'And you are . . .?'

'My name is Grace Malik. My husband Samir is the foreman here. I work in the shop and around the farm.'

'Is Len around?'

She waved a hand dismissively. 'That man is like sand in a windstorm. He cannot stay still.'

Anya couldn't help but smile. Grace was affable and warm. 'I can imagine.'

'We can see if Mr Dengate is in his office. He would like to meet you, I'm sure.'

'We met yesterday.' Anya decided not to mention that he'd pointed a shotgun at her at the time. Grace led the way inside the shed.

There were potatoes on a long conveyer belt which passed inside a covered area about half its length. A hiss sounded.

'What happens in here?' Anya asked.

'This is where we spray the food with water to clean it,' Grace said above the noise. 'The water is recycled in a tank for strawberries and stone fruit in one of our greenhouses.'

A man at the far end of the shed washed down the floors. Anya had to admit, the place was cleaner and far more high-tech than she had imagined an organic farm to be. And on a much larger scale. The potatoes dropped into a section of the conveyer belt that secured them in plastic bags marked with the Livelonger logo. A worker at the end placed them into large boxes and stacked them on a wooden pallet. He turned and waved to Grace. His smile matched hers, and his black hair was cut short. He had on safety goggles, ear protection and worker's boots. Signs on the walls warned about back injury prevention and safety first.

'How many people work here?' Anya was curious as to the size of the operation.

'Mr Dengate is always working. He lives in the house on the hill. Samir and I live in the cottage behind. Apart from that, there are three more workers and others come to help harvest the stone fruit.'

'Looks like you take safety and care very seriously.'

'We do. We are all proud of what we do, and the opportunities we have here. Mr Dengate is a fine man and very good to us. No one else would give us jobs when we came from South Sudan. We are refugees.' She waited, as if expecting some kind of reaction from Anya.

'Sounds like he made a very wise choice employing you both.' Anya felt her jeans pocket vibrate and excused herself to check the message.

Source of infection identified for some of the cases. Farm called

Livelonger Organics. Recall about to happen. Media being notified. Steve Schiller.

Anya took a breath. Grace, her husband and the others could be about to lose their jobs.

A noise outside had caught Grace's attention. She and Grace stepped out into the bright light as a convoy of cars arrived, led by a patrol car.

'Why are the police here?' Grace took a step behind Anya. 'We have done nothing wrong.'

A ute hurtled down the road and skidded to a halt. Len jumped out of the vehicle and slammed the door. A kelpie was at his side.

'What the hell's going on?' He turned to Grace. 'Go inside, love. I'll handle this.'

'I'm sorry, Len,' a uniformed police officer said. 'This is official.'

Eight people exited the vehicles. Some in suits carrying folders, the others in overalls holding kits similar to the one the health inspector had taken to Evelyn's home.

'Hammond, the Maliks and all my employees are here legally. You and your immigration raiders can bugger off. You're trespassing, the lot of you.'

No one moved. The dog stood its ground and barked.

Len warned, 'I've got a gun . . .'

The policeman stepped forward. 'Mate, you don't want any more trouble. This is serious. We have an order to close the place down.'

'Like hell you do. You have no right.' Len clenched both fists and stared the group down. 'Now get off my property or so help me—'

Anya owed it to her mother to put herself between Len and further trouble. He couldn't afford to make the situation worse.

A woman in a black suit explained from where she stood. 'Mr Dengate, we're here from the Department of Health. I'm afraid your produce has been identified as the source of an outbreak of a virulent type of E. coli infection.'

Len laughed. 'That's the stuff found in manure and meat. There's no livestock here, only fruit and vegetables. You're after PT. Go back to the main road, turn right and you can't miss it.' He waved beyond the hill. 'Always said the bastards would kill people one day.'

The policeman raised both hands, palms outwards. 'Len, there's no mistake. Trust me, I double-checked. Your spinach is infected. These people have proof.'

Dengate waved a finger, but he seemed less confident. 'Now that's just not possible. We're accredited, got reviewed only last week in fact. I'm telling you, you've got the wrong place.' He turned to go back to his vehicle. The dog followed.

'I've got the paperwork right here.'

The woman in the suit cleared her throat. 'Sir, the source of the infection has been positively identified. We were able to collect samples from the homes of people so far infected. A number grew E. coli and they came from your farm.' She was no-nonsense. 'They were in your own labelled packaging.'

'Ha!' He stood triumphant. 'That's your mistake. We sell bags that are recyclable and prolong the shelf-life of vegetables. Your so-called samples weren't from here, they were just stored in our bags.' His shoulders relaxed. 'You can leave the way you came in.' He turned and took a few steps towards the shed.

'Mr Dengate.' The woman spoke again, this time with a raised voice. 'We've now identified six people who purchased spinach from Livelonger Organics and were infected with what is a potentially deadly bacteria. The evidence is irrefutable. I suggest you comply or we'll be forced to take aggressive action. Trust me, this will go better if you cooperate. Human lives are at stake.'

He turned on his heel. 'You're seriously blaming me for this? What the hell?'

Anya stood silent, ready to intervene if necessary to protect the owner from doing something stupid. He was her mother's friend, and he was in serious trouble, legal and otherwise. These people had jobs to do and he couldn't interfere with them.

The woman continued, 'Up to an hour ago, there have been fourteen cases reported. Two deaths have been recorded: a gentleman in his seventies, and a child.' Although the source of Emily's infection hadn't been determined, it could still have been the Dengate farm.

Anya held her breath. The news had to be devastating to the owner.

'Old people, children. This just keeps getting better.' He stepped up to the policeman. 'Simon, you have to be in on this. How much are they paying you? Huh? How much?'

The officer stood his ground. 'Len, don't do this. I'm going to forget you ever said that. I don't like it anymore than you, but two people are dead because of something your company sold. There is a protocol and it has to be followed. If you obstruct these people, you will be arrested. That is my job.'

'Lies!' Len clutched his head with both hands. 'God, these people have everyone in their pockets.' He began to pace. 'You've got to hand it to them. It's a great story, saying there's a child. All they need to do is start a rumour. If they shut me down long enough, I lose all cash flow.'

Len was sounding more paranoid and irrational than before. She wondered if anyone would put his responses on the record and hold them against him at a later date. She tried to reason with him.

'It isn't a rumour. It's fact. The dead girl's name was Emily Quaid. She was ten years old and has a mother and little sister. I saw her body and was at the post-mortem. I promise you no one invented the cause of death.'

Len shook his head in disbelief as she continued.

'These officers need to find out how your crop became infected. They have to run some tests on your equipment. The sooner you get it sorted, the quicker you can get back to business.'

The department of health officer handed him a piece of paper.

Len turned to Anya.

'Is this really true?'

She nodded.

'How? . . . I don't understand.'

Anya felt sorry for a man who had spent his life building a business. Working the land was unforgiving, hard work. He was at the mercy of the weather and had still managed to make a successful living. Until now.

She placed a hand on his shoulder.

'All my life.' He wiped his forehead with one forearm and bent down to pat his dog. 'Good boy, Ros.' He looked up. 'I grow nutritious, wholesome food. Nothing adulterated, nothing unnatural. You tell me. How can that be a crime?' The dog placed his chin over his master's forehead. 'They set Reuben up. Now they've done it to me.'

Anya wondered who Reuben was, and how this must sound to everyone present. If this became a criminal case, she would make sure he was psychiatrically assessed to establish whether or not he was mentally fit to be interviewed by police.

Grace returned to Len's side. 'We should all go into the office and talk. Samir is inside. He'll know what to do.'

Len breathed heavily and locked eyes with Anya. 'You have no idea what they're capable of. They've got to me. Mark my words, your mother will be next.'

19

Anya returned to her mother's house. There was nothing she could do for Len Dengate now. The health inspectors were interviewing him and taking samples as per their protocols. As sad as it was for Len's business, Emily and the elderly man had died, and numerous others, including her father's cousin, were seriously ill. The infection may have been found in the spinach, but the original source still needed to be identified, and they needed to find out whether it was resistant to washing. The potential illness it could cause if uncontrolled was of epidemic proportions.

Inside the house, Anya smelt eggs cooking. Her mother was dressed and at the stove.

'Want some?' She stirred the pan. 'No bread, so thought I'd just scramble eggs. There's plenty if you grab a couple of plates.' She gestured towards the cupboard.

Anya obliged, surprised there was no hint of yesterday's argument, and no mention of where Jocelyn had been in the night.

With a wooden spoon, Jocelyn shovelled the eggs onto respective plates. 'Good thing about keeping chickens, you always have food.'

Anya carried the plates to the table.

Jocelyn plonked the pan in the sink and brought the salt and pepper shakers with knives and forks. 'I'll get some groceries later.'

Anya assumed she hadn't heard anything about Livelonger yet. Soon it would be all over the area and in all the media.

'I need to talk to you about Len.'

Jocelyn had a mouth full of eggs and managed, 'Good idea. There are things about him you should know before you judge him. He was different before his fiancée died.'

Anya was curious now. 'What happened?'

'Patsy Gallop was a researcher at the Tasmanian Institute of Agricultural Advancement.'

The name and story registered. 'The Gallop murder?' Anya remembered the case. A colleague had murdered Patsy Gallop, supposedly in a jealous rage. Dr Reuben Millard was convicted. The case had made national headlines. It didn't escape Anya that Len had mentioned that name just this morning. Reuben. He'd said, 'they', whoever 'they' were, had set him up. He hadn't mentioned Patsy.

'Did his behaviour change after she died? It must have been a horrible time.'

Jocelyn put down her fork and took two mugs from a stand beside the sink. 'If you're suggesting for one moment he's mentally ill, you're wrong. He is a clever businessman and a true friend. There's nothing wrong with that mind.'

Her mother really seemed adamant that Len was fine, despite the incident with the shotgun the day before.

It was now or never. 'You're going to hear about it soon. Evelyn and the little girl who died were infected with an unusual strain of bacteria.' Anya swallowed. 'One of the sources has been confirmed. The infection came from Livelonger Organics.'

Her mother paused, leaning forward against the sink.

'That place is immaculate. He's put everything he owns into it. Everything Patsy had too.' She turned around. 'Does he know yet?'

Anya nodded. 'The health inspectors are there now. A policeman was with them. I think his name is Hammond.'

'Simon's a good man. He should keep Len calm. I'd better go, before he does something that will get him into bigger trouble.'

'Mum, please wait. Len seems to have some . . .' She tried to find a diplomatic way of mentioning Len's delusions, '. . . fixed beliefs about someone inventing the E. coli and the child's death, just to set him up.'

Jocelyn stopped. 'Fixed beliefs depend a lot on your concept of truth. One situation can be seen in multiple ways, from any number of viewpoints. Every person's truth is real for them, and equally valid. Like I said, don't judge him.'

Anya couldn't understand why her mother was being so cryptic. She touched her mother's arm. 'He said that "they" had got to him. And that you were next.'

Jocelyn pulled away. 'I need to go to him.'

'Mum, do you know what he meant? Was he threatening you?'

Her mother wasn't listening. She headed down to her room and grabbed her bag. Anya was right behind.

'Please listen. He didn't sound rational.'

Jocelyn pulled open the front door. 'His livelihood has just been ruined. If what you say is true, he's lost everything. How do you expect a man to sound?'

She slammed the door behind her.

Anya had finished another load of washing when Jocelyn returned two hours later.

'Grab your things,' she announced. 'We're going out.'

'Wait,' Anya said. 'What happened with Len? Will he be all right?'

'That's what I want to find out.'

Anya slipped on her shoes at the front door. 'Where are we going?'

'For pizza.' Jocelyn was already outside.

They drove in silence on the way into town and stopped in the main street outside the Longford antiques shop. They headed to the back of a long brick building. The Convict's Delight was a restaurant. A waitress who was on first name terms with Jocelyn greeted them before the maître d'. She crossed off what appeared to be a reservation.

The waitress chatted as she led them to a table by the wall. For lunchtime, the place was surprisingly quiet. A drinks waiter polished wine glasses. A sliding partition door closed off a section of the restaurant and bore a sign that read *Private Function*.

Anya glanced around at the decor. Exposed beams featured above polished wooden tables, highlighting the lemon brick walls. Flickering candles added to the feel of a centuries-old English inn. They could have been in the New Forest near Southampton, in almost any time in the last hundred and fifty years. It was one of the things she liked most about Tasmania. Parts resembled England, others Scotland and Ireland, while others could have been New Zealand, or a European snowfield. All on one small island.

'These walls don't have ears,' Jocelyn said. 'Six bricks thick.'

Anya looked around. On closer examination, she could see fingerprints and what looked like a convict arrow on one brick, then another.

Jocelyn ordered a lemon, lime and bitters for herself. Anya requested a glass of pinot gris. Like a house mouse, the waitress was gone.

'The bricks were all hand-made by convicts. Every nail in these tables, as well.' Jocelyn was a font of information on the area. 'People take history for granted these days, but it's what makes us who we are. You can't just sweep it away. You of all people should appreciate that.'

Anya wondered what point her mother was making. Jocelyn still had the grey-blue eyes, but her cheeks were sunken and the bags under her eyes had become increasingly puffy. 'Mum,

I need to talk about yesterday. I cut my heel on the security door and was only looking for a Band-Aid. That's why I went into your bathroom.' She expected a resurgence of Jocelyn's anger at the invasion of privacy.

'Were there any in there?'

'Yes. Next to the bottle of Thyroxin . . .' She waited for a response.

Jocelyn was distracted by something at the entrance. The maître d' was overly effusive in greeting two men who stood with their backs to Anya's table.

The waitress returned with their drinks, whispering, 'The high and mighty are here. We had to get out the good silver.'

'Be careful they don't steal it,' Jocelyn replied, po-faced.

The waitress smirked. 'Never can trust politicians. I'll be right back for your order. Anything with spinach, like the Moroccan lamb pizza, is off the menu for now.'

The Livelonger recall had already affected restaurants.

The two men laughing with the maître d' turned and Anya recognised both faces. 'Isn't that Christian Moss and his assistant?'

Jocelyn squinted. 'How would you know them?'

'I met them in Hobart at the conference. Moss wanted to talk about a new GPS monitoring system for domestic violence offenders. His assistant's name is . . .' She searched in her bag before coming up with his card. 'Ryan Chapman.'

The waitress reappeared and Jocelyn ordered a Wagyu beef and marinated tiger prawn pizza with asparagus. Anya opted for spicy lamb and vegetables on a garlic pizza base, garnished with yoghurt, mint and lemon.

'Moss calls himself Mr Progress.' Jocelyn took a sip of her drink. 'More like Mr Sellout. Our state Minister for Agriculture, Community Services and Policing, Planning and Employment. No conflict of interest there. A real man of the people – that is, if you're big business or a multinational wanting to own the state. That assistant must be extremely good at damage control. Every scandal just seems to glide right off the great Christian Moss.'

'So tell me what you really think of him.' Anya grinned and tasted her wine.

'Progress is a misnomer. He's approved the sale of four hundred acres at Emerald Vale to a Chinese consortium, or in other words, the Chinese government. Some choice. Farmers have to sell up or face financial ruin.'

Anya wondered why it hadn't made big news. 'How is it possible anyone from overseas could buy so much land?'

'The federal government allows sales of up to $320 million to avoid review by the Foreign Investment Committee and public attention. Anything less than that goes straight through. That means foreign interests could buy the whole state, providing the vendors break it up into smaller parcels for sale. Up to $319 million if they want.' She took another sip of her drink. 'It's reprehensible.'

Anya saw Moss weave his way across the room to them. He had a suit and shirt on, minus a tie today. 'Dr Reynolds, so good to see you again.' He turned to Anya and extended his hand. 'Dr Crichton. I had no idea you two knew each other.'

Jocelyn refused to make eye contact. 'Christian, this is my daughter.'

A well-groomed eyebrow raised slightly despite the fluorescent smile. 'I didn't make the connection. Dr Crichton, I am more than keen to discuss the GPS initiatives you talked about. My chief of staff will set up the meeting.'

The waitress reappeared. 'Your table is ready, Minister, and your other guests have arrived.'

'We should get together and talk over a meal some time. Enjoy your lunch. If you'll excuse me.'

He left but turned back. 'Oh. Not sure if you've heard, but Len Dengate's involved in this terrible fatal infection outbreak. The department of health has instigated a product recall for Livelonger Organics and shut him down. Ironic, given he has been so vocal about the benefits of chemical-free food.'

Anya noticed her mother's cheeks redden. 'It's a shock all right. All these farms using toxic chemicals and Len Dengate's is the only one investigated for a problem.'

The minister looked solemn. 'I came as soon as I heard the news. We're having a crisis meeting right now, in fact. We have to work out a way of managing this travesty. It could affect tourism, exports and countless other industries.'

Jocelyn's jaw tightened. 'The investigation is in progress. From what I hear, not all the cases can be attributed to Len's farm. You could be facing far wider contamination. If I were you, I'd be considering that before burying Len's business. And as the Minister for Police as well, shouldn't your priority be to find the missing child and her mother?'

'I've got the best teams working on it.' His face gave nothing away. 'Why, I'm informed even your daughter is providing valuable assistance with the investigation.'

Chapman, wearing a suit and tie, greeted them all before asking for a word with his boss.

'If you'll excuse us.' The men were suddenly involved in quiet conversation as they headed back to the bar.

'Arrogant pig,' Jocelyn blurted, a little too soon for Anya's liking. The politician could have heard. 'How dare he suggest you played a role in bringing Len down.' Her voice became louder.

'I went to the house to speak to the mother, and saw the blood at the scene. That's how Emily's body was found, and why I attended the post-mortem. I had nothing to do with tracking the source of the infection. He's just trying to get a rise out of you.' Anya spoke quietly as she watched the men enter the private room. 'You and Moss obviously have some kind of history.'

'I was on a health committee with him a couple of years ago. We didn't agree on much.'

Anya didn't know many people who agreed with all her mother's views.

Glenn Lingard entered the restaurant, in a crisp shirt and

dress trousers. Ryan Chapman emerged from the private function and ushered him over. Anya wondered why Glenn would
be attending a crisis meeting dealing with a bacterial outbreak.

Jocelyn continued to vent and didn't seem to notice.

'Why would Moss care about the region's reputation, when
he's sold most of it to overseas interests?'

She was obviously very close to Len and the business but Anya
wanted them to enjoy a meal together, without making a scene.
A factual discussion would be more prudent right now, even
though what her mother was saying sounded a little far-fetched.

'What do the Chinese want with the land?'

'To secure a food supply for the future, for their citizens.'

Anya had read of the Chinese government buying up land
in Scandinavia, but that was to store grain in underground
silos. There were rumours about them doing the same on arid
land in the centre of Australia.

'Who would sell incredibly fertile land that's likely to have
been in families for generations?'

'Who wouldn't is a better question.'

The pizzas arrived and smelt flavoursome. Both women
picked up their knives and forks to eat. Anya realised she and
her mother had always eaten pizza with cutlery. It was less
messy and cleaner in a restaurant setting.

'You two must be related. Most people eat pizza with their
fingers,' the waitress mused before leaving.

'Len may *have* to sell because of the E. coli.'

Jocelyn didn't answer. 'Don't you think it's odd that he's the
only one whose food's been affected?'

By definition, organic farmers couldn't spray with chemicals.
That meant it was more difficult to control insects and vermin.

'His crop could have a particular infestation.' It still
bothered Anya that not all the infected people could be traced
back to Livelonger Organics. There could be another source of
the infection.

'What you're expecting me to believe is,' Jocelyn used her
fingers to mimic quotation marks, '"shit" happens. I used to

think so. But if there is an avalanche of shit, you better start finding the arseholes responsible and fix the cause. The way I see it, Len's been pushing diarrhoea uphill with a toothpick for a very long time. This area's got some giant arseholes that need plugging. How do you know he wasn't sabotaged?'

Jocelyn was sounding as paranoid as Len Dengate.

Anya sighed. 'Isn't it possible Len was under financial pressure? Farming is tough right now. He might have been trying to save money by cutting corners.' Then something else occurred to her. 'What if somehow the bags had come into contact with the bacteria in the production stage and were already contaminated when the spinach was packed?'

Jocelyn took a bite of pizza and waved her knife. 'You could be on to something. Someone could have set that up.'

Anya was becoming increasingly frustrated. 'Mum, not everything is a conspiracy.'

'Interesting you chose that word. Conspiracy theorist or whistleblower? Terrorist or freedom fighter? It depends on which side of the fence you're on.' She pointed at the entrance as two more men entered, each dressed in shirts and jeans.

'Craig Dengate – Len's older brother – and Graham Fowler, the CEO of PT, the company that took over Emerald Vale. Explain what they're doing here.' The first was a dead ringer for Len Dengate, only less solid. The second was shorter with sharp features and thinning grey hair.

Maybe they were just having lunch, Anya thought. She needed to make Jocelyn see the bigger picture. 'Because of Livelonger's spinach, an elderly man has lost his life and Evelyn is in a critical condition, facing kidney failure and dialysis. It still might have been the source of the infection that killed little Emily Quaid. Who knows, her mother and sister could have been infected and are somewhere in need of help too. The priority is to prevent further infection. You of all people know that. And don't you think the families deserve reasons, not excuses? What's happened to Len is sad, but he isn't a martyr or a victim here. The people who died or are fighting for their lives are.' Anya stabbed at her food and picked off a piece of lamb.

Jocelyn's hands trembled and she put her cutlery down. 'You think answers will stop those people's grief?'

'No.' Anya knew from personal and professional experience that closure was something psychologists and police talked about, but was never really possible. In reality, grief had no end. Time eased some of the pain, but the most insignificant sight, sound or smell could trigger it all at any moment. For her, the hint of lavender sent her back to the lavender farm she and Miriam had visited. 'I understand that in a crisis, people need to feel like they understand what went wrong, and need to believe no one else will suffer. Sometimes there is no reason. Tragedies just happen.'

Jocelyn's eyes darkened. 'You've been sheltered from the real world, the people who have to live on, for too long.'

Anya suspected they were no longer talking about the E. coli outbreak.

'Look over there at Craig. That fool would bet on two flies going up a wall, always chasing a big win. He's lost everything he ever inherited. Real estate's his latest bandwagon. Graham Fowler didn't get to where he is by tolerating fools. Wouldn't have picked them as allies. Look pretty cosy huddled together talking like that.'

Both men were led into the private room.

Anya knew her mother was harbouring some tidbit. 'It isn't a coincidence we came here, is it?'

Jocelyn grinned. 'The owner's wife is a patient of mine. She boasted that this was Moss's go-to place when he wanted private meetings and didn't want the media to find out. That room was booked for him over a week ago. Audrey knew Glenn would be here today for a meeting with Moss.'

If it was true, her mother was right. This so-called 'crisis meeting' was planned before anyone even got sick with the E. coli infection.

Jocelyn picked up a fork full of pizza and took a giant

bite. 'It's as if Moss knew this would all happen. By today.'

Anya put down her knife and fork. 'Can you hear yourself? Are you honestly suggesting a minister deliberately contaminated Len's crop and killed people. Planned the whole thing so it would all blow up today?'

Jocelyn conceded it sounded ridiculous. 'I know how that sounds. But consider this. A month ago, Len's property was valued at $180 million. With this scandal and the fear of the infection contaminating his land, he'll be lucky to get a tenth of that tomorrow if he put it on the market. Suddenly Graham Fowler from PT crawls out of the woodwork with Craig's brother, a real estate agent? You tell me that's not a coincidence.'

Anya had to admit, if PT wanted to buy Len's property, things had definitely turned in their favour. Christian Moss said the dinner was a crisis meeting. Then why was it booked a week earlier?

20

Anya and her mother returned home after lunch. While Jocelyn saw a couple of emergency patients in the cottage, Anya filled the kettle and switched it on. As she waited, she decided to tidy some of the files that had been dumped on the floor in the dining area. Each folder contained the medical records for every member of a single family unit. On the front of each folder was written a large number in thick black ink. A pile by the wall had all been marked with a zero.

Another stack had folders marked with 5+ and the name of a town. The name Evandale appeared on a number of files in that group. Anya wasn't sure what exactly her mother had been auditing, and why she hadn't transferred the information to a computer program that assisted with clinical audits. GPs could work out how best to implement preventive health strategies in their practices, depending on the prevalence of disease and risk factors in their patient base.

She looked inside one of the folders marked 5+. Diagnoses on the cover page for the first patient read prostate cancer, type 2 diabetes, hypertension and cardiovascular disease. The next family member's cover page documented hypertension, hypothyroidism and asthma. The third, a child, had been born with

Down syndrome. Another child was well, apart from asthma and peanut allergy.

Anya tried to work out what the number five represented. It wasn't the number of patient notes in the folder.

She suspected that there was some order to the mass of files that had covered the kitchen table and chairs when she had arrived. Two more piles contained files marked with the number three. The top folder was for an elderly couple. Between them, they had cardiomyopathy, high blood pressure, kidney disease, coeliac disease, diabetes and rheumatoid arthritis. From the numbers, it wasn't possible to work out what conditions of demographic her mother had been auditing, or whether she was somehow ranking severity of illnesses.

The kettle boiled just as Anya's phone rang.

'Dr Crichton, this is Beatrice Quaid.'

Anya sat on a dining chair to take the call. 'I've been thinking of you, wondering how you're coping.'

'I'll do better if what the police said is true,' she said. 'About the farm having poisoned Emily and all those other people.'

Anya rubbed her temple with her spare hand. 'A farm outside Longford has been identified as the source for some of the infected food. But they're still not sure where Emily got the food that caused her illness.'

'Are you saying it's possible this farm may not be responsible for my granddaughter's death?'

'I'm saying that Emily might have eaten some infected spinach from there. If she didn't, there is possibly another source. I haven't heard yet whether the bacteria was found in Jenny's garden beds. The health inspectors would have tested the fruit and vegetables she'd been growing.'

'So if they shut this farm down and there are no more cases, it proves they infected everyone. If more cases come up then they won't have been caused by Livelonger Organics . . .' Beatrice's voice trailed off.

Or people wouldn't have seen the recall announcements in time and consumed infected spinach, Anya thought. 'If new cases keep appearing once Livelonger is shut down, there has to be another source.'

'I see. I want you to tell me exactly what Emily went through.' The grandmother remained composed. 'How much did she suffer?'

The question wasn't that easily answered, especially as Emily didn't seem to have been given any medical treatment. 'She probably started feeling nauseated, and developed some vomiting and diarrhoea. After a while, she would have had abdominal pain, fever, and become dehydrated fairly quickly.' Anya could imagine the scene. Evelyn had deteriorated so quickly. Emily's illness could have come on and been fatal within a few hours.

'I need to know *everything*. Don't think you're protecting me by withholding information. Ignorance is much worse than knowing what happened.'

'I understand that. Pretty soon Emily would have started passing blood, then vomiting as well. The whole thing would have come on very quickly. Kidney failure would have happened next, so she stopped producing urine, then her other organs would have begun to shut down. She probably lost consciousness after that.'

'Was she alive when she was put in the box?'

Anya couldn't say for sure. 'I don't know. There is some evidence that Jenny did call for help though. A naturopath had been treating her and the kids, and she called him. Except that something interrupted her and she must have dropped the phone. My guess is that's when Emily vomited blood in the bathroom.' Without a car, Jenny had no way of getting her child to a doctor, or even to Heyes. 'It's most likely Emily died there.'

Anya could picture the mother panicking, trying to clean up the blood with the first thing she could reach – the towels. She didn't leave her daughter to get a mop or bleach. That suggested it hadn't been a calculated plan to clean up evidence of the blood. Besides, Mia could have been watching on, terrified for her sister.

'Thank you . . .' Her voice dropped a tone. 'I need to know how my granddaughter was . . . put . . . in the box?'

Anya closed her eyes. This must have been so painful to hear, but Mrs Quaid had a right to know.

'She was on her side, as if she was sleeping peacefully. There was a soft toy, a yellow duck, placed in her hands.' Anya honestly believed that the last was a loving gesture, not a cold, indifferent act.

The phone was silent for a few moments.

'And if Mia and Jenny ate the food as well, they would have experienced the same things?'

'We don't know if they did. Emily was on a special diet.' The best outcome would be that Jenny had panicked and gone into hiding because she feared Mia being taken away. She chose her words carefully. 'The police are using all their resources to find them.'

'But if they did eat the contaminated food, could little Mia survive this long?'

It was unlikely. If Jenny was ill, she wouldn't be capable of looking after her three-year-old. 'I know you're trying to prepare for the worst. Truth is, it's pointless even thinking that until the police know more.'

'I've been approached by a lawyer.' Beatrice sounded as if she were confessing. 'He is putting together a class action, to sue Livelonger Organics for everything they have, and to make sure they never hurt anyone again. After what you've told me, I've decided to join the lawsuit.'

After hanging up, Anya sat thinking about how Len Dengate would respond to the news about being sued. She hadn't told her mother that he would also be under investigation for possible criminal charges. If he'd had any idea the food was contaminated, or had failed to comply with quality standards, he could be charged with manslaughter or even negligent homicide.

As the sun set, Anya found Jocelyn in the cottage, asleep at her desk on a pile of papers. As the door clicked shut behind

Anya, her mother sat upright and rubbed both eyes. 'How long have I been here?'

'A few hours.'

'How could you let me stay here this long?'

'I saw the last patient drive off and assumed you had work to catch up on.' Anya had taken the opportunity to go over Tom Quaid's post-mortem notes and edit some reports on the chair out the back in the shade.

'Let me freshen up.' Her eyes were more drawn than earlier. Jocelyn splashed cold water on her face from the consulting room sink.

'Who are all those files for?' Anya pointed at Jocelyn's desk.

'They're from the Longford surgery. I'm auditing their files as well as my Launceston ones. Since no one bought the practice there, I brought them all with me.'

Anya leant against the door. 'When was the last time you took time off and got away?'

'A change is supposed to be as good as a holiday.' She dabbed her face with a paper towel. 'I moved house and surgery. Besides, I couldn't get a locum to cover me even if I did want a break.'

'It doesn't sound like your workload is any lighter than in Launceston.'

'We all have our crosses to bear.' She ran a comb from the drawer through her hair. 'You married Martin . . .'

Anya felt her temper flare and didn't want another argument. 'Please don't start this again.'

Jocelyn threw her hands in the air. 'Fine. I was only half-joking. Now. We have work to do.'

About five hundred metres from the turn-off to Livelonger Organics, they saw a dark sedan stopped by the roadside. It was an odd place to leave a car, off the main road.

Jocelyn slowed and then pulled up directly behind it. The headlights illuminated two silhouettes in the car. Before Anya could stop her, her mother jumped out and marched up to the driver's window. The headlights showed her handing something across, as if she were mailing a letter in a post-box.

Jocelyn strutted back to her car, tugging on her scarf.

'Right,' she said with a satisfied expression, and clicked the seatbelt in place.

Anya had no idea what had just happened. 'Are you going to tell me what that was all about?'

'Don't worry.' Jocelyn hit the blinker and turned into the road to Len's. 'I gave them my card to save them tracing my number plate. Who knows, I could get business if they get sick while they're in town.'

'Them?' Her mother's sense of humour appeared at the oddest moments. 'Who on earth are they?'

'Minister's henchmen. They had the public servant look.' She accelerated, leaving dust in her wake. Two kilometres down the road, they saw the lights of the main house.

Outside on the gravel drive, a white Honda was parked. It had a rental sticker on the back window.

'Right.' Jocelyn stepped out and collected a bag from the boot.

'Are you going to tell me why those men were really sitting out there in the dark?'

'Good question.' She wore a cheeky grin Anya had never seen before as she leant over and touched the bonnet of the hire car. 'We're right on time.'

Anya was confused and concerned. 'Mum, are you all right?'

'An old trick I learnt doing house calls. If people tell you they can't leave the house and you find their car bonnet is warm, you know they've managed to get out in the last hour. You'd be surprised how many people think the doctor is a free home service but don't think twice about driving to the shops or chiropractor.'

Her mother had a sensible answer for most things. There was nothing to suggest the slurring or forgetfulness Damien said he'd heard.

They climbed the four steps to the front door. Jocelyn waved to a camera above the door and let herself in. Anya followed. Len's house was immaculate. His kelpie lay obediently on a small mattress near the wall opposite the sassafras kitchen table. He sat up when Jocelyn walked in and raised his chin so she could scratch underneath. Len looked more dishevelled than before. He hadn't exactly dressed for company. It was difficult to miss a large flat-screen TV mounted on the sideboard. Wherever he was in the kitchen he could see it. The screen was on and split into four black and white views. The front, sides and back of the house were being monitored. Without rising from his seat at the kitchen table, he introduced a woman with a mane of honey-blonde hair who stood and straightened her navy jersey wrap dress. Her exposed skin was pale and her face free of makeup, marks and blemishes. The hair around her face was layered and held off her face with simple clips. 'Hi, y'all. I'm Alison Blainey. I'm here to lend POWER's support for Len to get through this.'

Alison explained she was originally from South Carolina and worked for an international humanitarian organisation called Protecting Our Water, Environment and Resources (POWER) in Hobart. Anya knew they attracted attention, media and donations when they protested against whaling, rainforest destruction and pollutant chemicals.

Jocelyn stepped forward and shook Alison's hand.

'When did you arrive?' Anya asked, curious as to why a powerful lobbying group would want to be associated with a company responsible for an E. coli outbreak.

'The contamination has been all over the news,' she said with a Southern American accent. 'I was in Hobart for a conference on Antarctica. I don't normally drive, but I hired a car and came straight here.'

Len pulled Jocelyn aside. Anya could hear every word without trying. 'Can we trust your girl? How do you know she isn't working with them? She was at my farm today when it all happened.'

'Don't be ridiculous. She and the police found the body of the child and Anya was involved in finding out the cause of death. She had no part in the public health investigation.'

The large man nodded. 'If you trust her, I do.'

Anya felt more than a little unnerved being in the home of someone who had pulled a gun on her just over twenty-four hours earlier.

Two framed photos sat on top of the sideboard. One was of Len and an attractive woman with dark hair and a bright face. Anya presumed this was Patsy. The other was of the same woman flanked by a large group of people, all wearing sports clothes. Len noticed Anya looking. 'That was the last picture taken of my Patsy. She was so happy that day.'

'She was stunning.' Anya tried to ease any tension.

'Too good for me, some said.'

Jocelyn scolded. 'She loved you, no one else. Never forget that.'

The host busied himself with a coffee pot and produced two extra china mugs. They arrived on a tray with a Royal Albert sugar bowl and milk jug. 'Alison's been aware of the goings-on in the area for a while. She thinks she can help save Livelonger. I was supposed to meet her late next week for advice to help promote the business.'

'So I came a little early.' She patted Len's hand. 'We need to go on the attack quickly. We should strike back with carefully placed articles and interviews reinforcing how sustainable and superior organic farming is. Non-organic producers argue there's no nutritional difference, so we have to focus on the health benefits gained from cutting out pesticides and toxic chemicals.'

Len poured the coffee as Alison continued.

'We'll bring up health concerns about pesticides. That always gets attention, particularly for pregnant women and babies. Then we'll shift the focus to the overall health benefits of organic foods.'

Anya felt increasingly ill at ease listening to the conversation. It disturbed her that the people most affected apart from

Len were not even considered important enough to mention. 'I'm sorry. Can we spend a moment acknowledging who was affected by the bacterial contamination? A ten-year-old girl died after being fed raw foods her mother believed were healthy.' The image of Emily's body and Beatrice Quaid's grief came to mind. 'An elderly man who prepared his own food died. One of our own relatives is in a critical condition. She was in perfect health until she ate the spinach. Now she's on kidney dialysis.'

Len's eyes darted to Jocelyn and back to Anya. 'I had no idea. I wish I–'

'No point dwelling on what could or should have been,' Jocelyn instructed. 'Anya is right. There are numerous people in hospitals fighting for their lives as we speak. This has to be about more than just damage control. What about prevention and making sure other crops don't get infected? At least turn this into something worth fighting for. Something Len has fought for all along.'

Anya pointed out, 'You'll have an even bigger problem if the missing mother and three-year-old are infected too.'

Alison swished hair from her shoulder and lifted her coffee mug. 'From what I hear, there were concerns about that mother's competence to look after children. And the elderly gentleman could have been confused and had questionable hygiene.'

'Are you blaming the victims?' Anya knocked the table, spilling her drink. Len was quick to wipe it up with a serviette.

'I can see where this is going but we all have to stay calm,' Jocelyn intervened. 'I wanted Anya here for precisely this reason. She's seen the victims and dealt with the police already.'

Anya wondered if her mother was including, or using her.

Jocelyn's phone vibrated and she excused herself a moment. Due to the worried expression on the GP's face, the others waited in silence.

'First, can you describe the diarrhoea for me?' Jocelyn's face soon relaxed. 'His poo was completely blue and solid? All right, what's he eaten today?'

Anya felt relief as well.

The questions continued. 'No blueberries? . . . Was he playing with playdough or plasticine yesterday or today?' Jocelyn nodded knowingly. 'And what does he look like above the nappy, in himself? . . . Drinking his bottle is a very good sign. I think you'll find he ate some blue playdough and has passed that in his nappy. It's safe and just goes through kids like food.'

The woman's voice was audibly apologetic. 'Never be sorry for being an advocate for your child. If you have any other worries, don't hesitate to call. It's what I'm here for.' She hung up and turned to Alison. 'People are scared. They're panicking. And it's understandable.'

The POWER representative was unfazed. 'I feel for the families. But this is about something bigger. All of the organic farms are at risk if the public loses confidence in them. Multiple studies have proven that there is no significant difference in the number of E. coli infections from organically grown food compared to non-organic produce.' She turned to Len. 'This didn't occur because you are an organic farmer, and that's what we have to demonstrate.'

Len dug his fingers into his scalp. 'I still don't understand how any of this happened. I want to do what I can for those people and their families. It's only right. Joss, if I need to sell up to do it—'

'That is the last thing you want to do,' Alison interjected. 'PR 101. Deny, deny, deny, denounce. Do not admit liability until there's no other choice.'

The woman spoke like a lawyer. Denounce meant blaming the victims. That was her plan.

'Let's stick with what we do know. Did you have any advice on the packaging?'

'Our label recommends washing before use. And we spray everything with water prior to packing.'

Jocelyn asked, 'Is there a chance that small amounts of bacteria survive on the leaves in spite of spraying and washing?'

Len conceded, 'It's impossible to scrub between every nook and cranny on anything with leaves.'

Anya thought of Jenny Quaid. Being illiterate, she couldn't have read a warning label on anything.

'You spray and wash the food. Good,' Alison reasoned. 'I suggest we run an old-fashioned campaign showing grand-parents teaching grandchildren about how to grow REAL food, that sort of thing. The current affairs shows lap all that up when you have images of fast food that won't decompose and how kids today can't name vegetables and don't know where their food comes from. Your image needs rehabilitation, and that's a great way to do it. Or . . .'

'What?' Len's eyes darted to Jocelyn, who was shifting in her seat.

'The ultimate damage control,' Alison suggested, 'You close the business and start up under a new name. Take a lower public profile yourself, The general public has short memories so you wouldn't have to lay low for too long. We could do focus groups to help you re-establish your return to the limelight.'

'Excuse me, I need some air.' Anya pushed back her chair and left the room.

Jocelyn followed her to the door. 'I don't like what she's saying any more than you do,' she said. 'It's like a game to that woman.'

'How can you stay then and be a part of this plan to sully the names of those poor people?' Anya wanted to know.

'Because Len is my friend. And there's a question we haven't answered for those people. We don't know how this bacteria got into the crop. You said it was a rare type. Is it a mutation? Did you know that PT, the company bordering Len's property, is involved in genetic modification? The head of that company, Graham Fowler, was in the meeting with Moss, remember? Why would he have been there if he has nothing to do with any of this?'

'What are you suggesting? Please don't say it's a conspiracy.'

'The whole thing's rotten. I don't know how yet but I'm convinced Len's been set up.'

21

Anya could not believe her mother had bought into Len Dengate's conspiracy theories.

'Len is paranoid, and quite possibly unstable.' She thought about all the electronic surveillance in the house, on the shed. That's how he had seen the police and health inspectors arrive at the factory. He had probably been watching her talk to Grace as well.

'He has every right to be concerned.'

'If someone had contaminated his crop, don't you think one of those spy cameras would have picked it up?'

Jocelyn stood, hands on hips. 'There's so much you aren't seeing.'

'Mum, I think it's pretty clear.'

Len appeared, moved past them and opened the front door. A minute later, Grace and Samir Malik came inside. They greeted Anya and Jocelyn and went to meet Alison.

'Please. Stay,' Jocelyn pleaded. 'If you still want to go in half an hour, I'll take you home.'

Anya stood, undecided. 'This damage control and discrediting people is wrong. Evelyn is one of the people that woman wants to malign.'

'Evie is one of the reasons I'm doing this.' Jocelyn's eyes

were determined. She tightly clasped Anya's hands between her own. 'Len is too involved. I can't solve this on my own.'

Anya shook her head. 'What if there is nothing to solve? No conspiracy?'

Jocelyn released Anya. 'If you look at the evidence and that's what you conclude, I'll accept that.' She placed her hands on Anya's shoulders and locked eyes with her. 'You are the brightest, most ethical person I know. I'm asking you to help me. For a day or two.'

Part of Anya was touched by the compliment. The other wondered if her mother had another agenda. She wanted to give her the benefit of the doubt. Staying a couple of days was not too onerous and the source of Emily Quaid's infection remained unclear. She owed it to Beatrice Quaid to finish the job she had started.

'I'll let my assistant know tomorrow.'

Jocelyn clapped her hands. 'Let's get to it.'

In the dining room, Alison was discussing a corporate structure of some sort while Len served supper. 'It always concerns us when a group like the Chinese consortium buys up big sections of land in foreign countries. This isn't the only location they've targeted.' She selected a series of papers and maps from her files. 'They trade under a number of names, usually friendly to each specific country. For example, here they go by the name Pure Tasmania, or PT. Their slogan is, "Nature's Finest Produce".'

Anya had seen their products in Sydney supermarkets, and admitted to herself that she'd bought them because she had assumed the company was Australian and providing locals jobs.

'The parent company is Clarkson Evergreen, which is consistently voted one of the top five evil companies in the world.'

Alison let that sink in. Len took the lid off a Tupperware container full of biscuits.

'All the profits go overseas,' Alison continued. 'These companies manage to pay very little tax as well. They're notorious for employing transient workforces for harvesting and paying them considerably less than union rates.'

'How are they legally able to do that?' Anya knew of the mining industry lobbying government for fly-in, fly-out workers from overseas to fill vacancies and the public outcry it had created at the time.

'In this state, they lobbied the government that they couldn't fill the jobs with locals, so obtained exemptions to fly in Chinese workers at peak periods. Regional governments around the world are more often than not very accommodating to the company. They classified this as an area of need.'

'They feed and house the workers on site.' Len offered around the plate of biscuits. 'We were told it would be a boon for local businesses, but extra supplies are shipped in by the company itself.'

Jocelyn added, 'I've seen a couple of workers who've been injured at work, but otherwise, they're pretty invisible to us. Galls me to see our state logo on all the stuff they ship out.'

Samir spoke next. 'In Sudan we have many problems with soil and erosion, many pests and insects that destroy our fields. The government set up a research facility that collected every species of plants and seeds. We thought, "This is a good thing." My family grew snake cucumber. It is only found in my country. We were no longer allowed to grow this without paying the research people.'

Anya didn't follow the logic. 'Did they impose a levy or a tax on farmers?'

'No more growing without paying.' He interlaced his fingers on the table. 'Now you have to pay for seeds. Every year. My family is ruined.'

Alison drained her cup. 'The research was funded by Clarkson Evergreen. They took advantage of international laws and patented the indigenous seeds. It's what they do.'

Anya glanced across at her mother, who had begun to perspire. She could see the pulse in her neck bounding at a rapid rate.

'Mum, are you all right?'

'I just feel a little . . .' Jocelyn's eyes rolled back and she tipped to the side. Len caught her.

'She's fainting, lie her down.' Anya remained calm, and was quickly at her mother's side. Len lifted then lowered Jocelyn gently to the floor. Grace rushed to the sink for a glass of water and a wet cloth.

Alison moved out of their way. 'Will she be okay?'

Len stroked Jocelyn's hair as she regained consciousness. 'You're right, Joss, just one of your little turns.'

Anya couldn't believe this had happened before. Fainting wasn't normal. She felt her mother's pulse. 'You need to stop the Thyroxin. You're tachycardic.'

'It's why I didn't take it.' Jocelyn tried to sit up.

'Then why do you have it?'

'Damn tests said I had an underactive thyroid. I got the script but haven't got around to starting them.'

Anya thought about her mother's weight loss and rapid heart rate. Those symptoms were more consistent with an overactive thyroid. The tests could have been wrong.

Her mother took the water from Grace and sipped. Len helped her to sit up and wiped her forehead with the tea towel. He really seemed to care about Jocelyn.

'And don't look at me like that, Anya. I hate fuss. It was a simple faint. I obviously haven't drunk enough fluid today. End of story.'

She pushed everyone away and Len helped her back to the dining chair and sat next to her. 'You were saying something, Alison?'

The others rejoined them. Grace moved along a seat to allow Anya to sit close to her mother.

'I was talking about how the company has a team of lawyers around the world looking for loopholes in each country's patent laws. If they genetically modify a seed, it's patented. In some cases, they put in a terminator gene so it won't regerminate and is unusable twice.'

'Farmers in my country are desperate,' Samir said. 'They buy seeds that promise four times the amount of corn or grain and say you do not need to spray with much pesticide. Because the seeds cost ten times more, they must go into debt. The farmers believe they are doing good things.'

Grace reached for her husband's hand. 'The insects still come. Then the company that sells the seeds tells farmers they must use their special pesticide. Still the crops fail. My father could not afford to live.'

Her husband took over. 'Like many other farmers, he became sick. One day, he burnt down his farm. Then he killed himself.'

Anya felt for the woman and the family her father had left behind.

Grace dabbed her eyes with a tissue.

'Sadly,' Alison added, 'this case is not unique. The seeds were considered pesticide resistant. But farmers were always going to have to spray pesticides to kill weeds. The theory is that the resistant crop grows without competition and produces a much larger yield. The company selling the seeds also makes the pesticide and charges a fortune for it.'

'Grace, do you know why your father burnt the farm?' Jocelyn gently probed. 'The crop could have been harvested and sold to pay at least some of the debt.'

'The soil turned hard and looked like salt. Nothing would grow in it except the expensive seeds, and again, they did not grow like we were promised.'

Instead of finding their way out of poverty, Anya realised, the poor farmers become indentured slaves to this company and had to keep working to pay off their increasing debt. She doubted it was a coincidence that South Sudan was a poor country with a large population and food shortage.

Alison pressed on. 'In case you're wondering what this has to do with Len's business, we're getting to that. The clever thing about Clarkson Evergreen is how they recruit top businessmen in the countries in which they operate. They have a revolving door of CEOs and board members, who, coincidentally, also rotate through positions heading their nation's agriculture departments, food and drug administrations or their equivalents.'

Len collected a folder from the centre of the table and extracted a document. 'They're major contributors to political campaigns as well. Here's a copy of an internal email sent from the CEO of PT to Clarkson Evergreen. It reassures the board members that the company's interests will be well represented, no matter which party wins the forthcoming state election.'

He handed it first to Alison, who reviewed the contents. 'How did you manage to get this? It's highly confidential and PT normally takes security very seriously.'

Len lowered his head. 'I can't say. Just got lucky.'

Alison glanced around the table as if to verify the source of the email. If anyone knew who had disclosed it, they weren't admitting it. Anya began to feel uneasy about what Len intended to do with the leaked internal email. Jocelyn had a glazed expression and Anya knew she should take her home soon.

'I'd love to know your source, it could really help our case,' the lawyer said.

The discussion was moving completely away from Len's problems.

'What case?' Anya suspected that this supposed good Samaritan and her organisation had their own agenda, and were using Len for some reason to raise their profile and push their own cause. Len needed practical help and advice, not campaigning right now. 'What does this have to do with defending Len against litigation and charges regarding the food poisonings?'

'PT is growing genetically modified crops next door to this very property. Two hours ago I assessed Len's crops with a strip test kit. In the northeast, three out of six samples were positive for GM plants. In the northwest, sixteen out of thirty were positive. If PT has contaminated Len's land and ruined his business, they'll be up for enormous damages and the loss of lucrative income. The non-GM premium for Len's crops is around \$40–60 per tonne.' She placed a hand on her host's shoulder. 'Once organic status is lost, it cannot be regained for at least thirty years.'

Grace covered her mouth with her hands, and Samir looked devastated. Len remained unmoved. In some ways, the almost catatonic response was more disturbing than his anger. Anya wondered if there was a possible link between the GM foods and the E. coli infection, but had no idea what it could be.

'Don't worry,' Alison assured. 'We might not save this farm in its current incarnation, but at least Len won't face financial ruin. PT will be accountable for their seeds contaminating his crops.'

'If I'm going down,' Len finally said, 'I'm taking those mongrels with me.'

22

Alison checked emails on a mobile. 'It's all arranged. A protest has been organised for tomorrow at PT headquarters in Emerald Vale.' She looked at their host. 'Len, I think it's better if you aren't seen there.'

'They set me up—' Len stood and began pacing the room. 'They've shut me down.'

'Minister Moss is scheduled to make a big announcement at midday. It's a good opportunity to deflect publicity from Livelonger Organics. If you're seen there, the media will make you the feature, not PT's wrongdoing.'

Anya was surprised at how quickly the organisation had rallied. As in many regional areas, environmentalists were seen by many as radicals, regardless of their scientific arguments. They were perceived as obstructionists, people who stopped jobs and got in the way of 'progress'.

The campaigner said good night and left.

Anya wondered if Alison realised what she was up against. Many of the farms had been in these families for generations. Some farmers had sent children to study agriculture at university so they could return and improve the quality and quantity of their yield. The problem they now had was dividing land amongst surviving children. With each generation, the land pool diminished significantly. Making a living off the land had never been more difficult. Companies investing in the state were seen as saviours, not enemies.

Before Grace and Samir left, Anya asked them a question that had been bothering her.

'How much spinach would Livelonger have distributed in, say, the last two weeks, up until today?' She was worried about the incubation period and the potential scale of E. coli infections they may expect. Not everyone would see the recall warnings.

Samir looked to his wife. 'Grace does the books and invoices.'

She was quick to answer. 'This time of year we average eighty kilograms of baby spinach a month. We pack it into quantities of two hundred grams.'

Anya did the maths. Around forty kilograms distributed per fortnight meant two hundred bags were available for sale. Multiply that by the number of serves in a bag – four – and they were looking at a major epidemic. It was miraculous there hadn't been more cases by now.

'Thanks. Have a good night's sleep,' she said to the couple. Jocelyn was engaged in a private conversation with Len in the lounge room. There was no more hint of low blood pressure or any more faints. Anya needed to address what was going on with her mother's health. Clearly, something wasn't right. But getting her to admit it was a battle that could wait until morning.

Anya occupied herself washing the crockery. She was glad Jocelyn had a good friend, but was also concerned about what would happen to the farm, with the E. coli investigation and fallout. Len was odd, impulsive and could be overly aggressive, yet was like a gentle bear around her mother.

After finishing the washing up, Anya took the opportunity to quietly phone Steve Schiller. If Jenny and Mia Quaid were alive, another night outside wouldn't be easy, especially for the toddler.

A woman answered and handed over the phone.

'Sorry. I thought you might still be at work.'

'Ducked home for a late dinner. It's going to be a long one.' Schiller sounded fatigued.

Anya instantly regretted dialling. He may not be impressed with her reason for calling.

'What's up?'

'Is there any news on Jenny or Mia? Did Dylan Heyes have an explanation for why Jenny was on the phone to him?'

'No word yet. Dylan Heyes says he can't remember Jenny calling. He's such a busy man healing the sick, performing miracles, like he does.'

Anya was curious why he would lie. He didn't have a motive for hurting Mia or her mother, that they knew of. So why deny a phone conversation unless he was hiding something?

'Did you press him?'

'Refuses to say anything else or answer any more questions. His lawyer friend made that pretty clear. If you ask me, he's guilty of something involving those two, we just don't know what. He's under surveillance and probably knows it. That's the best we can do until we get something solid to go on.'

'Any new reports of food poisonings?'

'Touch wood, not that we know of.'

At least that was something positive. Anya thought carefully about her next comment.

'I'm not sure how this is going to sound, but there are some people who think Livelonger Organics could have been set up. That the infection was deliberately introduced to the farm's spinach.'

There was a long pause. 'What possible reason would anyone have?'

'The farm land is prime real estate. There are buyers waiting for the company to fail. An environmental group called POWER were so quick to contact Len Dengate as well. A representative was here within hours.'

Another long pause. 'From what I've heard, POWER jumps on bandwagons for a living. Organic farmer versus big bad corporations is right up their alley so it isn't that far-fetched. My guess is, they're concerned about the reputation of organic farming.' Schiller hesitated then asked, 'What do you think?'

Anya was tired and knew how ridiculous the set-up plot sounded. She remembered that Schiller's background was in environmental science. 'To be honest, I'm not sure. I'm staying for a couple more days to see what I can find out.'

'Keep me informed, would you?' He sounded concerned.

'Likewise.'

Anya checked her messages. Bob had just texted. Evelyn was responding to haemodialysis. She was still on life support, but doctors were optimistic she would survive. Anya breathed out with relief.

She offered to drive her mother home. For once, there was no argument. Without hesitation, Jocelyn handed over the keys before hugging Len. She promised to check on him tomorrow.

Without streetlights, the roads were pitch dark. Visibility was limited to what the headlights illuminated. Jocelyn closed her eyes and Anya concentrated on the drive. On the intersection to the road to Jocelyn's house, she noticed a white car stopped on the verge, headlights on and driver's door open. It looked like Alison Blainey's hire car.

She tapped her mother, who gave a short snort and opened her eyes.

They parked a few metres behind. Both climbed out. Anya's gut contracted. There was no sign of Alison. The keys were still in the ignition. The airbag hadn't engaged. Papers were blowing out onto the road.

'Alison!' Jocelyn called. No response. 'Can you hear me?' she shouted louder.

A soft moan came from somewhere in the grass. Anya moved quickly towards the sound and saw movement. It was Alison, lying on her side, legs curled up.

'She's here.'

Jocelyn rushed over.

Where she was positioned, it was difficult to see more than an outline. Anya pulled out her phone and used its light as a torch. Alison's face was battered and blood streamed from her nose. 'I'll get my bag.' Jocelyn ran back to her car. Anya knelt on the ground to better assess the injuries, careful not to move anything.

'What happened?' she asked gently. Alison's dress was tattered but still tied at the waist, as it had been at the house.

'A woman. She waved and said she was out of petrol. She had a child in the car.' She spat out blood. 'I got out to help.'

Anya instantly wondered if it had been Jenny and Mia.

Jocelyn skidded to her knees, doctor's bag in hand. She pulled out a torch, which Anya held. The extent of Alison's facial injuries became apparent.

'Where does it hurt?' Jocelyn began to examine her. Eyes first, swinging a pen torch from her examination tools. 'Pupils equal and reactive.'

She held up four fingers. 'How many can you see?'

'Four.' Alison coughed and winced, clutching her ribs. She tried to sit up.

'We'll get you up in a minute.' Jocelyn eased her back down.

She listened to both lungs with her stethoscope. 'Air entry equal both sides.'

So far, even if she had fractured ribs, they hadn't punctured a lung.

'That's good,' Jocelyn said, feeling the wrists and arms.

Alison flinched on palpation of her left forearm.

'That could be broken.'

Anya looked around in case whoever had done this returned. 'Did the woman beat you?'

'I don't think so. I was talking to her. Something hit me from behind. I fell forward on the ground. Someone started kicking me, again and again. I could tell from his voice it was a man. I curled up and begged him to stop. All I could think of was protecting my head with my hands.' She took short, shallow breaths.

Anya noticed that her stockings were torn at the knees, but still in place.

'What happened then?'

'I don't know. He called me a whore and stopped. Then I heard the car drive off. I was so scared they'd come back.' She squeezed Anya's hand tightly.

'Any pain in your stomach or back?' Jocelyn asked.

'My side.' She clutched her ribs.

'We're going to try to get you up and take you to the hospital.'

'No. I don't need—'

'I'm going to be the judge of that,' Jocelyn asserted.

They slowly helped Alison to her feet and into the Mazda. In the light from the interior, her swollen cheek and eyes became more obvious. Anya helped her with the seatbelt.

'I'll take her to Launceston. They can do X-rays and a CT.'

Alison had significant head injuries and needed further assessment. Her fractured arm looked displaced as well.

Anya dialled the police. A patrol car arrived within minutes.

The officer who had been at Len Dengate's property, Constable Hammond, stepped out, accompanied by a burly uniformed sergeant.

'Where's the victim?' The older man surveyed the car and its position.

'My mother's about to take her to hospital.' Anya pointed at the Mazda.

He looked Anya up and down. 'And who would you be?'

'Jocelyn Reynolds' daughter Dr Anya Crichton. She's in the car with the woman who was assaulted.'

Hammond bent down to see inside the driver's side window and spoke to Jocelyn before standing up. '

'Dr Crichton, this is Senior Sergeant McGinley.'

Anya relayed what Alison had said, and mentioned her concern that the woman and child might have been Jenny and Mia Quaid. Hammond had a large torch, which he shone from shoulder height. They could make out scuff marks on the dirt and drag marks.

'Are we looking at sexual assault? Better breath test her.'

'What does her blood alcohol level have to do with anything? She was stopped and assaulted. You should be looking for whoever did this. Alcohol has nothing to do with sexual assault.'

She was tired of men like McGinley suggesting that if a woman drank, she was asking to be raped. The same people believed that the rapist was somehow less responsible if the woman was drunk and not even culpable if he had been drinking.

The sergeant hitched up his belt. 'You might think you're pretty important but you have no authority here. I want the woman breathalysed. If she's over the limit, we need to take her in.'

Hammond stood, head down. 'Are we looking at sexual assault?'

Anya preferred to deal with the more junior officer. 'I don't think so.' Victims were often loath to admit they had been raped. 'With her broken arm, it wouldn't have been easy for her to get her stockings back on.' Anya added, 'Do you have a photo of Jenny Quaid?'

'We were all issued with them,' Hammond said, and retrieved it from his patrol car.

Anya immediately showed the photo with Jenny's round face and cropped hair to Alison with the interior light illuminating it. 'Is this the woman you spoke to?'

Alison shook her head. 'I don't know. The woman I saw had long dark hair. I guess it could have been a wig.'

Anya thought of Beatrice waiting for any news. 'Did you see the child?'

'Not well enough to describe them. I'm not even sure if it was a girl or a boy. I'm sorry, it all happened so fast.'

Anya moved back to Hammond.

McGinley took notes. 'So Len Dengate recruits the Greenies to save his place. This one leaves his place, gets ambushed, then bashed. And you say a dark sedan was watching the property,' he said. 'If you buy into this, you're as crazy as Dengate himself.'

Anya heard Hammond mutter, 'What the hell has Len started now?'

23

After a restless night, Anya awoke. Jocelyn was already gone, presumably to her Longford surgery. Anya fed the chickens, collected the eggs and showered. There hadn't been an opportunity to get groceries after Len's farm had been shut down. She decided to get some things for dinner during the day.

First, she headed south to have a look at PT before the protesters turned up. It was a long shot, but if she could identify other locations of Clarkson Evergreen farms, there may be a correlation with outbreaks of E. coli infection in those areas. Before leaving, she also checked the internet. Information provided by the company was vague at best.

On the way, a roadside diner provided coffee, toast and news. The front pages of the *Hobart Sentinel* and *Launceston Herald* both showed photos of an angry Len Dengate with his arm raised in protest. She wondered where the photo had come from. The coverage of Livelonger Organics had relegated the search for Jenny and Mia to page two. At the time of print, there had been no new developments. Anya hoped that once Alison felt better and had recovered from her concussion, she might be better able to identify the car or woman who had stopped her last night. She flicked through both newspapers.

So far, the count for confirmed cases of E. coli infection was fifteen. Anya wasn't sure whether or not to be grateful for the relatively small number, although the survivors could be left with lifelong medical problems.

Around ten-thirty, she drove further south to Cressy, past paddocks of wheat and vegetables. Although Cressy had begun as a wheat belt, she hadn't seen any growing as a child. This was all new, at least in the past decade. In Anya's childhood, summer days were long, with hours spent shelling peas. Every chance she'd got, she would sneak away to read. To her special place: a secluded corner in the barn, which was occasionally shared with the odd chicken or rabbit. Damien, being more of an outdoors person, could never wait for summer holidays when he could be outside and run wild with his cousins. Riding on a tractor was his favourite. Her grandparents' farm was somewhere Anya had felt safe, away from the gossip of people who barely knew her.

Her great-aunt thought girls should learn to cook and sew. 'Books fill a girl's head with fancy notions,' she would say. 'Won't help an ounce in the real world.' Great aunt Maisy had been a robust woman who cooked for the farm hands from sun-up to sundown. Somewhere in between kitchen duties, she also managed to clean clothes and sheets, tend to the animals and care for her own, demented sister. For many women of that generation, formal education was never an option.

Anya reflected on how many people in her mother's family had been struck by dementia. Their experience wasn't unique. Some claimed pesticides were responsible but the most likely cause was vascular, the same risks for heart disease and stroke. They lived on a diet comprising mostly dairy and meat. Freshly made damper, fried eggs, bacon, baked beans and potatoes were the essential breakfast. Morning tea constituted three types of cakes like lamingtons, cream sponges and tea cakes. Lunch was a roast, lamb or beef, with at least six vegetables, most of which were smothered in butter, cheese or hollandaise sauce. Then came afternoon tea, pavlova with seasonal fruit, custard, or a slice. Dinner was made of leftovers cooked in lard, and often encased in pastry. She couldn't believe she had eaten so much animal fat growing up, and how much that increased the risk of vascular dementia. Dementia was always in the back of her own mind, as was the question of whether or not it was inevitable that she would develop it too.

She thought of her mother, who had been fairly quiet at last night's meeting, and the fainting episode. Jocelyn's pulse rate had been over two hundred as she fainted. Jocelyn denied taking the thyroid replacement, and the bottle hadn't been opened the day Anya arrived. She wanted to see the results for the blood tests her mother had had. Her mother had self-diagnosed, which was dangerous. She just had to broach the topic tactfully tonight.

Before too long, a series of signs announced she had now entered Emerald Vale, the home of Pure Tasmania. A montage of dairy cows on green pastures, corn, potatoes and green vegetables looked like a utopia. There was no mention of the land being owned by Chinese interests, or Clarkson Evergreen.

Anya followed some signposts promoting an information centre. Majestic pencil pines lined the road. They gave the impression of a path to a first-class, exclusive resort.

Before a boom gate, a sandstone cottage invited visitors to learn about Pure Tasmania. Anya parked in the designated area and followed a family of six into the centre. 'Welcome,' greeted a woman in her early twenties wearing a long white skirt, linen shirt and apron. On her head was a white cotton cap with a frill around the face. She looked as if she'd just stepped out of *Little House on the Prairie*, or a convict settlement. *SALLIE* was printed on her Tasmania-shaped badge. 'You're all in luck. The audio-visual presentation is about to start.'

The children, aged in their early teens, dragged themselves into the theatrette, complaining about having to be there. Anya wasn't in a hurry and her hesitation had the friendly staffer at a loss.

'How did you hear about us?' She smiled as if her lips refused to close.

'I saw some of your products recently in Sydney. Can friends and family get them at other places as well?'

Sallie pressed a button outside the cinema room, presumably to begin the presentation. 'Well, we do get a lot of wonderful feedback about our products but most of them go overseas. We're one of the biggest exporters in the state. We do post anywhere in the world. If you let me know specific suburbs, I can also look up distributors for you.'

'I travel a lot, and was just enquiring.'

'I'll just check.' Painted nails tapped on a computer next to an old-fashioned cash register.

On the wall behind were a number of plaques presented to the company for community support of local schools and clubs. Certificates announcing first place accompanied blue ribbons from the state's regional shows. Pumpkins, zucchinis, strawberries and dairy products featured.

Anya glanced around. Blue and white gingham curtains were held with silky tie-backs, giving the place a country, heritage look. Merchandise on glass shelves included jams and sauces presented with frilly matching gingham on the lids, bags of flavoured popcorn wrapped in cellophane and ribbon, all giving the impression they'd been hand-made. Anya selected a bag and looked at the ingredients. Corn syrup was mentioned, but there was no listing of anything genetically modified. Not surprisingly, she didn't see her mother's brand of powdered iced tea. A number of other varieties were available.

'Do you have different labels depending on where you sell your products?'

'You must be in marketing.' Sallie lifted a folder from under the desk and opened it for Anya to browse through. 'A lot of research goes into things like packaging and labels. I love ours, they're so old-fashioned. People really like the country feel of them.'

Anya flicked through the labels pressed in plastic sleeves. None mentioned Clarkson Evergreen and each seemed to promote a cottage industry feel, as opposed to a Chinese mega-company. She recognised one as a tin her mother had in the kitchen. She bet Jocelyn had no idea she was buying a PT product. It wasn't listed anywhere on the label, instead being described as Tasmanian made and owned with a trademarked title. Their products were pervasive and difficult for consumers to trace.

Sallie was back at the keyboard.

'We have branches at Ipswich in Queensland, and Elizabeth in South Australia for now, and of course, Blacktown in Sydney.'

The distribution was based in poorer areas, presumably where land was cheaper.

'Would you like to sample some of our special treats?' Sallie moved towards a table with baskets containing different types of popcorn. 'I thoroughly recommend the salted caramel, but the pumpkin pistachio is to die for.' The latter was surprisingly edible.

'Thanks very much, you've been a great help.'

'Come back again,' Sallie said, with the same smile. 'Don't forget to tell all your friends and have a great day.'

'You too,' Anya replied out of courtesy.

On a revolving stand near the door, postcards and brochures were on display, with the word *Complimentary* printed above them. She collected a couple on the history of the company and its range of products.

Outside, the sound of hydraulic brakes hissed. As Anya exited, a tourist coach opened its doors and a group of senior citizens filed out. The bus driver had already stepped down and handed out coupons to the willing passengers. He warned them to stock up but not fill up because next stop was lunch. Some of the women tittered in groups.

It seemed PT was doing everything it could to gain favour with visitors. No doubt kickbacks went to the coach companies.

Anya walked around and took photos with her camera. In a distant paddock, cattle roamed freely. PT bred animals as well as producing fruit and vegetables. She checked her watch: 11.15 am.

A white Commodore drove into the car park, followed by a van emblazoned with the name of the local television station. A familiar figure in a charcoal suit climbed out of the back of the first car, pointed to the front of the cottage and seemed to be giving instructions to the TV crew as they unpacked. It was Ryan Chapman, Christian Moss's chief of staff.

The camera set up with what looked like a view of the PT logo. A sound operator held a fluffy boom microphone. A young male reporter in a suit bared his teeth at a hand mirror. Within minutes, the car park had filled with people carrying recording equipment marked with the names of radio stations. Anya asked the sound man what was happening.

'Minister's about to make some big announcement.' He shrugged. 'We just got the memo to turn up.'

Nearby, the TV reporter glanced down the road and made a circle with his index finger to the cameraman.

Ryan Chapman noticed Anya and came across to say hello.

'We just keep running into each other,' he said, smiling. The man was definitely charismatic and enthusiastic.

Before Anya could respond, a female reporter with a phone held out to Chapman approached. 'I heard there was going to be an announcement by your minister,' she said. 'Any hints as to what that's going to be? I could make it worth your while.'

Ryan deftly deflected the question. 'Don't think my boss would approve of me selling favours. I can promise you it will be big and a major boon for the area.' He turned back to Anya. 'Nice seeing you again, doctor.'

She stepped back to watch what would happen next. Were the media aware a protest had been planned? It would have been unlike Alison Blainey not to notify them and miss a publicity opportunity. The real question was whether the minister and his team were aware of what was planned?

A series of coaches rolled along and stopped in the distant end of the car park. A large group formed at that end, comprising both older and younger people, some with babies and toddlers. The luggage doors opened and people collected placards and posters.

The cameraman rushed over after a reporter. Anya moved closer to listen, but kept far enough away to be out of it.

'Who are you representing today?'

A woman in her twenties held up her hand. 'We represent all Australians: the battlers, the taxpayers, the mothers who want the best for our children. We want a world they can inherit, that will still be here for their grandchildren.'

They began an interview as three minivans approached. Groups of men wearing soiled jeans, work boots and akubras joined seniors to disembark. The locals had rallied support, and Anya suspected it wasn't for the protesters.

'Go back to the mainland, you bloody Greenies,' an elderly woman from the first van shouted. 'You don't care about us, our jobs or our families.'

'We don't want you here. Piss off where you came from,' a male voice chimed in. 'We can't eat trees, we need to earn a living.'

The two groups exchanged insults, initially from a distance.

The protesters had a megaphone. 'You've sold your souls to the devil. Pure Tasmania belongs to one of the most evil companies on the planet,' shouted a man with dreadlocks who was holding a sign painted with the skull and crossbones beneath the words 'POISON PEDDLERS'. Another sign read 'FRANKENFOODS'.

Anya had seen protesters carrying similar signs outside the conference in Hobart. So far, there was no sign of Alison Blainey. She could still be recovering from the assault overnight.

'PT put us on the world map!' a local shouted.

'Yeah,' another shouted. 'PT saved our town.'

'They rape our country and take the profits offshore.'

'Get a job, you bloody dole bludgers.'

The two groups moved closer. Anya worried that with tempers and emotions rising, physical confrontation was likely.

From behind the boom gate, a number of security staff hurried towards them. A couple of minutes later, two police cars arrived.

Constable Hammond climbed out of the first car and put his cap on. He straightened his shoulders, pushed down his belt and took in everyone who was there. His first action was to meet the security crew. After a short discussion, PT's reinforcements retreated towards the boom gate.

Radio reporters scurried amongst the crowd, shoving microphones in people's faces for comments.

Anya stepped well back to observe the melee. A placard with a giant colour photo of a three-legged frog was unmissable.

A few moments later, another white Commodore pulled in. The minister had arrived. The protesters tried to block the car as it approached the boom gate, but the police and security team managed to keep them at bay. The car was allowed through, as were members of the press. A barricade was formed against anyone else passing.

'We want to give the minister a petition,' a young woman shouted over the din. 'We have ten thousand signatures!'

The representative from the protesters was petite, dressed in a peasant skirt with a snug, black T-shirt. Her red, wavy hair was pulled up into a ballet bun. She could have just come from a dance class and instantly caught the attention of the TV reporter. This spokesperson was, as they say, 'good vision'.

Before moving through the boom gate, a reporter stopped to interview her, to the irritation of one of the security team.

'Let the invited guests pass.'

'I'm president of the Medical Students' Association. We care about what our children are eating and what it's doing to the land,' the protester shouted.

Anya moved amongst the crowd to hear better.

This was no off-the-cuff rally, it was a carefully orchestrated grab for media.

Only the security guards weren't being compliant.

Without warning, Anya was hit from behind.

24

As Anya hit the bitumen she saw one of the security men dragging the medical student across the ground. The young woman squealed in pain. In response, locals surged forward. Two fellow protesters fought off the security guard. The reporter who had tried to interview her came running back, cameraman in pursuit. Just then, another woman screamed and everyone converged. Anya scrambled to her feet, having no idea who or what had hit her in the head. She saw an elderly man stumble, blood teeming down his forehead.

Anya squeezed through an opening to get to his side.

'Give him some space,' she urged, and felt another shove from the side. A hand steadied her. Constable Hammond. They forced and jostled through to get the man to safety. By now, a fist fight had broken out. Seemingly out of nowhere, local youths arrived in truckloads and joined in the rumble.

'Someone's going to get killed if I don't stop this,' Hammond shouted.

'I'll look after this man,' Anya managed.

Another police car approached, siren wailing and lights flashing. The noise seemed to scatter the crowds.

Anya applied pressure to the man's head with a handkerchief provided by an onlooker. He was lucid, but angry at the protesters and wanted to press charges against whoever had injured him. Drawn by the mayhem, the press had returned, abandoning the minister.

Anya looked across and saw Alison Blainey with the medical student. A coat hung over the environmentalist's shoulders, like a cape. She could only been discharged from hospital a few hours ago. Her arm was covered in a cast and long sleeves. There was little chance of disguising her bruised cheeks, even with oversized sunglasses. She must have been in the background before the altercation broke out.

Anya couldn't hear Alison's exchange with the medical student but from where she stood, it looked less than friendly. The older man's knees buckled and Anya reached out to catch his arm, before helping him to the cottage shop. The shop assistant had locked the door, but opened it when she saw them through the window.

'This is so going viral,' she enthused, mobile phone in hand.

'Do you have a first aid kit?' Anya pressed. 'If so, can you put a dressing on the gash?'

Sallie's initial response was incredulity.

'It won't take long.' Filming and disseminating the drama outside could wait a few minutes.

Returning to the car park, Anya saw that the protesters had retreated behind their buses. Simon Hammond was questioning the medical student, and some members of the press were lining up to talk to her as well. Alison Blainey had melted into the background. The rest of the media were far more interested in a violent exchange, and interviewed some of the men who had arrived in trucks.

'We don't want them here. No one does.'

A TV reporter near Anya turned to face the camera. 'The protest turned violent only metres away from where Minister Moss gave a press conference unveiling some of the largest investment ever seen in northern Tasmania. PT is donating $2 million for equipment in local schools and another $3 million for a state-of-the-art youth club in Longford. That's in addition to their $80 million investment here. This is a coup for our state and we'll be following the story as it develops.'

He signed off to camera. 'That's a wrap.' He pumped his fist, as if he'd just won a tennis match at Wimbledon. His story may have just made the national news.

Anya saw Alison Blainey emerge from the crowd to speak to the jubilant reporter after his sound man had finished. It was as if she was working the car park like a networking conference. The man appeared receptive to whatever she was saying and handed her his card. Anya had to give the woman credit. She was turning a PR disaster into a story hook for television's keenest reporter. Her assault injuries hadn't impeded her ability to do her job. Anya returned inside to check on the elderly man.

The minister and his chief of staff entered the shop.

'Sir, I'm so sorry you were harmed in this outrageous attempt to sabotage what should have been a day for celebration.'

The elderly man shook hands with Moss. 'You're doing a fine job,' he said. 'You've got my vote.'

'Thank you, sir. Ryan, see to it that this gentleman is seen safely home. Will you?'

'Yes, minister. Were you harmed, Dr Crichton?'

The heels of both of Anya's palms were grazed from falling. She had a small lump on the back of her head from the blow.

'I'm fine,' she said.

Moss pulled her aside. 'How is your mother's friend Dengate holding up? I heard he was threatened with arrest for obstructing health department officers.'

Anya assumed Hammond had told him. 'I was there and he was merely advised not to obstruct the investigators. And he complied.'

'That man has been a loose cannon for a long time. The potential damage he has caused to our export trade and tourism industry is incalculable. Holidays have already been cancelled on the basis of the outbreak of food poisoning. It's going to take a lot of time to undo what he's destroyed in such a short

period. You and your mother would be advised to stay well
clear of him and his employees.'

Anya felt her irritation rise. 'Why do you care who my
mother and I associate with?'

'You are an intelligent woman, doctor. You should know
that if you lie down with dogs, you wake up with fleas.'

It almost sounded like a threat.

'They were your men watching Len Dengate's house last
night.'

'I pride myself on knowing the people I represent. Repeat
that accusation and you'll sound as unstable as your mother.'
He leant in closer and the smell of tobacco and aftershave
reviled her. 'I hear the Medical Board may be investigating her
before too long. Something about her prescribing the wrong
medication.'

Anya's blood rushed. Did he know something or was it
another threat? She held her tongue. Something said on impulse
could make the situation worse for Jocelyn.

'Minister,' Ryan Chapman interrupted, 'it's safe to go.'

Moss straightened his old-school tie. 'One more thing,
doctor. People around here say the walls have ears.'

Anya felt her mouth go dry. They were the words Len
Dengate had used. In Jocelyn's house. Two days ago.

25

Anya drove back to Longford replaying the conversation with Christian Moss. What he'd said had had the desired effect. She had been rattled and he must have known it.

What did he mean by her mother being unstable? And how would he know about a possible Medical Board investigation? She wondered if Jocelyn had made some kind of error, or a patient had had an adverse outcome and decided to complain to the Medical Board through the local member of parliament. She thought about Jocelyn fainting last night. Len had said it was one of her turns, implying they had happened before. Was it possible Damien had spoken to her as her blood pressure dropped, which is why he'd heard her slurring and forgetful?

The self-prescribed Thyroxin bothered Anya even more. What else was her mother taking? She had access to pharmaceutical samples through the surgery. Also, if Len was a patient and someone thought they were involved in a sexual relationship, that could be grounds for a complaint. Was one of the other doctors in the surgery concerned? Her head ached with questions and no answers.

Len could have been known for saying 'the walls have ears'. It didn't mean the house was bugged. She could only imagine how paranoid that would sound if she mentioned it to anyone.

Politicians were manipulators and located weaknesses in their enemies. Moss must have viewed her as either an opponent or a threat, or he wouldn't have said anything. He could have just been bluffing, for his own reasons, whatever they may be, to make her dissuade Jocelyn from supporting Len. Maybe it was better for his portfolios if the scandal went away with the close of Len's business.

It still niggled that his crisis meeting had been called well before the E. coli outbreak. What crisis were they really discussing? One that had not yet become public?

Her mother was doing paperwork when Anya arrived at the group practice in Longford. Jocelyn had already heard about the violence at the protest. She'd even patched up one of the local boys, whom she suspected had fractured some bones in his hand hitting someone or something. He was apparently vague on the details.

'Have you had any lunch?'

'I did in between patients.' Her mother typed computer notes while Anya sat in the patient's chair.

Anya picked up an electronic blood pressure monitor. 'Do you find consultations out here are more complex, given the shortage of doctors and the time it takes to get an appointment?'

'They tend not to come in with minor complaints.' Jocelyn stopped typing and looked over her reading glasses. 'Why?'

'From what I can tell, you're under even more pressure than before.'

Her mother peeled off the glasses. 'Who's been talking to you?' She raised her voice. 'What have you heard?'

'I'm talking about last night when you fainted. Len said it's happened before.' Anya peeled a sticky note from a pad. 'I'm concerned about you.'

'Well don't be. I'm fine.' Jocelyn started typing again.

There was a tap on the door before it opened. A male doctor asked if Jocelyn could review a patient she'd seen the day before. A rash had developed after she had given samples of an antibiotic for a sore throat. Anya could hear the discussion with the doctor outside the room.

'It was most likely glandular fever, Epstein Barr virus,' Jocelyn announced. 'Haven't you seen the rash before?'

The male doctor spoke quietly but firmly. 'I have. I was wondering why you gave the teenager antibiotics if you thought it was viral. I mean, is there a reason you didn't order viral antibody tests? For diagnostic purposes?'

'One dose of amoxicillin from a sample pack gives you the diagnosis. The virus interacts with the antibiotic and causes a non-allergenic rash. You diagnose glandular fever more quickly and cheaply than with a barrage of unnecessary blood tests. The government didn't have to subsidise a prescription. And the patient avoided pathology bills they could ill afford. You should be thanking me,' Jocelyn argued. 'The boy was grateful he didn't have to have a needle.'

'Not anymore with a rash on top of his other symptoms. Jocelyn, we've been through this. For medico–legal reasons, we have to do what is considered best practice. And he's sitting final exams soon. He needs the diagnosis confirmed with blood tests anyway.'

'I can still write a certificate. You have to treat the whole patient, not a disease. Did you know his mother lost her job and is alone supporting three kids?'

Anya sensed the tension in her mother's voice.

'What is really going on here?' Jocelyn demanded.

The male doctor remained calm. 'If he'd had an allergic reaction, giving him that antibiotic would have been indefensible.'

After that, a door slammed and there was silence outside.

The mobile phone on the desk rang. Anya thought it could have been Len, or a patient, and answered it.

'Jocelyn Reynolds's phone.'

The caller paused then surprised Anya by asking who she was.

'This is her daughter.' Anya looked for a pen and grabbed the sticky note to take a message.

'Excellent.' The caller's enthusiasm was evident. 'This is Eloise Johnson, from the *Hobart Sentinel*. We're running a feature on child murders in the state and wanted to talk about the disappearance of Miriam Reynolds.'

The woman's insensitivity jarred. Despite the years, the scars still felt raw when opportunists like reporters tried to capitalise on the family's misery and Miriam. As if time had meant the family could talk about it like a bodily function, or reveal something that implicated one of them as a killer.

'The readers would really love to know how the family is doing, what everyone is up to, and how the disappearance affected your lives. And how you feel when you hear about other cases like Mia and Jenny Quaid.'

From the sounds of the caller, she hadn't even been born when Miriam disappeared. Anya tightened her grip on the handset. 'No comment!'

'I understand that like Jenny Quaid, the family was under suspicion, and the readers would appreciate–'

Anya hung up, hands shaking. She had been caught off guard. Being back in Tasmania made what had happened to Miriam so much uglier and more . . . real. There was no escape from it.

Her mother's obsession went far beyond normal grief. From what she had just overheard, Jocelyn's medical decisions were questionable at times too. Anya had never known her to cut corners or take risks with patients. Maybe Christian Moss was right. Jocelyn was facing a Medical Board investigation and was keeping it a secret. It might explain why she was obsessively going over all of her patient notes – attempting to defend herself.

It still left the fainting episodes and supposedly abnormal thyroid function unanswered. Last night was not an anxiety attack. There was something medically wrong with her mother and she was self-medicating with who knew what.

On top of that, she was supporting Len Dengate and his farm. If patients were being placed at unnecessary risk, Anya had little choice.

She knew that Jocelyn would never forgive her.

26

After leaving the surgery, Anya decided to stick to her original plan to buy groceries and cook a meal for her mother. They could talk in private without any interruptions, in a non-threatening atmosphere. She bought a leg of lamb to roast, steaks and a chicken to marinate and freeze. She unpacked bags of fresh vegetables, bread, sugar, milk and some staples that the pantry had been lacking.

She was wiping down the fridge shelves when the door banged.

'What did you do?' Jocelyn threw her bag on the table as Anya turned.

'I just bought some—'

'How dare you!' Her mother's face was flushed.

Anya had no idea what was wrong. She closed the fridge door.

'Don't stand there acting innocent. You've been in Miriam's room. Again. After I told you to stay out.'

Anya was shocked by the aggressive tone. Jocelyn's mental state had rapidly deteriorated; mood swings, paranoia, now delusions. She needed urgent help.

She spoke gently. 'Mum, I haven't been in Miriam's room. We need to talk about what is going on.'

'Don't you turn this on me. The photos were moved. I know exactly where they were and they've been moved.' She stood rigidly, hands on hips. 'There are only two people in this house and it sure as hell wasn't me.' She stepped forward. 'What else are you lying about?'

Her mother was completely irrational, and was beginning to frighten Anya. 'That room is special to you, and I respect that. Mum, can we please sit down and talk. I can make us a cup of tea—'

'You're deceitful, just like your father.'

Anya felt her own anger and hurt well up. She struggled to stay calm. 'This has nothing to do with Dad. I haven't lied to you about anything, or kept anything from you. I don't know why you keep—'

'What about the phone call you took and didn't tell me about?'

She reached into her pocket and held up her phone. 'I check every number and didn't recognise it. I called that woman back and gave her one hell of a story.'

Anya felt sick. Her mother must have ranted about the conspiracy by PT to poison Len's crop. If it ever got to print, she would appear completely unhinged and paranoid. Christian Moss had used the word unstable.

Jocelyn slammed her fist into the wall, scaring Anya even more. 'What the hell were you thinking?' She stormed down the corridor and out the front door.

Anya's mind raced as she chased her mother, who was at her car. Instead of getting in, she paced on the gravel drive, shouting.

'You had no right to gag me. I want to comment. I want to talk to every damn reporter about my missing child.'

'Wait. You wanted to talk about Miriam? To a reporter? They're parasites, dredging up our past to sell papers.'

'You have no idea. Why would you? You moved away the first chance you got, made your own life. Just like your father and brother. You'll never understand. Miriam was' – she punched her chest – 'MY child.'

Her mother let the words hang.

Seeing her mother like this was heartbreaking. Anya fought to hold back tears.

But she also felt decades of anger and hurt rage. 'And she was MY little sister. Do you honestly believe we all just forgot? Damien may have never met Mimi, but there wasn't a day he wasn't affected by it.' Anya could not stop once the pain began to pour out. 'You might have lost a child that day, but Damien grew up without an emotionally involved mother. As far as he knew, your patients meant more to you than he ever did.'

'You have a hide lecturing me about my son.' She hit her chest again, this time her mouth contorted in anger. 'You have no idea what it takes to parent a child.'

Anya's heart drilled as her eyes welled with tears. Her mother was good at going straight for the jugular.

'You barely even know Ben.'

'And now you're giving that useless pig another chance. So you've learnt absolutely nothing.'

Anya sucked in a breath and tried to calm down.

'God, Mum. This is just like you. Turning everything around to be my fault.'

'Everything *is* your fault. My Miriam would be here now,' she screamed, 'if it weren't for you! You were supposed to be watching her. All you had to do was hold her hand while I looked after the injured player!'

So that was it. After all these years, Jocelyn Reynolds had admitted who she held to blame for Miriam's disappearance.

The pair stood, emotionally wasted.

Anya felt like a knife had ripped through her core. Her childhood finally made sense.

Wiping her eyes, she took a staccato breath. 'I'll get my things.'

Jocelyn grabbed Anya's arms. 'This could be my last chance to get Miriam back. Someone out there knows what happened to her.'

After a moment's silence, Anya turned to go inside.

The Mazda door clunked and the engine revved. The car skidded as Jocelyn turned out of the drive.

27

After an hour, there was no sign of her mother and no answer on the mobile. Dark clouds massed in the sky. The temperature had dropped; the air had a sudden chill to it.

Anya opened the door to Miriam's room. There had never been a memorial or funeral. Mimi had been suspended in a timeless limbo. Forever young, forever innocent. Forever three. Except that Anya was no longer five years old.

The photos on the tallboy were all happy ones. Anya couldn't remember most of them being taken. Colours were fading and yellowing with time. The sight of two skinny girls poking their bellies out for the camera made her cringe. Hers was a deep crimson terry-towelling jumpsuit and Mimi's was green. The high elastic waists made their legs look like stilts. She wondered if Ben's children would make fun of his knee-length board shorts and long rash vests in years to come.

In another frame, Miriam held Anya's hand and looked up adoringly. They were dressing up. Miriam had always wanted to be the princess and had a cardboard cone on her head with a scarf poking through the pointy end. One of Anya's creations. An elastic around the chin kept it in place. As the prince, Anya wore a bed-sheet cloak to rescue the damsel in the tower from the naughty man, as Mimi called him. Fairy tales were the seeds of their imaginations and were never meant to have happy endings.

The truth was, Anya still felt guilty about letting go of Mimi's hand that day at the football match. And nothing could take that pain away, or bring her sister back. Saying a quiet prayer for Miriam, she left the room and closed the door again.

She cried for her sister, and herself. Deciding to wait, another hour passed and Anya became concerned. Jocelyn always had a quick temper, but cooled off quickly. She began to worry more.

Calls to Len and Audrey confirmed neither had seen or heard from Jocelyn. They promised to let her know if there was any word. Bob Reynolds answered his phone on the first ring. Anya asked about Evelyn, whose condition hadn't changed. Her father sensed something was very wrong, but Anya didn't want to burden him now. Another hour later. Still no sign of Jocelyn. Anya switched on the evening news. The only thing to do was wait for her mother to come home in her own time.

Leading the news was the minister's announcement of the major investment in the region. Anya hit the remote control and turned the sound up. Footage of the exchanges preceded comments by locals, who appeared more than happy to have been interviewed after the event.

'These dirty layabouts wouldn't know what work was. They're chardonnay-loving, latte-sipping Greenies who tell the world how to live. They're not from here. These protesters go around looking for trouble and find it everywhere.' The grey-haired gentleman stared into the camera. 'You can quote me on this. Bugger off back to whatever dirty hole you crawled out of. Nobody wants you here.'

There was a voice-over about a representative attempting to gatecrash the minister's conference without any mention of a petition. Surprisingly, there were no images of the medical student, or the numbers she represented. The protester in the dreadlocks was in an image behind the newsreader, mouth open wide in anger. The newsreader then led into the press conference inside the main PT building. The minister candidly apologised for the harassment of the press and tourists by the protesters, who were, he said, clearly puppets for anti-progress extremists and had been shipped in from the mainland specifically to target the good people of the northwest.

He was photogenic and knew how to charm the press. He announced that PT was doing Tasmania and the country proud. Then the reporter flicked to more interviews. Anya recognised some of the people from the bus tour to the cottage.

'PT is the best thing to happen to us,' one blurted. It could have been an advertorial, not a news item. There was little balance in the coverage. And it didn't in any way represent both sides of the story Anya had witnessed. Jenny and Mia Quaid weren't mentioned in the bulletin. There was a knock at the door and Anya hurried to answer it.

Constable Simon Hammond appeared, police cap in his hand. 'Sorry to disturb. Audrey Lingard said you rang and I thought I'd see if Jocelyn's turned up.'

Anya felt nauseated. 'Not yet.'

'Is it out of character for her to take off like that? I mean, she isn't a missing person until twenty-four hours have passed, but she's pretty important to a lot of folks around here.' He glanced around at the skid marks on the gravel.

'I don't know anymore.'

'I see.' He put his cap back on. 'If you like, we can check out the obvious places, make sure her car hasn't broken down . . .'

He didn't need to say what Anya had been thinking. That the Mazda might have run off the road or hit a tree, given the way Jocelyn had sped off.

'I'd appreciate that.' She grabbed her phone and slipped on the jumper Jocelyn had left on the bed for Anya to use during her stay. She closed the door and locked it with the spare key. If Len was on guard, any intruders would swiftly meet his shotgun.

By 6.30 pm, they had exited the driveway and rain clouds opened. It drizzled on the way to Longford. They drove past the bakery, antiques shop, restaurants and past the park. No sign of the Mazda. By the time they hit the highway, the windscreen wipers pounded at full speed, struggling to keep up with the downpour. Anya closed her eyes and listened to the hypnotic sound of the metronomic swipes.

The car cabin was stiflingly warm.

'Temp okay for you?'

Anya opened her eyes and nodded. 'Mum's jumper would hold up in Antarctica.'

He glanced at her. 'She wants to protect you. She's very proud, you know. Private, but you can tell she's proud of you.'

Anya had an elbow on the base of the window. She bit her tongue.

'Don't mean to pry, but can I ask why she took off?'

Anya looked at the man beside her. He had none of the regular hallmarks of a country cop, despite knowing most of the locals. The easiest way to avoid a question was to deflect with another. She had a lifetime of experience in that department.

'How long have you lived around here?'

Simon glanced sideways with a hint of a smile.

'Born in Hobart but my father got work at the pulp mill in Bernie. He had a dream of breeding the perfect Wagyu beef. He loved the marbling of the meat and knew there would be a big market for it in Asia, the Middle East and America.'

'*Had* a dream?'

'Yeah, he saved for years and started a small herd. Spent time on King Island learning everything he possibly could. He died of multiple sclerosis last year.'

'I'm sorry.'

The wipers swished away. 'Your mother was very good to him. Made sure he died the way he wanted – at home. On the upside, with all the cattle, I learnt how to cook a mean steak.'

In the distance, a hunched figure in a long coat and baseball cap trudged along the side of the road. The headlights caught him, but he didn't stop, instead, waving them on with one arm without even glancing around.

Simon slowed the car and pulled over. The man stood on Anya's side of the car. Anya wound down the window.

The man stopped for a moment then wandered over, through puddles and mud, to the passenger side.

'Need a ride?' the officer enquired.

The stranger leant down and forward, placing a forearm on the door. Anya moved her hand to shield her eyes from the rain and noticed letters tattooed on his nicotine-stained fingers.

'No thanks, mate. It's all good.' He stepped back.

Anya suddenly felt someone grip the back of her head and slam her face down into the dashboard. Pain seared through her forehead as a deafening bang rang out. Disoriented, she turned to Simon and saw the policeman exit the car, his gun out. She could smell discharge. Her heart lurched in her chest.

Hammond shouted, 'Stay down.'

Anya's mind spun. The man had refused a lift and the policeman had pushed her out of the way to shoot at him. It made no sense. She couldn't see either man and didn't know what had happened. She grabbed her phone, pushed open the door and clambered onto the road verge, head pounding.

Simon was squatting next to the man's body, gun still ready, reaching to feel for a carotid pulse with his free hand. Anya handed him the phone and fell to her knees and unbuttoned the man's coat.

Then she saw what looked like a yellow plastic water squirter by his side.

'It's a pool toy,' she screamed, and plugged the hole in his chest with her fist. 'A kids' toy!'

'Help me,' he gasped. His breathing was rapid and he moaned in pain. The hat had slipped off, revealing an almost shaved head. Blood oozed through his T-shirt. She pulled off her jumper and pressed it hard against the wound. 'Call for help!' she ordered. 'He needs an ambulance!' The pulse was thready.

The policeman stood motionless, gun still pointed at the man on the ground.

'You've got to get help. He's bleeding to death!'

Anya caught sight of a pink plastic drink bottle in the man's left hand as he spilt its contents across his body and hers. The smell stung her nose and lungs. Petrol.

Simon's boot kicked the container from the man's hand and he yanked Anya backwards, hard.

She tried to get a grip on the ground with her shoes but the officer was too strong. With the strength of two men, he flipped her onto her feet.

'RUN!' he commanded, ripping her arm as he propelled them along.

Whoomph.

The burst of heat from behind threw them both forward. As she turned, flames engulfed the man, metres from them. An animalistic howl was quickly consumed by the sound of the fire. The stench of burning flesh filled her nostrils as the policeman hurled her further away. She stumbled and landed on all fours. Coughing, she tried to clear her lungs. Simon ripped off her shoes and hauled her to her socked feet.

'Get your clothes off. Now!' he yelled, and began to rip down her trousers. Still struggling to inhale, Anya punched at him.

'He doused petrol on them.'

Realising the risk, she hurriedly complied while he ripped his boots off and hurled them into the distance.

'Stay well back.' He ran to the car boot and extracted a small fire-extinguisher, just as flames licked the side door of the car.

Anya watched, trying to make sense of what had just happened. The man had poured petrol on her and tried to set her alight. But why? Instead, he had set himself on fire. How had the officer known what the man was going to do? Simon blasted the man's body with flame retardant. Why had he shot so quickly?

There was no hint of movement on the ground.

'He's beyond help. I'll do what I can to stop the fire.'

Anya approached. The man's lifeless face was charred and unrecognisable. Free skin hung off contracted bones of the left forearm and hand. The right hand was meshed with the plastic weapon by his side. Clothing had melted into his skin. The only remnant identifiable was one white sneaker with a green stripe. She covered her mouth and nose. Of all the smells she had ever experienced, this was the worst. Self-immolation. An agonising way to die.

Whoever this man was, he had tried to kill her along with him.

Anya's heart hammered. She coughed again. This time her stomach muscles convulsed. She resisted the urge to vomit.

A loud whoosh sounded. She turned to see the car interior alight. Simon shook the extinguisher then dropped it. He snatched a rug from the opened boot. 'Run!'

Anya didn't need to be told twice. She took off, with what was left of her strength. The policeman was quickly at her side again, yanking her by the wrist this time. She moved her legs as fast as possible in the slippery, uneven ground. Hammond's strength and speed kept her upright more than once.

Pops and hisses sounded behind them in the blaze.

Finally, struggling to breathe, Anya fell to the ground and gasped for air. Rain ran into and out of her mouth. Simon bent over, chest heaving.

Body soaked and rain still bucketing, Anya began to tremble, trying to comprehend what had happened. The shivering became uncontrollable as rain pounded their bodies.

Officer Hammond removed his jumper and knelt at her side. 'Put this on.'

Teeth chattering, she complied. 'How . . . did you . . . know?'

He wrapped the rug around her legs.

'Something about him. When we stopped he walked straight through two giant puddles, didn't even try to go around them.' He rubbed her arms. 'When he got closer I saw he had something under the coat.'

Anya's mind flashed to what she had seen of his sneakers. He wasn't a farmer. Boots were the footwear of choice for locals. The car was now gutted with flames. Like rice breakfast cereal, the fuel snapped, crackled and popped. Petrol must have transferred to the side door when the man leant into the car. Anya's side. Either it had leaked or he had deliberately tried to incinerate them. Simon's quick reactions had saved both their lives.

They sat staring at the blaze in the distance that was the police car.

'Most of the locals drive diesel cars and trucks. Smart thing would be to stay with your vehicle in this weather.' Simon shook his head. 'Didn't you see the way he locked eyes right on you as he headed towards us . . . He was dangerous.' This time he shivered.

'Thanks,' was all Anya could think of to say. She hadn't even noticed the man was looking directly at her. One word didn't cover what she was feeling, but words failed her right now.

'The area command won't be thanking me. That beast of a vehicle was only two months old.'

A plume of black smoke erupted. Then a rumble. The explosion thrust Anya forward. The policeman's body took the brunt of it.

28

Anya could feel the heat intensify on her covered legs. She didn't move, bracing for further fireballs.

The policeman remained a heavy weight on top of her, motionless. She reached up and back with one hand for a carotid pulse. Bounding. Thank God. She moved to roll him and he pulled back. A cough expunged muck from his airways as he propped himself up on his elbows. The explosion must have concussed him.

Plumes of black and orange surged upwards from the wreck. Grass by the roadside had caught alight and spread to a nearby fence. There was nothing they could do but wait for someone to come along. In the light from the flames, Anya caught sight of Simon's blistered hands.

They had to be painful, unless they were full thickness and had burnt through the nerve endings. His hand function could be compromised if they didn't get him medical help soon. She moved the saturated blanket to cover their heads, but most importantly, his hands. She took the weight of the wet wool with elbows on her bent knees.

He glanced down but didn't acknowledge the injuries. 'It used to drive my father mad. The way cars crashed and automatically exploded in the movies. He said it was almost impossible for a fuel tank to explode. Guess he underestimated me yet again.'

His words weighed heavily. The fire sounded like snapping twigs in the distance. There was no sign of headlights.

'Do you have my phone?' Anya asked.

'Sorry, dropped it when I went to grab you. Someone on a neighbouring property will likely see the smoke and call 000, or come to see how they could help.'

'If this car was new, what happened to your last one?' She was assessing his mental function.

'Rammed by a drunk driver when I tried to pull him over. And the one before that was hit by a truck.'

Anya wondered if it was safe to be in a car with him. 'Seriously?'

'Hey, it was parked and I was inside the station. Accident investigators said the truck's brakes failed. The car was totalled. My cousin's a smash repairer, but I'm beginning to wear out the relationship. Seem to have a knack for being in the wrong place at the wrong time.'

Right now, Anya disagreed. If it had been anyone else who had pulled up to assist the man in the rain, they could have been burnt to death. There was no way the man could have known a police car was on its way along this road. He had to have had criminal intent.

'Cars don't matter. All I know is that you have great instincts, and they saved our lives tonight.'

'Never killed a man before.' He sat staring at the residual flames, nursing his injured hands.

Anya had seen police recklessly taser suspects to death. She had also seen the bodies of police killed in the line of duty. For survivors, the scars of death rarely healed. 'You may not have. He could have survived that gunshot wound. If the bullet had ruptured a major vessel, he wouldn't have survived long enough to pull the trigger on . . . whatever that was. He died trying to kill us.' She meant 'me', but couldn't bring herself to say it. 'Or he preferred death to arrest.' In that case, it was probable he had a criminal record.

'Instincts didn't pick a flamethrower.'

Anya had seen a kids' water squirter. 'It looked like—'

'A toy? I know. Saw it when he was down and I smelt the propane. It was connected to a tank and hose. I've seen home-made flamethrowers on the internet. They often end up killing the idiot holding the trigger.'

Building a flamethrower and attaching it to his body required organised thinking and a knowledge of basic science. Someone who was psychotic was unlikely to be capable of premeditation and planning to that extent. In a moment of paranoia, a knife, gun or even a box of matches were more accessible. Anya thought of the tattoo on his knuckles, though she couldn't make out the letters. It had looked homemade too. Like something done in prison.

'Why have petrol and propane?'

'I don't know. Maybe one was backup. Or a diversion in case he got caught.'

Anya hadn't seen what had ignited the fumes. 'How did he . . .'

'One of those gas stove igniters. He wanted to burn something pretty badly.'

Prison tattoos, kids' supplies. He could have been a serial arsonist who'd been caught before.

'Guess we'll never know what the hell he was planning.' Simon shielded his injured hands again against his chest.

'At least I've got a credible witness to the shooting.'

Anya hadn't seen the shooting. Simon had pushed her head forward and she'd hit the dashboard. It still throbbed.

A set of headlights appeared in the distance, followed by another. Two vehicles thundered towards them.

Simon crouched down, blocking Anya from view. 'Can you shoot a gun?'

'What—? I have shot—' She had shot a man at close range once. Simon didn't need to know the details. 'I could if I had to.'

He held up two burnt hands.

'I need you to reach into the holster. Now.'
The trucks were almost on them.
'Hurry. We don't know if he was acting alone.'
Her heart raced as she lifted out the recently fired weapon.
The first truck screeched to a halt and four men jumped out.

29

The men in the vehicles hadn't seen the pair. They sprinted towards the burning car.

Anya and the police officer crouched silently for a few moments. 'It's okay. I know them,' Hammond said.

Anya placed the gun on the ground and helped him to his feet.

'Here,' she hollered, hugging the sodden rug tighter, barely able to feel her feet on the sloppy ground.

Two burly forms headed their way. The larger man wore a full-length oilskin coat. The other had on a lighter, more modern jacket with fluorescent strips on the sleeves that caught the fire's light. Both men had on hats and heavy boots. She picked up the gun and reholstered it for the policeman.

'This one's burnt real bad,' someone declared in the distance.

The charred body had been found.

Without exchanging words, Anya was swept up by the larger of the men. 'We'll take care of you, little lady,' he said, and carried her to one of the trucks. Anya didn't recognise him under the hat. She was capable of walking, but wasn't given the choice. The wet oilskin coat had the same smell as her father's jacket in the rain, thirty years earlier.

'Simon's burnt. His hands,' she urged.

Hammond had already joined the mob trying to extin-
guish the rest of the flames. Anya was deposited inside the
cabin of the first truck. Large calloused hands ripped away the
wet blanket and replaced it with a multicoloured crocheted
blanket covering her front to the knees. She gripped it with icy
fingers. The man used a towel from the floor to rub her lower
legs – hard. 'Better get the circulation going. You're probably
in shock.'

'Please. You need to help Simon,' she said. 'I'm all right.'

He looked up and the cabin light illuminated sunspots on
his cheeks and temple. He was in his fifties, but had a face that
had seen a lot of sun over the years.

'You've got to be Jocelyn Reynolds's kid.'

He hit the heater button and a gush of air gusted about her
face. 'I'm Bill Whitehead. I'll let her know you're safe.'

'First, Simon needs medical attention.'

'Just like your mother.' He reached into the back seat.

'Do you know where she is?' Anya needed to know she
was all right.

'I wager on her being at the Wilson property by now.
Whole town is heading there, to fight the fire.'

He slammed the door before she got a chance to ask. What
fire? The fire was here. The man in the coat had set fire to
himself, and tried to kill her. She could hear male voices outside
giving orders but sat still, trying to process what had happened.
He had to have committed a heinous crime to die the way he
did. And he was prepared to murder in the process of taking his
own life. The image of the homemade tattoos filled her mind.
Prison tattoos.

She replayed the events. The man had refused a lift in a
storm. It was odd but Anya hadn't thought much of it. When
he'd stepped back, Simon said he'd reached for a weapon. Anya
hadn't sensed any hint of a threat, but she hadn't been expecting
one. She was focused on finding her mother. Within seconds,
her forehead had hit the dashboard and the man was on the

ground, shot through the chest. If the policeman hadn't acted so quickly . . .

The realisation hit that she had come very close to dying. Her body shook. All she wanted was to hear Ben's voice. Her phone was on the ground somewhere, near the cremated body, and undoubtedly a mess of melted plastic by now.

A police car arrived as the last of the flames was extinguished. Black smoke still billowed from the car wreck.

A female constable came to Anya and opened the door.

'You okay?'

Anya's teeth knocked when she spoke. 'I can't stop shaking.'

The woman rubbed her shoulder. 'My name's Rhonda. You've had decent shock. But you're safe now. It's over.'

Her eyes flicked back to the car wreckage. She kept her hand on Anya's shoulder and Anya was grateful for her presence. She couldn't see where Simon Hammond had gone. Rain spat on the constable's clothes.

'You're getting wet,' Anya managed, teeth chattering less. 'There's a towel here somewhere.'

'It's just water.' Rhonda pulled her collar tighter. 'Can you tell me what happened?'

There was a shooting, an incinerated body and an exploded and burnt police car. Images flooded Anya's mind. She hadn't witnessed the threat or the shooting. Only what Simon had told her. Had the policeman shot someone before? What wasn't in dispute was the fact that the man had tried to immolate her with him.

She repeated the story as she remembered it happening, still attempting to process the details.

Rhonda let her tell it without interruption. Then she asked, 'Did you recognise the man? Have you ever seen him before?'

'No, but he had tattoos and a shaven head.' Anya tried to picture his features but it had all happened so quickly. The hat had obscured his face when he'd leant down near her window. When the hat came off, she was concentrating on the bullet wound in his chest.

'Could he have recognised you?'

Anya paused. It hadn't occurred to her that she could have been the specific target. It seemed far-fetched. She shivered again and looked around. The car still burnt. 'I don't know. Are the fire crew far away?'

'You didn't hear?' Rhonda said. 'There's a fire out of control at the Wilsons' place and it's spread to PT. These boys were all on their way there. When they came out of Langleys Road, they saw the car blow, called us and doubled back.'

Anya could hear the police radio on the constable's shoulder. 'The wheat's gone up like a firecracker. Never seen anything like it. We've had to send for extra units from Lonnie.'

Launceston was at least fifteen minutes away.

'You need to be checked out properly,' Rhonda said. 'This lot will make sure you're safe and are seen by a medic. We can take your statement once you get the all clear.'

Anya nodded. She didn't have any energy to argue. Her body was replete of adrenalin.

'Goddamn Greenies. Bet they're behind it all. The bastards.' The man who had carried her to the truck climbed into the driver's seat, and three other men crammed into the passenger seats behind. They smelt of sweat and wet oilskin. 'A nurse is standing by at the Wilsons'. She can check you out there.'

Anya's thighs had begun to sting. She suspected the petrol had leeched through her clothes and burnt her skin before Hammond had ripped them off.

'Then we'll help out with the fire.'

The female constable clicked in Anya's seatbelt. 'I have to set up a crime scene and block off this side of the road. Hobart homicide detectives are on their way.' She pulled the hood tighter over her head. 'I'll see you as soon as this mess is sorted.'

She closed the door and tapped on the roof. The driver pulled out and accelerated. The Colorado hit a pothole further along and Anya's backside lifted from the seat. She had the luxury of a seatbelt. The four men squashed in the passenger seats didn't.

Anya thought of the man with the flamethrower. He could have started the Wilson fire.

'Did you see an abandoned car on your way here?' she asked the driver.

'A rental job was stopped on the verge, a kilometre or so away.' He flicked his eyes from the road to Anya and back. 'You think that dead guy could have left it there?'

Unless he'd been dropped off by someone else. Tracks would have led from the car to where Simon had pulled over. Then again, in the rain, they would be obscured. If he'd been dropped off, he hadn't been working alone.

No one asked her what had taken place, how a man had ended up shot and burnt alive. Country people knew that if someone wanted to talk, they would, when they were ready. The shooting and the policeman's burnt hands were stuck on a loop in her mind. The smell of burnt flesh remained with her.

By now the rain had eased. The windscreen wipers clunked more slowly than before.

'Is Simon Hammond all right?'

The driver swerved to avoid another pothole. 'I bandaged his hands, but we've only got a small first aid kit. They looked pretty bad but he won't go to hospital yet. He's in the ute behind us.' He glanced occasionally at Anya. 'Hell of a night.'

The men in the back were quiet.

'Reckon your mum's already there. From what I hear, she'd be one of the first to help out.' The driver turned sharply down a road to the left. 'Ever thought of setting up practice with her?'

'I'm not qualified to work in general practice. I work in forensic medicine.'

'We'll take any doctor we can get,' he said.

'Dad,' a man from the back spoke. 'Remember when the vet stitched me up?'

'See,' the driver said. 'Vet, doctor, you're all the same to us.'

She wondered about Bill's comments about Greenies. 'Why do you think environmentalists started the Wilson fire?'

The wheels clunked into another pothole. Anya braced herself with her hands on the dash this time.

'Bastards want to shut down our farms. A busload arrives from the mainland. Now this. You join the dots.'

Outsiders were still viewed with suspicion. Some of the community had never even ventured to the south of the state, let alone to mainland Australia. Anya wasn't sure why she was treated like a local, after all these years.

An orange glow lit up the sky ahead. The mood in the cabin grew sombre. The fire was massive. By the time they arrived, a number of trucks, rural fire service volunteers and two fire engines were already on the scene. Despite the rain and gusting winds, Anya no longer felt cold. Adrenalin pumped through her again. People ran towards spot fires with hoses and buckets.

'We need to know how many people are here volunteering.' Hammond had arrived first in the other utility. 'We don't want anyone else killed or hurt.'

A long coat covered his saturated uniform, presumably lent to him by one of the farmers. The dressings on his hands were already soaking wet.

'Right,' Bill Whitehead announced. 'I'll start a sign-up sheet. Find out who's here and before anyone else starts helping, they sign up. Before they leave, they sign themselves out.'

A man Anya recognised from the lunch at the restaurant with the minister approached. He was in a heavy coat and hat but he had a loping gait similar to his brother's. Craig Dengate.

'We set the homestead up as headquarters. We're all taking shifts. Food and drinks inside. The wives are bringing extra blankets and supplies.' He looked exhausted, as if he'd been at the blaze for a while. 'Heard you were injured, Hammo.' He squeezed the constable's shoulder. 'Nurse is inside. You need to get those hands seen to.'

Craig turned to Anya. 'There'll be a change of clothes and something to cover your feet inside. If you need to see the nurse . . .'

'I'm okay. Has anyone seen Jocelyn Reynolds?' She needed to know her mother was safe.

'Could be anywhere. It's been chaos, as you can see, until now.'

Her mother knew how to look after herself. She'd grown up in the country, Anya had to keep reminding herself as she helped Simon towards the house.

In the distance, cows lowed in distress. Rain bucketed in paroxysms.

While the nurse treated Simon's hands, Anya washed off and spread a thin layer of burn cream on her legs before pulling on a large borrowed jumper and an oversized pair of jeans, tightened with a belt. She finished with a spare pair of thick socks and boots.

A small woman in overalls stood in the doorway of the house and called for any spare hands for the feed lots.

The nurse explained that all able volunteers had just gone to a new breakout on the western border of the property.

'Give me a minute,' Hammond said.

The woman took one look at Simon's hands. 'You'll be more use here.' She turned to leave.

'Wait,' Anya stopped her leaving. 'What do you need?'

'To get about a thousand cattle to safety.'

Anya braced herself and headed out into the firestorm.

30

Anya climbed into the passenger seat of a black Range Rover.

A small woman sat on a custom-built cushion in the driver's seat, started the engine and introduced herself. 'Jeanette Egan. I'm a vet up at PT.'

'Anya.'

'Thanks for coming. The wind gusted and the fire is headed towards the herds in the feed lots. We're the only hope they've got.'

They entered a side road and stopped at a sliding gate. The area was surrounded by a three-metre-high electric fence. The vet had to get out of the car to punch in a security code. The gate opened. She was quickly back in the driver's seat and accelerated through.

She had to be under five foot tall and had her hair cropped short, pixie style. It was difficult imagining her being physically able to birth breech calves or sheep, but she was no-nonsense.

The area was lit with floodlights. It almost felt like an agricultural university campus. Anya noticed a sign outside a large brick building. The Tasmanian Institute of Agricultural Advancement (TIAA). Glenn Lingard had described it as the pinnacle of industry, science and government.

'How far are we from PT?' Anya said.

'We're in it. Covers all Emerald Vale. Kind of like the land of Oz.'

Glenn hadn't mentioned that the TIAA was on PT-owned land. She hadn't understood why Glenn had been at the restaurant crisis meeting with Christian Moss and the head of PT. Now it made sense. The TIAA and its research were important to the conglomerate.

They turned off down a dirt road and bumped along surfaces damaged by rain and heavy vehicles. Anya hung on to the handle over the passenger window. Jeanette picked up speed at every opportunity.

Anya tried to keep her mind off what had just happened at the roadside. 'How long have you worked here?'

'About two years. It gave me a foot in the door with the locals so I could buy into a private practice.' She turned into a narrower road that divided crops of corn. 'People take one look at me and assume I'm not up to the job.'

Anya knew what that felt like. 'As an intern, I got kicked off orthopaedics before I even started the rotation. The consultant deemed me inadequate to hold up a leg during hip replacements.'

'They don't get it. It's not the size of the dog in the fight that counts . . .' the vet began.

'It's the size of the fight in the dog.' Anya knew the saying. 'PT are equal opportunity employers then?'

'Did the interview over the phone.' Jeanette grinned. 'Put on my professional phone voice. Should have seen the look on the execs' faces when I arrived.'

The distant smell of burning flesh hit the car before they drove past a silo and saw the flaming shed, less than a hundred metres away from where cattle pressed against a fence, trying to escape the heat and smoke. The PT feed lots were enormous, much larger than Anya had imagined. There was no gate to let them through.

Jeanette stopped the car, headlights aimed at a section of

cattle. She grabbed bolt cutters from the back seat, pulled on thick gloves and began to cut a hole in the fence.

'This is worse than I thought. We're going to have to let them all out here.'

Anya helped speed the process by pulling back the thick wire. Without gloves, the task was difficult. The rain made the wire slippery. She pulled the jumper sleeves over her hands as makeshift gloves. The vet continued to cut links in the fence to as high as she could reach.

Anya peeled back a section of wire. 'Are we safe from the bulls once they're released?'

Jeanette put her boot on a break in the wire of the second tier of the fence and yanked back towards the fencepost. 'These have all been castrated.'

Anya somehow didn't feel any safer knowing they lacked testosterone. Being trampled or gored was still a possibility.

'Still, make sure you're on this side, near the fencepost, when they start coming out.' She handed Anya the bolt cutters and headed into the feed lot. 'Here's hoping!'

The car headlights allowed them to see what they needed to.

The animals were becoming more agitated with each passing minute. Anya separated wire as quickly as possible. A few minutes later, with Jeanette herding them from behind, the first few lumbered through the open section into the adjacent paddock.

A white utility bounced towards the fence and lurched to a halt. Samir Malik leapt out. He was holding a baseball bat and booming, 'Stop now. You cannot let them on Mr Len's property.'

Anya had been disoriented in terms of direction. She hadn't realised this fence bordered Livelonger Organics.

'If we don't, they'll burn to death. We don't have a choice.' Jeanette whistled and slapped another cow through the gap. 'Move!'

'You must stop. They are not allowed on this land.' The man raised the bat, as if he were about to hit a home run.

'I can't let you continue.' He adjusted his grip. 'I am begging you to step away from the fence.'

The Sudanese farm worker looked more afraid than threatening.

'Like I said. If there was any other way.' Jeanette gestured to Anya to keep cutting.

'Stop,' Samir shouted. 'I will not tell you again.'

Anya hesitated. He sounded desperate. Cows bustled and collided. Some climbed the backs of others.

His wife left the ute and went to his side. She held out both arms. 'We must let them go. It is the humane thing to do.'

Without further protest, Samir dropped the bat and nestled into her shoulder. Grace held him tightly and escorted him back to the vehicle. They drove off into the night.

'Go, go, go!' the vet urged.

Anya squeezed hard on the bolt cutters. 'Are these cows identifiable?' By law, she thought, they had to be electronically tagged.

'They are.'

Anya separated another section of fence and noticed some of the steers had plugs behind their ears.

'Is that what the plugs are?'

Cattle continued to forge through. Jeanette pushed a couple more steers and moved next to Anya, protected by a set of posts. 'That's a cartridge of slow-release hormone growth protectant. It's injected between the skin and cartilage at the back of the ear. This lot have been vaccinated and given antibiotics as well.'

More steers moved through, starting a faster procession. The smoke from the shed seemed to be dissipating.

'This is working.' Anya felt relieved she could help make a difference.

'Not for the guy from next door,' the vet explained. 'We've just released them onto an organic farm. We've most likely cost him his organic status.'

'You said the herd was identifiable. As soon as the fire's under control, they can go straight back to their side of the fence.'

'It isn't that simple.' Jeanette stood to the side as more cattle surged through. 'These animals are fed GM corn. Once they deposit manure, the ground isn't considered organic anymore.'

'Is the fear that undigested kernels get into the soil?'

Alison Blainey had already found genetically modified plants growing on Len's land. It was why she'd suggested he sue PT for compensation.

'Does changing their diets from grass affect the cows?'

'Corn alters the acidity in their stomachs—'

A team pulled up at the shed.

'We've got back up,' Jeanette wiped her forehead with a forearm. 'You can get dry in the car if you want. I want to make sure they all get through.'

Anya preferred to stay with the vet for now. 'Why use corn instead of grass? These cows have huge amounts of grazing land.'

'It's all about the money. Corn is much cheaper. They can pack more cattle per square feet. Human growth protectant speeds up the rate of growth and muscle, so they go to the abattoir quicker, and consumers don't know the difference. Most people care about the price of the meat. It's all about the bottom line.'

'What do you think about the practice?' Anya was interested to know.

'If they're going to do it anyway, better to have a vet who cares look after them.'

Jeanette's phone rang. She whipped off a leather glove and answered. 'Who?' She turned to Anya. 'Are you a pathologist?'

Anya nodded.

'It's for you.'

Anya presumed it was about giving her statement concerning the shooting and death of the man with the flamethrower. She put down the bolt cutters and took the phone.

Simon Hammond spoke quickly. 'Can you head back to Len Dengate's? Your mother needs you.'

Anya's heart accelerated. 'What happened? Is she all right?'

'It's . . . She isn't speaking.'

Anya immediately thought of a stroke. 'Is she conscious, can she move both arms and legs?'

'She looks physically all right. Anya, she isn't speaking . . . We just found them. Len Dengate's dead. Your mother's covered in his blood.'

31

With the cattle filtering through into the adjoining field, Jeanette drove across the top paddock and followed the path Samir's utility had taken and back around to Len's home.

'I don't believe he's gone. Len gave me a leg up when I arrived. Half the locals had never seen a woman vet and didn't trust one. He called me a pocket dynamo and acted like I cured Roswell of every potential disease.'

Anya's mind raced. Why would her mother be covered in Len Dengate's blood? And why was Jocelyn unable to speak? She was only half-listening to the vet. 'Did you just say Roswell?'

'The best trained kelpie I've ever seen. Named after the place in New Mexico. Len believed the American government covered up a UFO crash seventy or more years ago.' She whistled. 'He sure loves. I mean loved a good conspiracy theory.'

Anya hoped her mother was all right. Simon Hammond hadn't given any details.

They slowed on the hill up to the house. Five vehicles were parked out the front, including an ambulance and two police cars. The reality of Len's death seemed to confront Jeanette. She stopped the car short and pulled on the handbrake.

'If there's anything I can do . . .' She wrote down her number on a notepad and ripped off the page. 'Len was a good, decent man . . . I'll hang around a few minutes out here.' She wiped her nose with the back of a hand. 'If anyone needs me to look after Ros, I'll take him with me.'

'Thanks,' was all Anya could muster. The vet didn't want to enter the house. It was clear the body was inside. Anya became more concerned for her mother's mental state.

The outside lights were on. There were no disposable over-alls, shoe covers or a sectioned-off crime scene. She glanced up at the camera on the porch and hurriedly slipped off the muddied, borrowed boots. She knocked, but no one responded. The door was ajar so she stepped inside, careful to walk as close to the skirting boards as possible.

Inside, the body was already in a body bag on a gurney, flanked by two ambulance officers. The dog held vigil by the gurney's side. It had blood on its jaw. Anya's initial thoughts were that the dog had turned on its master. There was a smell of petrol in the house, and she had a flashback to the man on the side of the road. In the living area, a trail of blood from the leather lounge pooled in the centre of the patterned rug. Her next thoughts were that Dengate had had gastrointestinal haemorrhaging from an E. coli infection. Then she saw the shotgun and a fine mist of blood on the floor. She cleared her throat and began demanding answers.

The first question was to the ambulance officers by the gurney. 'What are you doing?' There didn't appear to be anyone documenting events. The process normally took hours. 'This should be a crime scene.'

Before either could answer, Senior Sergeant McGinley, in plain clothes, entered the room barking orders. 'Get the body out. Let's wrap this up.'

Anya challenged him. 'Have the SOCOs already finished?'

The sergeant shoved a phone into his trouser pocket and stepped close. 'Who the hell do you think you are? You're lucky to even be here.'

Anya felt her heart pound and felt her fists tighten by her sides. 'I'm a forensic pathologist and I don't believe you have secured a possible crime scene.'

Simon Hammond appeared in the doorway to the kitchen. His head was crusted in mud, soot and dried blood. The rest of him hadn't fared much better.

'Anya, you mother's out here. She won't even say if she saw what happened.'

Hammond let the doorframe take some of his weight. He looked as if he'd been in a war zone.

Anya moved through the room to see her mother sitting at the table with her face in her hands. She shouldn't be here, but at least she was safe.

Anya returned to the debacle of the death scene. 'Why hasn't the house been secured? Why are people walking in off the street, destroying evidence?'

'Excuse me?' McGinley's left upper eyelid twitched with a tic. 'You're only here because Doc Kancharla couldn't get sense out of your mother.'

'Who?' Anya hadn't heard the name before.

'I called him to assess the body before we moved it.'

'He's retired from general practice,' Simon interjected, gaze locked onto Anya. 'He certified Len's body.'

She realised the police officer had wanted her here. It wasn't just about her mother.

'Leave everything alone. Don't touch anything else,' she commanded the ambulance officers. They didn't hesitate to stop.

'Who the hell do you think you are?' McGinley blocked her way.

'I told you. A forensic pathologist. I have reason to believe this could be a suspicious death, and foul play needs to be excluded.'

'Well, missy, we've examined the scene and it looks pretty straightforward. In case you didn't know, tonight there's been a fire we suspect was deliberately lit and one of our officers was involved in a fatal shooting. We have limited resources and I can't waste time on something that's clear-cut.'

Anya couldn't believe his arrogance. 'A murder could have been committed but you're too busy or too under-staffed to investigate it properly. Even when a member of the public tells you there are grounds for suspicion?' Anya felt her face flush with anger. Her pulse bounded in her temples. 'I've got a comment for the reporters,' Anya fumed and spun around.

McGinley grabbed her arm. 'You will do no such thing. Hammond, restrain this woman. She's interfering with a police investigation. If she resists, charge her with obstructing justice.'

Simon didn't move.

Anya pulled free her arm. She had no intention of leaving. 'Are you refusing to follow protocol?'

'This is my beat. And I make the calls. If you have a problem, take it up with the Integrity Commission. They'll be round to investigate Hammond here soon enough for that shooting. You were there too which means they'll be looking at you with a fine tooth comb as well. Funny how you arrive in town and people start dying.' He waved to the ambulance officers to continue removing the body.

This man's gall and stupidity far exceeded his negligence and incompetence. 'Don't touch a thing!' Her voice was louder and more shrill than she'd intended, but effective.

'How about we talk to the authorities now,' she said. 'Give them the heads up about this case as well.' She addressed the ambos again. 'If you move that gurney, you can be charged with a crime.'

They backed away to the entrance.

The veins in McGinley's neck and temples distended. 'You're in way over your head, missy. You don't know who you're dealing with.'

'Oh.' She stared him down. 'I do know. You're a small-town copper. Big fish in a little pond, used to throwing your weight around. You've had your fill of free meals from restaurants and takeaways in your day. Bet it galls you that's considered corruption these days.'

'That's enough!' His face engorged with blood.

Anya was only just getting started. He had audaciously compromised a possible homicide investigation.

'You make decisions you're unqualified to make then blame your subordinates when anything goes wrong. Thirty years in the force and drinking buddies in senior ranks make you believe you're untouchable.'

'Hammond.' He clenched his fists. 'Get her out of my sight. Right now!'

Anya's blood surged and she tried to hide the anger flooding through her.

'Simon, may I borrow your phone?' she asked as calmly as possible.

He didn't need to be asked twice, quickly handing it over.

She phoned a police friend in Sydney, without taking her eyes of McGinley. 'I need the name of that detective you worked with. The one from Internal Affairs. It's urgent.'

'This is a bluff. Hammond, remove this woman now.'

Anya reached into Simon's top pocket with her spare hand and removed a notebook and pen, then wrote down the name and private phone number she heard and thanked her friend.

'Hammond, I'm giving you an order.'

The constable remained still. McGinley seemed loath to touch Anya himself.

Detective Oliver Parke picked up after one ring. He listened to Anya's comments about destruction of a possible crime scene, then calmly asked to speak to the officer in charge.

'He wants to talk to you. Internal Affairs like to record their calls so you may want to speak clearly.'

Sobered by the fact that she was not bluffing, McGinley sheepishly took the phone. Len, his family and friends deserved at least the best she could do.

'Yes sir. I believe the case to be a straightforward suicide. The deceased was unstable and was facing bankruptcy . . . So far we haven't located a suicide note . . . Um . . .' he mumbled. 'One, sir . . . Pardon?' He looked at Anya. 'You want me to ask? Now? . . . Just a moment.'

He closed his eyes and slowly opened them. 'He wants to know how many homicides or suspicious deaths you've worked on.'

Anya didn't hesitate. 'Hundreds.'

McGinley relayed the number to Parke then listened, eyes downcast. It was a minute before the sergeant spoke again.

'I take your point. Sorry to have disturbed you so late. Have a good evening, sir.' He hung up and tightened his grip on the phone.

'Doctor, what do you need from us first?'

'Who photographed the scene?'

'I did.'

'Talk me through what you found.' Anya rolled up her sleeves. 'Anyone have spare gloves?'

One of the ambulance officers gave her a fresh pair, blue, non-sterile.

She squatted down and unzipped the body bag, releasing the distinctive smell of death, blood and petrol. Len Dengate had a single gunshot wound to the lower portion of his chest. It was about an inch in diameter, surrounded by soot. It had crenated, or slightly scalloped, edges. The shot had passed through the shirt, just to the left of the midline, beneath the rib. She didn't move the shirt or attempt to get a closer view of the skin wound. That could be done after it was cleaned, just prior to the post-mortem. The less disturbed the body, the better, for now. The face was pale with a bluish hue. The beard around the mouth was bloodied. The skin was cool to touch. Both hands were to the sides, fingers curled.

Propped in the corner was the shotgun.

'Simon, can you or someone put fresh gloves on and get me some paper bags and elastic bands, without disrupting anything else in the kitchen, if that's possible. They'd most likely be in one of the drawers.'

'I'm on it.' One of the ambulance team took large strides to the kitchen.

'We need to bag his hands. I assume you already checked for gunshot residue. But you'd know that if he was in the room when a gun went off, he may have it on him anyway.'

McGinley remained silent. He hadn't thought to test for it.

'Where was the body found?'

'He was on the floor when we arrived.' He sullenly pointed to the rug. 'It looked as if he shot himself. From what we can tell, your mother found him on the lounge and dragged him there to try to revive him. We believe that's how she got his blood on her.'

'Did you test her hands for gunshot residue?' Anya hated to say it, but there could have been a struggle. Maybe her mother tried to stop him from shooting himself. She needed to be tested as part of procedure. It could also help clear her of suspicion - if it ever came to that.

'I'll get on to it,' Hammond said, with a sympathetic look.

McGinley eye's narrowed. 'You're calling your mother a suspect?'

Anya surveyed more of the room. 'Of course not. But if you don't run the tests now, there are no second chances to get this right.'

In a coroner's case, whatever medical interventions were put in place had to be left in situ. There were no drip stands or evidence of intervention going by the size of the body bag. For ambulance officers not to have intervened, Len would have had to have been deceased when they arrived. She tried to picture the events. Blood smears on the floor could have been from her mother's knees and hands.

'You said Mum hasn't spoken.'

'Alison Blainey was with her,' Simon explained. 'She was the one who called us. She's in shock so one of the constables took her back to the motel she's staying at.'

'Where was Mum when you arrived?'

'It wasn't easy getting her away from Len. She was holding his head in her lap.'

Anya could imagine her mother's grief. 'You'll need to take fingerprints. Len's, Alison's, Mum's and anyone else who's been here. The room, doors and weapon have to be dusted as well. The dog's face should be swabbed and photographed too.' There was blood residue on Ros's nose. If someone had threatened Len, the dog could have bitten them.

The paramedic returned and Anya placed a paper bag around Len's right hand. In the left, she noticed a small torn piece of paper stuck to his palmar crease. She asked for plastic tweezers from the ambulance's kit and carefully removed it to a separate bag, before instructing McGinley to accurately label the object, location on the body and time.

'Could be part of a suicide note,' he mumbled.

It was impossible to say. There was no sign of more paper.

Len's dog whimpered by the gurney.

'God, what happened? I got a message to come straight here.' A male voice boomed from the hallway. Craig Dengate barged in. He was a slightly smaller version of his brother. 'Len—'

The body bag was in view. Craig stopped, arms dropped to his sides. 'Oh God, no.'

'Get him out,' Anya directed and stood between him and the body.

McGinley moved over, but only to restrain the brother from touching anything. 'I'm sorry, Craig. Looks like Len shot himself.'

The elder Dengate stepped back. 'That's impossible. He would never leave Ros.' He pleaded with McGinley. 'He can't have. He wouldn't have.'

Anya felt her anger simmer again. The scene was out of control. The police sergeant had already made up his mind, and was convincing the brother there was no possibility of foul play.

She moved to examine the blood splatter on the floor.

'Sorry, mate, but I'll need you to identify the body,' McGinley said. 'Might as well do it now.'

'That can happen at the hospital. Later.' Anya didn't want any more contamination. And no relative should have to identify Len's remains in the state he was currently in. Hospital staff would cover the wounds with sheets to minimise the impact on a family member. This would be their last memory of their loved one.

'He's here now. Let's not make this any more traumatic,' McGinley almost growled.

'The scene's been contaminated enough. No one touches anything,' Anya ordered.

Ticking the boxes and filling in the paperwork seemed like all the policeman was interested in. He seemed to have no regard for what had happened or how the death had occurred. These moments were critical in establishing the truth and could save a lifetime of questions from other police and family members, not to mention insurance companies and lawyers. It would be in Craig's best interests to let them do their jobs.

Before Anya could stop him, McGinley further exposed Len's face. The sergeant was beyond incompetent and destructive to the scene.

Craig blessed himself and said a prayer. When he had finished, he wiped tears from his eyes.

McGinley was impatient to get on with what needed to be done. 'I need to ask you about Len's gun. Is there anything distinctive about it?'

Anya had seen it briefly, from close up to the barrel, but wasn't aware of anything specific.

Craig stared towards the fireplace. 'Dad got it made for his twenty-first. His initials are engraved under the barrel. The butt was carved in a flourish of the South Esk River.'

There was no doubt the shotgun was unique. Craig stepped towards the weapon in the corner, leaving muddy prints in his wake. 'That's it. I'd know it anywhere. It never left his side.'

'Don't touch anything!' Anya urged, but Craig already had hold of the weapon. 'First Mum and Dad, then he lost Patsy.'

McGinley made no attempt to stop him. He seemed more concerned with comforting the brother than investigating Len's death. 'When was the last time you saw or spoke to him?'

'This afternoon. I heard about the department of health closing him down. I rang to tell him it was just a setback. I offered to pay for all his legal expenses. He said he'd think about it . . .' Craig shook his head. 'I was going to come over tonight, then word came through about the fire.'

The older Dengate bent over and cried. Hammond slowly led him out the front door.

Anya took more photos with McGinley's camera, looking for any evidence of blowback blood spatter.

32

After all the sample testing and photographs, the body was removed. Roswell was delivered to Jeanette, who had been called back to check on stock at PT.

Spent, Anya ventured into the kitchen and removed her gloves.

Simon sat next to Jocelyn. She clutched an untouched cup of tea between her hands. Dried blood stained her fingers and the front of her shirt. There was no blood splatter on her face or clothing, nothing to suggest she'd been present when Len was shot. That was a vital observation.

'Simon, can you witness and record that Mum doesn't have any blood spray or drops on her face?'

'I can do better than that.' He pulled out his phone. 'Jocelyn, do you mind?'

Anya felt a crushing tightness in her chest seeing Jocelyn staring into space, a hollow version of herself. Len's death would have been difficult enough for her to deal with. Finding his body compounded the trauma.

Simon clicked some photos and emailed them, presumably to a work address.

Craig Dengate had not wanted to leave the property until Len's body had been taken care of. The case was, by definition, coronial, and an autopsy would be performed at the first opportunity. He would forever be haunted by the memories of blood on the floor and the last time he saw his brother's face.

Anya knelt down and lightly touched her mother's back. Jocelyn didn't respond or even react to her daughter's presence. She was virtually catatonic.

'Can't believe Len would shoot himself,' Craig said, to no one in particular.

Only that morning, Anya had described Emily Quaid's death to the distraught Len. It was possible the guilt he'd felt over the deaths from the E. coli had overwhelmed him. He was facing total ruin, from his point of view, and had already suffered the loss of parents and his fiancée. Even winning a lawsuit against PT couldn't bring back the company he had built from scratch. The organic status of the land was already ruined.

Death wasn't the answer, Anya knew. The people he left behind would suffer even more.

'Guess Len went out with one big act of payback.' McGinley helped himself to the coffee pot on the stove. Craig pulled up a chair near the wall.

Anya wondered if anyone had bothered to check if there were more than one mug out when they arrived at the scene. Had Len entertained anyone before his death? Had he eaten, been interrupted? All those things were critical to the investigation. Her focus, however, remained on Jocelyn's mental and emotional wellbeing.

Simon challenged his superior. 'How is suicide payback?'

'Makes everyone else suffer. It's gutless. Not being able to face the consequences of your actions.' McGinley waited for acknowledgement.

None came.

'Doesn't anybody else get it? It's obvious and it all fits. Len lit the fire tonight, to sabotage PT,' the sergeant bleated. 'Didn't you smell the petrol on him?'

Simon didn't buy it. 'Why would he set fire to those fields?'

'Everyone knows Len had whacky ideas about PT. Look at the way he accused them of contaminating his crop. He had motive and opportunity,' McGinley was on a roll. 'PT has an electric fence. It's too high to get past. Setting fire to the Wilson boundary meant it easily spread to PT's crops and feed lots.' The coffee he poured looked more like syrup than a drink. 'Before he checks himself out, he tries to destroy the people who ruined him. He wasn't fiddling while it burnt like that Nero character. Maybe he thought he could but then got the guilts when it became so out of hand. Who knows what a deranged mind really thinks? Oh, sorry Craig. No disrespect.'

Anya recalled Len's comment at the meeting with Alison Blainey. That if he went down, he was taking PT with him.

Craig Dengate lifted his head. His eyes were bloodshot. He looked broken. 'He was against violence. I didn't think he'd do anything this crazy.'

Anya wondered. He'd held a loaded gun to her head only days before.

'That makes absolutely no sense,' Simon argued. 'Len wouldn't use a pesticide because it harmed insects. He was all bluff and wind. I don't believe he'd risk anyone getting hurt, even by accident.'

Jocelyn raised her gaze a little, as if she were listening.

'In terms of suspects for lighting the fires, the suicidal pyro-maniac we stopped to has to be number one. He tried to burn Anya alive with petrol and had a backup.'

Jocelyn turned her head. Her voice was strained. 'What man?'

'From what I hear,' McGinley slammed the mug back on the sink, 'that dead guy had a plastic toy water squirter. But you didn't know that until after you'd blown a hole in his chest.'

Anya was about to argue the facts when Jocelyn spoke again.

'Alison Blainey said there was an attack planned for tonight. A group from POWER was just supposed to cut down the wheat with whipper snippers as a way of protesting against GM experimental crops.'

'Sounds like Len was keen to jump on a bandwagon,' McGinley said. 'He went along, got carried away and started the fire. Then he panics, thinking someone's seen him. He comes back here and—'

Craig hung his head as Samir came into the kitchen via the back door.

'Is it true what people are saying?' He stood, hat in his hand. 'About Mr Len?'

Anya rose. 'We're so sorry. Len died tonight.'

The foreman seemed to be frozen in disbelief.

'Don't believe what anyone says.' Jocelyn stared at the sergeant. 'I know for a fact Len didn't kill himself.'

Craig Dengate pushed his chair back slowly. 'There's only one way you could possibly know for sure Doctor . . . You're the one with his blood on your hands.'

Jocelyn threw her chair back as she lunged towards Len's brother. 'You've always been a fool. You'd sell Len out in a heartbeat.'

Anya quickly moved between them.

Dengate's face was bright red, his lip curled. 'Everyone here is a witness. She isn't denying it.'

Sergeant McGinley hoisted his trousers. 'This isn't helping. Jocelyn, if you know something, damn well say it.'

She took a series of rapid breaths. 'He wouldn't have done this. To PT or to me.'

'I have to agree. If there was ever a time to take revenge,' Simon concluded, 'it was when his Patsy died. We're talking about someone who testified *for* Reuben Millard, the man accused of killing Len's fiancée. Does anyone really believe a man like that was capable of revenge?'

There was no answer.

Jocelyn straightened her shirt and slowly walked out the back door. 'I want to go home. You can get my formal statement in the morning.'

'I'll drop you home,' Simon offered. 'I'm sorry. By morning, I'll probably be on suspension pending the shooting investigation.'

The implication was that McGinley would be the one to take her statement.

Anya wanted to go back and check the lounge room again. Something bothered her about the whole scenario. She thought her mother could probably do with some time to herself too.

'How are your burns?' she asked Simon.

'Our car's automatic, power steering. The bandages won't affect my driving. You do what you have to here. I'll look after your mum.'

As Hammond and Jocelyn headed out of the house, McGinley took a call and listened with little input before hanging up. 'That was the homestead. Sounds like the fire's out, but it's one hell of a mess. Millions of dollars' worth of damage, they reckon.'

'Any protesters or volunteers injured or not accounted for?' Anya asked.

His phone rang again. 'Right. Launceston Crime Scene are out on Langleys Road. Hobart detectives are right behind.' He moved past Samir and called out the door to Simon, 'Hammond, better brace yourself. You started one hell of a shitstorm.'

Anya had a thought and rushed out to the front of the house. She caught her mother getting into the muddy blue Mazda. Jocelyn wound down the passenger side window. 'Mum, I need to know. Where was the gun when you found Len?'

Without hesitation, she answered. 'Between his legs.'

'Are you sure? I know this is difficult, but it's incredibly important. Can you remember *exactly* where it was?'

Jocelyn closed her eyes. 'I'm so tired. So very tired. I need to rest.'

'I know, Mum, but we need to understand. Think hard. Please.'

Her eyes opened. 'The barrel was leaning on the lounge between his legs, and the shoulder piece was against the inside of his right leg. That's right. I had to push it away to drag him on to the floor.'

'Thanks, Mum.' Anya moved some hair out of her mother's eyes. 'I'll be home to check on you when I can.'

'Check the generator,' her mother said.

'What generator. Why?'

'He could have heard about the fire and got it ready in case the power was cut.'

Anya went back inside to go over the scene again.

33

Anya entered her mother's house at 4 am. The front door was unlocked. She left the borrowed boots out on the verandah and checked inside. Jocelyn lay asleep on top of her bed, fully dressed apart from her shoes. Anya quietly stepped to the linen cupboard and removed a spare blanket and clean towel. Her mother didn't rouse when Anya covered her to the shoulders and closed the door behind her.

Anya undressed in the main bathroom. For the first time she noticed red marks on her skin where the petrol had chemically burnt her legs. Dark bruises covered her knees and forearms from when she had been thrown forward onto hard ground when the police car exploded.

She washed off the mud in the shower and scrubbed her skin, careful to avoid the chemical burns. It took two washes with shampoo for her hair to feel close to clean again. She towel-dried her hair and pulled out yoga pants and a T-shirt from her packed case. The rain had passed, but the wind whistled through the bathroom window. With a mohair blanket from the lounge wrapped around her shoulders, she unlatched the back door.

The wind picked up and buffeted her hair around her face. She sat on the bench, knees tucked up to her chin. Without city lights or clouds to hinder the view, the stars looked like tiny droplets of paint splattered from a child's paintbrush thousands of miles away. Her grandfather had once said that everyone had the ability to travel through time. All they had to do was look at a star. By the time its light reached your eyes, it was already thousands of years in the past. The concept impressed Ben just as much as it had Anya.

She wanted to hear her son's voice. And the truth was, she missed Martin more than she had imagined. She would call them in a few hours, when they were both awake.

Anya's thoughts turned to Len Dengate and the ramifications of his death. Whether Beatrice Quaid would ever receive justice for Emily, and if they would ever understand how the spinach crop had become infected in the first place. There was no justice in anything that had happened in the past few days.

She heard the door to her mother's bedroom squeak and the padding of feet. Anya headed inside. Jocelyn wandered around the living room, picking up and putting down files.

'Mum?'

Jocelyn seemed oblivious as she paced and mumbled to herself. Suddenly, she turned on her heels and shuffled back up the corridor, past her bedroom, files still in hand.

'Mum?'

Her mother opened the door and stepped into Miriam's room.

Anya ventured to the doorway. Jocelyn had curled up on the bed and was breathing deeply, files clutched to her chest.

She was asleep, and had been all along. Anya had never known her mother to sleepwalk. It could explain the exhaustion in the daytime. Anya covered her with the mohair blanket and went to bed herself, leaving the door open.

By morning, Jocelyn was in her own bed again. Anya had woken at eight, unable to settle. Sleepwalking could explain some of the things her mother thought were out of place. She put three teaspoons of black tea leaves into a china pot and took it to the kettle. After that, she turned the pot three times.

'You do that exactly like your grandmother.'

Anya hadn't heard her mother enter the kitchen.

'She taught me. Guess some habits are hard to break. Do you still put in a teaspoon per cup and one for the pot?'

'Is there any other way?' Jocelyn rubbed her eyes. 'What time did you get in?'

'Around four.' Anya collected two mugs and a strainer from the draining tray by the sink. She poured the tea and put sugar and milk into both of them.

'It's as if you're channelling Grandma right now,' Jocelyn said. 'When we were upset or sad, she'd always say a cup of tea would make everything better. Who'd have guessed science would prove her right years later?'

'Grandma always had good instincts.' Anya stirred the drinks. In the light, her mother looked more tanned than before.

'I saw your bag was packed in the bedroom. Have you been called to another case?'

Anya sat next to Jocelyn at the table. 'After what you said yesterday, before the fire, and Len . . . I thought it was better if I went to a hotel. I wanted to see how you were first.'

'Len is dead, dammit, and you're offended by something I might have said?' She held her mug with both hands. 'I won't apologise. Martin is a schmuck.'

Anya sat back. Her mother didn't seem to remember why she'd driven off, or the other hateful things she'd said. The trauma of finding Len's body must have pushed it from her mind.

When she'd returned to Len's living room the previous night, Anya had thought about how quickly the scene had been contaminated and how difficult it now was to work out what had taken place. Multiple people had traipsed through, including police, ambulance officers and even Craig Dengate. Alison Blainey and her mother had been at the scene before anyone else. The blood stains were still on her hands.

No other rooms had been photographed or video recorded. Anya spent the remaining time at the house filming. The entire house was tidy, but no one had seemed to check if anything was missing. In contrast, the Quaid house had been far better examined when Emily's body was found.

When Jocelyn was up to it, Anya would show her footage in case she could identify something out of place.

The Hobart homicide detectives had attended the scene by the road with flamethrower man but hadn't come to Len Dengate's house overnight – at least not while Anya was there. Suspicions about the death might otherwise have never come to light.

Jocelyn blew on her tea. 'Len had every reason to live.' She bent across and whispered, 'There were people who wanted him out of the way. Some very powerful people.'

'Why are you whispering?'

Jocelyn frowned, and pointed at the walls and ceiling. Her mother thought the house was bugged.

Anya sighed. The conspiracy theory again. She tried not to confront her mother, but lead her to a logical conclusion.

'Mum, the house isn't bugged. Sometimes tragedies happen. Len was a good man under incredible pressure.' It bothered her that a suicide note hadn't been found, yet there had been that small remnant of paper in Len's hand. 'When you arrived, was there a note in his hand?'

'No! That's what they want you to think. That he committed suicide. Len was under pressure. Because he knew they were after him. They'd already got to Reuben and Patsy.'

These were delusions. Her mother was more unwell than she had imagined. 'Please, Mum, you have to stop this,' she begged. 'Or you'll lose your medical registration. You need help.'

Jocelyn's description of the gun placement when she found Len was what had convinced Anya that Len's death was suspicious. It was now obvious that Jocelyn's version of events was completely unreliable.

'Stop what?' Her mother's eyes filled with tears.

Anya pressed her fingers into her temples. Tiredness and frustration boiled over. 'Stop pretending that you're all right and the rest of the world is at fault.' She took a strained breath. 'Len was your friend. He was in crisis and you think it was a huge conspiracy to ruin him, then someone murdered him. You're delusional. You have to know you need help.'

Jocelyn's chin began to quiver. 'That's it then. You think I'm losing my mind. Just like my mother and aunts.'

'Mum.' She knelt down to plead. 'Look at the files all over the house. This isn't you. You're even sleepwalking. That's how things get rearranged in Miriam's room. Last night you took two files in there and slept holding them to your chest.'

Elbows on the table, Jocelyn buried her face in her hands and sobbed.

Anya placed a hand on her mother's back. 'I can help. If you let me.'

'Fine. First, I need you to hear me out. I deserve at least that.'

Anya lifted herself back on to the chair. For the sake of peace, she would listen.

Jocelyn was already on her feet, headed for the back door. She slipped on her gumboots.

'You coming? There's a spare pair in the shed.'

Reluctantly, Anya followed. Obviously, Jocelyn believed the house was bugged.

'After this, have me committed, do whatever. If you won't believe me, no one will.'

Jocelyn grabbed a crowbar from a tool box under the wooden bench and marched towards the chicken pen.

'What are you doing?' Anya reached for her arm.

'Len would never kill himself.' She pulled away and opened the latch to the wooden door. Chickens flurried as she entered.

This was insane. Anya ducked her head and followed, closing the door behind them.

Jocelyn was already at the roosting area. With a shovel from inside the back section, Jocelyn scooped away mounds of straw, shredded paper and manure. She tossed the shovel aside and dropped to her knees.

Anya felt helpless. She believed her mother was out of control but had no idea how to stop her without causing physical harm.

Jocelyn hacked at a section of wooden flooring with the crowbar as chickens squawked. Anya decided the only choice was to call the mental health crisis team, and turned back towards the house.

A crack sounded. Her mother made a yelping sound.

Anya hurried back to her mother's side. Blood dripped from her left hand.

'Now I can prove I'm not mad.'

'Okay, Mum. First, let me look at your hand.'

'Not until you see these.' The broken floorboards lay to the side, exposing a plastic-covered, taped-up bag of documents. Cautiously, Anya lifted it out.

Jocelyn sat back. 'Read these and tell me I'm crazy.'

Anya was more concerned with the cut hand.

Jocelyn held her palm upwards. Anya noticed something for the first time. 'Let me look at your other one.' The creases in the palms of Jocelyn's hands were dark.

'Do you use a self-tanning cream?'

'Don't be ridiculous.'

Anya realised why her mother had been so exhausted, had a racing heart, appeared so tanned and had lost so much weight.

'How long have your palms been pigmented?'

Jocelyn looked closely. 'I didn't know they were. People keep asking if I've been on holiday.'

Jocelyn was acutely unwell, but the cause was physical.

'We need to get you to hospital.'

She helped her mother to her feet. And collected the bag of documents.

34

Jocelyn lay in the emergency bed in Launceston. Her blood pressure was 70/60 and the monitor showed 130 beats per minute. She drifted in and out of consciousness and didn't flinch when the intravenous cannulas pierced her skin. For the first time, Anya saw how vulnerable her mother was. And how alone.

The registrar, Dr Megan French, had been in emergency when they arrived and was quick to make an assessment. Jocelyn was in acute adrenal crisis. The tiny adrenal glands above her kidneys had failed. The situation was critical. The diagnosis fitted with all of her mother's symptoms. Her body couldn't produce the hormones needed to process carbohydrates, fats and proteins, which explained the dramatic weight loss. Added to that, she couldn't produce adrenalin and cortisol or keep her blood sugars up, which was why she was fatigued, exhausted to the point of sleep walking. It could be why her memory seemed to be failing. She was trying to function without adequate sleep, with dangerously low blood pressure, given the adrenal glands were responsible for regulating the body's fluid and salt levels.

It all made sense. Anya looked at the blood results. Low sodium, high potassium, low glucose: the signs were all there.

Dehydration, severe hypotension, muscle wasting, pigmented skin and palms. A dextrose infusion treated the hypoglycaemia, and aggressive fluid replacement would increase Jocelyn's worryingly low blood pressure.

Anya was relieved her mother had cut herself on the wooden planks in the chicken pen. If not, Anya may not have noticed the pigment on the hands. She thought about how her mother wore gloves to wash up, clean, and treat patients.

The registrar, Megan, returned and delivered an injection. The next test took about twenty minutes. At first they injected a substance into the blood stream and monitored the adrenal's hormone response. Initially, they needed to watch carefully for an allergic reaction to the injection. Instead of leaving the task to nursing staff, Megan surprised Anya by pulling up a chair.

'Your mother's a strong woman. Is determination a family trait?'

'You might say that.' It was one of Jocelyn's greatest strengths, and weakness.

'I'm wondering what precipitated the deterioration. There's no sign of infection as far as we can tell, but we're waiting to get a urine sample. Is there any family history of cancer, or endocrine disease?'

'Not that I know of.'

'Any immune disorders?'

'Nothing apart from hay fever.' Anya went through a mental list of causes of adrenal disease. 'No travel, no tuberculosis. No other physical stressors come to mind.' The emotional stress of finding Len Dengate could have precipitated the collapse. Her body didn't have the capacity to produce any cortisol, even when faced with a life or death situation. 'Last night she found her close friend shot to death.'

Megan was quiet for a moment. 'That is horrible.'

Anya felt incredibly guilty. She had completely misread her mother. 'I was beginning to think she was suffering from early dementia. There's a strong family history.'

'Alzheimer's?'

'No, vascular.'

The registrar wrote in the notes. 'We see a lot of that around here. What's her mental state been like?'

'Forgetful, misplacing things, defensive. I think she was worried about losing her mind.' She couldn't believe she had misjudged her mother so badly. 'There wasn't much food in the house and I assumed she was forgetting to eat. And last night I saw her sleepwalking for the first time.'

'They can all be explained by her illness. She was completely physically and mentally exhausted. It's a wonder she managed to keep working.'

'What next?' Anya asked.

'We have to exclude adrenal tumours and check the pituitary as well. I suspect your mother has Addison's disease. As you know, there may not be a cause. It's just that the adrenal glands can't do their job.'

Anya was impressed by how knowledgeable the registrar was in what was supposedly a rare condition. She hadn't hesitated to make the initial diagnosis, before Anya mentioned it.

'Have you seen many other cases like this?'

Megan watched the monitor. 'I'm seconded from Melbourne. I'd seen one case at med school until I started here six months ago. The number of immune disorders in this area completely blows me away.' Her pager beeped. She stood and put the chair to the side. 'Must be something in the water.'

35

'Your mother has a visitor,' the nurse advised. 'I told him she was sleeping but he's asking for you.' Anya looked up. Simon Hammond stood at the entrance to the high dependency unit. He was in full uniform and carried his cap.

She was relieved to see him and slipped outside the room so as not to disturb her mother.

'How are your burns?' The palms were dressed in a clear skinlike dressing over a white cream.

'They'll heal.' He opened and closed one fist, then the other. 'Have to keep doing this to stop scarring.'

'Any word on who the man in the sneakers was, or what he was doing?'

'Not yet. Dental records may be the only way.'

'I imagine they're checking people recently released from prisons. Maybe someone will recognise the tattoos.' She pulled her cardigan across her chest and crossed her arms. 'I didn't properly thank you. For last night. You risked your life to save mine.'

'Don't mention it. Just part of the service.' He rotated his cap in his hand. 'How's your mum doing?'

Anya looked back through the window. The nurse had opened the venetian blind on the other side. 'Better than before. She was much more ill than anyone realised. How did you know she was here?'

'Secretary called us when she didn't go to the surgery, and there was no answer at home or on Jocelyn's mobile. Basic policing. She didn't look too good last night either.'

Anya realised there were advantages to living in a small place. If her mother had collapsed at home, it wouldn't have taken long for someone to find her and get her to hospital.

'She is a great lady. A lot of people care about her.' He pursed his lips, creating a left dimple. 'You'll probably have a year's supply of casseroles and cakes when you get back to the house.'

In a way, that was mildly comforting. It's what country people did in a crisis. The first instinct was to cook and make sure no one went hungry.

'Oh, sorry about the bruise on your forehead,' he winced. 'It looks nasty.' Her carry-on and laptop bags were by his side. Following her gaze, he said, 'Brought your things when I checked your mum's place. Thought you may need more clothes, toothbrush and that. Lucky for me, your stuff was already packed.'

It was a kind thought, but more than a little unsettling. And presumptuous. 'Thanks. McGinley let you back on duty?'

'He wasn't happy but needs all hands on deck after last night. I had the first interview with the Office of Police Integrity aka Internal Affairs this morning. Your contact, the one who put the wind up McGinley. Guess you'll be seeing him later.'

Anya's friend had spoken highly of Oliver Parke. She was glad someone competent would be investigating the police shooting. McGinley would have to be on his best by-the-book behaviour. She wanted to know if Alison Blainey had given a statement yet.

'Has Alison said what happened when they got to Len's last night?'

'She says Len was shot before they got there. The door was open so they walked in. She'd never seen a body before and panicked. She ran outside. We'll find out more when your mum's fit enough to talk.'

Anya felt relief that her mother hadn't been in the room when the shooting took place. Alison's statement also cleared her mother of involvement and suspicion.

'I checked Len's generator last night after you left. It was in the shed, full and ready to use. An empty tin was near it, smelling like petrol.'

'So we were right. He didn't set the fire.' Simon spun the cap again. 'Can we talk?'

'I thought we were.'

The dimple appeared again. Simon asked a passing nurse if there was somewhere to speak in private.

'There's a relative's lounge,' the nurse replied, and said to Anya, 'Your mother will be fine while you take a break.' An alarm bleeped for another patient and she excused herself. 'Across the other side,' she pointed.

Simon and Anya found the room. The police officer seemed nervous as they sat in adjacent chairs. 'About last night . . .'

Anya straightened. She felt sorry for the officer, who had innocently stopped to offer a man a lift in the rain and now his career was at risk. It was unethical to talk about the shooting before she gave her statement.

He put up a hand, as if reading her mind. 'I mean Len. Thank you for what you did.'

Anya was taken aback. Simon seemed more concerned with Len's death than his own future.

'In what way?'

'I can't shake the feeling that the big guy was murdered.'

Anya sat forward. 'Why?'

'Some people wrote him off as a crank, conspiracy theorist, an anti-progress, fruity Greenie. But something felt wrong from the moment we got there.'

Anya listened. This officer had excellent instincts.

'You hesitated when you looked at the wound to his chest,' he said.

He was right, just as he had been when he'd noticed flame-thrower man's sneakers and how he'd walked through puddles to the passenger side of the car. He'd read the man's face and body language perfectly and realised a lethal threat when Anya hadn't.

'He was shot through his shirt. It always raises alarm bells with a supposed suicide.' In her experience, people who committed suicide, whether by knife or gun wound, always exposed their skin before wounding themselves. Pulling the clothing out of the way was one of the most reliable signs of a self-inflicted injury. 'It's hardly proof of anything, but it does raise the question.'

She thought about how McGinley had been so quick to dismiss the death as suicide.

'Most jumpers take off their shoes and leave them behind.' He nodded. 'Techs say there weren't any fingerprints on the gun's pump mechanism.'

'That's not unusual.' Lack of fingerprints on the gun's wooden component was insignificant. And they had all seen Craig pick up the weapon at the farce of a crime scene.

He picked something minuscule off his cap. 'I went back to Len's place this morning.' He pulled out his phone. 'Took more photos, but unless there's something you can see that I've missed . . . I couldn't find a suicide note anywhere. Or whatever that piece of torn paper in his hand came from. I checked the rubbish and chicken scrap bucket, just in case. Len kept notes on everything.'

Anya had known relatives and friends to remove suicide notes, for their own reasons. Sometimes these were religious, if suicide was deemed a grave sin and excluded them from a specific burial, or for privacy reasons if an admission or scandal was revealed in the note. 'Mum still had on last night's clothes when we came to hospital.' They were in the plastic bag the nurses put all her personal belongings in, and it had come with her to the ward. 'If she took a note, it could still be in one of the pockets.'

'I assume McGinley'll check his computer, see if he emailed anyone or wrote an email without sending it.' Emails could also provide evidence of whether anyone had threatened him over the E. coli infections or in the past. That was another possibility Jocelyn hadn't considered. She had been adamant that Len had not committed suicide. Her reasons, though, sounded completely nonsensical. As did the whispering as if the house was being monitored. Then again, Christian Moss had said, 'the walls have ears'. How would he have known both Len and Jocelyn believed that?

She thought about the multitudes of writings in the scrapbook under the bed, with the word CONSPIRACY circled. Her mother was terrified she was in the process of losing her mind. She was trying to solve something while she could.

The hoards of patient files had to contain something to help her find the answers she was searching for.

Anya wondered if some of the answers were in the papers that had been hidden under the chicken coop.

36

When Simon had left and the nurse disappeared to lunch, Anya peeled open the bag and pulled out the wad of documents. Anya looked across at Jocelyn, who was resting peacefully despite the flurry of activity around other patients. Monitors alarmed and phones rang incessantly in the ward.

Anya slowly tore open the layers of plastic covering and exposed the collection of papers.

On top was an envelope titled *Last Will and Testament of Leonardo Dengate*. She opened it and unfolded the paper. Signed in ink, and dated less than a year ago, the document was filled with legal jargon about revoking previous wills. Her eyes scanned and stopped.

I hereby leave the entirety of my estate to my closest friend, Dr Jocelyn Reynolds. In the event of Jocelyn Reynolds pre-deceasing me, I leave the entirety of my estate to her daughter, Anya Crichton.

Anya sat back, stunned. She had no recollection of meeting Len Dengate before this visit. She could appreciate him wanting to leave the property to her mother, but in the event of Jocelyn's death, surely he would want his family to inherit.

There was an accompanying letter addressed to her mother and marked personal. She hesitated, not wanting to further violate her mother's privacy.

The will could not have been clearer. Included was a psychiatrist's report that gave Len a mini mental state examination score of thirty out of thirty, and declared him free of mental illness on the date the will was signed. It would be impossible to claim that he was not in a fit mental state to change his will. Len Dengate was as determined as Jocelyn. They would have made a formidable pair.

She thought of Craig Dengate, who would have inherited Len's land and farm prior to this will. If there was suspicion of homicide, police looked first at the person most likely to benefit from the death. Being the sole beneficiary of the will, Jocelyn might just have become a suspect if questions were raised about possible foul play. Anya's head pounded.

Jocelyn suddenly sat upright.

'I didn't mean it.' She began to sob. 'Please forgive me.'

A nurse hurried in and hit the fluorescent light behind the bed, which flicked on, off then on.

'It's all right, Dr Reynolds, it's just a bad dream. You're in hospital.' She wore navy culottes, a white shirt and navy cardigan, and had a pen lanyard around her neck. Her face was round and kind. 'It's not uncommon when you start having corticosteroids.'

Jocelyn blinked a number of times and recognised Anya.

'How long have I been here?' She turned her head as the monitor beeped seventy per minute.

'A few hours.'

'What happened?'

Anya moved her chair closer to the bed. 'You slept. It's a good thing.'

'I had the most horrible dream.' Her eyes filled with tears and her hand reached out.

Careful not to knock the taped-in cannula, Anya stroked her mother's fingers.

'In it I said vile, cruel things to you. None of it was true.' She licked her dry lips.

Anya reached for a glass of water and held back her own tears, wanting to believe that her mother hadn't been in a fit state yesterday to know what she was really saying. 'It was just a nightmare. Dreams are never real.' She wiped a strand of hair away from Jocelyn's forehead. 'Your body's been struggling without cortisone for who knows how long. The endocrinologist thinks you have Addison's disease.'

Jocelyn looked again at the monitor. 'Could it be cancer?'

'Not according to the MRI scan.'

She let her head flop back against the pillow.

'Do they serve food in this place?'

Anya grinned and relief filled her. 'Looks like the hydrocortisone has kicked in.'

'I can get you stewed unidentifiable fruit or custard,' the nurse said, checking the machine delivering intravenous fluids.

'On second thoughts, you could crank up the good juice in here.' Jocelyn pointed to the cannula. 'Whatever it is, it's got a decent buzz.'

'Steroid and sugar hits will do that to you.' The nurse smiled. 'There's a vending machine outside but don't let on I told you. It has Burger Rings, chips and Twisties.'

'I'm on it,' Anya said, relieved her mother was all right and making light of the situation.

Jocelyn tightened her grip on Anya's hand. 'Please don't go.'

The nurse left the light on and retreated.

'I need to tell you something.'

Anya assumed it had to do with Len Dengate.

'Annie, I've never told you how proud I am of you. How lucky I've been to have you as a daughter.' The heart monitor beeped in regular rhythm.

All her life Anya had hoped to hear those words, but not under these circumstances. 'Mum, you don't have to–'

'Yes I do. I've been so wrong about so many things. I promise, things will be different from now on.'

They remained in silence for a while. Anya grabbed a tissue from the table and blew her nose.

'Did Simon Hammond come to see you?'

Anya nodded.

'He's reliable and kind-hearted. You could do worse than him, you know.'

'Excuse me?'

'Okay.' Jocelyn had the spark back in her eyes. 'Maybe everything being different was a stretch. Consider me a work in progress.' She reached for the bed controls and slowly sat the bed more upright.

'That's a decent bruise on your head. Are you all right?'

Anya nodded, astounded at the change in her mother over such a short period of time.

'Did you bring the papers?'

There was nothing wrong with her mother's short-term memory. 'Are you sure you want to . . .'

'It's what Len wanted. I owe him that much.'

Anya reached down to her bag.

The nurse returned with a full plastic food tray. 'Foraged some contraband. Sandwiches, some carrot cake from a birthday morning tea. And thought you might like a nice hot cup of tea.'

This nurse's face was a true indicator of character.

'You didn't have to—'

'There's nothing wrong with being looked after. Enjoy it while it lasts.' She placed the tray on the mobile bed table and wheeled it into place.

Jocelyn licked her lips and took a sip from the brown plastic mug. 'It always tastes better when someone else has made it.'

'If only my husband understood that.' The nurse smiled warmly. 'If there's anything you need, just call.'

Anya waited until they were alone and then pulled out the wad of papers.

Jocelyn chomped into an egg sandwich. The smell of it made Anya nauseated.

'Did Len tell you he changed his will last year?'

'No.' She took another bite. 'We were friends, but he kept some things very private.' She chewed and swallowed. 'What are you–?'

'He left everything to you.'

There was a moment's silence. 'I had no idea. His family will challenge it.'

'He proved that he was of sound mind with a psychiatric report saying he was fully mentally competent.'

Anya tried to read her mother's face. This was a large parcel of land. Even after the E. coli scandal, she doubted Jocelyn would sell it.

'Sneaky bugger. Got the last laugh after all.'

'There was a personal letter addressed to you.'

'What does it say?'

Anya hesitated. 'I didn't open it. It's private.'

'I don't have my reading glasses.'

Anya suspected her mother would be less likely to get overtly upset in her presence. She used the knife from the tray to tear open the envelope. The letter was written in fountain pen, and the handwriting was like calligraphy. She looked at her mother, who nodded for her to continue.

Dearest Jocelyn,

You have been my loyal confidante and friend for many years and nursed me through the tragedy of losing my beloved Patsy. You have neither asked for, nor expected, anything in return. For that, I admire and respect you. You are one of life's true altruists. The pain you have suffered with personal loss has not jaded your sense of fairness and justice.

Anya paused to check her mother, whose head lay against the pillow, eyes closed.

'Go on.'

You have struggled for many years and waived payment for medical services, or accepted token gifts in lieu, such as fruit, vegetables or the odd rabbit. Now I am in a position to repay your kindness, only not in kind. By the way, I apologise for the menagerie I have inflicted upon you over the years.

'Must be at least ten years he'd drive to Launceston to see me. Said he couldn't trust anyone local.' Jocelyn chuckled. 'Chickens, lame ducks; four months ago there was a salamander. Who gives away a salamander?'

'He was a character,' Anya agreed.

Livelonger Organics was my life's dream. This may come as a surprise to you, my dear friend, but I have been prone to occasional moments of reason. This is why I have accepted legal advice to separate the company from the farm equipment and land. Livelonger Organics has no assets and leases the land from me. If the company is forced into bankruptcy, creditors' or other vultures' attempts to acquire the land will be unsuccessful. The land will remain in my name until my death, either premature or otherwise.

Anya stopped reading. It was as if he had suspected the farm produce would be sabotaged or compromised. More than that, it implied that Len had known his life might have been in danger. The gunshot wound could have been more important than anyone realised. She wanted to be at the post-mortem to see for herself.

Jocelyn opened her eyes.

'There's more,' Anya explained.

I hope that you will continue your good work and reveal PT and its co-conspirators for the murderers and evil manipulators they are. Sadly, if you read this, they have silenced me, or so they believe. Step carefully and securely at all times. My greatest regret is not being able to protect Patsy, Reuben, and you.

Her mother felt the need to explain. 'Patsy was a vibrant, intelligent, witty woman. Even though Reuben is serving a life sentence for her murder, Len always believed he was set up. He was the chief research scientist for TIAA. Patsy was worried about some top-secret study they were conducting.'

'Is that why Len testified for Reuben in court?'

Jocelyn nodded. 'Is there more?'

Anya continued.

With the culmination of your findings, I believe you and your beloved daughter will be able to prove the crimes against humanity and nature. Many more lives depend on it.

Yours in undying friendship, respect and appreciation,

Len

Anya silently reread the last few lines. It was dated three months ago. Len Dengate had wanted Anya involved in his case. Her mind raced. What crime had been committed against her mother?

'If anything happened to him, even it if seemed accidental,' Jocelyn said, 'he wanted you to be involved in the investigation.'

Anya needed to know what Jocelyn and Alison had found when they arrived at Len's home. Jocelyn had to be questioned by police, despite her health problems.

'Mum, can you tell me what happened last night?'

Jocelyn seemed to shudder and her eyes glazed. 'When Alison and I arrived, the door was opened. Len wouldn't leave it like that. Ros barked and straight away I knew something was wrong. I ran into the room and saw him. Part of me knew he was already gone but I guess I couldn't accept it. You asked me about the gun. It was propped between his legs and he was slumped back on the lounge.' She swallowed hard before continuing. 'I couldn't resuscitate him like that so I moved him on to the floor.'

That explained the pattern of blood smears from the upholstery and the rug.

'Where was Alison?' Anya asked.

Jocelyn cocked her head. 'She screamed when she saw him and ran outside. She must have called the police and ambulance.'

'I tried to bring him back, but he'd lost too much blood. I even swore at him that PT would win if he didn't fight . . .' She plucked at the bed sheet. 'It sounds so stupid. I just didn't want it to end like that for him. Still can't believe it.'

Anya reached across and took her mother's hand and held it until Jocelyn drifted back into a fitful sleep.

She tried to process what her mother described, and the information in Len's letter. After a few minutes she released their hands and began to flick through some of the papers. She stopped at the front page of the police report into Patsy's murder.

Senior Sergeant McGinley had been the first person on the scene.

37

While Jocelyn slept, Anya went home to grab her mother a change of clothes and toiletries. She wondered why Jocelyn would develop Addison's disease. The comment the medical registrar made about the prevalence of immunological conditions took her by surprise. Jocelyn had no family history of Addison's disease, and it was supposedly rare.

Anya replayed conversations and scenes from the past couple of days in her mind. She thought some of the answers might be in the Conspiracy notes under Jocelyn's bed. Len had been worried about being destroyed and now he was dead.

She also wanted to meet with Jeanette Egan. Something the vet had said during the fire got her thinking. Anya rang the number she'd placed by the bed. Without hesitation, Jeanette agreed to be over within the hour.

Kicking off her shoes, Anya immediately noticed something out of place across the hallway. The door to Miriam's room was ajar. She had deliberately closed it before the ambulance left for the hospital.

She pulled it shut and pushed on it again. The mechanism wouldn't release. The only way it would open was manually. Timidly, she searched inside. Nothing appeared out of place, considering Jocelyn had slept in there during her sleepwalking episode. Stepping into the living room, goose bumps spread across her shoulders and arms. Piles of patient files remained, but a stack now obscured the lower portion of the television. She had moved them to the side to watch the news the other night. Now they had been moved back. This had to have happened while she and her mother were away.

Anya held the phone handset, ready to call the police. But what was she going to say? That someone had rearranged some files? So far nothing appeared to be missing. She ventured into the kitchen area. The benches were clear and glistening, papers and files stacked into neat rows beside the table.

'Whoo hoo.'

Anya startled at the noise at the back door.

'Anyone here?'

Audrey Lingard stood in a patterned, loose-fitting shirt. She was the only person Anya knew who could make purple, black, white and orange work together. Matching tangerine necklace and bracelets complemented the ensemble, which included black cigarette pants and sparkly thongs. While Jocelyn had dressed more conservatively over time, her friend had become more colourful.

'Oh, darling.' Audrey embraced her goddaughter. 'I hoped to have come and gone by the time you came back. I came to help when I heard your mum was in hospital.'

Anya looked around. 'What are you doing?'

'I have a key so I thought I'd tidy up a little. Don't worry, I won't throw anything out, although just between you and me, Josie has to get over this hoarding papers business.'

Under the circumstances, hoarding was the least of Jocelyn's problems.

Anya needed to know. 'Have you been in the other rooms?'

'Darling, I popped in yesterday and did a bit of tidying, cleaning, just making the place a bit more presentable. Wellwishers will be coming once she gets home.' She unloaded pyrex dishes from an insulated bag into the freezer. 'You can thank me later.'

Anya wasn't feeling grateful, more like Audrey had intruded. 'Can I ask you a question? Did you move any papers in the living room, near the television?'

'Of course not. Your mum is fanatical about two things: patient notes are confidential. I wouldn't even look at the names on them. And that room in the front, the private one no one's supposed to enter. She could stash dead bodies in there for all I know, but half the fun is not knowing.'

'Has anyone else come inside the house?'

'Only Glenn. He helped me with the sheets. My sciatica stops me making beds.'

As if summoned, Glenn Lingard wiped his feet and came through the back door.

'It's all hung up.' He stopped when he saw Anya. 'Mum said you wouldn't mind us doing a bit around the house while Jocelyn's laid up.'

'I took the washing home and did it overnight. I'm just about to make a cuppa,' Audrey said, 'then you can feed the chickens.'

'Please. I can do that,' Anya said. She didn't want anyone seeing the hole in the pen, where the documents had been buried. 'I mean, you've already done enough.'

Glenn washed his hands in the sink and sat at the table. 'Heard you helped save some of the livestock during the fire.'

'We all helped where we could.' Anya hadn't remembered seeing Glenn that night, but there were plenty of people helping out she hadn't seen either.

'I drove past your institute. I didn't know it was actually within the PT grounds. You have to get through electric fences to get to work.'

'It's the price you pay for being innovative. Plenty of ignorant people don't appreciate what we do. They call it Frankenscience. People like Len Dengate and his organic cronies, who wanted to shut us down.'

Anya clicked on the kettle then found the new tea bags while Audrey chastised her son for speaking ill of the dead.

'I thought you would have been in favour of the principles of organic farming,' Anya said.

'Not when people risk dying from eating the food. Look at the E. coli outbreak. It's a perfect example. What if we could prevent the infections in the first place by harnessing science and making bacteria and viruses work for us?'

'You advocate genetically modifying food?' It wasn't what she'd expected him to believe.

The kettle boiled and Audrey filled cups.

'The way I see it, people have been selectively breeding crops and livestock for thousands of years. It's well documented in the Bible: look at Jacob and Rachel.'

She couldn't remember the Bible promoting injection of one species into another's DNA, but she listened. He must have known more about PT research and programs than she had imagined.

'People have always bred crops to become resilient, grafting plants whenever possible. Animals are chosen for breeding. Prize bulls, rams, roosters, racehorses, greyhounds. Even these chickens were bred to be good layers. Women use sperm banks to try to breed the next Nobel Prize winner.'

'Surely there's a big difference between selective breeding and adding the genes of fish to tomatoes to prolong shelf life.'

'Not necessarily. Famine affects millions of people,' he argued. 'If the technology exists to save whole populations, it's criminal to deny its use when it's safe, effective and affordable.'

Audrey placed the mugs on the table, and some homemade scones with jam and cream. Glenn helped himself without interrupting his speech.

'Rice, infused with Vitamin A, can cure blindness in third-world countries. A third of the world has zinc deficiency. In extreme forms it causes mental retardation, and in mild cases impairs the immune system and reduces resistance to infections like malaria, pneumonia, diarrhoea. It causes almost a million deaths a year around the world, and affects billions of people. It's possible to modify grains to take up more zinc from the soil and environment. If we have the capability, we would be morally culpable not to utilise that. We could potentially solve the world's food crisis.'

Jeanette Egan pushed through the back door. 'The same was said of AIDS medication in Africa, except that pharmaceutical companies owned the medication and are anything but charitable organisations.'

Glenn rolled his eyes. 'Who brought her?'

She took her boots off once inside and was instantly even smaller. 'Hi, Audrey, Anya. The world doesn't have a shortage of food, it's a distribution problem. Instead of distributing excess to those most in need, it gets dumped. To keep up market prices, at the expense of lives.'

Glenn shoved his finger into the table. 'Populations grow, land doesn't. We need to become even more efficient in terms of yields and nutritional value.'

The idea had appeal, in theory.

'Who's going to fund it?' Anya had to ask.

Glenn sat forward, forearms on his thighs. 'That's the great thing. Governments, at least this state's, and China and the US are already working on solutions with growers.'

Jeanette challenged him. 'You failed to mention Europe and the UK legislating against GM products.'

'They knee-jerked with blanket bans. It's a very political issue and there's a lot of ignorance and scaremongering going on. The countries in most need, third-world countries, are crying out for help. If we develop the seeds, they can grow crops that are drought resistant, mould resistant, that increase yield and thrive where nothing else grew before. In Nicaragua, two per cent of the adult population suffers from pesticide poisoning. Thousands die every year, and millions suffer severe side effects. By producing pesticide-resistant plants, farmers can spray a lot less and kill the weeds, not the crop itself.' He shoved the scone into his mouth as if in triumph.

'You twist facts to suit yourself.' The vet stood, arms folded. 'Who funds all this great research? I know, the companies who profit from it? Where's the peer review of the science?

Oops, it's buried by government-approved self-regulation of your industry. And who's on all the committees? Reps from PT, your research unit, which is another name for PT, who recommend self-regulation of the science. You aren't a scientist, you're a puppet for big corporations.'

Glenn stood and pointed his finger near Jeanette's face. Despite a considerable size difference, she was not going to be intimidated. 'You are a hypocrite who wouldn't even be asked to treat a pet hamster if it wasn't for PT giving you work when no one else would. You don't seem to have any problems taking pay cheques from PT.'

'At least I'm honest about it. I treat their animals. It is what it is. I'm not trying to profit from the most vulnerable people on the planet. Len Dengate was a great man, and he knew exactly what you were doing.'

Glenn turned and slapped the door jam before storming out the back door and slamming it behind him.

'So,' Jeanette said. 'Any more water in that kettle?'

Audrey tugged on her plastic beads. 'You shouldn't bait him like that. You know he has a temper.'

'If he didn't act like a silverback every time he made a point, maybe I wouldn't.'

Anya followed him to make sure he wasn't near the chicken pen. He was loading his boot with gardening tools. 'She doesn't have a clue what we do.'

Anya seized the opportunity to find out more about the company Len feared so much. 'I'd love to find out more.'

He stopped and looked at her. 'If you're really interested in the science, I'd be happy to show you around the lab sometime.'

'Sounds great.'

Glenn opted to tackle the overgrown grass in the garden while Anya trekked to the chicken pen. The crowbar and displaced planks weren't visible to anyone looking from the back of the house. Chickens squawked when she approached. Inside, things were exactly as she remembered leaving them, apart from the new deposits of chicken poo.

She shooed the poultry aside and knelt down, peering into the hole her mother had made. It was too dark to see. She inserted her hand and reached around. Leaning in further, she scraped her upper arm on one of the splintered boards.

Then she felt it. More plastic. She left it in place and went back inside.

Jeanette was finishing a scone and a coffee. Audrey collected her insulated bag and placed a tea towel on its rack inside the cupboard. 'I'll leave you two to it,' she said. 'Don't mind me, I'll see myself out.'

'Thanks, Audrey.' Anya stood and hugged her mother's friend. 'Mum's lucky to have a friend like you.' She meant it.

'Now, I'll be in to see her as soon as you say she's well enough for visitors.'

When Audrey was out of earshot, Anya turned back to Jeanette. 'What was that about with Glenn?'

'He's a pompous ass. And he was no friend of Len's.' She looked up over her mug. 'What did you want to talk to me about?'

'Cows and their stomach acidity.' Anya grabbed her keys. 'Do you mind driving while we talk?'

'It's what I do.' Jeanette left her mug in the sink and they headed out in her black Range Rover to the northwestern border of Len Dengate's property.

'It's been bothering me how the E. coli got into Livelonger's spinach. And going by the volume of spinach they produce each fortnight, there should have been a lot more cases,' Anya began.

'That's if all the spinach was contaminated.' Jeanette headed out towards the entrance to Livelonger Organics. As they passed Len's house, they remained silent. A crime scene van was outside, with the area cordoned off.

Jeanette spoke first. 'Do you think it's possible someone deliberately contaminated part of his crop?'

'It seems pretty far-fetched but Len expected something like this to happen. Can you tell me again about the effect a corn diet has on the cattle?'

'Pretty simple. They're stomachs are designed for grass feeding. Corn alters the acidity of the stomachs, although it isn't a permanent state. If they go back to a grass diet, the digestive acid levels revert to normal in about five days.'

'Does that affect the bacteria in the gut?' Anya wondered. Animals and humans needed a balance of organisms to digest food.

Jeanette thought. 'It would. Some of the organisms wouldn't survive the change in pH. Others might appear that weren't there previously.'

Anya had researched the strain responsible for the food poisoning. 'The infective E. coli was a toxin producer that hasn't been seen around here before in humans.'

'You think it's crossed over from an animal population?'

'I'm just trying to understand what happened and why.'

The Range Rover pulled up along the boundary. Cattle were grazing through what remained of Len's crops in that field. Anya asked the vet, 'Can you find out if the bacteria affected the animals?'

Jeanette removed her laptop from the back. 'I remember a colleague treating a multi-resistant organism in a leg abscess while I was on holiday a few months ago. In the feed lots, the animals have to stand in their own faeces and sometimes get infected wounds. They're packed pretty tightly, as you saw.' She looked up her files.

'It was a Shigella-producing E. coli. A rare strain.' She showed Anya the test result data on the screen.

'That's it. The same bacteria that killed Emily Quaid and infected the others,' Anya concluded. 'If it was on the leg wound, it was most likely in the dirt, or manure.'

'OK. The corn diet could have been responsible for the new, virulent strain. But how did it get into the spinach?' Jeanette considered the possibilities. 'The cattle were contained behind those fences and Len didn't use the manure to fertilise his crops. He wouldn't buy anything from PT on principle.'

Anya was reminded of something the medical registrar at the hospital had said. There must have been something in the water here. All Livelonger's produce was sprayed and washed before packaging.

She thought out loud. 'If the water supply had been temporarily infected, he could have washed the bacteria onto the spinach without ever knowing.'

Jeanette tapped the steering wheel. 'You could be on to something.'

For the first time, Anya felt like they could find an answer to why people died and who might be responsible. If only they knew how Emily Quaid acquired the infection. The only person likely to answer that was Jenny Quaid, if and when she was found. Still, the other victims deserved to know how and why they acquired it.

'Do you have any maps of the water supplies, and where the South Esk River runs?'

A few more clicks and the maps were on the screen. The purest water came through the river that flowed through the properties owned by PT. It deviated through Len's property at the north-eastern quarter before meandering through Jocelyn's property.

Seeing the maps was revealing. Suddenly, Len and Jocelyn's theories made some sense. It would explain why PT were so keen to acquire Dengate's land, and no doubt, her mother's as well. With the addition of those two properties, PT would exclusively control the entire area's irrigation supply. They could run all competition out of business. By then, they would have acquired all the land and it didn't matter if they alienated the locals. No one could afford to buy them out.

Jeanette had already proven invaluable help.

'Len irrigated from the river, if that were contaminated, you'd expect a lot more cases. It wouldn't have been in his water supply then.' Anya felt frustrated by the dead end. Or maybe not. The next question she had was where on the property was Len's spinach grown? Jeanette made a call to the office. Grace answered. Spinach was seasonally grown in the southeastern and northwestern fields. Downhill from the feed lots.

Jeanette retrieved the testing kit from the back of the car and removed some swabs and specimen jars.

Anya asked, 'If it's in the cattle faeces and was flushed down into the spinach crop, are you sure you want to be the one responsible for finding out? You'll probably lose your job, and they may come after you for breaching confidentiality or harming the company. They'll think of something that may affect your future employment prospects in the state.'

Jeanette remained silent.

It seemed unlikely PT knew about the E. coli in the manure. If they did, they could have reverted the cattle to grass feed, and the evidence would have been destroyed in a few days. Once the acidity in the animals' stomachs returned to normal, the E. coli would no longer thrive.

Anya didn't want Jeanette to suffer. She'd already helped so much. 'I'm happy for you to walk away and leave the swabs with me. There's a class action in progress and they'll come after PT if our theory is proven correct.'

The vet pondered for a few moments. 'Len's gone. Nothing will bring him back. I can make sure his good name is protected. If he isn't responsible for the E. coli outbreak, I want to be the one to clear his name.'

Anya was impressed by the loyalty Len Dengate still inspired and felt the hairs on her arms stand up. The big man had said that if he went down, he'd make sure he took PT with him. She and Jocelyn needed to brace themselves for the backlash that would head their way if the E. coli grew. Manure samples had never been so valuable.

38

The following morning, a clean-shaven man in a pressed grey suit, pale blue shirt and mauve tie spoke to the nurse outside. He looked more like a police officer than a doctor.

Jocelyn was still dozing.

The friendly nurse popped her head in. Seeing the patient asleep, she whispered to Anya, 'There's a detective out here who wants to talk to you.'

'Did he give his name?'

'No, but for what it's worth, he's pretty cute and very polite.'

Anya put the files she'd been reading under her bag on the chair and folded the spare blanket on top.

The slim, tall gentleman held two takeaway coffees in a cardboard tray. He extended a hand. 'Oliver Parke. I'm sorry to turn up unannounced but rumour has it you aren't answering your phone.'

'It got burnt along with a squad car.' She shook his hand. 'Long story.'

'Your father called the Longford police when he couldn't reach you or your mother after the fire.' He pulled a piece of paper from his pocket. 'A female constable wanted me to pass this on.'

Rhonda was the policewoman she had met the night of
the fire. Anya read the note. *Evelyn is improving, and coming off
dialysis. Please call when you can.*

'Thank you.' Another advantage of a smaller town where
the police knew the locals. 'Constable Hammond mentioned
you were in town.'

'I came to Hobart for the conference you spoke at. I've
been looking into complaints about how police handle child
abuse cases in the state. Just after you rang, I heard about the
police roadside shooting. I brought you a proper coffee.' He
held out the cardboard tray. 'Didn't know how you take it, so
there's one with milk, one without.'

Anya chose black. 'Thanks.'

'Then I found out you were a witness to the shooting, so I
put my hand up. As you know, an outsider has to be brought
in to investigate the local constabulary in cases like this. That
way we avoid potential conflict of interest and the public
get the investigation they deserve.' He gestured to the exit.
'Do you mind if we step outside? It's cooler out there.' They
passed through the double doors to a corridor and sat on plastic
waiting-room chairs. 'So Hammond just happened to mention
to you that I'd interviewed him?'

Anya quickly corrected him. 'He came to see how my
mother was. I assure you we didn't discuss what happened
the night before last. He was completely ethical.' There was
nothing like an internal affairs investigation to make everyone
nervous. She lifted the cup. 'Is this a bribe?'

'I prefer negotiation offering. I know it isn't a good time
for you. I need to get your statement this morning. Here or at
a station.'

'Accepted.' It was difficult to believe that she had almost
been killed a couple of nights ago. Anya's fingers moved to the
bruise on her forehead and back to the warmth of the cup.

She needed to know about the man who had tried to kill
her.

'Have they identified the body on the road?'

'Hobart boys recognised the description of the tattoos. Dental records confirmed the ID. Thadeus Leske, aka Mincer.'

'Mincer?'

'With a first name like Thadeus, can you blame him? Released from Risdon prison two months ago. Standover man, debt collector and occasional arsonist. If anyone welshed on their debts, his signature move was putting their fingers in a meat grinder.' He tapped on the side of the coffee cup. 'Real charmer from the sounds of it. Medical records show he had inoperable lung cancer. Not surprising, he was a chain smoker.'

That was why he had nothing to lose, she thought. He may not have wanted the rest of his days to be spent in prison.

'Did anyone think to check for his fingerprints at the Dengate house?'

'What are you thinking? I chased up on the case you rang me about. McGinley is convinced Dengate's fatal wound was self-inflicted.' Parke turned to face Anya. 'There's an *interesting* character, by the way.'

Anya wondered what that phrase really meant to an internal investigator. She was thinking about Mincer Leske. 'A known arsonist and standover man is in town the night a major fire started and he happened to be carrying a home-made flamethrower?' She sipped. 'McGinley mentioned Len's body smelling like petrol but I didn't pick that up. McGinley assumed that was proof Len started the fire then shot himself out of guilt. Mum said he would have filled up a generator when he heard about the fire, in case power went out. I found an empty can next to it in the shed. Sounds like Mum was right and McGinley jumped to a dangerous conclusion.'

'Yeah, well, the sarge has only ever worked one homicide. Do you know of any connection between Leske and Dengate?'

A wardsman wheeled a patient on a bed along the corridor. The wheels squeaked. A nurse carried a large bag of X-rays with the patient. The ward was getting a new admission.

Oliver moved to open the ward door for them. When the patient was inside, he returned. 'What made you think Dengate's death was suspicious?'

'Len wrote a letter to my mother. We found it in documents that included his will. He specifically asked for me to investigate his death, whether it looked accidental or otherwise.'

'McGinley claims Len was more than a touch eccentric.'

Anya knew exactly what that implied. 'He was lucid and had enough foresight to organise psych assessments that confirmed he was of sound mind when he changed his will three months ago.'

Oliver smiled. 'Smart guy. Okay. He worries something's going to happen to him. Then it does.' He swigged on his coffee. 'First question to ask if you suspect a staged suicide: who benefited from his death?'

Anya knew the fact that her mother had been first on the scene and had Len's blood all over her was enough to raise suspicion. Being the sole beneficiary could be used against her. She could not prove that Len hadn't told her about changing the will. And the papers had been buried under her chicken pen.

'Not necessarily. Maybe we should be asking who *believed* they would benefit at the time of Len's death.'

'I'm liking the way you think, doctor.' He checked his watch. 'Can I give you a lift to the station? If we get the formal interview over with, I can look into whatever else is necessary while I'm still here. That scene was a complete cock-up. If nothing else, McGinley deserves a rocket where it's likely to hurt him most.'

Anya felt a wave of relief. The chances of Len Dengate's death being dismissed as suicide were decreasing.

'I'll grab my bag. Oh, and is there any chance I can attend Len's post-mortem? Can you find out when it's scheduled?'

He pulled out his phone and dialled as Anya left a message with the nurse about where she was going.

Oliver hung up as she returned. 'We're in luck. It's in half an hour, just a few storeys below us. We can both go then head

to the station for your statement. There's even time for breakfast if you want.'

'McGinley will just love seeing us again,' she quipped. He
had been in the same job for years, with little experience in
crime scenes. She pulled on her cardigan. 'Do you know about
the other homicide case McGinley worked on?'

'Constable Rhonda did mention it. Guy called Reuben
Millard is serving life in Risdon.'

'The victim, Patsy Gallop, was Len Dengate's fiancée. Len
always believed Millard was framed.'

Oliver raised his cup. 'McGinley just got a lot more
interesting.'

39

Steve Schiller was already in the autopsy suite office when Anya and Oliver arrived. He stood as soon as he saw them.

'Thanks for coming,' Oliver said, finishing off an egg and bacon roll. 'This is—'

'Doctor, good to see you again.'

Oliver rolled the wrapper into a ball and lobbed it into a wastepaper basket. 'Should have known. Five hundred thousand people in the state and they all know each other.'

'We met over the E. coli poisonings,' Schiller explained. He was far more formal in the presence of a Police Integrity officer. Oliver seemed to have that effect on people.

'Heard your relative is doing better.'

'She's lucky, compared to some of the others.' The news stations and papers had been more occupied with fires and shootings. 'Any word on Jenny or Mia Quaid?'

He shook his head. 'It's weird. They just vanished. The way that little girl was left with the toy. You wouldn't think they'd miss the funeral if they had a choice. If Heyes knows something, the mongrel isn't talking.'

What he didn't say was that with each day, the odds of them being found alive decreased.

'On the upside, no new cases have been reported.' He turned to Oliver. 'The government is in damage control over the outbreak. The Attorney General is putting heat on to charge the directors of Livelonger Organics with negligent homicide, or manslaughter.'

'Len Dengate was the owner.' Oliver wiped his hands with a handkerchief. 'He's inside on a slab.'

A woman wearing an ID badge entered the office. 'Dr Ashton's ready to begin.'

Anya had worked with Ashton before he moved to Launceston. He was thorough and very experienced. They followed the assistant along a short corridor, through plastic doors and into the autopsy suite. Oliver explained that he had invited Schiller as part of the homicide unit. If the death was suspicious, they needed to become involved as soon as possible.

Anya grabbed gloves from a dispenser on the wall while cursory introductions were made. Schiller stood back. Oliver crossed his arms and stepped forward.

Len's body lay naked on the gurney. On the whiteboard, his height was listed as 190 centimetres. Weight 120 kilograms. He hadn't appeared that tall in person, Anya realised, because of his habit of stooping.

An assistant photographed the only apparent wound. 'No external contusions or bruising,' the pathologist announced. 'This is what I'm told you had specific questions about, Anya?'

Anya glanced back at Oliver, who nodded. 'The scene wasn't preserved, and there is the possibility of a staged suicide.'

McGinley pushed through the doors in uniform. 'Why was I summoned here?'

Oliver acknowledged him. 'Thought you'd appreciate being kept in the loop.'

The sergeant glared at Anya and Schiller. 'This is a waste of all our time. Dengate was crazy. Everyone knew it. He shot himself because he couldn't face what his farm had done to those people. He caused the death of a child, an old man, and couldn't deal with it. He took the coward's way out.'

'Suicide, like martyrdom, is arguably the bravest of acts.' Dr Ashton looked up. 'My first day in medical school we were taught that. And every hypochondriac dies of a genuine illness.' He turned everyone's attention to the hole in the left upper abdomen.

According to the scale, the entrance wound was around an inch in size, consistent with a twelve-gauge shotgun. What struck Anya was its shape. It was oval, with a wider margin of soot on its central side.

'What is it you're seeing?' Oliver asked.

'This wound captured my attention immediately,' Dr Ashton said.

'Obviously, it blew one hell of a hole.' McGinley didn't have the insight to keep quiet.

'It's not the size, it's the shape that concerns me.'

The detectives stepped closer.

'See,' Anya explained. 'There's more soot on the side closest to his middle, or the left, if you're facing the body. That and the oval shape mean the contact wasn't as tight on that side.'

Dr Ashton asked for a telescopic probe and extended the column.

'Does that mean he could have hesitated?' Schiller asked. 'It wouldn't be easy to hold a gun to yourself and make sure the barrel was evenly pressed against your skin.'

'Think about it,' the pathologist said. 'One hand is larger, more muscular. He was right-handed. Let's assume he shot himself and aimed upwards for the heart for maximum damage.'

He held the probe against his plastic apron, to stimulate the shotgun. 'You'd expect greater pressure applied to the right-hand side of the wound, if he aimed the gun upwards and towards his left shoulder.'

'The location of the entry point is on the left side of Len's upper abdomen. Through his shirt, which in itself is suspicious.'

'X-rays show most of the damage was done to the right lung and aorta, which appear to have been virtually shredded.' The assistant switched the lights on the viewing box.

'It's a typical "billiard ball" effect within the chest. The pellets strike each other and bounce more widely than normally expected, causing massive amounts of tissue damage,' explained Anya.

'Death would have been within seconds,' Ashton concluded.

It would prove to her mother that nothing or no one could have saved him once the shot went off. 'What about the trajectory pattern?'

'The damage is almost exclusively to the right side of his chest. Dengate would have had to have reached *across* to his left and down to manage to pull the trigger.'

'Exactly.' Anya felt relieved Dr Ashton appreciated the significance.

'And that would have been pretty awkward, even for a big guy,' Oliver added.

Schiller considered the information. 'For the barrel to be pressed more heavily on that side, someone else must have held the gun and fired.'

McGinley looked as if he'd just been delivered a knockout blow to the face.

40

After the post-mortem, Oliver drove Anya to attend the Launceston police station where she sat in an interview room with Oliver, who introduced himself and named Anya for the video recording. Schiller sat in. This was an internal investigation of Simon Hammond's actions.

'Have you ever seen this man before?' He slid across a mug shot.

'It looks like the man who tried to set me on fire, but it was dark, and he had a hat on.'

'Can you please tell us more about the circumstances under which you encountered this man. What sort of mood was Constable Hammond in?'

Anya was tired, but recalled every moment of that night, as if it were a slow-motion movie in her head. Oliver let her speak. She gave him the facts as she saw them, without embellishment. She tried to be as logical and cogent in her recollection of that night's events as she could. Hammond had been kind enough to offer to help locate her mother. He didn't appear to be intoxicated or under the influence of any substances. He was calm and controlled, in her opinion, doing his job.

Both detectives took notes in addition to the recording.

Anya recalled how she had been confused when the gun was fired, momentarily disoriented after hitting the dashboard. She described seeing Hammond move in front of the car, gun poised to fire again, and the moment when she dropped to her knees to stop the chest haemorrhaging. She shut her eyes and breathed in.

'What is it? What are you noticing?' Oliver encouraged.

'Petrol. It didn't register before. I smelt it *before* the gunshot. It must have been on the car door.'

'Anything else?'

'There was another smell, even in all that rain. I couldn't pick what it was.'

Schiller flicked through his notes. 'The constable reported propane.'

'Propane is odourless,' Anya said.

'They put an additive with it so you can tell if a canister's leaking,' Schiller explained. 'That could be what you noticed.'

It was logical. She tried to capture the exact order of events. 'Leske must have splashed the car door with petrol just before, or even as, Simon fired.' It had to explain why he'd walked straight over to the car, eyes fixed on her. He'd approached and leant down through the window, and hadn't tried to hide his face, apart from with the hat. 'He did see me notice his tattoos. He didn't try to conceal them.' A former prisoner would know they were easily identifiable. She stared at the table, with a clear image.

Seconds later, when she had attempted to stop the bleeding, Mincer Leske had splashed her with what remained of the petrol and Hammond had yanked her away, just before it was lit. 'I think he intended to kill us both from the second Simon pulled over to offer him a lift. Simon was being kind to a stranger in a storm. If he hadn't read the situation so quickly and reacted . . .'

The enormity of what could have happened hit her harder than before. She clutched her abdomen.

'Let's have a break.' Oliver noted the time and moved over to stop the video camera.

He pulled his chair around to Anya's side of the table.

'Is this the first time you've talked through what happened?'

She felt a tightness in her chest. 'I guess with everything that's gone on . . .'

'You've been running on adrenalin since what was a life-threatening event. Your mother's friend dies and it's up to you to preserve a crime scene. A critically ill mother and hardly any sleep last night . . .' He lowered his chin to meet her gaze. 'Have you even told the people who mean the most to you?'

Anya still hadn't spoken to Ben or Martin. 'I didn't want to worry them.'

'For what it's worth, loved ones usually want to share what you're going through, and not just the good times.'

She wondered if he was speaking from personal or professional experience. His job involved investigating corrupt and self-destructive behaviour, as well as innocent police who were caught up in extraordinary circumstances.

'How about we leave you for a few minutes to make those calls.' Oliver left his phone on the table and closed the door on his way out.

Grateful, she dialled Martin's number. 'Hi.'

He immediately knew something was wrong. 'I've been trying all night to call you. I saw the news. The fire near your mum's place.'

'I'm okay, but Mum's in hospital after an adrenal crisis. She's been unwell for a while, and no one knew.'

'Hey, maybe that's why she never liked me,' he joked. 'If she's cured . . .'

She smiled. 'Medicine has its limitations. For that we'd need more than a miracle.' It felt so good to hear his voice again.

'Annie, what's wrong? You don't sound yourself.'

'It's been a hard few days.' She told him about her mother's friend dying, and how she had to stay a few more days to help Jocelyn handle the stress.

Martin understood completely. 'She's lucky to have you. So are we. Hey, if you want, we can come down–'

'No, please don't.' As much as she would love to see Ben, and his father, the time wasn't right. 'Everything's a mess here. I'm involved in a case and have been a witness—' She stopped herself. 'Trust me. You and Ben are far better off where you are. I'll see you as soon as possible, I promise.'

'Annie, it isn't just Ben who misses you.'

'It's mutual.' She looked outside the window. Oliver was waiting. 'Is my gorgeous boy around?'

'Right here, with ants in his pants, wanting to talk.'

'Hey, Mum, I don't have ants in my pants. Dad's being silly.' She heard him bouncing something like a ball on the floor. He normally did more than one thing at once. 'When are you coming home?'

'I've been with your nanna. She's sick in the hospital, but getting much better. I'll be back as soon as I possibly can.'

'Is she sick like Nita?'

'Her illness is different. I'm sorry, sweetie, but I have to go now. There are some policemen who want to talk to me.'

'Are you in trouble?'

She laughed. 'No. I'm helping them, it's my job sometimes. How about I call you later, then we can talk longer. Okay?'

'Dad, Mum has to go. She's gonna call later.' Anya loved the way Ben often repeated information. 'He says it doesn't matter if it's late.'

'All right then. I better go. Love you, and I'm sending you the world's biggest hug. To infinity and back again.'

'Love you too, to infinity and never back again.'

She hung up and held the phone, as if it still had a connection to home.

Oliver came back with Schiller. 'All good?'

She admitted he had been right.

Outside the room, Senior Sergeant McGinley boomed, 'I don't take kindly to threats.'

Through the glass window, Anya saw Samir Malik being escorted to a desk. 'I have a right to know what this is about.'

Oliver's attention was diverted. 'Excuse me for a minute.

Can you have a look through these and tell me if you recognise anyone?'

He laid out a number of photographs. They were from the protest she had witnessed at PT. He gestured for Schiller to go with him.

Anya recognised the spokesperson, the medical student, in a number of the pictures. Some of the vocal elderly tourists looked familiar as well. Then she saw something that surprised her. In the background, taller than the women, stood an imposing male figure, even beneath that cap. His mouth was open, fist raised, as if he were one of the protesters. She hadn't seen him arrive off any of the buses. She would have remembered someone with such a distinctive appearance. Mincer Leske had been in the crowd that day. What was a violent man like him doing at a food protest?

41

Anya watched through the window. Samir Malik sat, looking up. McGinley stood over him. Samir intermittently shook his head, then cast his eyes downwards.

Detective Parke ushered the senior sergeant away for a private word. Anya couldn't hear what was said, but Oliver stood with arms folded, while McGinley spoke in his ear, counting on his fingers. When he finished, the Internal Affairs investigator said something the sergeant baulked at. Oliver slapped his colleague's back and re-entered the interview room.

'Why is Samir here?' Anya asked.

'McGinley says the guy has a history of violence and couldn't account for his whereabouts when Len Dengate was shot.'

His gaze remained focused on Anya's.

'I saw him at the fire. He was on the northwestern boundary of Len's property when we released the cattle.' Anya wondered why the foreman hadn't disclosed that information. She decided not to mention the baseball bat. The man had looked desperate and was trying to protect the farm. All Grace had to do was speak reason for him to back down. 'His wife was with him. He wanted to stop the cattle from being released onto Len's paddock, but Grace said it was the only humane thing to do. He agreed.'

Oliver's brow furrowed. 'For some reason, McGinley omitted that piece of information.' He closed the blinds in the room, turned his chair around and straddled it. 'I was warned, unofficially of course, that this place is about to be on centre stage. The state government want to turn the island into a feed lot for Asia, and environmentalists are applying international pressure to stop development. Len Dengate seemed to be at the epicentre of one giant storm.'

'Not Len. PT was at the centre. He was convinced they wanted him ruined. His fiancée died at the research facility. Which is funded by PT and on their well-secured grounds.'

Oliver rubbed his chin. He scribbled something and tore off a piece of paper from his notepad, which he handed to Anya. 'We might give the interview a break. It's been a rough couple of days, and again, thank you for taking the time to assist in the investigation. We could resume tomorrow morning if it suits.' He stood up, collected his papers and turned the chair back to the table. 'All the best for your mother's speedy recovery.'

She looked at the note he'd written. On it was the name of a cafe in the main street of Longford and the time, 1 pm. She headed outside and shielded her eyes from the glare.

Across the road from the station, two women were involved in an animated discussion. From the back view, Anya recognised Alison Blainey's long hair. The other woman was petite with red hair swept back into a bun. She was the protest leader who had wanted to give the petition to Moss at PT.

Their conversation was heated and from the body language, argumentative. The representative for POWER crushed a cigarette beneath her shoe and headed towards the station, briefcase in hand. She slowed when she saw Anya and peeled off oversized sunglasses. Her makeup was heavy but couldn't hide the bruises or swelling on her face. Her left forearm was splinted with a fibreglass cast.

'How's the arm?' Anya asked.

She moved the fingers on her cast side. 'Don't know how I'll cope with six weeks of this, but it could have been a lot worse.

I'm grateful you and your mother found me, and helped the way you did.' She cocked her head and her hair flipped down her back. 'Is your mother all right? I heard she was rushed to hospital. I was in shock, but what she must be going through right now . . .'

Anya didn't want to talk about her mother with Alison, who may or may not have been involved in the fires, despite the fact that she'd been with Jocelyn when Len's body was found. She looked across the road. 'I've seen her before. Do you know who she is?'

'Madison Zane. She's a member of POWER's branch based at the university. They've been questioning her too, about Len Dengate, about the fire. Unfortunately, things go wrong when rogue amateurs try to make a name for themselves. They should have left the crop cutting to the experts.'

Anya squinted. 'Are you saying she's responsible for starting the fire?'

'We don't put lives at risk. There's a vast legal difference between vandalising a crop and arson. We know it. Do they?' She looked up at the door and straightened before going inside. 'Thank you again for what you did the other night. Helping me.'

'Do you have any idea who attacked you? Or why?'

'Could be a redneck who sees environmentalists as a threat. For all I know, I was in the wrong place at the wrong time.'

The woman across the road was on her phone. Anya waited for a passing car and crossed over.

'Excuse me,' she said, approaching as the conversation ended.

The woman looked back with a blank expression. 'I don't have anything to say.'

'I'm not a journalist, or police,' Anya explained. 'I was at PT when you tried to present your petition. My mother's a GP in Longford who was friends with a man who was killed that night.'

She looked around, as if checking Anya was alone. 'It's just . . . I can't believe any of this is happening.' She retrieved keys from a backpack on the ground and levered it over her shoulder. 'Now Alison Blainey wants the police to believe we set fire to PT. Why don't they ask her what she's playing at?'

Before Anya had the chance to ask what she meant a car pulled up and the student climbed in the passenger side.

Before closing the door, she called, 'Check out the video of the night. It's already gone viral. No one's admitting to posting it, but you figure it out.'

While Anya waited at the taxi stand, she searched for POWER and PT on her phone. A number of video clips came up. The third clip was a recording of a group of six wearing plastic hazard overalls and air filtering masks. Each carried whipper snippers and sliced through a crop of wheat. The clip was dated the night of the fire.

42

Anya got a taxi back to her mother's home and extracted the heavy parcel from the chicken pen. Thankfully, it was still in place and no one else had been around. While still hidden from view, she carefully unwrapped it. Inside were four A4-sized notebooks containing scribbled notes and handwritten data. None of it looked familiar or was immediately decipherable. It was already 12 noon. In an hour she was supposed to meet Oliver at the cafe. She took the notebooks and hastily replaced the floorboards as best she could, sliding hay and newspaper over the top. From outside the pen, nothing appeared altered. It was the only place she knew of that was safe. Someone had moved things inside the house, searching. But for what? It had to have something to do with Jocelyn's patient files. There was no reason to disturb them otherwise. Thieves would have taken the television, not moved papers across in front of the screen.

She thought of Simon Hammond collecting her carry-on bag and bringing it to her at the hospital. Maybe he had been looking for something and had used her bags as an excuse for being there. He had been so quick to shoot Mincer Leske. She strained to remember even the smallest detail. Had the stand-over man recognised the police officer? Was he the one Leske had wanted to kill, and Anya was just collateral damage? Had the plan been to kill Leske all along?

Simon had seemed to be doing the right thing after Len Dengate was killed. He and McGinley could have intentionally stomped all over the crime scene. By the time she had been called, the room had already been disturbed and altered. Was the fire a diversion to distract attention from Len's murder? The police should have honed in on what a violent criminal, just released from prison, was doing with a homemade flamethrower. Leske had to be a suspect in the fire as well as Len's death. Proving it was another matter.

Anya dug her fingers into her temples. She was beginning to sound paranoid and was seeing conspiracies all around her. Just like her mother before hospitalisation.

Wiping dirt and dust from her jeans, she headed back towards the house.

The only thing Anya did know for certain was that Oliver Parke had set up a secret meeting. He had to have a good reason. Or maybe some information that could help answer their questions. Grabbing her mother's keys, she locked the house and headed for the cafe in the hire car.

Within fifteen minutes she was at a table in the corner, with a white coffee and her laptop, checking emails. An email from Beatrice Quaid's lawyer was straight to the point.

Mrs Quaid is aware of Mr Dengate's unfortunate death and no longer wishes to claim damages or pursue litigation. She is concentrating on finding her daughter and grandchild, and will sue for custody if the situation arises. She wishes to thank you for your kindness and assistance.

Anya reread the message. The grandmother no longer wanted to mount legal action. It was possible she felt guilty after hearing of Len's death, or had lost the desire to seek revenge. She wondered what Quaid's response would be if she knew PT could have been directly responsible.

It didn't matter to Anya. Ben had a new-found obsession with *Star Wars*. Martin had attached a video of her son. It began with him standing beside a whiteboard with magnetic letters that spelt out the title of the movie series. As Ben hummed the theme song, he used both hands to slide the letters from the top to the bottom of the board. 'That's the opening titles bit,' he declared, and then proceeded to give a summary of the story about good guys 'versing' bad guys. Martin's voice whispered from behind the camera, 'Warning, retelling may take longer than the actual movie.' Ben acted out a battle with a toy lightsabre. Her gentle little boy was evolving into a child who liked nothing better than a fight scene. Still, she couldn't help but grin.

'Hope that's legal, whatever you're doing.'

Anya looked up to see Simon Hammond standing by her table. She snapped closed the lid of her laptop.

'Sorry, didn't mean to sneak up on you.' He surveyed the specials blackboard. 'Detective Parke asked me to drop this off and mentioned you were a fan of this place so I thought I'd try to be here first.' He seemed to be waiting for a response from Anya.

She shrugged. 'What can I say? According to Mum they do great coffee.'

The officer presented her with a sealed envelope and headed over to order from the counter.

She opened it and carefully removed the contents. Inside was the PM report for Patsy Gallop. Anya slid it back into the envelope. 'Thanks for bringing it.'

'Mind if I join you?'

Simon Hammond pulled back a chair. His hands were now wrapped in crepe bandages.

She reached across and helped. 'How are the wounds today?'

He sat and slowly wiggled each finger. 'Stiff and sore. How's your mother?'

'Doing better. Suspect she'll be dangerous after a couple of days' rest. Can you imagine her on steroids?'

He laughed and Anya tried to read his face for any sign that could reveal whether or not he was hiding something. A waitress arrived with a quiche and placed it down on the table in front of him.

'What did Parke want you to see?' He cut off a large piece of quiche and chewed with his mouth open. Steam came out.

'Len's post-mortem,' she lied. She didn't want anyone knowing she was looking into Patsy Gallop's death as well.

He finished chewing. 'Would it be a little . . . easier . . . for you if I read it?'

'No, but thanks. I was there this morning. Did you hear?'

'The big guy could have been murdered. I had a gut feeling, which is why I called you the first chance I got.' Hammond swallowed his mouthful. 'You know McGinley's questioned Samir Malik. Next he wants to question your mother. At the moment, he's pushing her as the number one suspect. No one saw her between when you had that fight and when Alison Blainey called the police at Len's. McGinley thinks the environmentalist was so hysterical when we got there, a lawyer could rip her statement apart in court. If your mother can't account for her movements, she'd better get a lawyer before saying a word.'

43

Anya sat in the car with the door locked. Tiredness flowed through her veins and she took a moment to mould her back into the car seat, feeling the warmth of the sun on her face. Oliver was unofficially helping out with a review about Patsy's death. She wondered if Len's murder was related.

Oliver had made sure she received a copy of Patsy's post-mortem report as soon as possible. Hammond had been keen to know what was inside the envelope. She dismissed suspicions about his possible motives as paranoia, and peeled back the envelope flap to slide out a series of stapled pages. The report lay on top. She wound the window down a little and sorted through the pages, stopping at the medical report on Patsy Gallop.

According to the notes, thirty-one-year-old Patsy had gone for her usual lunchtime run. She normally worked out of the TIAA building but was utilising facilities at one of the laboratories inside PT headquarters. Around 3 pm, she complained of acute abdominal pain, diarrhoea and dizziness following a meeting.

According to a secretary who suggested getting the company nurse to review Patsy, Reuben Millard instead demanded an ambulance be called, and the paramedics found her to be hypotensive, with a critically low blood pressure of 75/50. On arrival in the emergency department at Longford Hospital staff were concerned about an abnormality on her electrocardiograph, what was described as a prolonged QT interval. It could occur as a rare congenital condition or be brought on by certain medications. Either way, it was life-threatening.

She was having trouble breathing and arterial blood gases showed normal oxygen concentration, but a low level of carbon dioxide. She was hyperventilating and developing acidosis. One of the nurses noted her breath smelt strongly of garlic.

The doctor on call organised for urgent transfer to Launceston Hospital. The emergency team there continued fluid resuscitation and an infusion to increase her blood pressure. Blood tests showed high levels of potassium. She had begun to have short runs of a life-threatening abnormal heart rhythm. By now, her kidneys were failing and she was vomiting continually, despite administration of powerful anti-vomiting drugs.

She was transferred to the intensive care unit on a ventilator. Two hours later, she suffered a cardiac arrest. Despite every effort by the staff to resuscitate her, she was pronounced dead just after 7 pm.

Anya considered the possible diagnoses. A flu or gastroenteritis, in someone who had a predisposing heart condition. It did not escape her that food poisoning from E. coli was a possibility, although that seemed to be quickly discounted. An alternative cause was acute poisoning. The intensivist's notes described Patsy's breath as garlicly and her teeth slightly reddish.

Anya flicked through the pages to the post-mortem report, dated the following day.

The most notable features were oedema – fluid leakage into the lungs and brain. The liver was badly damaged, necrosed. Once she'd presented to hospital, Patsy's death was rapid and unpreventable.

Len Dengate had been at work in Hobart and hadn't made it back to the hospital in time. A toxicology screen was performed and, according to the report, results were pending.

Three knocks on the window jolted Anya out of her thoughts. She pulled the papers to her chest to hide the contents then relaxed when she saw Oliver Parke's face peering in.

He moved around the front of the car to the passenger side. Anya leant over and unlocked the door so he could join her.

'Anything interesting?' Inside, he opened a briefcase and pulled out an apple before clipping it shut.

'I haven't got to the toxicology report yet.'

'Selenium.' He bit into the crunchy fruit. 'They use it to make glass, rubber, photoelectric cells.'

She rested her head back. That explained the garlic breath, acute abdominal symptoms and reddish teeth. Selenium was an important component of the human diet, but it was easy to overdose on. Or be poisoned with. 'You forgot to mention that some antidandruff shampoos contain it. And it's in cold-bluing solutions to help stop guns rusting.'

'Which means almost everyone with a firearm could have it.' He sat forward and scratched the back of his head with his spare hand. 'She was dieting for the wedding, apparently, and watching everything she ate, exercising like mad. Could she have taken it as a supplement for a health reason – shiny hair, whiter teeth, some latest fad?'

'Only if she had prostate cancer, which I'm pretty sure we can rule out.'

He glanced sideways at her with a half-smile. 'I'll take your word for that.'

'Besides, regular small doses didn't kill her. She died from acute ingestion, so has to have consumed the selenium within hours of her symptoms becoming apparent.'

Oliver chomped down again on his apple. 'She worked in an agricultural laboratory. Any chance she accidentally ingested it, or spilled it on herself? Maybe inhaled it? I'm wondering if selenium was already in her system and her saliva. That's why it was found in her drink.'

'That isn't possible. Do you know where and how it was kept in the lab?'

'In the chemical cabinet. The only fingerprints on the bottle belonged to Reuben Millard. And,' he chewed, 'the bottle was empty. According to the prosecution, records indicate he'd ordered a new supply the week before Patsy died.'

She was impressed. Oliver had extracted a lot of information from the files in a short period of time. 'So the police think he ordered more so he could poison her?'

'Now, that's the thing. It hadn't arrived. The empty bottle they found was months old. And before you ask, McGinley seized the sports drink bottle from Patsy's belongings at the lab. It tested positive for selenium.'

The toxicity screen would have taken days, at least, to come back and selenium had to be specifically tested for. 'What would make a country cop automatically think of that? It could have been a flu, gastro, or heart failure for all anyone knew.'

Oliver rotated what was now an apple core, nibbling on anything edible that remained.

'Here's the thing. McGinley got lucky. Seems an anonymous caller tipped him off before Patsy Gallop's body was cold. The caller alleged Patsy and Millard had had an affair and Patsy had called it off. Jury took less than two hours to convict the vengeful, jilted lover.'

Anya knew how unusual a short deliberation for a guilty verdict was in homicide. If the jury were so quickly convinced, Len Dengate's support of Millard was even more remarkable.

Oliver exited the car and deposited the core in a bin, then took off his suit coat and lay it neatly across the back seat.

'What are you doing?' Anya asked as the detective walked around to the driver's side.

'Well, McGinley cocked up a crime scene, deliberately or through breathtaking incompetence. And now there are questions raised about a related case which, coincidentally, he was involved in. I have a job to do and thought you'd want to come along. Find out from the horse's mouth, so to speak. Unless you want me to go to Hobart by myself. No one visits Reuben Millard anymore. Didn't you hear? I got an anonymous tip-off, something about the investigation wasn't up to scratch.'

'Why are you standing there?'

'I like to drive. It helps me think. And you can read on the way.'

Anya hid a grin and climbed out.

'Fine.' She liked the way his mind worked and was interested to know what Millard had to say.

There was still hope that the truth Len wanted told would come out.

44

They headed south on the Midlands Highway.

'What do you make of Alison Blainey and POWER?' Oliver asked. Anya was surprised by the question.

'Not a lot. She instantly appeared after the health inspectors showed up, saying she could launch an offensive with the media, and deflect negative publicity by suing PT for ruining Len's organic status. She also helped organise the protest at PT the next day.'

He had one hand on the steering wheel, the other arm rested on the top of the driver's door sill. 'Where the ubiquitous Mincer Leske turned up. That brawl reminded me of the rumble between the Jets and the Sharks from *West Side Story*. And before you ask,' he hit the indicator and changed lanes to overtake, 'a girlfriend in high school made me sit through every movie musical from *South Pacific* to *Grease*.'

'Held you down and forced you to sit through all those films.'

'What can I say? It was the chivalrous thing to do. Mind you, Olivia Newton John in those black pants was the fantasy of a generation of teenage boys.'

'And the nightmare of adolescent girls who thought the only way boys would like them was to dress like that.'

He became serious again. 'Back to Alison Blainey and POWER. The way I see it, they promote themselves as David versing Goliath Corporations.' He tapped his wedding band on the steering wheel.

'Did you just say "versing"?'

'Technically, language is evolving and my kids use it as a verb all the time.'

'My eight-year-old does too.' It was something Anya had to adapt to.

'I'm curious about POWER,' Oliver said. 'Why would an international organisation bother with a small organic farmer who caused a deadly outbreak of food poisoning? It's not exactly a PR win for them. There's got to be another agenda.'

Anya reflected on the meeting at Len's home. 'Like GM crops. She said she tested for GM plants in Len's crop with a kit she carried. His spinach causes a bacterial infection never before seen in Australia and instead of concentrating on its origin, she tests his crop for GM contamination.'

'Maybe she thought the two were related. Could the GM seeds contain the bacteria?'

'I asked the vet to do some tests. I suspect it came from run-off from the feed lots, from the cattle manure next door at PT.'

'You and a vet worked this out but an environmental organisation couldn't.'

Anya wasn't sure whether to be offended or not.

They overtook a van with more than a dozen pushbikes on top. The tour bus was full.

'That's something I'd like to do some day. Cycle around this state.'

Anya preferred the car. It was safer on the roads.

'Do you think POWER employed Mincer Leske to provide some aggression at the protest and then set fire to the crop the next day?' Oliver asked.

Anya wondered. 'Alison was assaulted and had her arm broken. There was no sexual assault, just a beating, and it

sounds like it could have been Mincer's handiwork, although
Alison said a woman stopped her car and she didn't see who hit
her. She didn't exactly deny destroying the crop, but from what
I can gather she was trying to implicate a university branch in
the fire lighting. Penalties for arson are much higher than for
vandalism, it seems.'

'She should know. She is a lawyer.'

'Do you mind if we look into the medical student from that
branch who was arguing with Alison this morning outside the
station? Her name's Madison Zane.'

'No problem. If you can spare the time.'

Anya could. She decided to start looking through the notebooks she'd found under the chicken pen. She reached into the
back for the calico bag in which she'd stashed them. Inside one
of the books was a series of documents and PT emails. She first
looked at a flow chart: names circled with arrows connecting
them in various configurations. It looked like something her
mother had drawn in her giant scrapbook.

'What have you got?' Oliver enquired.

'I'm not sure. It's a whole lot of company names in a flow
chart. And individuals as well. Names I haven't heard of.'

'Try me.' Oliver quickly looked over, then turned his attention to a log truck ahead of them.

She read them out. Clarkson Evergreen. PT. Christian
Moss's name was on it. 'Minister Moss, Mr Progress, as he
calls himself, is on a committee about giving approval for GM
trials. It's also got the CEO of PT on it, Graham Fowler. He,
coincidentally, is on the board of the therapeutic medicines
association, responsible for approving medicines in the country.
Mum and I saw him and Christian Moss in a private meeting
the day before the fire.'

'Not surprising, they'd be meeting.'

'Moss said it was an emergency meeting to save tourism
and minimise damage to the economy following the E. coli
outbreak. Craig Dengate was there as well as Moss's chief of
staff. It was a private meeting but had been arranged well before

the E. coli scandal even became public. A researcher from the Tasmanian Institute of Agricultural Advancement, which is on PT property, was there too.'

'Curious.'

The car slowed. They were temporarily boxed in by trucks.

Anya followed the links from Christian Moss's name. They extended to a Chinese name at the top. The Chairperson of Clarkson Evergreen. PT was beneath, alongside four other companies. Graham Fowler was also on the board of a government-appointed committee on science and development.

On the surface, it looked like a large number of companies, but the same names kept coming up, like an incestuous family.

One name she hadn't seen before was on an email. She checked. 'One of the men who works for the legal department at PT is mentioned. His name is Jerry Dyke.'

'How do you spell it?'

Anya spelt it out.

Oliver pulled over into the emergency lane and stopped. 'Can I see?' He looked across at the flow chart. 'Something's missing.' He pulled out a pen and wrote before handing it back to Anya and returning to the traffic.

Reuben Millard.

'What's the connection?' Anya had no idea.

He tapped the page with his left hand. 'Dyke is the lawyer who defended Reuben Millard in the homicide trial.'

45

A phone call to the university was put through to Madison Zane in the Department of Medicine building at the university. As head of the Medical Students' Association, she was easily locatable.

She recognised Anya immediately and looked alarmed when Oliver walked in.

'Am I being arrested?'

'No, we just want to talk to you, about the protest and the night of the fire,' Anya said, explaining that Oliver was present for unrelated business.

Madison seemed resigned to another interrogation. 'The other researchers have lectures today, so we have this place to ourselves.'

'You made good time coming back,' Anya said.

'I had to. I need to get experiments set up.' Her flat shoes made a short scuff on the lino floors. She moved gracefully, back straight, feet slightly turned out. She could have been walking onto a stage at the ballet. 'I still can't believe the minister didn't take our petition.'

'What was the petition about?' Oliver asked.

'We want a moratorium on the government approval for PT to conduct human trials of GM foods like corn, soy, linseed and wheat in Australia, at least until their safety is actually established.'

'Who's we?' Anya was curious to know how wide-reaching their organisation was. The one Alison Blainey accused of being amateur.

She recited a list. 'Medical students, Doctors for a Better World, mothers' groups, senior citizens, Wise Up Australia–'

'Okay, that's a lot of people,' Oliver admitted.

Anya wanted to know, 'Are you aware of the outbreak of E. coli cases at Livelonger Organics?'

'I read it was a new strain and resistant to antibiotics. That was just the first one that went public.'

'Do you mean there have been other infections?' Anya was surprised the doctors hadn't mentioned it. 'How do you know?'

'Half of our state is a laboratory for GM experimentation. PT and its owners are in the business of creating mutations. They inject bacteria and viruses into plant DNA, and animal DNA into plants. Nature evolves to survive and they found a way to inject a suicide gene into seeds.'

'Can I ask something?' Oliver interrupted. 'Why would you want seeds to die?'

'So they only survive one planting.'

Oliver looked perplexed.

'That way you sell more, because to grow the plant again next season, you'll have to buy more seeds That's what they're in the business of selling. Suicide genes mean there'll always be demand.'

He raised his hands in surrender. 'Why don't people just buy seeds somewhere else.'

Madison squinted her eyes as if trying to work out whether he was joking or missing her point. Either way, the discussion was going nowhere. What about other infections. How many other children like Emily Quaid would suffer?

'You mentioned other infections?'

'They may take some time to appear. There's no guarantee that the organisms they inject into DNA and RNA will be broken down by normal digestion. For the past twenty years, people have been consuming what are essentially foreign bodies, things to which our bodies have not previously been exposed. Is it any wonder food allergies are a pandemic? Our bodies haven't had the chance to evolve to cope with it all.'

Anya was surprised the medical student knew so much about it. She looked around the lab. Bottles of energy and sugared drinks were lined up in a row, each labelled with a number from one to ten. In front of each was an index card of ingredients. They included the iced tea her mother regularly drank.

'PT and companies like it make it difficult to trace anything back to its source. Sure, they try to cut down on the risk of things like infection in their foods.'

The medical student had a broad knowledge and moved from one topic to the next. The mention of infection piqued Anya's interest. Len Dengate's spinach had been infected and he had some of PT's plants growing in his fields.

'You said they cut down infection risk. What sort of infection risk do their plants have?'

'Sorry. I didn't explain. They don't just manipulate plants and seeds. They produce Frankenmilk, beef and other meats too. They use toxic chemicals on top of the chemicals they've already introduced into the food chain. Did you know PT change the animals' diets, castrate them, then inject artificial hormone replacement to accelerate growth. If that isn't enough, after slaughter, the company either irradiates the meat products or washes them in ammonia. It looks like red meat, but what part of it is natural?'

'Makes you want to become a vegetarian,' Oliver shook his head at the concept. 'Is that even legal?'

It must have been. Anya had seen the cattle with the plugs behind their ears releasing growth hormone and other chemicals like testosterone on the night of the fire. 'There is some logic behind it. Castrated cattle are easier to control and produce leaner meat, which is what certain markets demand. They are manipulating nature for maximum profits.'

Madison was on a roll. 'PT has its fingers in lots of money making pies. The parent company, Clarkson Evergreen, already makes pharmaceuticals, so why are they investing in things like malaria vaccines or vitamins incorporated into rice? Why not just give people the vitamins or vaccines?'

It was a good question. Glenn Lingard mentioned the potential for augmented foods but Anya hadn't questioned the true motive.

Oliver nodded for Madison to go on.

'Because a vaccine would cure the disease. Eventually there's no demand, like for smallpox. But . . .' She hoisted herself onto a bench. 'If they put it into the rice, people will be dependent on those seeds, ones that can't be reused, to maintain their immunity. It's extortion. They're drip-feeding nations with a cure that only works if they keep eating the product.'

'That's completely illogical, not to mention morally questionable,' Oliver concluded. 'Why are these companies so keen to own land here? Between higher wages and the costs to reach their export markets, how is business even viable here? Why not just produce in China?'

'I wish our politicians asked the same question. Our laws say you don't have to label GM foods if they are used in restaurant meals or processed food. Export markets to Europe, Canada and the UK have dried up because of public opinion forcing legislation to outlaw them. This is the only country in the world that has approved human trials for GM wheat. It appears in Tasmanian bread and no one's told.'

Anya understood the reasons for concern. 'Because bread is considered a processed food.'

'Look,' Madison said, sliding down from the bench. 'Don't get me wrong. It's possible that GM wheat with increased fibre and a lower glycaemic index could be a good thing, and prevent things like bowel cancers. My thesis,' she pointed to the bottles of drink, 'is looking at GM sugar inserted with leptin.'

Oliver interjected, 'Isn't that the hormone that switches off hunger?'

Madison's face brightened. 'Right. In theory, it's a great idea. We need to find out more about how it affects consumers. People I know who drink these are weight conscious, but never drink just one. They're supposed to be full, but they guzzle at least two to three a day.'

Anya thought of her mother drinking the iced tea from a bottle. In preference to almost anything else.

'Clever marketing?' Oliver offered.

'It has to be more than that. So far, people are going back for the drinks that contain the GM sugar. It's as if it's addictive. At least, that's my hypothesis. I have a year to prove or disprove it.'

Jocelyn wasn't likely to fall for the marketing blurbs aimed at young people. It had to be something in the taste or delivery of the drink. Anya wondered if it had anything to do with her mother's new immune condition.

'The iced tea. Is there a chance that has GM sugar in it?'

Madison grabbed a pen. 'Yes. Why? Do you drink it?'

'My mother does and she's just become unwell.'

'In any of these drinks, preservatives and even the artificial sweeteners can contain GM bacteria as well. How many of us have a clue as to what we are really putting in our bodies and how much that contributes to the incidence of disease?'

Oliver rubbed his chin. 'Then how can long-term effects be measured? Surely it's got to be a nightmare to trace back.'

Anya knew that in the past fifteen years there had been an unprecedented increase in the numbers of allergies, immune conditions like coeliac disease, and food intolerances diagnosed. Not just in Tasmania, but worldwide. It also coincided with an explosion in the number of cases of autism and attention deficit disorders. Doctors were better at diagnosing all of those conditions, but that didn't necessarily explain the exponential rise. That period of time was how long GM foods had been in the food system, in multiple forms.

'You get it.' Madison's shoulders and neck relaxed. 'They can't be accountable for any long-term consequences. In US supermarkets, up to ninety per cent of the products contain corn syrup made from GM corn. Now corn has become one of the top food allergies around the world. Only no one's withdrawing corn syrup from the market or banning it in schools.'

The facts were staggering.

'Medicines are controlled and are only approved after rigorous, peer-reviewed long-term studies. The process of publishing medical research is arduous and many studies get rejected, which means the results can't be considered valid. The same standards don't apply when our food is manipulated and chemically or genetically altered. PT can do their own testing, and select which results they make public to support their cause.'

'So how do we get the government to intervene?' Oliver seemed enthusiastic about taking up the cause himself.

'All we want is more independent scientific rigour. Not just the three-month studies on pigs or rodents that the laws stipulate. Like I said,' she picked up the iced tea, 'this stuff could actually help with the world's obesity pandemic. But what if the sugar or its substitutes turn out to be as addictive as cocaine?'

Madison was well informed and remarkably articulate about the facts. Anya wanted to know why she and Alison Blainey had argued. 'Aren't you and POWER on the same team?'

'We're considered a branch of POWER but recently we've become disillusioned by them. We want facts and civil discussion. They're only interested in campaigns that bring them lots of publicity and donations. POWER's campaigns aren't evidence-based. They're reactionary.'

'What you're saying,' Oliver ventured, 'is your enemy's enemy isn't necessarily your friend.'

'You should be investigating Alison Blainey,' Madison added.

Anya moved away from the sample drinks. 'Why?'

'She's supposed to be this big shot crusader against PT. What's the first thing she does when she gets to Livelonger Organics?'

Anya flicked a glance at Oliver. 'Tested the crop for GM contamination.

'The kit was in her car, right?'

'That's what happened,' Anya agreed.

'Then she offers to sue PT. If she's so clever, why didn't she know that no one's ever won a case against them? It's the way Clarkson Evergreen and all its companies like PT operate. The moment they know their seeds are on someone's property and that property hasn't paid for the right, they sue for breaching their patents. Courts don't care if the seeds blew in or were washed into their fields. They always find in favour of PT.'

'If it isn't the farmer's fault?' Oliver argued.

'That doesn't matter. Farmers in Canada, Mexico, and the US have been bankrupted because courts determined they had infringed seed patents. PT is a powerful company. They have *never* lost a case like that.'

Anya let the statement sink in. Alison Blainey did have her own agenda, and it had nothing to do with saving Livelonger Organics. As a lawyer who was familiar with Clarkson Evergreen and PT's histories, she would have known they would not win a case against the company for contaminating Len's organic crop.

It was as if her actions worked in favour of PT. Maybe someone knew she was working for the enemy and the assault was a warning.

Whatever her real agenda, the assault hadn't deterred her. Alison seemed determined to finish what she started.

46

At the prison, Anya left her bag in the visitors' locker, wishing she'd had more than a brief glance at the material that had been buried under the chicken pen. Oliver carried a notepad and pen. She carried two of the journals. After being scanned, patted down and quizzed, they were led into a room with eight plastic tables fixed to the floor. Nothing in the room could be smashed or used as a weapon.

Anya felt claustrophobic in prison visiting rooms. This was a maximum security facility for some of the state's most violent and deadly offenders. One had shot six people from his workplace. Another had beaten a police officer to death.

They had the space to themselves. A female officer waited with them.

'What sort of prisoner is Millard?' Oliver casually asked.

The Amazonian corrective services officer stood with her hands clasped in front of her. 'Decent. Never talks back, never causes trouble. Keeps to himself but sure loves getting his magazines.' She huffed. 'Gets a real spring in his step a couple of days before *Scientific American* arrives.'

A small, thin, stooped and bespectacled man was led into the room, hands cuffed together.

'There you go, Dr Millard,' the male officer said. 'These

are your visitors.'

'Thank you, you've been very kind.' The small man rubbed his wrists once the handcuffs had been removed and studied Anya and Oliver. 'Have we met?'

'No,' Oliver explained. 'I'm Senior Detective Parke and Dr Crichton is a pathologist and forensic physician. We wondered if we might ask you some questions.'

'Let me guess. I'm a suspect in the Lindbergh baby kidnapping? Shooting Martin Luther King?' He signalled to the guard. 'Experience has taught me the hard way. You can interview me with my lawyer present. If I still have one.'

Oliver took the lead. 'I'm reviewing a case that may be connected to yours. It may shed new evidence on what happened to Patsy Gallop.'

Soft brown eyes widened and Millard inched forward a little in his chair. He reminded Anya of a wounded animal unsure whether or not to trust someone offering help.

'New evidence?'

'Len Dengate was found shot.' Oliver let the news sink in. 'He's dead.'

There was no hint of pleasure in the news. Millard shook his head. 'Poor fool. Just couldn't leave it alone. Are the police calling it suicide?'

Oliver glanced at Anya. 'Leave what alone, doctor?'

The prisoner sat back and slowly shook his head. 'It's over. There's nothing anyone can do now.'

Anya wanted to know why Millard assumed Len's death had been deemed a suicide, and why he didn't seem to accept that Len could have killed himself. She lifted the book from her lap. Seeing it, Millard reached across the table with one hand, the blood draining from his face. The female officer stepped forward.

'No physical contact, Reuben.'

'Sorry.' He pulled his hand back. 'I just . . . It was Patsy's.' He almost seemed frightened. 'Did Len give it to you?' His eyes darted back and forth between them. 'God, that's why he's dead. You don't have a choice. If you have families of your own, you have to destroy it.'

Oliver shifted in his seat and Anya felt unnerved by the reference to their families.

'Can you tell us why you're so worried?' She gently slid the book across to him.

He stroked the cover with one finger before opening it.

'We studied rats to test the safety of some of the seed crops being developed at PT. This is one of Patsy's logbooks.'

It looked like a kind of shorthand, interspersed with figures and tables. Recorded observations, methods and outcomes. 'Can you decipher it?'

'I'm the only one left who can. I know it by heart. But, like I said, it has to be destroyed.'

The trio sat in silence for a few moments.

'Is that all?' Reuben moved his chair back.

Oliver sat, elbows on his thighs. 'It's not as if you have a revolving door of visitors.'

Reuben looked to the guard in the room.

'Man's got a point,' she said. 'What's it gonna cost you to talk a few more minutes?'

'Okay,' Oliver asked. 'Why did you keep liquid selenium in the lab?'

'Simple, there was a deficiency in the local soil. Sometimes the mice were fed diets from food grown in other areas. By excluding selenium deficiency in all the subjects, we excluded an important variable that could have affected the results. The liquid was easy to administer to the animal feed in droplet form.'

'Was that documented in the study findings?' Anya asked.

'Most definitely.' He opened the book and flicked through a few pages. 'Patsy recorded the daily doses.'

He found an example and turned the book around for Anya. 'Se', the chemical symbol for selenium, was the abbreviation used.

'She recorded the dose in terms of micrograms and drops. You see,' he pointed to a line on the page, 'they were the equivalent of two-ounce, or 59 ml to be exact, bottles, containing twelve teaspoons or twenty-four half-teaspoons. Each half-teaspoon contained one hundred micrograms of selenium. With this viscosity a half-teaspoon contains twenty drops of that specific liquid formulation. Therefore, five drops were the equivalent of ten micrograms.' He sat back, arms folded.

'Why were you the only one allowed to touch the bottle?'

'I wasn't. Patsy pipetted the dose out each day. She wore protective gloves so her skin wouldn't be burnt by spills.' He looked as if he were watching the scene.

'It's understandable. Working so closely together. Same goals and passion for science?' Oliver left the comment hanging.

'I've never been attractive to women, detective.' Millard let out a sigh. 'I deeply admired her. She was exceptional. Vibrant, extremely intelligent and insightful.' Another sigh. 'I was never even in her league. Len was good to her. She shone every time she saw him. Anyone could see it. If you're asking if I ever had intimate relations with Patsy, the answer is no.'

'Did she know how you felt about her?' Anya asked.

He made eye contact with her. 'Patsy was the best research assistant and friend I ever had. Why is it so difficult for people to understand that it was enough? I didn't want anything to change that.'

Anya believed he was being honest.

'Why were the police convinced you two had an affair?' Oliver questioned.

Millard inhaled and looked upward. 'They claimed they found love letters, emails from my computer to hers.' His eyes became dull. 'I saw her every day and she was engaged to another man, also my friend. We worked at a research centre, but everything was owned and paid for by PT. The computers were company property. Why would I have done that?' His leg began to jiggle beneath the table. 'Not that it matters anymore.'

The man sounded innocent, yet seemed defeated, as if he were resigned to his fate.

'Why did your lawyer fail to offer a defence on your behalf?' Oliver knew more about the case than he had let on, particularly about what had become of the lawyer.

'He said the jury would see through the prosecution's lies.' He placed both hands on the table. 'Is that it?'

Oliver leant closer. 'Jerry Dyke was wrong. He didn't even put you on the stand to defend yourself. He failed in his duty to you.' He paused, letting the words sink in. 'And within weeks he was on the payroll of PT.'

The convicted killer's expression remained bland. 'Unfortunately, detective, there are no laws against that.'

There was no hint of anger in his voice. In psychiatric terms Millard presented with a flat effect. Lack of emotion or variation in mood. Anya wondered if Patsy's death, the conviction and prison had broken what spirit he had. Or he really was a cold-blooded killer, without a modicum of remorse.

She wanted to know if anything could get him more animated. 'From a scientific perspective, do you regret working there?'

Millard cocked his head and licked his lips. 'In the beginning I was hopeful of the new technologies. In the field of molecular genetics, possibilities are only limited by our imaginations.' His eyes began to lighten, and for the first time, there was expression in his voice. 'In the right hands, this technology could change the world. Just like Salk did with the polio vaccine.' His eyes moved between Anya and Oliver. 'Do you know he could have made billions but decided not to patent it, as a gift to the world? I wanted to be like Salk.'

Anya genuinely wanted to know, 'What changed?'

'Funding. Universities are now reliant on corporate funding for research. Look at the USA for a prime example. Research is purely there now for commercial development. Inserting a gene to make a rose blue isn't going to help the world, but if there's a dollar to be made by fans of blue roses, funding will back it.'

'What if the research isn't favourable to the company?' Oliver asked. 'Scientists are supposed to declare financial interests, conflicts of interest, in publications.'

Millard was beginning to warm up. 'I was reassured my work would not be censored.'

Anya shifted in her seat and the chair leg scraped the floor. The guard looked up from a magazine, and they continued. 'Was it?'

'It's no coincidence that companies that make the most toxic chemicals known to mankind – tobacco, chemical weapons and pesticides – now control the food industry. Ask yourself what would make them even wealthier? Is it any surprise they're buying up patents for vaccines and medicines? Inserting genes into some of the pesticide-resistant plants resulted in the creation of new, unintended proteins. They were fed to cattle without being adequately tested. Was this reported?'

The question was obviously rhetorical.

'In the US, they get away without adequate testing because they *miraculously* fall into the category of GRAS.'

Anya was unfamiliar with the acronym.

Oliver knew. 'Generally Recognised As Safe.'

'Exactly!'

Oliver's knowledge seemed to impress and engage Millard.

'Because they're seeds,' his forehead and eyes became more dynamic as he made the point, 'they automatically get a free safety pass. No proof required.'

'It's difficult to get how that is even possible,' Oliver added.

'Money is power. You pay off government officials everywhere. Anyone against GM foods, like a lot of Europe, is accused of restrictive trade practices, and being anti-progress. The funny thing is, regimes that were big on genetic engineering and using people as human guinea pigs were known to commit some of the worst atrocities in history. The Nazis were the ultimate fascists. How is this different? Of course, third-world countries are the first to be taken advantage of. Clarkson Evergreen has planted their own people in important government positions in countries like Indonesia, Brazil, Bangladesh, Sudan, now Australia, New Zealand, Canada, and the US.'

It sounded like something from the Cold War, with 'sleeper' agents infiltrating influential government agencies, except that this was considered capitalism, adeptly practised by a Chinese communist government. Anya thought of Samir and Grace, and the tragedy their families had suffered. 'What sort of health issues can the new proteins you mentioned cause?'

'Allergic reactions, cancer, immune diseases . . .' He stopped himself.

It was exactly what Madison Zane had said.

'Believe me, I was idealistic and thought I could make a difference. Only it's all about profit. Industry funds universities. Whoever controls the funding controls the outcome.'

Anya felt for this man. Instinct told her that Len had been right about him. 'You could appeal your conviction. Your lawyer obviously had a connection with your employer.'

He offered a half-hearted smile. 'I don't believe in God or the afterlife. It may not be much of a life in here, but I have more than Patsy. And now poor Len.' He bowed his head.

Anya had one more question. 'What do you think happened to them and why?'

'You seem well intentioned, but you have no idea what you're dealing with.' He slid the book back across to Anya and stood up. Before the guard escorted him out, he turned back. 'You need to destroy this and any others you may have, while you still can.'

'Before we go,' Oliver casually enquired, 'know anyone who goes by the name of Mincer Leske?'

Millard's shoulders tightened and his blinking became rapid. 'Never heard of him.'

47

It was late afternoon by the time they left the prison. Anya felt rung out after the events of the past couple of days. She had no objections when Oliver asked if he could drive on the way back.

She held the books tightly in her lap. It seemed odd that Reuben Millard wouldn't defend himself or challenge his lawyer's advice. He had assumed Len's death was a staged suicide. But hadn't said why.

'What are you thinking?' Oliver asked.

'Two scenarios. Reuben Millard loves prison life, or he really thinks he'd be killed if he appeals his conviction now.'

'Did you see his reaction to hearing about Len's death?'

She had. There had been a hint of sadness, but no surprise or shock. 'Not what you'd expect from someone who wanted vengeance if Patsy had chosen another man over him.'

'I agree. There wasn't the slightest sense of satisfaction, or relief.'

If he'd been acting, there would have been little to be gained by feigning sympathy for Len. Millard had also refused any offer of help looking into his case.

'Maybe he believes in karma.' Drizzle began to fall. 'The windscreen wipers are on the left side.'

'Thanks.' Oliver kept his eyes on the semi-trailer in front of them. 'Why do you say that?

'I think he feels guilty about the work he did for the company. He may think he's paying the price for other wrongs.'

'That's the bit I don't get. If he felt that guilty, and there was something revealing in Patsy's logbooks, why not expose them? Why does he want them destroyed? What possible incentive does he have for remaining silent?'

Anya tried to see it from Millard's point of view. His colleague was murdered and he had been framed and imprisoned. Now Len was dead, and he believed it would be written off as a suicide. If he were innocent, what would prevent him trying to prove it? 'Maybe someone else has been threatened. Does he have a family?'

'Father died years ago.' Oliver checked the rear-view mirror. 'Mother passed away last year. No brothers or sisters. Never married.'

'You said he didn't get visitors anymore. Who used to go see him?'

'Vince Chan, vice president of product development at PT.'

It was definitely time to take Glenn up on his offer to tour the laboratory. 'I know someone who's working in that area.'

He seemed interested again in the rear-vision mirror. They were headed north, back on the Midlands Highway. Anya checked her side mirror. Behind them was a red Torana followed by a white Commodore.

'Why did you want to take this car to Risdon?'

'Someone's pretty interested in what we're doing. Don't turn around, but we've been dogged since we left the prison. We weren't tailed on the way down to the university. My guess is, someone at the prison tipped off our secret admirers.'

He slowed and hit the blinker before pulling over to the side. The rain was constant but not heavy. He stopped and hit the hazard lights before stepping out and opening the bonnet.

The Commodore slowed and cruised by. Tinted windows disguised whoever was inside. It looked like a government vehicle.

Oliver climbed back in and rubbed water from his cropped hair. 'Let's see if they loop back. There's a U-turn bay not far ahead.' He was studying his watch.

'Two minutes.' The car appeared on the other side of the road.

Anya knew the road well. 'I can get us onto back roads from any of the turnoffs.'

'We have another couple of minutes before they loop back on us again. They may assume we've taken the next one, so let's shake them up.' He watched until they were out of sight. Anya quickly closed the bonnet and they headed north again.

She found the calico bag behind the driver's seat and put the logbooks away.

'How nervous do you think we should be?'

'I'm not sure. You were at Len Dengate's PM. Chances are he was murdered and it was staged to look like a suicide. Reuben Millard seems nervous for our lives then we're followed. I'm thinking there really is something important in those books.'

Anya had to agree. 'The sooner we find out, the safer we'll be. I still subscribe to the "knowledge is power" concept. Besides, if they know we've got the logbooks, they're going to assume we've at least read them.'

It would take a few hours to go through them without interruption. Anya had an idea. 'I know somewhere at Arthurs Lake. A cabin we can use where no one will disturb us.'

'Is that our only option? You should know. I'm married and I would never–'

Anya exclaimed, 'Neither would I! I am just trying to get us to a safe place.'

'Just felt duty-bound to clear up any possible miscommuni-cation.' His face reddened. 'Will a car arriving cause a problem for neighbours?'

'Cabin used to get rented out so they'll assume it's tourists.'

He stopped briefly at a service station. Anya refilled the tank while Oliver went into the shop. As she went to pay, Oliver returned with two full shopping bags. Bottled water, bags of chips and Twisties were visible through the plastic. The man's stomach seemed like a black hole.

Back in the car, he pulled out a packaged car cover. 'Just in case.'

Reuben Millard's instructions to destroy the logbooks had definitely rattled him as well. Anya drove from there. The roads were better than she remembered, but the weather made them difficult to navigate. Passing through sheep farms, rain now sheeted down. The windscreen wipers swished at maximum speed as the wind buffeted the car in gusts. A log truck passed in the opposite direction and the car rocked with the closeness.

Oliver's arms tensed on the dashboard. 'Are you sure you don't have to be a mountain goat to get in and out of here?' They passed fewer farmhouses on the way up to the mountains. Soon the vegetation was sparser, and the terrain rockier. Still, the occasional dead Tasmanian devil lay squashed on the road, casualties of nocturnal travels.

Anya thought of the snow chains her father always kept in his boot. The cabin had been known to have snow around it, even in summer. After what felt like hours, she steered down the familiar gravel drive to the wooden cabin. Outside, the air was at least fifteen degrees colder than it had been at the prison. Oliver patted his arms and offered her his suit coat but she hoped wet weather gear was still kept locked in an inside cupboard.

'Not a fan of the weather, but this is pretty amazing.' Oliver surveyed the view of the lake. It was still and the quiet was only disturbed by the rain and occasional duck call on the water. A mist had already begun to descend on the surface. 'Guess this belongs to a relative.'

'Something like that.' Anya's father had spent many weekends fishing with friends up here. He still rented out the shack in winter to tourists who appreciated the snow and remote location. Her father wouldn't be there now. 'Trout fisherman's paradise.'

Going by the amount of dirt and dust on the wood pile cover, it hadn't been visited in a while.

While Oliver put the car cover over the Commodore, Anya moved to the back section of the wood pile and reached her hand under. A hand-carved wooden box still hid a key with a leather tag attached, embossed with the words, *Love Shack*.

'So much for security.' Oliver rubbed his hands together. He took some deep breaths, which condensed as he exhaled.

'From memory, it's colder inside.' Anya grabbed some logs of wood, careful to check for spiders, and unlocked the door.

Oliver followed with some kindling from a box next to the chopped wood.

Anya had remembered rightly. Little had changed inside the cosy cabin. She wiped her feet in the wet area designed for boots, coats and waders. The room contained a wooden table with four chairs, a small stove and an oven adjacent to a sink. Against the side wall was a bar fridge.

She switched on the power in the fuse box inside the door and shivered. The temperature was rapidly dropping as night approached. She prepared a fire as Oliver explored the basic bathroom and two small bedrooms, each just large enough for a double bed. The same key unlocked the cupboard, and she produced two waterproof jackets.

'This is really homely. My kids wouldn't like it, no freezer for the ice-cream.'

'In winter, you just bury it in the snow.' It had been one of the things she'd loved doing with her father. 'Once we left the milk in the car. Next morning it was frozen solid.'

'Speaking of milk. . .?'

Anya suspected he was thinking of his stomach again. She arranged the kindling and pointed to the cupboards above the sink. 'Try there.'

'We'll never run out of long-life milk packs.' He pulled out a couple of cartons. 'Just in case anyone pops in, there's still six months left on them.' He rifled through the cupboards. 'We have two-minute noodles, cup-a-soups and . . . four tins of tuna in oil, instant coffee, tea bags and biscuits. I call dibs on the chocolate chip ones.'

She wondered how many brothers and sisters he'd had growing up, or if fatherhood had made him more childlike at times. 'You sound like my son,' she mused, appreciating the lack of pretence. Ben was always fun to play with, and not remotely interested in the self-imposed inhibitions of adulthood.

She lit the fire starters, kindling and a large piece of wood in the combustion stove. Within minutes, radiant heat filled the kitchen area and the kettle was on the stove top. A warm drink would take away the chill she felt in her bones and help her concentrate on the task at hand.

Oliver set up a work station at the round all-purpose table.

Something had been nagging at Anya all day. If PT knew what their products could do, they were potentially responsible for the deaths of anyone who consumed those products. Without accurate labelling of products, it would be impossible to source the illnesses or allergies back to them. Anya thought about what Madison had said about the way PT treated its beef.

'If PT did irradiate or wash the beef in ammonia in the abattoirs, they must have known the cattle could carry infections. They wouldn't want it being traced back to their meat products.'

'Which means they did make some effort to make sure their products were safe.'

'At what cost? The consumers don't get a choice. Would you deliberately feed your children meat that's been irradiated, or washed in ammonia?'

'No way,' Oliver said. 'To be honest. I don't get it. Has society gone that litigation crazy that producers are having to protect themselves even if the meat is eventually served under-cooked on someone's table?'

A piece of wood cracked in the fire.

'The cattle are packed into feedlots and stand in their own manure. Faecal material is all over their hooves and lower legs. It could transfer to the carcasses in abattoirs and end up on the meet in the skinning process.'

'Does that sound crazy to you? Instead of moving the cattle out of their own manure, you introduce radiation or toxic chemicals to the beef, so people won't get sick.'

He was right. It sounded like something in a comedy skit to prove people had lost sight of the point of eating: nutrition and sustenance. 'They either didn't think about the possibility of water contamination or run-off from the feed lots, or they knew and ignored it. It's made worse because of what the cattle are fed. Corn alters the stomach acids, so new forms of bacteria can find their way into the manure.'

'And therefore the food chain.' Oliver put his hands behind his head. 'You'd think farms produce the best, freshest and healthiest food. If spinach you think has been washed can kill you, what hope is there?'

Anya moved over to place more wood in the fire. 'The vet said one of PT's cows developed a leg abscess a few months ago, with a new strain of E. coli identical to the one that caused the food poisonings. She's checking the manure samples now. If they match, it would explain how Len Dengate's crop became infected. The feedlots are upstream from where he planted his spinach.'

The detective returned to his laptop and started clicking away.

'PT brings whole new meaning to what the protesters called Frankenfoods. Take a look at this.' He showed her a picture from POWER's website of dairy cows pumped with hormones to increase milk production. The udders were abnormally huge and must have been painful for the animals.

'What a mother eats or drinks goes into her milk. So they're pumping hormones into cows that will get into the stuff we force our kids to drink to be healthy. How many of us have no idea?'

Wind lashed the branches in the trees outside the cabin.

Anya thought of how quickly Evelyn had become critically ill. It was only luck that had prevented hundreds of deaths. PT was playing roulette with people's lives. And it was owned by one of the most profitable companies on the planet.

Oliver's phone rang. He checked the number before answering. 'Speaking . . . She's here now.' He handed across the phone. 'It's Steve Schiller from Hobart homicide.'

'Hi Steve.'

'Just wanted you to know. We found Jenny and Mia Quaid. Alive.'

Anya drew a deep breath and imagined Beatrice Quaid's relief. 'That's fantastic news. Where, how?'

'They were hiding out in a yacht down in the harbour. Owners were overseas and hadn't accessed it for a month. Someone reported a break-in and we found Jenny cowering with her little girl. They haven't eaten much, but doctors say they'll be fine.'

'Does Beatrice Quaid know?' The grandmother's prayers had been answered.

'She's on her way to the hospital now.'

'Beatrice may not know that Jenny can't read or sign anything without help. She said her daughter ignored the lawyer's letters, but she may not have been able to read them, so may not know about the custody fight that's taking place.'

'I'll talk to the grandmother. Jenny's been to hell and back. She thought she'd killed Emily by not preparing the food properly. Been off the electricity grid and hadn't seen or heard the news. At least now she can be there to bury her child.'

'Will she be charged with anything?'

'Doubt now the prosecutor would go for negligent homicide or manslaughter for not getting medical attention in time. Maybe interfering with a body, but the way Emily was placed wasn't disrespectful and she died in the house so it might be difficult to make that case. Jenny didn't report the death. My guess is the chief prosecutor will think she's suffered enough.'

Nothing would bring Emily back. But hopefully, the Quaids could form a family again.

'Can you find out where she got the vegetables from for Emily's diet? We still don't know if there's another possible source of the infection.'

'Ahead of you there. The market she helps out at barters with seasonal employees of Livelonger Organics. She gives them bread for vegetables. No receipts, so we couldn't trace it, but she was sure it was Livelonger spinach.'

It seemed PT – through Livelonger Organics – was the only source of the infection. They couldn't argue contamination from other sources. Anya thanked him for letting her know and handed him back to Oliver at his request.

The kettle whistled and she lifted it off the stove. Collecting mugs from the cupboard, she made two cups of instant coffee. Long-life milk was optional.

She placed one in front of Oliver on the table.

'None whatsoever?' he was saying. 'It had been wiped completely clean. Thanks. Let me know whatever else you find.' He hung up and dumped two sugars into his coffee. 'Len Dengate's shotgun? The metal trigger had no prints on it. Pretty clever to shoot yourself in the gut and bother to wipe clean the trigger mechanism and dispose of the cloth in the couple of seconds before you die.'

Len's death had to be considered more likely to be a murder now, if both Alison and Jocelyn denied wiping the gun clean. The crime scene may not have been secured, but from what Simon Hammond said, no ambulance officers were present when the police arrived. McGinley was alone in the room when they were in the kitchen, but what reason would he have for wiping the trigger clean?

Oliver knocked his mug and spread coffee on his notes. He moved the cup away and pulled out a handkerchief to wipe down his files.

It reminded her of how the files at Jocelyn's house had been moved.

Her relief about the Quaids being found was short-lived. 'I think someone went through Mum's house while we were at the hospital.' She realised how odd it must sound but if Len had been murdered, maybe someone was looking for the documents he had hidden in the chicken coop. Whoever followed them from the prison could have begun at her mother's house.

'Some of her files were moved around. It doesn't sound like much, but I know exactly where they were left. To anyone else, the place looks like a horrible mess, but I know they were moved.'

'Anyone you suspect?'

'Two people I am aware of were in the house. My godmother and Simon Hammond. Simon brought my carry-on bag to the hospital so I'd have something to change into.'

Oliver squinted. 'Do you still have the envelope he gave you?'

Anya retrieved it from the calico bag. It was yellow and unremarkable.

'I put a dab of lemon juice from my salad across the seal.'

He moved over to a reading lamp by the sofa and held the envelope in its light.

A splodge appeared. 'If he'd opened the envelope and didn't want you to know, he would have just put the papers in a fresh one. This is the original I sent.'

'You were testing Simon Hammond's honesty with invisible ink?' She almost laughed. With all the advanced technology at his disposal, Oliver used a child's trick for secret messages.

'It works and it's legal. In my job, you can't trust anyone. I don't like that he's been in your mother's place without you there.'

'He's a country cop. It happens. It could have been someone else.'

'I still don't like it.'

'There was someone else who had been in the house. Glenn Lingard.' Anya remembered that he had made the bed because of Audrey's back problem and been at the crisis meeting at the restaurant with Moss, his assistant, Craig Dengate and the CEO of PT, Graham Fowler. If Glenn was somehow involved in Len's death, Audrey's life would be shattered as would the lifelong friendship between Audrey and Jocelyn.

She watched Oliver. Working the way he did and suspecting everyone he came across must be isolating. In some ways, she felt similar. She pulled out the logbooks.

'I know all about psych lab reports, but not so much about biological science,' he admitted.

The principles were the same. Three books documented a study over a period of three months, and ended two weeks before Patsy Gallop was killed. Anya selected the first book by the earliest date. Patsy had painstakingly recorded every aspect of the study.

There were four separate groups of female mice. Males were excluded to avoid pregnancies complicating the results. Each group contained twenty-five animals. One was a control group, fed non-GM grain from northern New South Wales. The second was fed GM corn from PT's crops. The third group lived on non-GM corn. The fourth was provided with a diet of GM grains. Each mouse was three weeks old at entry and weaned from its mother.

Every animal in the study was labelled so it could be weighed and measured – seven days a week. Every entry was in Patsy's handwriting. Either she had transcribed someone else's data, or checked every mouse herself each day for the duration of the study. Patsy even noted the batch numbers of food and the selenium bottle from which the daily doses were administered. Reading the behaviour and observations of the mice was tedious, to say the least.

Oliver stepped into the bathroom to make a call. She thought it odd that he was making a call in the coldest room in the cabin.

She began to read through the police report.

'Got anything?' He returned to the table and moved his chair closer.

'Patsy recorded every detail about what the mice were given, including the batch number of the selenium bottle. I can try to work out how much was used, and how much might have been left in the bottle the day she died.' It sounded even more like a long shot as she verbalised the thought. 'There had to be a reason Millard made a point of telling us about the drops and teaspoons in each bottle.' The detective didn't dismiss the idea. 'Consciously or not, I believe he wants us to investigate.'

Anya located the specific page. There was a photograph of the bottle, and another enlargement of the label, with batch number visible. She found Patsy's first notation for the matching selenium. On a separate piece of paper, she tallied up the number of drops each day and counted the days selenium was administered, in case the dose was intermittent.

She calculated that the amount of selenium added to the food sources totalled twelve drops per weekday, or sixty drops per week. That amounted to a teaspoon each week for the duration of this particular experiment. Each bottle contained enough selenium solution for exactly fourteen weeks. Anya double-checked her calculations. Before allowing for spillage or drips, there had to be a maximum of one teaspoon remaining after that time; a maximum of one hundred micrograms of selenium. That was not enough to overdose on.

The fatal dose of selenium could not have come from the bottle in Reuben's laboratory.

48

Oliver sat back down at the table.

'Are you absolutely positive there wasn't enough left in the bottle to give Patsy a lethal dose?'

Anya handed him the calculations to check again. He multiplied, added, then cross-referenced the bottle numbers.

'We know the second bottle hadn't arrived.' Oliver circled the final figure. 'There was a maximum of one to two millilitres left in the bottle, which is how much in dosage?'

'One to two hundred micrograms. It isn't enough to give Patsy the toxic levels that were discovered in her blood and urine.'

Oliver clicked his pen. 'So where did the selenium in Patsy's drink bottle come from?'

'And who else had access to it?' Anya flicked through the files. A forensic scientist had printed out a chromatograph analysis of what was left in Patsy's drink bottle. She had been running that lunchtime and left a small amount unfinished.

There were a number of spikes on the page, each one representing a different chemical. Selenium caused the highest peak, but there were also references for three other substances: sodium, sucrose and monopotassium. The chemist's report suggested the results could have been caused by previous substances contained in the bottle, or whatever it had been last washed in.

Obviously, Senior Sergeant McGinley and the prosecution team hadn't thought about the logistics of how he could have poisoned someone with the contents of a bottle that didn't contain enough to harm anyone. Neither had Millard's defence lawyer. Reuben could now have grounds for appeal, if he decided to change his mind. Jerry Dyke's employment at Clarkson Evergreen raised more suspicion now.

'Selenium is a supplement and can be bought over the counter at pharmacies, health food shops and even some supermarkets.'

Anya agreed. 'A lot of people can access it. Who knows how many people?'

Oliver was on his feet. 'Anyone could argue that Millard knew how poisonous it was in excess. He could just as easily have added tablets to her drink that day. Or . . .' He paced back and forth. 'He carefully extracted the selenium from the bottle in the lab, and replaced it with water. So Patsy was administering water, not selenium, in the mice feed.'

The second option didn't make sense. 'If he went to all that trouble, why wouldn't he just throw out the empty lab bottle and remove incriminating evidence that had his fingerprints on it?' Anya showed Oliver the report. 'Another chromatograph, of the dregs in the lab's selenium bottle, proved the liquid was pure selenium, not water. The contents can't have been replaced.'

'Then we need to find out who else had access to Patsy's drink container. My guess would be at least Len Dengate, the secretary in the lab, and maybe the cleaners if she left it there overnight.'

Anya's stomach quietly grumbled.

Oliver opened a packet of biscuits and offered her one.

She took it. 'Whoever killed her had to have motive and opportunity.'

The detective agreed. 'Reuben warned us to destroy these logbooks. If he really is innocent and knew the logbooks could prove it, it makes no sense that he wants us to destroy any chance he has of being exonerated.'

Anya thought back to how he believed being in prison was better than being dead. He was still scared someone would target him, even in prison. 'Mincer Leske was only recently released from Risdon, wasn't he?'

'Did you see Reuben's demeanour when you mentioned his name?'

She had. The blinking showed he'd been unnerved.

'Police haven't released Leske's name yet to the media. That meant Reuben wouldn't know he was dead. Seems Mincer's girlfriend and child haven't been located, so they haven't been able to notify them. Once they're found and told, the police will be free to make the news public.'

Alison Blainey had described being stopped by a woman with a child before she was beaten on the road. If Mincer committed the assault, he could have used his girlfriend to set it up.

If Millard was afraid of Leske, maybe he had good reason. 'Could Millard have been the real target and Patsy died by mistake?'

'Unlikely. According to the police report, the poisoned drink bottle was bright pink and had a printed label with Patsy's name on it.' He pulled up the image on his screen. 'Which means the killer is either unbelievably dumb or deliberately set Millard up.' Oliver devoured the bag of corn chips he'd bought. 'I need some protein. It helps me think.'

'There's tuna.' Anya reminded him of his early find.

He shoved his hands into his trouser pockets. 'My mother used to make this concoction with tinned food from the cupboard on a Friday night. Tuna, peas, creamed corn all together. Still gag at the thought.'

Anya would have settled for anything right now. Her head throbbed, and she felt like there were three-inch nails in the back of her skull. While the detective took notes in between handfuls of junk food, she grabbed some aspirin from a zip purse in her bag and swallowed it down with water from the bathroom tap.

Oliver swung his jacket around his back and slipped his arms inside. 'I'll bring us back something from that roadhouse we passed. Just in case, don't answer the door to anyone.'

Anya didn't have to be reminded. Someone had followed them from the prison. Whoever it was had more than a passing interest in who visited Reuben Millard. She moved to the door and clipped the lock behind Oliver.

She Skyped Martin's number on her laptop. There was no answer at home, or on his mobile. Next, she contacted the Launceston Hospital, who put her through to Jocelyn's bedside phone. She was surprised when her mother answered.

'Darling, I hope you're not working too hard.'

The chirpy tone took her by surprise.

'Mum, is something wrong?'

'No, darling, of course I'm doing what I'm told. Sergeant McGinley's here to take my statement about the other night. He says he also has some questions for you about the night of the fire.'

Jocelyn was warning her.

'We had a bit of car trouble and decided to drop in at Uncle Arthur's,' Anya lied, hoping her mother would realise where she was. Uncle Arthur was what the family jokingly called her father when, after weeks of planning, he spent a weekend at the lake and came back with only one or two fish.

'He'll be so pleased,' Jocelyn played along. 'Even if Arthur can fix the engine, you'll be too late getting back to drop in tonight. And don't worry about trying to call, the phone reception at your uncle's is impossible.'

'Talk soon, Mum.' Anya hung up. Her mother wanted Sergeant McGinley to think she had broken down and was out of contact. Jocelyn didn't like to be pushed, especially by men wielding authority.

Anya made another coffee and thought of Len Dengate. Someone had gone to the trouble of killing him and staging a suicide. Livelonger Organics was facing ruin but Len still would have owned the land. His small business wasn't large enough to threaten a corporation the size of PT. If getting hold of his land was the motive, then Craig Dengate had to be a prime suspect. That was if he were unaware of the will change. The police could argue that Jocelyn must have known about the will because it was hidden on her property, and she was first on the scene. Len trusted her implicitly and would have let her into the house. There had been no obvious sign of a struggle. To get that close to him, someone had to have surprised him or known him well.

Anya shuddered and folded her arms tightly across her body to stave off a draught. Len Dengate may have been killed for whatever was in these logbooks. He was convinced he was being watched and followed, which is why he buried them under the chicken pen. Jocelyn had even said 'These walls don't have ears' in the restaurant. Len's paranoia was looking justified now, especially since she and Oliver were followed from the prison. Someone still wanted the logbooks, whether they were incriminating or not.

She put another log in the combustion stove and closed the door, feeling the heat rise in her face and hands, and went back to reading about the experiments. A thud sounded outside. She stopped reading and listened.

Another thud.

Someone was outside. Oliver had been gone a few minutes. She moved to the window and looked out. No sign of the hire car.

Wind howled and the bedroom door inched open. Anya grabbed an iron frying pan. It was heavy and could do damage if swung hard enough.

Thump, then another thump. She edged towards the kitchen window and saw a kangaroo on the wooden verandah. It was foraging and bounded off when she tapped the window. After listening for another few minutes, she relaxed and returned to the table. The frying pan remained within reach.

For the first seventy days of the selenium study, it seemed everything was routine. All the mice fed and grew consistently, although it appeared the mice in the two GM groups grew bigger and heavier. Whether or not that was statistically significant was yet to be determined. The recordings and observations were repetitive and occasional words difficult to decipher. Patsy had used her own kind of shorthand at times, or her handwriting was hard to read. On day seventy-nine, two of the mice in one of the groups became sluggish and refused to eat. Their growth rate stalled over the next week. By day eighty-six, another two in the group had become unwell.

On day ninety-one, three of the mice in the GM seed group died. Here, Patsy's notes became more detailed. She performed necroscopies on the animals. Mouse 42 died earliest and was found to have a large stomach tumour. Mouse 46 had ovarian cancer. Number 28 had tumours growing in its liver and spleen.

Eight days later, another four mice were dead, including two in the GM corn group.

Anya wrote down the causes of death. Gastric tumours were the most common, followed by endocrine organ damage and bowel cancers. In the non-GM groups, all the mice survived and appeared to have been in good health.

Reuben Millard and Madison Zane had both mentioned allergic reactions as well. Millard had specifically said cancer. The GM foods in the experiment were causing cancer in the mice. A gust of cold air interrupted and the wooden door slammed closed. Oliver hung his coat on the back of his chair and warmed himself by the stove.

'A tree is down and blocking the road out. We'll have to make do with tuna and crackers.'

Anya turned towards the stove. 'I've found something.'

He vigorously rubbed both hands and stepped closer to peer over her shoulder.

'The study they were working on. The mice in two groups developed cancers after about three months.' She looked up at the detective. 'It was in the groups fed PT-grown corn and grain. Genetically modified varieties. Necroscopy showed damage to endocrine organs, like adrenal glands and the pancreas.' It didn't escape Anya that her mother had a rare immune disease affecting the adrenal glands. The registrar at the hospital had been shocked by the number of cases in the north of the state. It was possible GM bread and corn products sold to locals had something to do with the abnormal rates of disease. The locals were completely unaware due to the absence of labelling on the products. Madison, the medical student had made some interesting points.

'That would explain why there was selenium left in the lab bottle, if the research was shut down prematurely and the corn and grains abandoned.' He slid his laptop across the table to the adjacent chair. 'Let's just do a literature search . . . Seems there was something about GM seeds put out by the University of Tasmania eighteen months ago. Let's see if the mainstream media picked it up . . . Oh. This is interesting.' He sat back and moved the screen around so Anya could see. 'After extensive research and studies, the Minister for Agriculture proudly declared the seeds were safe, so could be planted, grown and consumed without risk or concern.'

So safe that PT was injecting millions more dollars into the area. Photographed were Moss and one of the men she and Jocelyn had seen at the restaurant: Graham Fowler, chief executive officer of PT.

'We just found ten million reasons to keep this study quiet. The crops are already in the food supply and have been for a while.'

Oliver stretched his arms over his head. 'Why not just sack the research team? Why kill Patsy? Reuben Millard was in charge. He was the one with the reputation in the scientific community.'

'Maybe he was the target after all.'

He rubbed his eyes with both hands. 'The pink drink bottle had her name on it.'

'Exactly. These logbooks exist and were hidden. The killer had no way of knowing they hadn't already been copied.'

'Or that they would surface one day, like now.'

It was beginning to make convoluted sense to Anya. 'If you can't destroy evidence of the study, the next best thing is to make sure no one would ever take the results seriously.'

'So rather than kill the lead researcher, you discredit him. And what better way to do that than have him convicted of the worst crime?' Oliver hit his forehead with a palm. 'Murder. And make it look like a scandalous love triangle. That way, you kill two birds with one stone, so to speak.'

Anya was relieved the theory made sense to the detective. 'Nothing Reuben says or does has credibility after that.'

Reuben Millard had been the target. Killing Patsy Gallop was a means to that end.

And someone else knew it and was now dead. 'Len Dengate had the logbooks so was aware of the cancers in the GM group,' she reasoned. 'Once Millard was charged, the logbooks lost their impact.'

'That explains why he supported Millard.' Oliver walked to the cupboard and pulled out two bowls before pouring out the Twisties. 'Want some?'

'No, thanks.' Anya refilled the kettle and put another log in the stove. The heat was making her mouth dry. She couldn't think of anything worse than salty snacks. With corn in them. She asked to look at the pack and read the ingredients. It was an Australian company but there was no mention of GM corn used in it. Madison's comments about labelling had been disturbing.

'Something has to have changed recently.' He crunched into a mouthful.

'Media and public health departments focused on Len when his crop became infected with E. coli. The POWER group heard about it and became involved.'

Oliver typed something into his laptop and then turned his screen towards Anya again. 'Your medical student's right. I did a search and it seems that PT's affiliate companies make a habit of suing anyone found to have PT's patented seeds growing on their property. It's their modus operandi. They've been getting away with it for years.'

Alison Blainey had tested for the GM seeds, with the promise of saving Len if his crop had been contaminated. She knew precisely what would happen when she made the information public.

POWER had organised the protest and taken responsibility for cutting down the crop, but denied setting the fire.

Alison Blainey was using Len and POWER for her own reasons. Anya just had to work out why.

49

At ten o'clock, Oliver went outside for the second time and was back within minutes.

'Two guys are using a chainsaw but said it'll take hours to clear the road. Are you sure it's the only way out?'

Anya hated being cooped up, but knew that driving in the storm would be more dangerous. If one tree was down, chances were that others had fallen as well. The wind howled outside the cabin as rain pelted the tin roof. A draught gusted beneath the front door, sending shivers up Anya's legs. As a temporary measure, she shoved rolled-up newspaper into the gap between the door and the floor.

Oliver's phone rang. He checked the screen before answering. 'Great . . .' He located the pad and pen and scribbled down some figures and a page of notes. Afterwards, he thanked the caller and put the phone down on the table. 'Looks like our thug for hire came into a fair bit of money recently. Over four days, Leske's girlfriend deposited sixteen lots of three thousand dollars into their account. Not bad for a couple who are unemployed.'

'Let me guess,' Anya said. 'She said she won it at the casino.'

Casinos were notorious for money laundering. Punters walked in unchecked with wads of cash. All they had to do was put money into poker machines, then cancel the transaction. The machine printed out a note to cash that didn't differentiate between a refund and a win.

'I've never won a cent at one, but guys like Mincer and his partner manage to consistently rake it in on slot machines. Uncanny, isn't it. If we get tapes from Launceston and Hobart casinos, we may find she won it in miracle time.'

Oliver referred to his notes. 'The money was deposited at different branches, in cash. Amounts less than $10,000 don't normally arouse suspicion. That same month he asked the prison to change his home address to a property not far from PT headquarters.'

Anya straightened. 'Craig Dengate was the only real estate agent at Cressy. Len's brother may have rented it to the girlfriend.'

'No renting. He paid a deposit with a $50,000 bank cheque from his account. Total sale price was $200,000.'

Leske hadn't struck Anya as the farming type, let alone an environmentalist keen to protest. 'Maybe having a child had made him want to reform. The land was his way out. He saved all the proceeds of crime.' Anya was reaching for an explanation but could no way see how a property would sell for as little as $200,000.

Oliver paced the small living area, hands on hips. 'You'll never believe it. Told his parole officer he won the money. Then the day he gets out, he sells the property. For a sweet two million dollars.'

Anya frowned. Mincer's actions didn't make sense. His presence at the PT protest just before the fire had bothered her. It had frightened her that the man had no intention of being taken in by Hammond. Mincer chose a quick death rather than capture by trying to set her on fire with him after the shooting. 'He had to have been into something big, like drugs, guns, murder. For him, arrest or even being recognised wasn't an option, even if he had weeks or months to live with his cancer.' She tapped the table. 'What if he was paid to stir up trouble at the protest and start the fire that night?'

The detective reached into his briefcase and pulled out a file. 'PT wants the protesters questioned about the fire. At the very least, they want them charged with trespass.' A series of ten-by-six-inch photographs was attached with a paper clip. 'Journalists took them. McGinley and his colleagues are trying to identify the alleged *insurgents* from police records.'

'You'd think he would have at least hidden his face better. Here, he's staring straight at the camera.' It was as if he challenged the photographer to click.

'Can you honestly see this guy working for environmentalists then bashing Alison Blainey?'

Anya couldn't. 'More likely he bought the Cressy place to set up a business away from prying eyes. It would be perfect for something like a meth lab.'

He chewed on another biscuit. 'If you're setting up a drug supply network, you'd want to keep a low profile in the area. Guys like this don't normally dirty their own nests.'

Anya thought about his eyes almost daring the camera to click. 'Protest groups are definitely about publicity. Endangering lives other than their own only loses them supporters and brings a barrage of criticism.'

'Isn't all publicity supposed to be good?' he asked. 'They certainly got it. Tasmania and the troubles at PT scored a feature on CNN news after that.'

Anya couldn't help wondering. 'What if Len Dengate was the real target that night? Mincer could have killed Len and started the fire to cover his tracks and divert attention. Almost worked, the way McGinley carried on.'

'Even if Mincer pulled the trigger that night, we'd need to know who he was working for.'

Anya's head ached. They were going around in circles. Someone had gone to a lot of trouble to destroy Reuben Millard. She kneaded her temples. Reuben had reacted when they'd mentioned Leske's name.

'You should get some rest,' the detective suggested. 'I'll let you know when the road clears.'

She had no energy left to argue. Anya decided to lie down in the first bedroom. She closed the door.

She was woken from a deep sleep by knocking. 'Anya, the road's clear. Thought you'd want to get back.'

The temperature in the room had plummeted without the heat from the stove. Her arm muscles quivered as she lifted off the woollen blanket and padded out to the living room.

Oliver sat hunched over his computer, looking as tired as Anya felt. He had notes spread across the table and a flushed face. She stood in front of the stove, drawing all the heat possible into her body. 'What time is it?'

'Two in the morning.' He arched his back and stretched his hands behind his head. 'Mind you, I think I've just got more work done in these few hours than I'd get through in a week at the office. Something about the air.'

'Or the peace and quiet,' she offered. 'It's why my father loves this place so much.' She filled the now empty kettle. A shot of caffeine would help her drive back. 'Any progress?'

'Not sure. As far as I can tell, everyone's connected.'

'Welcome to Tasmania,' she quipped.

'I'm not talking blood relations. I mean Christian Moss, the Minister for Everything, seems to be friendly with just about every business interest in the state. The state government has forged a special relationship with China, it seems. Christian is quite the traveller. From what's been in the papers, he's managed at least eight trips to Guangzhou, aka Canton, and all in the past two years. Guess where the global headquarters of Clarkson Evergreen is located? He keeps company with some pretty prominent Chinese politicians.'

He packed up his computer and notes. 'On the way back, we can check out the property Mincer bought.'

Anya wondered if he was in command of his senses. 'You're seriously suggesting we just pop in on a possible meth operation?'

'It's the neighbourly thing to do.' He grinned. 'We can check out the local real estate agent while we're there.'

Anya scraped her hair back into a bun with her fingers. 'You want to visit Craig Dengate as well. At this hour?'

'I hear country folk are early risers. May even catch one off guard.'

50

They drove on in the dark, Oliver using his smart phone as a GPS to guide them to the address of the property Mincer Leske had purchased. There was still a sold sign out the front. It described one hundred and twenty hectares of fertile land, the equivalent of more than five hundred blocks of land where Anya lived in Sydney.

The road was unlit and cloud cover made it darker than usual.

The headlights lit the sign. It described 'the potential for mixed farming with a proven history of high-yielding crops'.

'They mention poppies in the list of crops. Maybe Mincer was moving into the pharmaceutical trade,' Oliver suggested.

Anya got out of the car. The air was too cold and damp to stand out in comfortably. With the engine off, the place was eerily quiet.

Oliver climbed out of the passenger side, and accessed the torch app on his phone. He walked to the milk can mounted on a metal pipe that served as a letterbox and lifted the back. He reached in with one hand, then ripped his hand out. Anya rushed forward and saw an oversized spider scurry away. Out here, it could have been venomous.

'Did it bite you?'

He vigorously shook his hand before letting her see. 'I hate creepy-crawlies.'

'No puncture marks. You're fine.' Oliver may have been bright and intuitive, but he hadn't learnt not to stick his hand in a dimly lit hole without checking for hidden dangers. 'You always have to check your shoes before putting them on too.'

Anya hoped this was the end of his curiosity.

'Nothing here. No letters, flyers.'

She wondered what he had expected to find. She borrowed the phone and read the for sale sign more closely. It was a three-bedroom home with a bathroom. Soils ranged from red/brown loams to heavy black alluvial soils. Stock water was pumped to troughs from dam storage. The realtor had made a point of mentioning every potential feature. It must have had something horribly wrong with it to be sold for $200,000, even with the threat of fracking taking place within its boundaries.

'Good news,' Anya quoted. 'The property is not burdened with imbalanced capital improvements.'

'Sounds like my place. Only our agent referred to it as a renovator's dream.'

Anya wondered why anyone with a young child would buy this place. For the money, Mincer could have bought something a lot smaller and still made a living off the land if that's what he had intended.

'Come on.' Oliver was first back in the car.

'To Craig's place?' She clipped on her seatbelt.

'We should let him have a bit more sleep. Let's have a quick look around here. Like I said, if there's anyone there, we'll hightail it out.'

Anya didn't like where this could be headed.

'Mincer's dead. We know that. Partner's not here. Remember, his death still hasn't been made public. Police have already searched the place for her and you assume they would have found a meth lab if there was one here. Once word gets out about Mincer's death, this place will be buzzing with reporters.'

She started the engine. 'Then what do you expect to find?'

'Something. Anything that gives us a clue as to what he was up to.'

Anya drove slowly along the road to the house, manoeuvring over potholes and divots.

Oliver was right. The place looked abandoned. Even the shed was missing a side.

A rusted shell of a tractor, minus wheels, was dumped to the side of the house. It couldn't have looked less inviting to potential buyers.

'Looks like it's been abandoned for years,' she thought aloud.

'Anyone who bought it needed capital to get it up to liveable standard.' Oliver had the phone torch on again and was out, up the steps to the porch before she could stop him. 'Look out, there's an old rake. Don't tread on it,' he warned, directing the light at it.

'Five minutes. That's it,' she said, avoiding the rake. 'And first sight of anyone . . .'

Oliver peeked in the windows. 'Empty apart from mess.'

He pushed against the front door and it gave way. 'See, it was open, we won't have broken in.'

'Just illegally entering, trespassing,' Anya said, blowing into her icy hands. She was still outside. 'This is crazy.'

'Promise, we'll be quick.' The detective took a step and his foot disappeared through the board. He managed to keep his balance, and lift his leg out. Luckily, the suit trousers and his calf were undamaged.

Stepping back outside, Oliver shone the light on the splintered and crumbling wood.

'Mincer had to have wanted the land as an investment. This place is riddled with vermin. The house has got to be uninhabitable.' A loud bang made Anya jump. The door had slammed shut.

A gust of wind caught her hair and the porch rattled.

As they turned away from the house, they were met with a growl. Anya was no dog expert, but something like a pit bull terrier stood between them and the car, poised to attack. She dared not move or speak. Her heart instantly sped up. This was a vicious animal and judging by its bony frame, it hadn't been fed recently.

'Down,' Oliver tried in a non-threatening but firm voice.

From what she could see, the bone-crunching animal didn't have a collar on. It bared its fangs that caught the moonlight, and barked at them. And again.

Anya looked sideways for something to defend them with. A small broken piece of wood on the ground was out of reach and probably wouldn't keep the dog at bay anyway. Their only hope was to get inside, with it on the outside, but it was too close for them to make it in time. Anya stayed frozen.

Oliver gently slipped his arm out of his jacket as the dog barked again before growling. 'If it attacks, it should come for me.' He slid the other arm out with minimal movement and wrapped the jacket loosely around his left arm. The act seemed to inflame the dog further.

'I don't like this,' Oliver quietly shared her sentiments.

That was enough to provoke the dog. It shot forward and locked on to Oliver's forearm. Anya leapt over the railing onto the ground and grabbed the old rake – just as a shot rang out. Deafened, she spun around, rake in her hands.

The detective stood over the dog on the porch, suit jacket still in its mouth.

Oliver's gun was ready to shoot again.

She carefully approached. The dog was dead. 'Why didn't you tell me you had a gun?' she demanded.

'Didn't want to scare you,' he managed.

51

Oliver was given the all clear to leave hospital. He had been lucky to sustain only mild scratches to his arm. The jacket was the price he paid. She left him to be collected by Steve Schiller. They had homicide cases to discuss.

By the time she arrived in the intensive care ward, Jocelyn was already dressed.

'I feel twenty years younger,' she announced. The medical registrar was in the room.

'I don't need to tell you how important it is to take your hydrocortisone and attend for follow-up.'

'No you don't. I never want to feel that bad again.' They said goodbye. Audrey had been to visit. Glenn was going to be busy preparing for a business trip to China so had offered to show Anya around PT this morning. Otherwise it would have to wait until he returned. 'Should have seen Audrey's face when I said I wanted to chaperone you two.'

Jocelyn was definitely better. Her eyes were bright again. Nothing was going to stop her discovering the truth behind Len's death.

After a quick detour to her mother's so Anya could change her clothes, they arrived at PT and parked by the cottage shop before walking towards the boom gate. Jocelyn seemed to have more energy than Anya, with a full dose of hydrocortisone in her system.

A camera was visible on the guard's station. A guard looked Jocelyn up and down in her jeans, long-sleeved shirt and scarf. Clearly, she wasn't a high-flying business executive. Anya's business jacket over jeans received less overt scrutiny.

A call confirmed they were on the list for a visit.

'It's easier to get in and out of prison,' Jocelyn complained as they trudged up the hill to another car park and entered PT headquarters through a white metal detector. Their bags were placed on an X-ray scanner by one security guard and examined by another.

'Think we just left Kansas,' Jocelyn muttered once they were released inside a giant glass atrium. They could not take their eyes off the central feature. A circular glasshouse with lush trees and plants reached skyward. They could have been in a land like Oz. Green glass sculptures decorated the spacious and light-filled lobby. It was a stark contrast to the homely cottage shop beyond the boom gate.

A Eurasian woman scanned herself through train-station-style gates and greeted them with a beaming smile.

'Welcome to the future. Your host has been delayed, so we have time for a tour.' She led them through a door and down a white corridor to a number of parked golf carts. It felt like they were entering a movie studio.

Within minutes they rode through a number of hothouses containing strawberries, tomatoes and trees that produced both lemons and limes.

'Impressive, aren't they?' The guide proceeded with a monologue. There was little opportunity for interaction, and it definitely wasn't invited.

'Beneath us are silos for food storage. We believe we must be prepared for the inevitable food shortages that will come with population expansion.'

'How do you stop the products from going off?' Anya asked.

'Our wheat is mould and drought resistant. Imagine the potential for feeding people in Africa.' Given the security and underground networks, PT headquarters was more like a wartime bunker than a multinational corporation. She stopped the cart, stepped out and scanned her ID by the double doors to the lifts.

'She's either an automaton or was a pharmaceutical rep in a past life,' Jocelyn whispered. 'Memorise every word and never deviate from the script.'

Before the lift doors opened, the escort handed them each a glossy booklet. Anya flicked through the first few pages, filled with tables, photographs of scientists in white coats, farmers on the land and topic headings like *Sustainable Future*.

After a short ride in the lift, they stepped out into the foyer and were greeted by Glenn. The guide handed them to their host and Glenn led them through another security section, to another set of lifts. The building was much more extensive than it appeared from the outside. He scanned his ID.

'How do you get to come and go between buildings if you work for the TIAA?' Anya asked.

'As part of the arrangement with the Tassie government, PT funded the TIAA building and allows researchers to use their own laboratories which are . . .' his eyes widened, 'incredibly state-of-the-art.' He seemed genuinely excited to show them around. In a shirt, tie and dress trousers, Glenn looked every part the professional.

'So PT owns our supposedly independent Institute of Agricultural Advancement,' Jocelyn concluded.

Glenn ignored the comment. 'I'll show you the sensory lab first. It's like a Disneyland for food.'

They rode to the fifth floor. The antiseptic smell in the corridors gave it the feel of a hospital. The rooms were all glass-walled. People working inside were visible, like fish in an aquarium.

Around the lab, there were odd-looking machines on benches, with paper plates containing snack foods laid out.

Glenn's phone rang and he excused himself to take the call outside. Anya watched him through the glass.

Jocelyn moved to an end wall where she looked at a cabinet full of glass or perspex containers, each containing a single item of food. 'Is this an experiment?'

'No,' Glenn said as he came back in, and seemed a little self-conscious. 'It's PT's Hall of Fame.'

'That top one looks like a hamburger patty.'

'It is. As far as sensory-specific satiety goes, these foods are close to perfect.'

Anya glanced at her mother.

Glenn explained, 'People love something with flavour – at first. They might like, say, chilli con carne. But would they eat it every night?'

'Not in my house.' Jocelyn listened.

'They will buy a plain meat patty. It isn't full of flavour but satisfies everyone in the house.' Anya was curious. The centre obviously cost a lot of money to build and run. 'If people like plain things, and you are aiming to feed entire populations, why the need for a department dedicated to product development?' she asked.

'Food is complex. PT is keen to discover the bliss point.'

'That sounds counterproductive if you're trying to feed populations,' Jocelyn frowned. 'Isn't bliss like perfection? An end point?'

'It is the art and science of optimising each component in a product to create the highest level of craving. Making sure the food is good enough to eat, but not so great that a consumer tires of it. The perfect food or drink.'

Anya thought chocolate analysis would make more sense. It was the one thing she could never get enough of. 'Does that in any way relate to your work with vaccines and vitamins – rice, meat, fruit and vegetables?'

It was sounding as if the food being studied was highly processed, and could barely get further removed from nature.

'They all apply, to be honest. No point creating a new type of rice if not everyone likes it. Take what's called "mouth feel". The way something feels in the mouth is the second most important consideration after bliss point in terms of predicting how much a consumer will desire it. Colour, of meat, as an example, is another crucial determinant of whether or not someone will buy and consume a product. Too dark, or too light, turns people off. And different cultures tend to like their meat different colours.'

It was as if he was describing fine wine, not hamburger meat.

'Honestly, does it really matter that much? I mean, why go to all that trouble when it could end up burnt or overcooked?' Jocelyn had never been a big meat eater.

'Our research suggests colour is very important. Supermarket lights are maximised to make meat look red. Some companies and meat sellers are known to put sulphur dioxide into their products; it's known in the trade as a weekend special.'

'Isn't that illegal?' Anya assumed it would be.

'Of course it is. Meat starts to go pale when it goes off, so some butchers add sulphur dioxide because it's tasteless and instantly the meat looks redder and smells fresher. The alternative is adding heart or kangaroo meat to make meat darker again. Imagine instead if we could give them meat that never loses its colour?'

Rather than exposing meat sellers for breaching food standards, PT were competing for their business.

'Surely it's cheaper and more sensible to educate people in what meat really looks like. We are ridiculously pampered, if we think this is a problem.' Jocelyn wasn't impressed. 'All the money spent on this research could be going towards health, schools and nutrition education. It's hardly fulfilling your brief of advancing agriculture, either.'

'That may be, but government can no longer afford to subsidise research. In some cases, there isn't a bliss point, but a bliss range, which can mean massive savings to a company, increased employment and expanding into projects that benefit communities.'

Glenn passionately believed in what he was doing.

He indicated a potato crisp which had pride of place in the cabinet.

'The natural sugar – starch – in the potato is readily absorbed. It results in glucose levels rising, so creates a craving,' Glenn said. 'What I'm working on are potatoes with lower carbohydrates, which would be lower GI for the health conscious, and as a bonus, absorb less fat. My specific focus is maximising nutritional content of food.'

Anya doubted that the company had any intention of marketing the low GI potato to third-world countries. People in first-world countries would rush to buy anything containing a healthier potato, especially potato crisps that would still contain all the fat, additives, salt, and artificial flavours they were drawn to.

PT's goal was to have consumers addicted to its products, at any cost. With the full support of the state government and local people.

52

While Jocelyn sat and rested, Anya asked if it was possible to see the science facilities. Glenn seemed happy to oblige and showed her into an adjacent lab. A petri dish containing a grain of rice became his focus.

'I'm working on a type of rice that can vaccinate against malaria. If we increase the protein content, it will be a true superfood that actually saves lives. From there, we could breed it to grow in minimal water. The possibilities with the science are endless.' He had an almost religious fervour.

'Isn't the science still controversial?'

He crossed his arms and tugged at his beard. 'People in desperate need don't care where the food or life-saving treatments come from. If a company funds development of life-saving technology that otherwise wouldn't exist, humanity is better off. If we have the capability and don't utilise it, our neglect has cost millions of lives. I see it as a moral duty.'

'What about the anti-GM arguments?' Anya wanted to know if Glenn really was a zealot or had a balanced view of the topic; if he would mention studies like those performed by Millard.

He pulled up a laboratory stool and offered Anya one, which she took.

'Most of them are proposed by groups like POWER who declare to the world that they keep the bastards honest. It turns out they have become a monopolising corporate giant. Just like the ones they claim they want to destroy.'

Anya had seen the ads and contributed to non-profit groups like Doctors Without Borders herself. 'Except that they survive on public donations.'

'Two hundred million dollars isn't exactly small change. And in organisations that oppose and vilify, the most extreme and aggressive types get to the top. They fly business class, stay in top hotels, lobby politicians. How are they any different from business executives?'

He had a valid point. It hadn't occurred to Anya that an environmentalist group would be such big business. That money had to be managed. And to function, there had to be a structural hierarchy, just like in any large organisation. She wondered where Alison Blainey fitted into POWER.

'And there are arguments that GM foods so far haven't lived up to the promises of increased yields over the last fifteen years or more.'

He raised both hands. 'That doesn't mean they won't. It means we haven't got it right. Yet. I wouldn't be doing this if I didn't honestly believe that we can make a difference. Look how penicillin changed the world. It takes on average fifteen years for vaccines to get to poorer populations. What if we can get vaccines to people quicker in their food and overcome the challenges of growing crops in arid regions with large populations? How can that be wrong?'

Audrey's son had her intensity and knew the art of persuasion.

'What about the potential for corruption?' Anya argued. 'Giant corporations aren't charities. They won't feed the world without making a sizeable profit. It's in their best interests to generate terminator genes that stop farmers reusing seed they have already bought.'

'True, but look at medicines. The checks and studies are so rigorous it now takes up to $4 billion to develop, test and get approval for a new drug. Only the largest pharmaceutical companies can afford to bring them to the public. Most people don't have any idea how much work goes into a simple capsule they don't think twice about popping.' A machine beeped behind an interconnecting glass door. In the next room, another researcher attended to it.

Anya had been waiting for an opportunity to show Glenn the chromatograph report from the contents of Patsy Gallop's drink bottle. She pulled the piece of paper from her jeans pocket and unfolded it on the bench top. He had been in Jocelyn's house and could have been the one looking for something among her mother's files. And whatever Moss, Craig Dengate and PT's CEO were involved in at that supposed emergency meeting in the restaurant, Glenn was a part of.

She decided to challenge him and see his reaction to what she had learnt from the logbooks. 'I was wondering if you recognised this particular formulation.'

She knew Glenn hadn't been working at TIAA when Patsy was killed, but hoped he may recognise what else could have been added to the bottle.

'You're full of surprises.' He looked down the nose of reading glasses to study the page. He stared closer and ran along the bottom axis with his index finger before turning his back to the door. His face tensed. 'Where did you get this?' he whispered.

He clearly recognised something on it.

Anya's heart raced. 'It was involved in a crime.' She looked for any reaction.

'I don't understand . . . It's impossible.'

'Why? What's in it?'

He spoke in hushed tones. 'Our formulae are patented and top secret. We don't want competitors producing the same things. Industrial espionage is real,' he urged. 'This is important. What possible crime—?'

'It's the analysis of the remaining contents of Patsy Gallop's drink bottle.'

He put an elbow on the desk and leant on his hand. 'Can't be. The head of the lab poisoned her with the selenium solution. Mum sat in at the trial.'

'I have proof the toxin can't have come from that bottle in the lab.'

Glenn lowered his eyes to meet Anya's, as if double-checking the implication. 'If you're right, then someone with restricted access from inside PT killed her.'

Anya felt a galloping in her chest. Glenn could have denied recognising the print out. Instead, he was implicating someone within the company. She needed to trust him.

'Can you tell me what it is?' she asked softly.

He moved to a computer and typed a password while Anya looked towards the adjoining room. Within minutes he had pulled up a number of graphs and hit the print button. A worker entered and took her place at a microscope.

'This place is better resourced than anywhere I've worked in the world,' Glenn announced as he reached for the printer.

He laid a number of sheets on the bench.

The worker glanced over and then returned to the microscope.

Glenn scooped up the papers and bumped a petri dish with capsule shells in it.

'You can take these examples of printouts back to your pathology lab. They should consider one of these for toxicology. Expensive but well worth the investment.' He spoke a little louder. 'For security reasons the samples aren't identifiable.'

Anya presumed visitors could be searched before departure. Staff were possibly afforded the same treatment. She took Glenn's cue.

'Thanks so much for the tour, it's been fascinating. Very impressive.'

'Let's go get your mother and I'll walk you both back down to security,' Glenn said.

The colleague didn't look up or speak.

In the elevator on the way down, Glenn remained silent. She assumed the lifts were monitored.

Before he opened the glass barriers they'd come in through, he hugged Jocelyn, then turned to Anya and extended his arms. She felt awkward moving into his embrace.

He spoke into her ear. 'The selenium is freely available but the rest of the chemical composition is unique to us. A twenty-four-hour slow-release capsule casing.' He placed what felt like a capsule in her hand as she stepped back.

Anya kissed his cheek as the barrier opened so they could exit.

Someone had put capsules filled with selenium into Patsy Gallop's drink. And if they were slow release, there had been a large window of opportunity. She had died on a Monday, so anyone who'd had access to the drink bottle on the Sunday could have been responsible.

She and her mother headed for the doors.

'Excuse me.' The security man stepped in front of them. 'We have orders to search you.'

53

Anya curled her fingers around the empty capsule. Jocelyn placed her hand on her chest and protested.

'Do you seriously think we stole something? Here, go crazy.' She raised her arms to shoulder level. 'It'll be the first time I've been touched by a man in years.' She closed her eyes. 'Frisk away.' A female security guard joined them.

The male guard appeared embarrassed. 'Just doing our jobs, ma'am. No offence intended. It's standard procedure.'

'I bet you don't body-search Christian Moss when he comes to visit,' Jocelyn complained as her bra line, waist, legs and trousers were patted.

'Mum, please.' Anya coughed and covered her mouth. 'They're following procedure.'

'Your bag, ma'am?' the male guard said. Her mother offered him a used tissue and a piece of chewing gum that might have been a few months old before handing over the bags. The female guard moved to Anya.

Heart pounding, she held up her arms, fists closed. She had no idea what the penalty would be for theft of a top-secret capsule. The doors were metres away.

'Can you show me your hands, ma'am?'

Anya's heart sank. Someone had seen her take the capsule.

She slowly opened her fingers.

'Thanks, have a good day.'

They collected their bags and headed outside.

When they were at the car, Jocelyn asked. 'What did you do? You looked guilty from the moment we got in the lift.'

Anya pulled the capsule out from under her tongue.

'Was it that obvious?'

'To me.' Jocelyn grinned widely. 'Why else do you think I performed like a crazy woman?' She peeled open a piece of chewing gum, popped it in her own mouth and held out its wrapper. Anya placed the empty evidence inside.

On the drive back home, she explained about the chromatograph and what she and Oliver had discovered.

'I thought poor Len was in denial when he defended Millard. Even I thought Patsy could have . . .' She rubbed her eye. 'Why didn't he tell me what the books contained?'

'He has to have believed he was protecting you. You were the person he cared for most and trusted, enough to make you his beneficiary.'

The drive to her mother's house took less than fifteen minutes.

Once in the driveway, they saw a white Land Cruiser parked outside the house.

'That's Craig Dengate's car.' Jocelyn fiddled with the top button of her shirt. 'I guess the lawyer already sent a copy of Len's will to his family.'

Anya stopped about thirty metres back and Craig climbed out of the vehicle. He was smaller in build than his brother but still imposing as he stormed towards them.

'Mum, lock your door and don't get out.'

Craig yanked at the car handle. 'What the hell are you playing at?' He thumped on the window with a closed fist.

Jocelyn flinched.

'You crazy bitch!' He punched at the glass again. 'Do you know what you've done?'

Anya restarted the engine, placed the gearshift into reverse and swung the car around. Dengate was kicking the car with his leather boots as she accelerated forward.

'He's taken the news pretty well, don't you think?' Jocelyn tried to joke, but she was clearly shaken.

Anya headed straight for the Longford police station. Dengate was quickly in her wake. The Land Cruiser pulled alongside them.

'I think he's going to ram us,' Jocelyn warned.

Anya saw his left hand go to the top of the steering wheel. She took her foot off the accelerator and slammed the brake. The Land Cruiser swung in front of them, up onto the shoulder of the road, barely missing a fencepost. Anya managed to avoid a collision and pressed back on the accelerator. They were minutes from the police station.

Dengate manoeuvred away from the fence and continued to chase them.

'Mum, call the police, now. Tell them he's after us.'

She dialled as Anya kept watch in the rear-vision and side mirrors. They were fast approaching a semi-trailer up ahead. Dengate was gaining. She had seconds to make a decision. A van came into view heading towards them from the opposite direction.

Anya held her breath and blasted her horn, in the hope the semi-trailer would decelerate so she could overtake and warn the van.

'Don't!' her mother shouted.

The truck hit its brakes and Anya saw their only chance. She pulled around it and pushed on the pedal with all her strength, still pressing on the horn.

The oncoming van had slowed enough for her to fishtail through the narrow opening, back onto her side of the road.

Dengate hadn't been able to follow her. A stream of cars followed the van she had narrowly avoided. Dengate was suddenly blocked from overtaking.

It gave her a moment to breathe. Even so, she sped to Longford police station, cutting corners until the hire car slammed to a halt outside, in front of a patrol car.

McGinley lumbered out of the driver's side, followed by Simon Hammond. 'What the—'

Jocelyn and Anya sprinted towards the police.

'Craig Dengate's trying to kill us.'

McGinley sighed. 'Now I'm sure—'

Dengate's car almost slid around the corner and mounted the kerb, barely missing a telegraph pole. The driver appeared, a rifle in his hands.

'Boys, I don't have a problem with you.' Craig Dengate's chest heaved. He spoke with an eerie calm. 'This is between me and the doctor.'

'Mother of God,' McGinley appealed. 'What do you think you're doing?'

Anya saw Simon Hammond motion with his head to get Jocelyn inside. She grabbed her mother's shoulders and took a slow step towards the building.

'Stop! I swear to God I'll shoot you bitches.'

Kerbside, Hammond lowered to his haunches, gun drawn. From there, he moved around the back of the car, to get a clear shot at Craig.

Out of the corner of her eye, Anya saw Rhonda, the female constable, come around the side of the building. So did Craig. He fired into the ground. 'Nobody move.'

'Okay.' McGinley's shirt was saturated with perspiration across the neck and underarms. 'We don't want anyone to get hurt. So far, no one's in any trouble. Let's keep it that way.'

'Declares you, the moron puppet! Do you think anyone takes you seriously? You're the town bloody joke.' Craig began to sniff and wiped his nose on the crook of his left elbow, eyes still darting around the scene.

One hand next to his holster, the other outstretched, McGinley eased forward.

Craig raised the weapon in his direction. 'You still don't get it. It's already too late. Len pissed off some very powerful people.'

The sergeant took another step.

'Stay back or I swear . . .'

Jocelyn broke free of Anya, making herself the prime target. 'Wait. Len loved you. He knew you were a good man.'

It caught Craig's attention. 'You. You tricked the stupid bastard into leaving you the farm.'

'That's not true.' Jocelyn's arms were in front of her, palms outwards. She spoke gently but firmly. 'I didn't know until the will was found.'

'That's bullshit. You should have just stayed out of it. Because of you . . .' He almost spat the words. 'I'm a dead man.'

McGinley said, 'Craig. Nothing can't be fixed. Just put down the gun and we can talk. You've got us all twitching here with trigger fingers. For God's sake, put the rifle down.'

A woman with a wheeled shopping bag crossed the road. Simon waved her back from behind the car. She saw the rifle and hurried away.

'I didn't even know about the will. I promise you,' Jocelyn pleaded.

'Len was so damn stubborn.' Craig began to cry. 'He didn't get that he had to sell. His business was over anyway. I tried to talk sense into him.'

'Did you see him that night?' Jocelyn's voice rasped. 'To make him see sense.'

'He kept mocking me. Saying I didn't have the guts . . . I never meant it to go off. It happened so fast—'

The realisation hit like a blow to the chest. Craig had killed his own brother. By admitting it, Craig had nothing left to lose. Jocelyn moved to lunge forward and Anya grabbed her.

Simon was in place, poised to shoot.

'Think of your wife, your kids,' McGinley tried. 'They'll understand it was an accident. Just put the gun down.' He reached his arm forward again.

'Stop there,' Craig yelled. 'Everyone get back.'

For a tense few moments no one moved.

Craig let go with his left hand and lowered the shoulder of the gun.

Simon held his position.

McGinley took his hand off his holster and walked slowly towards Dengate.

Suddenly, Craig hoisted the barrel with his left hand.

Jocelyn pushed Anya aside and ran towards him.

Anya gave chase. She was almost in reach of her mother when Jocelyn screamed.

'NO!'

Two shots fired, in quick succession.

54

Jocelyn dropped to her knees, hands holding her chest. Craig Dengate lay on his back, right leg bleeding.

Simon Hammond took a look at the head wound and turned away for an instant.

There was no sign of life. Anya reached down and felt for a carotid pulse. Jocelyn shoved her aside and began cardiac massage. 'Get an ambulance,' she shouted.

Anya could see the efforts were futile. The head shot would have killed him instantly. Her mother was in denial.

Simon's face pleaded with Anya, who shook her head. There was nothing anyone could do to save Craig. He had made sure of that when he pulled the trigger on himself. Whoever shot him in the leg had caused peripheral damage, not hit a major vessel. Good luck or precision aim – it could have been either.

McGinley leant over Craig's car door, face buried. A woman screamed, and a crowd began to gather. Oliver's voice was in the background. 'Get back!'

McGinley composed himself. 'Get something to cordon off the street,' he ordered.

Rhonda quickly returned with a woollen blanket and two emergency space blankets. Hammond drove the patrol car backwards to block the entrance to the street.

'All weapons down,' Oliver commanded. McGinley reholstered his, still in a daze. Oliver took a blanket and held it up, blocking the view from the other end. No one had dared breach the perimeter from the station side of the road. Oliver handed Rhonda his car keys and asked her to block the road at the other end, but leave enough room for the ambulance to get through. 'I need the weapons of whoever discharged one.'

Jocelyn was panting, continuing the cardiac massage.

'Someone stop the prick mongrels taking pictures! This guy has a family, for God's sake!' McGinley yelled, pulses in his temples and neck throbbing.

'What the hell happened? Who was he?' Oliver demanded.

Simon returned and took the holster off his back containing the weapon he had fired. 'Craig Dengate. He came after the women. We tried to get him to put the gun down. Then he turned it on himself. I shot him in the leg. Guess I wasn't quick enough to save him.'

Oliver took the gun.

'For what it's worth,' Anya said, 'the police did everything they could. I thought he was going to kill Mum.'

Jocelyn was vigorously pumping on the chest. 'Come on, Craig. Stay with me.'

Anya knelt down next to her mother. 'It's too late, Mum. He's gone. We have to declare the time of death.'

The ambulance arrived and the officers stared silently. Jocelyn sat back on her haunches and rocked, staring at the blood on her hands.

The forensic team would be hours at the scene. McGinley took on the responsibility of informing Craig's wife, preferably before she could hear the news from any other source. The senior sergeant also had the unpleasant task of asking Craig's widow if they could search the house for evidence that he had been involved in Len's death. Anya was relieved that Oliver

Parke volunteered to accompany him. It was the best chance they had of finding out why Craig had done what he had.

They had to wait for a team to arrive from Hobart for the internal investigation. For now, Rhonda manned the phones and repeated the order, 'No comment,' before hanging up.

Oliver would take statements from McGinley first, followed by Simon Hammond. It was the second time in days he had shot a civilian while on duty. Craig Dengate had threatened to shoot Anya and her mother. As far as she was concerned, Simon Hammond could have just saved her mother's life as well as hers. Craig had killed himself or had intended to commit suicide by getting the police to shoot him.

Anya phoned the registrar at the hospital, who recommended increasing Jocelyn's cortisone dose under the circumstances. Her mother refused to go home and let it take effect. Instead, she asked Anya to help her in the bathroom. Once the door had closed behind them, Jocelyn pulled her daughter close.

'There's something I have to confess . . . I took something. From Len. I thought that's why he was killed but the murderer didn't find it. So I took it before the police and ambulance came.'

Anya tried to process what her mother was saying. 'You took evidence from a homicide victim that could explain why he was killed? Do you hear what you're saying?'

'Yes. And I'm not proud, but it's what Len wanted. It's why he told me where it was. In case anything happened. No wonder Craig missed it. He hated Roswell.'

'Mum. Stop. You're not making sense. You took something to do with Len's dog?'

'No. What I took was a small USB device. It was inside Roswell's collar.'

'Where is it now?'

'In my bag, inside a tampon box. I figured no one would look there.'

As crazy at that sounded, it was as reasonable a hiding place as any. 'You have to hand it in. You can give it to Oliver and explain you weren't well. You were hallucinating with the low cortisol and blood sugars, and you were in shock.'

She raised a hand. 'I knew what I was doing when I took it. Before you hand it over, I want to know what's on it.'

'We can take you home and look, but then we have to hand it in.'

'No.' Jocelyn flat-out refused. 'We can't use your computer or mine. They could be monitored.'

Anya was not about to start an argument about whether or not they were being watched. After being followed from the prison, she had to admit it was a possibility. 'Fine, then, but where can we check it?'

'Where better than a safe place?' Jocelyn said.

Anya realised her mother meant here. On one of the police computers. 'You can't be serious.' She couldn't believe her mother was even suggesting it.

'Think about it. They're all busy with the crime scene, the databases are firewalled, so they are less likely to be hacked. It's the perfect place. No one would expect us to use them, even if they are watching us from outside.'

Perversely, her mother's logic was convincing. 'All right. But first, you'd better wash your hands.'

For the second time in days, Jocelyn's hands were covered in Dengate blood. She began to scrub while Anya went to retrieve the USB without arousing suspicion.

55

In between answering the phones, Rhonda kindly showed her to a computer.

'You can't access any databases. Just the internet. Don't need to tell you the sites you click on can be tracked. Just in case,' the female officer reminded. 'It's a standard spiel. Anyone accessing a computer gets it.'

'I just need to log in, check emails and send my report, then I'll log straight out. You'll never know I've been here.' She hoped no one would find out what she was doing.

The USB could provide evidence as to who killed Patsy Gallop. This was, in an odd way, an ideal time, while the station was minimally staffed and in turmoil following another shooting.

Simon Hammond wore a distracted frown and gazed towards the front windows. He had been asked to write his statement before being formally interviewed for this shooting. He hadn't even had a chance to process the event or his involvement.

'Hey, Hammo, at least you didn't trash another car.' Rhonda tried to lighten the mood, unsuccessfully.

Jocelyn was still in the bathroom scrubbing her hands.

Anya could already see the headlines. Country cop kills again; radio shock jocks decrying police brutality. Violent criminals were more likely to be glamourised, even have TV series made about them. Simon's life and family would be picked over by reporters and there would be little empathy for how his life was forever changed.

Anya knew he didn't wear a wedding ring.

'Is there anyone I can call and let know you're safe?' She was concerned.

'No one here.'

'Anywhere else?'

'Not anymore. My girlfriend didn't want to leave her job in Melbourne. I didn't want to leave Dad. By the time he died, she'd found someone else.'

The phone rang again and Rhonda dutifully repeated, 'No comment,' and referred the caller to the department's media spokesperson.

Simon swivelled back to the desk and began two-fingered typing.

Anya plugged in the USB and pulled up the contents. The device contained hundreds of files. None was named; instead, each had been numbered. She decided to go methodically, starting at the first document.

Up came a copy of an email, sent from the CEO of PT, Graham Fowler, to Christian Moss. It praised the minister for his foresight and vision of the future. There was nothing suspicious or incriminating in it.

She tried the next file. It was an email dated months later, this time from Moss to the CEO.

I have every confidence that the MIV will be a phenomenal success and we will achieve our mutually advantageous goal. I guarantee this will be a state-of-the-art facility. Any further questions or concerns, do not hesitate to contact me, or my chief of staff, Ryan Chapman.

Their mobile numbers were included. Anya tried to remember where she'd seen the letter, MIV, before. Then it became clear. It had been circled over and over again on the scrapbook page under mother's bed.

She read through a number of banal exchanges, dates of meetings. It seemed the CEO was on the board of a committee known as CTGM, which stood for Controlled Trials GM.

She decided to search the internet to see who else was on it, but found only a number of names she didn't recognise. She kept the site open and returned to the documents.

Jocelyn had returned and sat down next to Anya. 'I feel like Lady Macbeth. The blood stains and this pigment are fading, but it's as if they don't wash off.'

Anya wanted desperately to assuage her mother's guilt. 'You didn't do that to Craig. Or to Len.'

'I only wish we knew why Craig did what he did. To Len and himself. His wife and kids didn't deserve this either.'

Anya had to ask. 'Do you know what MIV stands for?'

Her mother grabbed her wrist. 'It's what Len was trying to find out.'

Anya's thoughts returned to Craig's connection to Mincer Leske. He had sold Leske the property at Cressy. Mincer was dead. He wasn't a threat to Craig, if he ever had been. Whatever it was, Craig was obviously in way over his head. He'd said he was a 'dead man' once he found out Jocelyn had inherited Len's estate. She wondered if he owed a lot of money to someone dangerous. He was also closely associated with Christian Moss and the CEO of PT. He had been included at the lunch with Moss that day at the restaurant, in what was supposed to be a private crisis meeting. Except that it had happened to be organised prior to any crisis taking place.

Anya scanned more uninspiring emails among committee members. Then one stood out. It was dated August two years ago. Jerry Dyke had been appointed to the committee. She clicked back to the web and searched for the dates of Reuben Millard's trial. The lawyer had been appointed to the same government committee responsible for approving GM trials during the murder trial.

Anya sat back. Madison Zane had mentioned that trials only had to run for a period of three months. As Patsy Gallop and Reuben Millard's experiment had shown, none died within ninety days. Many became ill after that. Dyke had to have known the full study results when he defended Millard at trial.

Phones rang in the background. Hammond answered one, Rhonda picked up the other.

'Senior sergeant's on his way back,' she said, to everyone in the office. Simon's typing accelerated.

'What is it?' Jocelyn prodded.

Anya showed her the screen. She read silently and her mouth opened when she read Jerry Dyke's name.

Time was running out. Anya searched the files for 'cancer'. Nothing.

She tried Reuben Millard. Nothing.

Patsy Gallop. Nothing.

Finally, she typed Blainey. A file popped up.

Had correspondence from an Alison Blainey from POWER. The organisation plans to block MIV plans. Could be a problem.

The message was from Graham Fowler. Moss and his chief of staff were recipients.

Moss responded,

Familiar with POWER. Making name re Antarctica. Will organise a meeting. See what's negotiable. Our side will not compromise. MIV must be impenetrable – secure, private, disaster-proof.

Jocelyn read it as well. 'Len was a fox. He contacted Alison Blainey to find out more about this facility. He didn't antici-pate the E. coli infection but met her anyway. She has no idea he had this, obviously.'

Everyone in the office was preoccupied with phones.

'Maybe they're building a defence facility or a nuclear

power station,' Anya suggested. 'National defence and energy are way out of Moss's jurisdiction.'

The thought occurred to Anya that PT could have been brokering some sort of secret deal to benefit the Chinese government. Whatever it was, security was deemed paramount.

McGinley loped through the back door, followed closely by Oliver.

Anya escaped the screen and hid the USB in her jeans pocket.

'How did the wife take it?' Rhonda asked solemnly.

McGinley's face reddened. 'Four-year-old was asking when Daddy was coming home. The two-year-old was at a neighbour's. The wife has to ID the body later. If that's not lousy enough, she had to find out her husband shot himself in the street and was shot by police in the process. After breaking that news, we barge in and demand to search the joint for evidence he murdered his brother. How do you think she took it?'

'She seemed decent.' Oliver slouched into a chair. 'Your heart breaks for those kids. Looks like she was in the process of leaving him, although she denied it. Had a lot of the toys packed in boxes. His side of the wardrobe was full, hers was almost empty.'

Jocelyn cleared her throat. 'Anything to confirm he shot Len?'

McGinley conceded, 'He didn't smell of petrol that night like Len did. He'd already changed and washed before he came back to the scene. We found a blood-stained shirt buried in the shed. It was with a pair of old boots that look like they've got blood splatter on them.' McGinley leant forward, arms straight, hands on the desk nearest him. He paused, then became upright again.

'Also found a sale agreement. If signed, it would have had Len sell the property to PT. It had a small bit torn off the top. Think they'll find it matches the scrap of paper found in Len's hand.' McGinley stepped forward. 'Believe I owe you an apology, Dr Crichton.'

Anya could only imagine how difficult this was for the senior officer, in front of his subordinates. She chose not to remind him about the sanctity of a crime scene in front of them. 'The only positive is that the truth has come out. Inevitably, it does.'

'Not all of it.' Jocelyn seemed agitated again. 'Anya, we need to go. NOW.'

56

Jocelyn asked to be alone for a while to rest. Rhonda drove her home. Oliver asked if Anya would join him at a cafe in town. The team from Hobart would begin going over the individual statements and re-interview in the morning. She decided to tell him about the existence of the USB, just not where it came from. To protect her mother, she implied, by omission, that it was in the parcel under the chicken coop.

Inside the cafe, Oliver went to order. Anya scanned for a corner table, where she could sit with her back to the patrons, in case anyone recognised her. She still had the USB for safe keeping.

'I thought country life was supposed to be peaceful.' Oliver returned with coffees. 'Changed my mind about wanting to move here.' He sat down. 'While we were in Hobart, McGinley took Alison Blainey's formal statement about that night in Len Dengate's house. He also showed her a series of photos. She identified the woman who stopped her on the road as Mincer's girlfriend. His kid's name is Brutus, by the way. Seriously.'

Anya focused. 'Mincer did assault Alison Blainey after we met her at Len Dengate's place?'

'Looks like it. After what the medical student told us, I checked into Blainey's background,' he said. 'Degree in environmental law at the University of California. Worked for organisations like POWER ever since. She specialises in Arctic and Antarctic protection and opposing genetic modification, or genetically modified organisms, depending on what you read.'

A waitress delivered a hamburger and chips on a plate for the male detective. While he admired it, Anya helped herself to a chip.

'There's nothing in her background suggesting corruption. Earns a good living. POWER and companies wanting to go green fly her around the world business class. Unlike members of the police force who always go cattle class.'

'Len Dengate said she was attending a conference on Antarctica,' Anya reasoned. 'If Craig Dengate paid Mincer to light the fire, maybe he paid him to assault Blainey as well.' Although she couldn't work out a reason why he would do that.

'All right. Why go after Jocelyn then?' he asked.

'Because Mum inherited his brother's property.' Anya thought logically. 'Craig was trying to force Len to sign a sale agreement to PT before he killed him. He was so desperate for Len to sell that he threatened him with a gun. Even though,' she emphasised, 'he wouldn't get anything for it, apart from a real estate commission. If he thought he was the beneficiary, he may have had to kill Len to finish the deal?' It suddenly made sense. Craig had to have promised the property to PT and been unable to deliver once he discovered Len had changed his will. Even Jocelyn's death wouldn't help him. The land would then go to Anya. 'Craig implied his life depended on delivering Len's property to PT. It explains why he went after you two in a rage.' Oliver chewed on a couple of chips. 'All we have to do is find out what it is about Len Dengate's place that's worth killing and dying for.'

'I think I know,' Anya said. 'May I borrow your phone?'

He handed it across. She pulled up a map of the local area and PT land. 'See the South Esk? It flows right through . . .'

'What are all the orange shadings?'

'The land the Chinese own via PT.' Anya could barely believe how many properties on either side of the river had been amalgamated. Apart from a small section that broke the pattern. 'The green area is Len's land. His brother sold his share and the Chinese have been making offers on Len's section. They need it to monopolise the river for irrigation. They dam it, stop it flowing and strangle the downstream properties as well. They own most of the north of the state that way and monopolise the farming.' Attached to a corridor to the east was her mother's property. 'Or they need the pure water supply for something else as well.'

'Have they ever made your mother an offer?'

'Not that I know of. Guess there was no point unless Len accepted. He was the domino that wouldn't fall.'

It didn't have to be said. Now Jocelyn owning her and Len's both properties meant she was in their way.

Oliver dipped some chips into mayonnaise. 'It's worth finding out who else bought properties in and around Cressy a year ago, and what they paid for them. Maybe Mincer knew something we don't about the area's potential.' He took a mouthful of burger.

'How are you getting to spend time on this?' Anya had wondered. The detective was supposed to be investigating Leske's shooting by Hammond.

'This place is a smorgasbord for someone like me. Botched crime scenes, stuffed-up police investigations à la Patsy Gallop, a policeman shooting two people in a matter of days. I can take my pick. My bosses won't expect to see me for months.'

Anya smiled.

'I can get a team of forensic accountants to go through Craig Dengate's financials. There are sites that post the properties that have sold in the area in the last few years and the prices paid, and whether they were overvalued compared to others in the area. They'll let us know if there are likely to be hidden accounts.'

Anya slowly sipped her coffee.

Oliver wiped his hands on a napkin. 'The USB you mentioned. I'll need that as evidence.'

'Only if you let me see what else is on it.'

'Anya, this is serious. You could have been shot today. So could your mother. From what McGinley and you say, Craig Dengate didn't kill himself out of depression or because his wife was leaving him. He really believed he was a dead man once he found out he hadn't inherited Len's property. He failed to deliver and knew the cost. Whoever's behind this, they're playing for keeps and covering their tracks. The less you know, the safer you are. Please hand it over.'

'The more I know, the safer Mum is. Alison Blainey met with Christian Moss after Graham Fowler, the CEO of PT, emailed him. The emails mentioned words like "impenetrable" and "state-of-the-art" in reference to MIV.' Whatever MIV stands for, Alison is involved.

57

That evening, Oliver arrived for dinner. Audrey Lingard had left enough meals in Jocelyn's fridge to last a fortnight, but after the events of the day, no one apart from the detective had much of an appetite. Jocelyn couldn't rest until she knew why Craig had killed himself. Anya looked in the fridge for something people could graze on if they felt the need.

'They weren't made from PT beef, were they?' Oliver peeked under the lids.

'Audrey said she buys from the town meatworks.' She checked inside the foil of one package. Garlic bread. She did it up again. 'Any luck finding out what MIV means?'

'Weird that they use a code. If Moss is doing more deals with the Chinese consortiums, the feds would be pretty ticked off he's going behind their backs and compromising international relations with America. That's a delicate line in diplomacy they have going.'

Whatever the secure structure was going to be, it seemed odd that PT thought they had to negotiate with POWER and Alison Blainey.

'Maybe further development would harm the local flora and fauna, or threaten an endangered species.' Jocelyn appeared in the doorway and went to make herself an iced tea.

'Mum, there's wine. Oliver stopped and bought some, along with beer.' One drink wouldn't affect Jocelyn's medications.

'I'll have wine then, if I'm allowed.' Jocelyn seemed a little lost. She had dealt with so much in the past few days, including a potentially fatal illness. Considering that, she was holding up well.

Anya was curious. 'How did research into Craig's real estate office go?'

Oliver opened his notepad. 'Craig seems to have been quite the slick salesman. Nine properties were sold in the last fourteen months, to seven buyers. They were all decent sizes, from one hundred to four hundred hectares. First one was bought by Jerry Dyke.' For Jocelyn's benefit, Oliver added, 'If you remember, he was Reuben Millard's defence lawyer, turned PT employee.

'Next was Lydia Pilchard.'

Jocelyn poured two glasses of white and brought them over, along with a beer for Oliver.

'I went to school with her,' she said. 'She just happens to be Christian Moss's older sister. I don't recall any of her husbands being interested in farming, and she hasn't had to work since husband number two.'

'Thadeus Leske,' the detective continued. 'Ryan Chapman, whom I gather works with Christian Moss . . .'

'That's his chief of staff.' Anya had seen him a few times now.

'Well, he bought two properties. Then there was Margaret Nelson, whom Craig's secretary tells me is a widow. Margaret died a few months ago and left it to her nephew, the one and only Reuben Millard. A woman named Kimberley Oscrow bought one. Craig Dengate snapped up the other two himself. They were all bought in a disastrous slump and from what I can tell, for a bargain. Amazingly, they've all just been sold.'

'How recently?' Anya didn't believe in coincidence. All but one of the buyers were connected directly or indirectly to PT.

'Settlement took place yesterday on all but the

Dengate-owned properties. They were due this coming week.'

'Did any sell for a loss?' Anya thought that might explain Craig's pitiful grab for commission from Len.

'Astonishingly, each one was worth . . . wait for it . . . on average, ten times the price a year ago. And they were all purchased by the same buyer – Ethical Future.'

Anya whistled. 'Wow. This is like the pot of gold at the end of the rainbow. Mincer and his luck at the casinos, now this. Makes you wonder why he bothered with odd jobs.' She thought for a moment. 'You said all but Craig's sales were finalised.'

'That's right.' Oliver took a swig of beer.

'Mum, has there been any talk or whispers about new developments around here? Any new projects?'

'Not that I've heard.' Jocelyn frowned. 'That's an enormous amount of land. Surprised Craig could keep his trap shut about the record prices.'

'I had an informal chat to Dengate's assistant who said Craig did all the dealings in person with a representative from Ethical Future. She seemed to think it was so "hush-hush", someone famous had to be behind it.'

'They'd be more likely to buy an island than a chunk of land in the middle of somewhere, I'd have thought. This generation is completely celebrity-obsessed,' Jocelyn said. 'The rumours about fracking were picking up pace. Maybe this Ethical Future, whoever that is, heard the mining company didn't get the licence before anyone else.'

'The secretary photocopied this for me.' Oliver unfolded an A3-size document. 'I've marked the properties that turned over.' Pink highlighter stripes covered most of the map. The properties' boundaries outlined one mass of land.

'It's fertile land. PT and the Chinese have to be behind this. It'll mean they own at least a third of the state.' Jocelyn slapped the table. 'Moss and his cronies have a lot to answer for.'

Oliver jotted down some notes. 'I'll get my people to look into Ethical Future. Someone has to have signed for all the sales.'

Anya wasn't comfortable. 'PT have shown themselves to be shrewd businesspeople. The market was dead, and yet someone paid exponentially more than market value.' She wondered if Ethical Future was another Clarkson Evergreen company, like PT.

'And look who profited,' Oliver said. 'Not who you would think of as natural bedfellows. Millard looked terrified when we mentioned Mincer Leske's name.'

Anya had to agree. She left the table to put the food into the oven. 'Why did the turnover take just on twelve months?'

Oliver sat back, hands clasped behind his head. 'That's something I haven't worked out. My people did some checking. Graham Fowler was a major contributor to Christian Moss's re-election campaign in the two last elections. According to the list of donors, so were half the scientists and executives at PT. Including Patsy Gallop and Reuben Millard.'

'Patsy would never have contributed to Moss's campaign. She was vocal about supporting the Sustainable Tasmania Party.' Jocelyn clicked her fingers. 'I know why they all kept the properties for at least twelve months. If you keep if for at least twelve months and make it your primary residence for that time, you don't have to pay capital gains tax. In Mincer Leske's case, he would have made it the girlfriend's primary residence given he was in prison for most of that time.' She sat back. 'This is a conspiracy even Len missed. Craig was in it up to his eyeballs.'

Anya looked over Oliver's shoulder. He had listed the names of the real estate deal in a circle. 'Who's the lynchpin here?'

'As far as we know, Mincer didn't live in his place. It looked like it had been abandoned for years with rats as the only tenants. And the secretary said Craig Dengate did everything for those sales. Even handled the pest and building inspections for all the buyers.' He rocked the beer bottle in one hand. 'No conflict of interest there when the real estate agent's contacts give the all clear to a place. Talk about buyer beware.'

'Who was supposed to have done the inspections? I had a devil's job getting anyone to look at this place,' Jocelyn said. 'Craig knew I had trouble and didn't say anything. I distinctly remember Len asking him if he knew anyone reliable.'

A knock at the door distracted them. Jocelyn went to answer it and Anya took the opportunity to check the bread in the oven. The smell of garlic already filled the kitchen.

Jocelyn called out, 'We have company.'

Simon Hammond appeared in the hallway and looked around. He was dressed in jeans and a plain shirt. 'Sorry to interrupt, I just wanted to see how you were doing. After . . .'

'You're not interrupting.' Oliver was quick to invite him in.

Anya gave Oliver a quizzical look.

'Please, join us,' he said.

'No, but thanks anyway. I'm going on leave and just—'

'This is a bad time to isolate yourself,' Oliver interrupted. 'You don't want to cut yourself off from colleagues and support right now.' He didn't seem bothered about the documents on the table or keeping their investigation confidential.

'Company's great. There's plenty of food.' The detective got up and gave the constable a beer.

58

A nya added an extra dish of food to the oven.
There was another knock, this time on the back door.
Jeanette Egan apologised for the intrusion. She had printed out
the preliminary results of the cultures from the manure samples
she had taken. Anya and Jocelyn invited her in as well.

'I thought you would want to see these for yourself,' she
said, leaving her boots at the back door and handing over the
pathology results. 'You can look at them later.'

'No,' Anya said. 'These are important.' A quick read
confirmed the presence of the same organism that had killed
Emily. It was contained in almost every sample. Anya exhaled
slowly. PT was responsible for Emily's death. This proved it.
Jenny Quaid and the other affected families would be able to
sue PT for compensation, and the company would be forced to
modify its practices.

'Thank you,' she hugged Jeanette. 'Please join us for a meal.
It's been a long day.'

'I can't believe Craig killed his brother. I knew he had
money troubles.'

Oliver introduced himself and asked, 'What sort?'

'He liked to gamble. Ponies, greyhounds. Vets hear a lot in
the stables.'

Jocelyn brought Jeanette a beer and went outside to be with Roswell, who was sitting patiently on the verandah.

Oliver looked at the culture results. 'You'll lose your job over this, when they find out you tested the samples and showed us.'

'I know. But I did it for Len. He deserved a whole lot better.' She raised her drink.

The others did the same. 'To Len.'

Oliver quickly returned to business. The map. 'Do either of you know this area at all? It's around Cressy.'

Simon pulled his chair in closer, and Jeanette peered over his shoulder.

The constable studied the highlighted areas. 'I've been trying to work out what was going on there myself. Last summer there were an odd group of incidents. Like here.' He pointed. 'The old couple woke up to a Molotov cocktail through their front window. Seemed random. They were retired and never even had a parking ticket. No neighbour feuds, and we didn't find out who did it. I went back a month later to check on them and they'd moved out.'

'Anything else?'

'A car had its tyres slashed while the owners were asleep. Each had a steak knife in it. We assumed it was just kids out at night looking for trouble. Nothing was stolen, just the tyres wrecked. The old man who lived there was shaken that someone had been so close to his house.'

'Can you remember the address?'

'It was across the river.' Simon examined the map again. He identified it as the property bought by Kimberly Oscrow. 'People here aren't used to having homes broken into. Guess it was a violation he couldn't forgive.'

'Do you know the woman who bought the place, surname Oscrow?' Jocelyn asked.

'Should I?' For the first time, the senior constable appeared unsure of himself. Anya suspected he was feeling intimidated about being quizzed regarding places on the map.

'Do you know if McGinley owns any property down that way?' Oliver asked what Anya had already wondered.

'No clue. We don't exactly mix outside work.' He pushed back his chair. 'I should be going. Anyway, glad you doctors are okay.'

Anya felt he needed to be around people who had shared the trauma.

'At least stay for dinner. There's plenty to go around. And I promise to protect you from the interrogator. He has a one-track mind.'

'Speaking of food, something smells fantastic.' Oliver was back at the fridge and removed three more beers. Anya wondered who was planning on driving that night. She placed a pile of plates on the bench and counted out the knives before laying out trivets. Jocelyn steered Simon up to her end of the table, next to Anya. Jeanette grabbed the seat on his other side.

Jocelyn waited on Simon, who sat quietly. She chose a selection of foods for him. Jeanette and Oliver helped themselves. Anya served up her mother's food before sitting down herself. For the first time in years, she heard Jocelyn say grace.

The clinking of plates and chatter gave Anya some mental space. Jocelyn ate a hearty meal and told Simon stories about his father as a child.

Going back for seconds, Simon quietly asked Anya, 'Why did Parke ask about McGinley owning something there? Is he investigating him?'

Anya could honestly admit, 'I don't know. But in light of new evidence, it's possible that Reuben Millard didn't kill Patsy Gallop.'

The policeman's face moved closer. 'I knew it. Millard didn't have a bad bone in his body. He was the kind of guy who'd give you his last dollar and not expect anything in return. Len was convinced, too. I couldn't come up with anything to prove otherwise.'

'Do you think McGinley's corrupt?' Oliver was back with his empty plate, not mincing words.

'I've watched him ever since I got here. Laziness and bumbling incompetence are more his specialty. He was so quick to point the finger at Reuben, everything that happened after that was to prove that theory. If it didn't fit, it was thrown out of the brief.'

Oliver piled his plate with more garlic bread and lasagne. 'Any examples?'

'For one thing, no one searched her and Len's place for selenium tablets. Sure, they searched Millard's, but not the most obvious place.' Simon came to life, as if he'd been wanting to share his thoughts. 'Patsy had trained for a mini-marathon. Those athletes are fanatical. They use protein powders and concoctions they get online. I couldn't help but wonder if she might have accidentally poisoned herself.'

Anya chose not to mention the dissolved capsules found in the drink bottle. Over-the-counter tablets were swallowed, not normally dissolved in water. Someone had to have placed a powdered form of selenium in the capsules, then put them in Patsy's drink bottle. It was someone who knew she ran each day, and had access at PT and the opportunity.

Jeanette helped herself to some lamb casserole. 'She was pretty, I know that. Plenty of men fancied her. Maybe one of them couldn't handle rejection. Like in *Fatal Attraction*.'

That was what McGinley wanted to believe of Reuben Millard, Anya thought. Yet nothing had been found on his home computer, only on his work one.

'Did anyone else at TIAA or PT come under suspicion?' Anya asked. 'Even briefly?'

'She died on the Monday at work and Millard was the only person who'd been with her in the morning. She went for a run at lunchtime, before getting sick that afternoon. Toxicologists testified that the poison was fast acting. Everyone else at TIAA had been with others that day, and didn't have access to Patsy's drink bottle. Apart from Len, that is, before work.'

'What had she done that weekend?' Anya pressed.

'On Saturday she tried on wedding dresses in Hobart,'

Jocelyn reflected. 'She was so excited about marrying Len and thought she'd found the perfect one. On Sunday she did a fun run and weekly weigh-in.'

'After that,' Simon added, 'she went home. Len cooked dinner, they watched TV and had an early night.'

Anya remembered seeing a photo of Patsy at Len's house. She was in workout clothes with a group of people. Patsy was beaming in it. Len had said he kept it on display because it was the last photo of her ever taken. 'She won an award that day.'

Simon snapped his fingers. 'That's right. I'd forgotten. How did you know?'

Anya excused herself. 'Mum, do you remember where Len got the picture of Patsy taken the day before she died?'

'I do. I got it for him from the newspaper. They sell prints.'

Anya looked up images on her computer and typed in Patsy's name. A series of photos of her popped up. Many showed her with a much fuller figure. Anya scanned the thumbnails. Halfway down the page she found it: an image of Patsy with her medal. Pulling up the image, she couldn't believe the difference. The chubby man in the photo was familiar. He was much trimmer now, but the eyes were the same.

'Recognise him?' she asked Simon.

'That's Christian Moss's right-hand man, Ryan Chapman. He was at the protest at PT.'

Everyone in the group photo had access to Patsy's drink bottle that day, including Ryan Chapman. But which of them had access to PT?

59

The following morning, Oliver took homicide detective Steve Schiller with him to interview Christian Moss and Ryan Chapman about the real estate deals in Cressy. Craig Dengate had tried to force Len to sell his property to PT before killing him. They still had no idea what drove Craig to commit suicide or who he was so afraid of. Why he had said he was a dead man.

Oliver referred to these interviews as 'chain rattlers'. He'd ask what they knew about Craig Dengate and his business dealings, keeping his knowledge about the Cressy properties to himself. He would then casually mention rumours of dodgy real estate deals and see how they reacted. Anya would love to have been a fly on that office wall.

Anya left Jocelyn to sleep in, and went to the motel where Alison Blainey was staying. She had a lot of questions to answer about her connection to whatever MIV was, and why she was negotiating with PT. Was POWER even aware? Was it part of their strategy? And why had she offered Len help when she knew PT would ruin him, based on the way they sued anyone who they claimed infringed their GM patents? It seemed inconceivable that they could sue farmers for unknowingly fostering PT seeds that had blown onto their properties, but logic, morality and the law were mutually exclusive at times.

Anya parked in the car park. A restaurant was attached to the motel. As she pulled on the handbrake, a figure caught her eye. Alison Blainey stepped out in sunglasses and looked around. She appeared to be waiting for something, or someone. What caught Anya's attention was that she didn't have a bag with her, and hadn't stepped out for a cigarette. The time ticked over to 8 am.

Anya waited in her car to see what Alison was doing.

A black sedan pulled in. Alison crossed the car park and got into the back seat of the car. Tinted windows obscured any view inside. Anya craned to record the number plate and texted Oliver from her mother's mobile.

The sedan remained stationary and a few minutes later, the POWER worker alighted. The car pulled away, then stopped. The back window wound down and Anya could make out the face. Graham Fowler leant out. He said something and Alison laughed before he wound the window back up. The car drove off.

'Nothing like schmoozing the enemy,' Anya muttered. The pin-up girl for environmentalism and anti-GM campaigns was a fraud.

Alison looked around and headed back to the motel. Anya was quickly out of the car and following. Blainey entered the restaurant and headed for the ladies' room. Anya took the opportunity to go in after her. Alison washed her hands. She stood straight when she saw Anya.

'Hi.' She grabbed some paper towel. The bruises on her face were more purple today. 'I heard about your mother, and I hope she's doing all right. What happened to Len, oh my gosh, I heard his brother was involved. That's horrific.'

Anya agreed. 'I don't know if you heard; Len Dengate left everything to my mother.'

The news didn't take her by surprise.

'You must be a little nervous.' Anya began to wash her hands.

'Excuse me?' Alison dabbed one of her bruises with a little finger.

'I mean, suing a huge organisation like PT. Mum is pretty angry about their seeds contaminating Len's crops. We're lucky to have you on side.'

'I've been called away on another case but I'll put our best people on it, I assure you.'

Anya turned off the taps and shook the excess water into the sink. 'The MIV is more important then.'

The environmentalist scrunched the paper towel.

'I'm sorry, I'm preparing for a speech at an Antarctic conference. If you'll excuse me.'

'Maybe you forgot. You met with Christian Moss, and talked to Graham Fowler about it.'

Anya blocked the exit. 'I've seen the proof.' She waited for the words to sink in.

Alison tried to sidestep but Anya stood in her way.

'Did you take a bribe, or were you always going to back down?'

Alison bit her top lip and a crease formed between her eyebrows. The effect was particularly unattractive. 'That's defamatory. I negotiate. It's what I do best. As a result, Mawson Island is safe. The penguins, seal colonies, all of it. The Antarctic teams can stay and do their research undisturbed.' She continued justifying her actions. 'Clarkson Evergreen were always going to build a vault. China has planned it for decades. Global warming and climate change accelerated the schedule. You'd have to be blind not to see it coming. So you fight it or get the best possible deal for the environment.'

'You were supposed to fight for the environment. What about all the great work you've done to raise awareness of GM? How can you turn your back on that?'

Alison surged forward. 'Don't lecture me. I've been doing this job for years. Life's about compromise. Sacrificing land around here is nothing compared to saving Mawson Island. I had a chance to save something priceless and I took it.'

'You sold out the people here for a vault? Do you think

they – or their children – will thank you?' Anya was still uncertain as to what the vault was to contain.

'Who else has the power and money to build the most comprehensive bank of seeds in the world? Samples from every single plant ever known to have grown on the planet. In the case of man-made or natural disasters, countries can replant their own native crops and flora.'

Suddenly, it made sense. The structure was akin to a defence fortress. The Doomsday Vault was a precaution against nuclear war or global destruction. The memo had said it had to be private, isolated, secure and impenetrable. Disaster-proof. It all became clear. Whoever owned the world's seed bank controlled the entire food supply.

'Are you that naive? What's to say China will give seeds to countries that criticise or disagree with their policies? Or a country that can't afford to buy back its own seeds?'

'You don't get it. They're custodians with foresight. The vault will be the largest and most extensive in the world. Countries volunteer to send their seeds. They want to pay to have them stored.'

'Is that what you choose to believe? PT doesn't follow rules. They commit fraud, scientific fraud, and have no ethics. You told us. Governments are afraid to cross them. Look at their track record.'

'Grow up, Anya, this is the real world. It's called politics and everyone plays it. This time I did it well and POWER gets the credit for saving a natural treasure. It was a win-win situation.'

Anya tried to control her rising anger. The notion that it was even possible for PT to buy an island in the Antarctic region was abhorrent.

A woman entered the toilets and took in the scene. 'Everything okay in here?' She bore a striking resemblance to Alison, and the accent was similar.

'Fine, Kim. I was just coming.'

'Excuse me, I'm Anya. You are?'

'Kimberly. Alison's sister.'

Anya suddenly identified the mysterious buyer in Cressy. Kimberly Oscrow. Alison had been in on the deal with the others from the start. This wasn't just about a moral victory. She had orchestrated a million dollar deal in her sister's name.

'Congratulations on the Cressy real estate windfall. Twelve months waiting really paid off.'

Alison's face suddenly appeared pale. 'What are you talking about?'

The sister seemed to freeze, unsure how to react.

'Quite the team, you all made. And even Craig Dengate kept quiet about it. So did Mincer Leske. I wonder if he knew you were in on the Cressy deal when he assaulted you. Or was that some kind of set up to gain sympathy and get publicity?'

The colour returned to Alison's cheeks and she closed the bathroom door to any potential interruptions.

'Ally, let's just go,' the sister pleaded.

'Don't say a word, Kim.' She turned back to Anya, inches from her face. 'What the hell are you accusing me of?'

Anya held her ground. The lawyer was on the defensive. 'Corruption, fraud, misrepresentation, working for PT to get Len Dengate's land. There's also falsely accusing Madison Zane's group of starting the fire that night when Mincer Leske was behind that too.'

'Years in this business taught me to be realistic. As soon as the food poisoning went public, Len Dengate was out of business. His case would have brought unprecedented publicity to POWER in this country and PT would have got what they wanted.'

Anya could barely believe the moral vacuum in which this woman existed. The masquerade had conned a lot of people. 'You don't care about POWER or PT. You saw a chance to make money and grabbed it.'

'You think the work I do is forever?' Alison bleated, 'The moment I hit forty, POWER will want someone younger and prettier to front the cameras. The money Kim and I made is what POWER owes me. It's my superannuation and they won't have contributed a cent of it. Like I said. Win-win.' Her sister handed over a bag, which she threw over her good shoulder. 'My conscience is clear and I haven't done anything illegal.'

Anya shrugged. 'POWER, the Independent Commission against Corruption, the general public and even the department of public prosecution may all disagree. Once that happens, do you think Graham Fowler will still be chummy with you?'

Alison's body stiffened. 'He won't cross me. He knows the damage I can cause him and PT,' she snapped, face ruddy.

The lawyer had to have some dirt on the company and CEO that made her so sure.

'Funny, that's what Len said. If he went down, he's take PT with him. Maybe you're fulfilling his prophecy. Ironic, really.'

Alison stared at the wall, for once lost for words, then stormed out with Kimberley Oscrow in tow.

Satisfied with her own 'chain rattler' interview, Anya rang Oliver. 'They're building a Noah's Ark of seeds?' She tried to fathom the true significance. 'They own the original seeds, and can genetically modify any and every one of them and patent the results. They could hold the world to ransom.'

'I'm picturing Graham Fowler stroking a white cat with Chinese officials while he laughs maniacally.'

'Oliver, none of this is funny. Len, Craig, Patsy were collateral damage. They're dead because PT's end goal was so important.'

Whoever owned the food supply had ultimate power following war and natural disasters. Starving people didn't want cash, they needed food.

'I know. We arrived at Moss's electoral office, where he's supposed to be. Place is locked up. I'm heading your way now.'

'Okay, I'll meet you at the cafe.' She hung up and stopped to unlock the car door.

Something sharp pressed against her back.

A man's voice whispered in her ear. 'One sound and I won't hesitate to shove this between your shoulder blades.'

60

Anya took a breath and felt the sharp blade cut through her shirt.

'When we get to the car, you'll get in without a fuss. Your mother needs you to cooperate.'

Anya's eyes desperately searched for anyone who could help her.

'Where is she? She's got nothing to do with this.'

'She knows about the land, just like you do.' The voice was menacing but she couldn't recognise it, or see the man's face. 'She's where no one will find her if you don't cooperate. Her little medical problem could relapse at any time.'

A dark sedan was parked outside the restaurant.

Heart racing in her chest, Anya had no choice. The knife jabbed until she was shoved forwards into the back seat, hands behind her. Cable ties dug into her wrists as they snapped tighter. Her bag and keys landed on the seat next to her. If he'd left them behind, someone would know she was in trouble.

The man quickly climbed into the front, separated from her by a screen. The front and back door locks clicked simultaneously.

The car pulled out slowly, then accelerated as it hit the road.

Anya turned to see if anyone was following. They were

the only ones on the road. She struggled with the ties. The man had a knife, she knew that. Her mother had been safe at home when she left. Was she still there, or had she been taken?

Maybe they were after the USB. There could have been something more incriminating on it that she hadn't yet seen. Oliver had it anyway. She had nothing to bargain with.

She tried to think of a way out.

The car turned off and Anya recognised the road. They were headed to Len Dengate's house.

The wheels clunked over a bump and her head hit the ceiling. She struggled to get her hands free, but every movement only tightened the plastic cables.

When she failed to turn up at the cafe, Oliver would have to know something was wrong.

Anya tried to slow her breath and think of a way out. If she could release the lock, she might get the door open. She looked up and saw they were turning off onto the road to Len's house.

Anya moved to the right and reached down to her bag. Her mother's phone was inside. For the first time, she was grateful for having such long limbs.

The screen between the front and back seats lowered.

'What the hell are you up to? Sit where I can see you.'

She slid the phone under her thigh and tried to engage the man while she did her best to dial for help.

'Why do you want Len Dengate's property? What's on it that's worth killing for?'

'You're the one with all the answers.'

Before the screen raised again, she recognised the voice. Ryan Chapman.

The car jolted over a pothole, and despite her lunging to grab it, the mobile slid to the floor. She was filled with dread.

They pulled into Len's drive and Anya knew she had to take whatever chance she could to get away. She tried to remember the exact layout of the house. The car stopped. The car door opened and she saw Chapman's face. Taking a handful of Anya's hair in his free hand, he yanked her to her feet and nudged her again with the knife into the house.

From the corridor she could see that the house had been ransacked.

The rug had been discarded but the blood stain was still prominent on the floor. Jocelyn was in the kitchen, tied to a chair, her mouth stuffed with a gag.

'Sit down!' Chapman shoved Anya down into another chair.

The photo of Patsy and the group was missing. Kitchen drawers were upturned and their contents dumped across the floor. The wide-screen TV had been separated from the wall and smashed.

'Are you all right?' Anya asked her mother.

Jocelyn's eyes were watering, but she nodded.

'Shut up!' Chapman turned to Jocelyn. 'Where did Dengate hide it?'

He ripped out Jocelyn's gag. It smelt like vomit.

'We don't know what you're talking about. I thought you wanted me to sign over the deed.'

'That's only part of it.' He stepped forward and slapped Jocelyn hard in the face. She toppled sideways to the floor. Anya lunged forward then felt the knife on her neck. 'Tell me or I swear . . .'

He hauled Jocelyn to an upright position.

'Where is the computer and where did he keep the files?'

'What files?' Jocelyn said. 'I honestly have no idea.'

He raised his hand again. 'Everything he had on me. I know about Jerry Dyke's emails.'

There had to be something more incriminating than they'd already seen.

'Wait!' Anya said. 'She doesn't know anything about it. I found a USB when she was in hospital.'

Chapman turned his attention to her. 'Where is it? You have five seconds.'

'I don't have it with me. I put it back under the chicken pen, where Len buried Patsy's log books,' she lied. 'The police have them. They know all about the cancer in the mice. And that Reuben Millard didn't kill Patsy. They're probably searching your house right now for proof. It won't be long until they find us here. They don't have the USB though. That's still under the floorboards.'

'That's bullshit.' He began to perspire. 'Millard would never talk. You're lying.'

He put his face close to Anya's. She could sense his fear. He had taken a risk leaving Jocelyn alone. If he hadn't called someone to check the pen, he had to be working alone right now. So she hoped.

'You're right. Millard didn't say much at all. The police worked it out themselves. Mincer Leske was the key.'

Chapman began to pace the room. 'I told Fowler he was a screw up from the start. You can't trust someone who plays off both sides.'

Anya tried to buy time to keep them both alive. As long as Chapman wanted the USB and was too afraid to leave them alone, she might be able to bargain with him. 'What the police couldn't work out was why you paid him to bash Alison Blainey and set fire to PT after including him in the real estate deal?'

'You don't get it. Mincer was a low-life. Hell, he was blackmailing Fowler. The piece of scum said Millard gave him incriminating evidence that would bring PT down. He wanted money. Fowler wanted Alison Blainey intimidated and roughed up. If anyone questioned her motives taking on PT for Len Dengate, it would look like the anti-environmentalists had tried to stop her. Mincer was happy to do it for a price. And it worked.'

'What about the protest?' Anya could see he was panicky. She needed more time for someone to realise she and her mother were missing. The phone was still in the car. She wasn't able to get to it and call for help. Keeping Chapman talking was their only hope.

He moved closer with the knife. 'I'm going to ask you nicely one more time. Where is the USB?'

'The police have it,' she finally admitted.

'Liar!' He punched her in the face. The force threw her sideways and he hauled her back up. Her cheek and jaw throbbed. Blood dripped from her lip.

Jocelyn squealed. 'Stop it! Your fight's with me, not her.'

Anya could see he was at breaking point. She tried to get him to focus. 'I think PT wanted Mincer to start a fight at the protest. Get more good publicity for Moss and the company. Everyone would need it once word of the plan to buy Mawson Island got out.'

He squatted on his haunches and waved the knife. 'You don't get it. Tasmanians were crying out for PT to build in the area. They've resurrected the local economy. The people want PT.'

Jocelyn interrupted. 'Not when they discover what the food does. Diseases, cancers, food poisoning. Your boss will be out on his arse.'

'And that's the point,' barked Chapman.

He dialled a number on his phone. Whoever it was didn't pick up. He pitched the phone against the wall in frustration.

Anya's cheek throbbed and she swallowed blood. She could see he was about to lose control.

Jocelyn kept his attention. 'Moss probably wants to distance himself from you. All those years of loyalty and hard work were for nothing.'

'You're as stupid as Dengate. This was never about Moss. His career is over. Mr Progress spread himself too thin and he doesn't have the backing anymore. No one wants to back a loser.'

Anya thought about who had paid large contributions to Moss's last election fund. State elections were a year away. 'You didn't call Moss. That was Fowler who wouldn't pick up. If Moss looks like losing, they'll want to replace him with a new candidate. Someone loyal to their cause.' Clarkson Evergreen and PT was courting government officials as part of their business plan.

Chapman moved closer to Anya. 'Like I said, this was never about Christian Moss.'

'There is a little problem about all the illegal activities,' Jocelyn challenged him.

'We've done nothing illegal,' he hissed and moved over to her. 'By law, GM trials only have to go for three months. Millard's study went beyond what's required. If he hadn't gone to prison and the results had been made public, PT would have had to pull out of the state and go elsewhere. Then where would we be? Hundreds of millions of dollars down the drain.'

'We'd be a lot better off,' Jocelyn answered. She was slightly slurring her words. Anya wondered if she'd had her hydrocortisone injection before being taken.

'I didn't know you could live in two places at once,' Jocelyn managed. 'That's a lot of capital gains tax you've just avoided. A public enquiry might want to know how you and some of your cronies managed to make a fortune selling land to PT a year after buying it for a steal. Molotov cocktail? Not very sophisticated.' She tutted.

He grabbed the knife and stuck it under her chin. 'You've got nothing.' He turned his face to Anya. 'I want that USB. Or I kill her right now.'

'Bogus building inspections,' Jocelyn goaded. 'Craig was afraid you'd all be caught. Mincer Leske had nothing to lose. He wanted the money for his son before he died of his cancer.'

Anya saw the whites of Chapman's eyes flare. He drew blood from her mother's neck.

'So the bastard was dying. For a fee, he was supposed to light a small fire, not burn down half the feed lots and make the environmentalists out to be terrorists. The moron couldn't even get that right and burnt himself to death.'

He dug the knife deeper and Jocelyn began to pray out loud.

'The police know about the capsules!' Anya blurted out. She had shown Oliver the printouts after the visit to PT.

Chapman eased the pressure on the knife blade.

She continued, 'It took twenty-four hours for them to dissolve in Patsy's bottle. Police are at your home and office as we speak searching for the others.'

Chapman started pacing again, sweating heavily now and moving the knife between his hands.

'We're tied up, it will give you a head start,' Jocelyn urged. 'There's no phone here. You have a car. We don't.'

Ryan seemed to come to a decision. He collected the keys and stepped back.

Anya believed he would save himself and leave them alive.

Then he stopped. Christian Moss stood in the doorway.

61

Chapman put the knife behind his back.

'Ryan.' Moss took in Anya and Jocelyn. He quickly saw Jocelyn was tied to the chair. 'Tell me what's going on. You disappeared this morning.'

'These two are trying to ruin everything we've worked for. They know about the Cressy development.'

Moss stood, hands on hips. 'They can't prove anything. Those purchases and sales were all legitimate. You and I both know Graham Fowler has more to worry about than us.'

'You don't understand, Chris. These two want to ruin you.'

Moss walked slowly, and spoke quietly. 'My God, Ryan. What have you done?'

'You don't understand, Chris, they're going to lie and say you did illegal things. I'm doing this for you. All of it.'

'He's lying,' Jocelyn managed. 'Fowler's been backing him to run in next election instead of you.'

Moss inched forward. 'The truth always surfaces. Politics and marriage have taught me that.' He took another slow step. 'It's over.'

'Sit down, you chicken shit. After everything I've done for you,' Chapman wielded the knife, 'you're not going to weasel out of a bit of dirty work now. You're in this as much as I am.'

Moss stepped back, hands up. 'In what, Ryan? You're scaring me, and the women. Put down the knife and we can talk about it.'

Jocelyn spoke. 'He murdered Patsy Gallop.'

The shock on Moss's face looked genuine. 'Reuben Millard did that.'

'Jesus, Chris. Didn't you think it was convenient timing that the bitch was going to release the study results and the head researcher killed her?'

The muscles in Moss's face slackened and his lips parted. 'Is this true?'

'I had to prove loyalty to PT. It was the only way. Or they would have pulled out of everything we'd been planning and building.'

'My God. And you knew Craig Dengate gambled everything he had and more.'

'It wasn't hard to convince him the Chinese triads were behind Patsy's death. All he had to do was deliver his brother's property and he failed. Craig did everyone a favour. He wasn't supposed to kill the brother. That was a bonus. Then I just had to sort out Jerry Dyke.'

Moss clenched his jaw and tightened his fists. 'What did you do to him?'

'He's been leaking emails to Len Dengate who had them all on a USB. When I get that, we're home free.'

Moss sat, weight on his toes, as if he was ready to pounce. 'Where is Jerry Dyke?'

'Don't worry. He's being met by "friends" in China,' Chapman looked at his watch. 'In about two hours, it will all be over and we'll be in the clear.'

As mad as Chapman sounded, he might actually get away with everything. Unless there was something else on the USB that she hadn't seen. Anya knew she and her mother were the remaining loose ends. So far, Moss hadn't tried to overpower Chapman or help them escape.

'What are you going to do with us?' she asked, as calmly as possible.

'The old woman here is crazy and everyone in town knows it. Craig Dengate can't talk now . . .' he looked at Moss. 'She stabs her daughter out of grief and insanity, in the very place where her beloved Len died.' After that, he turned to Jocelyn, 'she kills herself and it's all over. I just want the USB and you get to die first, without watching your mother suffer.'

Moss stood up and placed himself between Chapman and Anya. 'No, Ryan. It stops here.'

Chapman wiped his forehead. 'How did you think things got done? Deals brokered, donations to your re-election campaign? You act like Pontius Pilate wiping your hands of anything you didn't see. That doesn't make you innocent. You're in this with me.'

Moss shook his head. 'This is wrong. I had nothing to do with Patsy Gallop's death. Murder? There's no way I was involved, or ever would be.'

Ryan grabbed the knife tighter. 'You're in it as much as me!'

Anya sensed he was about to act. She squinted at her mother then the back door. Jocelyn blinked then threw herself and the chair to the floor.

Chapman lunged at her with the knife. Moss dived and tackled him. The knife flew to the floor. Anya stood and kicked it out of reach. At that moment, Oliver and McGinley stormed in, weapons drawn.

'Nobody move.'

Simon Hammond followed. 'We've got medics outside.' Jocelyn remained on the floor.

'She needs hydrocortisone. One hundred milligrams IV, now,' Anya instructed.

'I'm on it.' He rushed out and brought in the ambulance officers. Anya felt her body relax as McGinley, puffing, hand-cuffed Chapman.

Oliver helped Moss to his feet.

'Minister, thanks for helping. Even so, you have a lot of questions to answer about seed banks and corporate corruption. On the bright side, you are going to be on top of the news cycle for a few days at least.'

Simon found a pair of scissors on the floor with the rest of the scattered cutlery and cut Anya's hand ties.

Oliver said, 'Glenn Lingard is on his way to Chapman's home with the police to identify the capsules when they're found. Turns out more than twenty went missing the week before Patsy's death. If it wasn't for Glenn doing an audit, we may not have known.'

'I want a lawyer!' Chapman shouted.

Anya hurried to her mother's side. Jocelyn hugged her tightly, only letting go so the ambulance man could deliver her injection.

Anya turned to Oliver. 'Chapman was after the USB you have. There's got to be more incriminating info on it.'

'Tech are looking at it, but so far it's just the emails. Seems Len was bluffing if he suggested he had something more implicating Chapman. Jerry Dyke's emails have been enlightening enough.'

Ryan's mouth gaped at the news as McGinley led him outside.

Anya couldn't understand how Moss and Oliver had found them so quickly. 'How did you know we were here?'

'Remember that talk you gave in Hobart at the conference? I was in the audience and thought the idea of tracking offenders with small GPS devices was clever.'

Anya rubbed her wrists. 'You didn't plant one on me . . .'

'Not exactly. I might have dropped one in your bag after we were followed that day at Risdon. Just so I could keep an eye on you in case of trouble. I ran into the minister as I was leaving his electoral office and he said Chapman was meeting your mother here. When you didn't answer the phone, I checked the GPS. Turns out, monitoring people who might get themselves into more trouble is a great idea.'

Anya needed to know, 'Minister, why was Glenn Lingard at that crisis meeting you said was about the E. coli outbreak but you arranged a week earlier?'

'He's passionate about the seed vault and his scientific knowledge has proven valuable. Glenn is involved in the planning but to my knowledge, wasn't involved with Chapman or any of the real estate purchases, if that's what you're really asking.'

Anya sighed with relief and helped Jocelyn to a car.

Reuben Millard looked surprised when he saw Anya and Oliver. 'To what do I owe the honour?'

'We have some news,' the detective announced. 'Yesterday, a man named Ryan Chapman was arrested for the murder of Patsy Gallop.'

Reuben didn't move or speak. For a moment, Anya thought he was catatonic. 'Did you hear us?' she checked. 'If he does a plea bargain, you'll be exonerated.'

'That's . . . I mean . . .' He looked at the prison officer for verification.

'It's true. Was in the papers this morning,' the guard said.

'I don't know what to say.'

Anya handed across copies of *Scientific American Mind* and *Nature* magazines. Millard's eyes brightened.

'What can I give you in return?'

'The truth,' Oliver admitted. 'At first we thought you were scared of Mincer Leske. We saw the way you reacted when we mentioned his name. But you weren't afraid of him. You were just shocked that we might have known you two were connected. Am I right?'

'This is your story.' Reuben placed his hands in his lap.

'Jerry Dyke did try to help you. He went on that committee that approves GM trials to see what PT were concealing in their new study. Landing a job with them was either planned or a fortuitous bonus. He found they were fraudulent in claiming the GM seed was safe. He started forwarding emails that incriminated PT to Len Dengate. That's why you didn't need our help.' Oliver put his hands behind his head. He was enjoying this. 'How are we doing?'

'Rather well, so far.'

'You'll be pleased to know we had Jerry Dyke intercepted at Canton airport and he's on his way back to Australia safely to testify. Any plans those thugs from Clarkson Evergreen had for him have been obliterated.'

Anya chimed in. 'The next bit is heart-warming. Jerry knew about the plans for a seed vault and how the land would be prime real estate once PT needed it.'

'It was interesting that your aunt, may she rest in peace, happened to invest at the right time then leave it to you in her will. It was somehow poetic justice.' Oliver leant forward. 'You'd have thought she'd want nothing to do with PT after your ordeal.'

'What can I say. Pragmatism runs in our family.'

Anya continued, 'Then we started wondering if Mincer was working for Craig Dengate, Christian Moss or even PT. We ruled out the environmentalists because they don't normally light fires.'

'Definitely,' Oliver concurred. 'He did some odd jobs for PT. Even so, we think you told Mincer about the real estate deal.'

Reuben blinked twice and pinched his nose. 'Careful, these walls have ears.'

It was exactly the phrase Len Dengate and Anya's mother had used.

They waited, and he continued. 'You've earned the right to know. Jerry told me about the real estate deal. I would have had nothing when I eventually got out of here, so I decided to be practical and capitalise on the deal. Mincer was an *interesting* character. Not well educated and a recidivist. I paid him to protect me in here and got to know him better. He had a keen mind for science, as it turns out.' He touched the cover of the

Nature magazine. In an unlikely friendship, the criminal and the researcher had bonded over science. 'Then he got the lung cancer diagnosis and wanted to leave a legacy for his son, so the child could have a better life. It was only reasonable for me to let him know about Cressy so he could cash in. All he needed was the deposit, which Jerry Dyke arranged through the girl-friend on my behalf.'

Anya couldn't believe they were talking about a man who tried to set her alight. 'He tried to kill me and a police officer the night of the fire!'

'I said he had a good mind for science. He didn't always make good decisions. None of us is perfect, doctor.'

Oliver raised his eyebrows at Anya, who sat back, amazed at Millard's loyalty to a violent criminal.

'We heard Graham Fowler paid him to light a small fire.'

'Well, Thadeus did like an adrenalin rush. I told him that wheat crop was to be trialled on humans. He probably thought he was doing us all a favour by setting fire to all of it. I certainly didn't ask him to. He did have a sense of justice, as misguided as that may have been. Particularly after becoming a father.' He rested his hand on the cover of the *Nature* magazine. 'He didn't want his child or family to be human guinea pigs. So I guess the opportunity was too good to resist. He had nothing to lose, only weeks to live, the doctors said.'

Reuben almost made Mincer sound noble. Prison would have changed anyone. Despite being innocent, no doubt Reuben had had to evolve to survive in here. Cultivating a friendship with Mincer ensured Rueben would survive. Anya wondered who he was paying for protection now that Mincer was gone. No doubt the scientist had a plan.

'You'll want to be looking into Ethical Future, which is part of Clarkson Evergreen. Graham Fowler will have a lot of explaining to do to the Chinese owners when they find out he made a personal profit on real estate at the company's expense.'

'Good luck,' Anya said, and stood.

'Thanks for the tip,' Oliver went to shake Millard's hand.

'Thanks again, especially for the magazines,' he said, clutching them to his chest.

Jenny Quaid asked to meet with Anya. They arranged to have a coffee in Hobart, before Anya flew back to Sydney. Jenny brought Mia along, and the little girl sat in a high chair. She looked healthy and was a real chatterbox.

'Do you have babychino?' Jenny asked the waitress.

'We can definitely do milk with froth on top.'

The three-year-old grinned.

'How are you doing?' Anya asked Jenny when the waitress departed.

'Every day is harder than yesterday. I don't know what I'd do without Mia. Emmy was my world.' Jenny's face was ashen when she spoke of her child. 'I heard you saw Emmy and looked after her. I mean, treated her with dignity.'

Anya could see the mother's pain. 'Emmy was treated with respect by everyone. And the duck stayed with her.'

Jenny picked up a board book and Mia flipped through it in her chair. 'There was so much blood. I panicked. Em wasn't breathing and I didn't know what to do. I tried CPR but she was gone. She looked just like Tom did after he passed.' Her face was tight but she tried to form a weak smile at Mia. Jenny pointed to a lion in the book. 'What sound does a lion make?'

Mia roared then giggled. Anya could see Jenny was barely holding it together but seemed to want to talk.

'Emmy used to play hide and seek in the wardrobe and so I put her in there and made sure she wasn't cold. Mia put Duck-Duck in her hands.' Jenny swallowed hard.

Mia made a quacking sound when she found the picture to match.

'Are you going to sue PT?' Anya asked gently.

Jenny sniffed back tears. She was resilient and presenting a brave face despite her incredible grief.

'Mum is helping me with it. She wants me to move back in so she can help look after Mia. I know it's hard on her, with her health, but I can cook for her and help out around the house.'

Mia turned over a page and pointed at a puppy.

Jenny barked softly in short, quick bursts. Other cafe patrons looked on, but Mia's response was infectious laughter. Jenny barked again. Her sad smile twisted as she gazed at Mia. Anya could see she was a good, engaged mother. Emily and Tom's deaths would always be tragedies.

'I have to learn how to read for her sake, and mine.' Jenny reached a hand to her daughter, the other held a tissue. 'They have classes at technical college with a creche in the room next door so we can still be together in between classes.'

This was great news. Once Jenny's secret had come out, she had discovered how much support was available.

'Mia looks like she's doing well.' Anya smiled.

'She's a great kid. Keeps me going. Just when I think I can't get up, she smiles and . . .'

Anya understood completely.

Jenny handed her daughter a toy phone. 'I made a complaint against Dylan Heyes. Did you know he tried to massage my spinal nerve?' she said.

That didn't sound so unusual, but Anya was no expert in remedial massage.

'Only, he does it to women from the inside. Without using gloves,' Jenny whispered.

'That's sexual assault,' Anya said quietly while Mia pretended to talk on the plastic phone.

'That's what the police said. Other women have come forward too.'

Dylan Heyes and his unproven therapies had undone him, so to speak.

The text alert on Anya's new phone beeped and she checked it as the coffees and demitasse of frothy milk arrived. It was a message from her mother.

Just finished first meeting with Megan French. We're writing up the cases and hope to submit to the Medical Journal of Australia!!!

Anya smiled. She had suggested an epidemiological study co-authored by Jocelyn and Megan French, the hospital registrar. Jocelyn's audit of patients at her practice had identified the numbers of immunological conditions in families and written the numbers on each file.

Megan French had performed hospital audits on cases like Jocelyn's. Both women had been right. The numbers were disproportionate to other areas, and increases coincided with the arrival of GM foods. Not surprisingly, the cattle remained free of disease. They were slaughtered before they were likely to develop illness from the GM feed.

GM food safety would be on the public agenda again.

She texted back: *Great news! Glad you're coming to visit next weekend. Ben can't wait to see you x.*

Cold Grave

Cocooned from the world on a luxury cruise, nothing can interrupt forensic physician Dr Anya Crichton's time with her precious six-year-old son.

The break Anya needs is shattered when the dripping wet body of a teenage girl is discovered in a cupboard. With no obvious cause of death and the nearest port days away, Anya volunteers her forensic expertise.

She quickly uncovers a sordid pattern of sexual assaults, unchecked drug use and mysterious disappearances. Shadowed by a head of security with questionable loyalties, Anya can trust no one. Her family's lives depend on what she does next.

One thing is certain. There is a killer on board.

Death Mask

Dr Anya Crichton's latest patient was a virgin until her wedding night, three weeks ago. She now has multiple sexually transmitted infections, yet her husband has none. Is this a medical phenomenon or has something more sinister taken place?

Anya's subsequent investigation attracts international attention and takes her to New York, where she addresses professional American footballers about the consequences of their sexual behaviour.

Then an alleged rape involving five football players and Anya is commissioned to investigate. She is immediately thrust into a subculture of violence, sexual assault and drug abuse and soon discovers a devastating truth.

Now lives, including her own, are in danger...

Blood Born

For pathologist and forensic physician Dr Anya Crichton, the death of a gang rape victim hours before she is due to give evidence at trial is a double tragedy. The violent Harbourn brothers, the girl's accused attackers, now look like they will escape prosecution.

But the Harbourns' trail of destruction doesn't end there. When two sisters are brutally assaulted and one of them is killed, Anya begins working round the clock to catch the Harbourns and nail their ringleader, the deviously clever Gary. With the help of Detective Kate Farrer and the surprise involvement of star litigator Dan Brody, she begins to discover just how twisted this family really is, and what they're capable of.

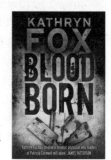

In Dr Anya Crichton's most difficult case yet, she must piece together the evidence before a killer's attention is turned on her . . .

Skin and Bone

Detective Kate Farrer returns to duty after three months of leave following her traumatic abduction. Partnering homicide newcomer, Oliver Parke, they are thrown into the investigation of a woman burnt beyond recognition in a house-fire.

The pair is also requested to look into the disappearance of a teenage girl. Suspicion falls on the unsavoury Mark Dobbie, a steroid user who is obsessed with the missing girl's sister.

While the pressure to identify the charred body and find the teenage girl escalates, a quadriplegic is burnt to death in his bed. Shocking links to all three crimes emerge and Kate Farrer's past demons come back to haunt her. But she must fight them – lives depend on it.

Without Consent

Forensic physician Dr Anya Crichton is on the trail of a serial rapist. When two of the victims are stabbed to death, police suspicion immediately falls upon Geoffrey Willard, recently released from twenty years in prison for the brutal rape and murder of a fourteen-year-old girl.

Unravelling the forensic evidence, Anya is confronted with the greatest ethical dilemma of her career. If Willard is innocent, she is about to blow the whistle and destroy a fellow pathologist's reputation. If he is guilty, her involvement has jeopardised the investigation and ensured a rapist–murderer goes free.

Only the killer knows that a mistake has been made. One that could prove fatal...

Malicious Intent

While investigating the drug overdose of a teenage girl, pathologist and forensic physician, Dr Anya Crichton, discovers striking similarities between the case and a number of apparent suicides. All of the victims disappeared for a period of time before taking their lives in desperate circumstances.

As Anya delves deeper, the pathological findings point to the frightening possibility that the deaths are not only linked, but part of a sinister game. Nothing can prepare her for the role she is forced to take in the deadliest play of all...